THE

LIGHT

OF

EPERTASE

Epertase Publishing
Second American paperback Edition

Republished 2021 Editing by Rebecca Brown
Cover art and author photo by Steve Murphy.

Visit Douglas R. Brown at epertasepublishing.com
Follow Douglas on Twitter @douglasrbrown22
Like Epertase on Facebook
Contact Douglas at epertase@gmail.com
ISBN 13 978 0 9899917 5 9

DEDICATION

For my aunt, Bobbe Ecleberry.
You have supported me and taught me at every step of the
way during this publishing journey. You are a talented editor and
wonderful aunt. I would not be writing books today if it wasn't for
you, and I sure wouldn't have gotten a publishing deal. I could
never thank you enough.

ACKNOWLEDGEMENTS

As I wrap up my Epertase trilogy, I am saddened to say good-bye to Rasi, Alina, Simcane, and the rest of the Epertasian gang, yet I am equally excited and relieved to move on to other stories. I am proud of my Epertase trilogy as a whole and hope you have enjoyed the journey.

I would like to thank a few people for their support. Thank you to my wife Angie and son Aiden for being my world. Thank you to the following people who have supported me in more ways than I can list: My mother, Lillian Dove; my sister, Amie; my brother, Brian; my grandmother, Lona Davis; my father, Dale, Aunt Bobbe and Uncle Tom; my cousin, Greg Ecleberry; friends like Darby and Hazel Blackstone; Cory and Amiee Knight; Kara, Bryan, Maggie, and Mason Young; Sean and Helena Wooten; Matt McNemar; Mick Cecil.

Thanks to Steve Murphy for being a great artist and a better friend, and to everyone at Columbus Fire Stations 15 and 22 (again except for John Galloway).

Thanks to the readers who have discovered the Epertase trilogy or *Tamed* and have written to tell me how much they loved them; to Brett Shearer for being Rasi on my covers, my son for being Cridon on this cover, and my wife for being Alina on *A Kingdom's Fall*; to Rhemalda President Rhett Hoffmeister and Vice President Emmaline Hoffmeister and Editor Becca Brown; and to Breanne Best for helping me get my start.

A special thank you to my proofreaders: Amy Penrose, Jeff Stanforth, Sean Wooten, my mother, and my aunt. Here's to many more adventures.

To my two friends fighting the tough fight right now, I'm thinking about you. Keep fighting, Bryan Oiler and Sean Tibbs. You've got a lot of friends pulling for you. Update: While Sean Tibbs is doing well in 2021, we unfortunately lost our friend Bryan. You're truly missed.

Special note: This trilogy has been completely revised in 2020. If you purchased a copy of any of the books in this series before Fall, 2020, then there are changes to the story. While most of the changes won't be too discombobulating, there is one that will throw everything off for you. The character you know as Terik from pre-2020 copies has had a magical name change. He is now known as Atticus. This change was made to help with the confusion of having both Terik and Tevin as prominent characters. With the revisions, the story remains mostly the same, however, you will no doubt find a few inconsistencies. I hope you will overlook those in light of the grander story. All that said, I believe this series is immensely better and I couldn't be prouder.

EPERTASE

INFINITE SEA

TEK ISLANDS

N

THE RISE OF CRIDON
THE LIGHT OF EPERTASE
BOOK THREE
BY
DOUGLAS R. BROWN

3

When kings make war, innocent men die.

THE STAR OF EPERTASE: CYRUS

In a time before Queen Alina and Rasi, before King Thadius and his son Matthew, and before the land of Epertase had a name, there was a young wizard named Cyrus. Cyrus was a short man, his eyes reaching no higher than the chest of most, but he was strong and fit from a lifetime of hard work. A coal-black beard and mustache, neither of which were well-trimmed, adorned his round face and drove his wife mad with its scratchiness.

Most of the people in Cyrus's village knew him, which made it difficult to get anywhere fast as he was repeatedly stopped with pleasantries. On the day he needed a new spade after snapping his in half shoveling some particularly rocky soil, it had taken him most of the morning to get to the carpenter. Though several people could make spades, Joss was the town's most skilled. If he made one, it wouldn't break so easily.

By the time Cyrus had finished entertaining a bevy of children with a levitating spell, he could see Joss's shop up ahead. Maybe he would make it home before lunch after all. It was turning out to be a fabulous day. Some days just felt like nothing could go wrong.

And then the dreaded battle horns blared. Cyrus froze, a knot swelling in his throat. The horns meant the dragons were coming.

The streets filled with panicked villagers in an instant. Their only chance was the underground bunkers.

Cyrus swallowed a belch of acid worry that burned his throat. He was too far from his home to get back in time if the dragons were close enough that the watchers had seen them. He prayed his wife and mother-in-law would heed the warnings, though he had his doubts. Before Cyrus came along, his wife's father had ruled the house with iron discipline until he died of rotten foot disease. Now neither could make a decision to save their lives. As much as Cyrus had tried to help them over the years, too much damage had been done. There was no way they'd leave without him. He turned and ran toward his home.

All three tower watchers pointed east and Cyrus's eyes followed their fingers. His stomach turned. For more than thirty years the villagers had lived near the forest at the base of the tallest mountain without ever seeing a single dragon. Now, the distant sky was black with a mass of fiery death.

Cyrus didn't like using magic on his own people, but he had no other way of getting through the crowd in time. He put his hands together and gently parted the throng of people with an invisible touch. Taking no notice of his spell, men, women, and children continued running past him as Cyrus ran north through the path he had created.

The first dragon to reach the village shot overhead. Women and children screamed. Men gathered spears and raced east toward certain death in an effort to buy the others time.

It was the cries of those brave dying men that filled the town first. Cyrus didn't look toward the massacre, but the flames touching the morning sky told the stories of their deaths. Maybe against one dragon the men would have had a chance, but no one could have imagined so many dragons coming at once.

He would never make it home in time.

The town darkened in the shadow of the dragons as though night had fallen. Cyrus was close enough to see his house, but not close enough to reach it.

The roar of the dragons overhead pierced his eardrums as the monsters dove. Six metal spikes as tall as men launched toward them from the edges of the city. They were the townspeople's best weapons against the fierce creatures. The dragons shifted and swooped as the spikes soared past. The launchers became their next targets.

Cyrus reached the outskirts of town. A dragon dove toward him and those fleeing nearby. The air heated. Cyrus planted his feet and conjured a spell above his head just as the dragon unleashed its firebreath at the crowd. His spell repelled the flames like the air was made of water. The diving dragon swooped past, the rush of air from its mighty wings almost tumbling Cyrus over. Though the closest homes and shops caught fire, Cyrus had protected many people from the flames. The effort took a toll on his stamina.

He focused back on his home. Once more, he prayed his family had already fled. To his horror, another dragon dove toward his house, too far away for Cyrus's magic to reach. His heart fell into his stomach. He barreled toward his home as the dragon ignited a wall of flames that engulfed his modest house. The heat pounded Cyrus's flesh.

Once close enough for his spells to reach the flames, he extended a feeler in hopes of catching his wife's essence. Nothing but death returned. He stretched his arms into a "T." His eyes rolled back and his blood boiled. A blast of air exploded from his chest and instantly smothered the flames like a child's birthday candle.

He pushed past the lingering heat into his home. Though most everything inside smoldered, small pockets of flames still flickered throughout. With an angry roar, he overturned the charred remains of the table that was his wife's last gift from her father. His eyes blurred behind tears that had nothing to do with the irritating smoke. Frantic, he spun toward the farthest wall and nearly vomited at what he saw. "By the gods." He dropped to his knees.

His wife and mother-in-law huddled together in the corner, their charred-black faces frozen in horror and agony. Smoke trickled from their gaping mouths. He shoved his hand over his nose to muffle the putrid stench of burning flesh. It was overwhelming. If someone had run a sword through his beating heart, it couldn't have hurt as badly as it did at that moment.

With seething hatred, he stared up through the disintegrated roof at the dragons circling overhead. He vowed the tears he now shed would be the last tears he would ever show the world. He whispered, "I love you both. I will return soon to give you proper burials."

Bubbling rage pushed him to his feet. He stepped onto what was left of his front stoop where he could see the flaming town.

In the south, the townspeople fled toward the forest. The dragons must have cut off the bunkers. They swooped down and plucked townspeople from the plains and carried them to their deaths. A few of the townspeople slipped from between grasping talons and thudded to the ground.

"Cyrus," a familiar voice shouted from behind. "Cyrus."

It was the only man Cyrus wanted to see at that moment—his closest friend and the fiercest warrior he knew, Uriah.

His friend carried a spear and wore a sword on his hip. "We must buy time for our people to escape," he shouted.

Cyrus looked away, not wishing to show Uriah his pain, but Uriah was no fool. Seeing Cyrus alone outside the shell of his house revealed everything. He went to Cyrus's side. "I am sorry, my friend. They did not deserve such a fate." He placed his hand on Cyrus's shoulder. "Help me save as many of our people as possible. Help me get vengeance on these beasts." Then he removed his hand and drew his sword. His shadowy, deep-set eyes told of his resolve.

Cyrus had nothing left to lose. He closed his eyes and pictured the two women who had held his heart for so long. With their images fresh in his mind, he looked back to the dragons methodically picking his countrymen apart in the plains outside of town. They were playing with their food.

Uriah said, "We will need every bit of your sorcery. Get their attention. Draw them to us."

Cyrus had never summoned what he had always felt was his truest power, afraid to lose control. Now he had no reason to hold back.

"Do it now," Uriah screamed, eyes burning with rage. "Before it's too late."

Cyrus drew his sword and held it high above his head. If he could stab the gods, he would. His anger fueled him unlike anything ever had. Words came to his lips that he had never heard spoken before. It was the language of the gods.

His sword began to glow. A beam of white light shot up from the tip, lighting the clouds with a thunderous boom. At first the dragons ignored his beacon, but then a single dragon noticed and pulled away from the horde. Then another one followed. And another. Soon all the dragons were drawn toward Cyrus's beam like moths to a flame.

With the dragons drawn away from the fleeing townspeople, the first villagers reached the cover of the forest. It was their best chance of escape since dragons only scorched forests to build nests—some unwritten pact they had with nature, Cyrus supposed. Or maybe it was just a myth and everyone would die soon anyway.

Uriah's knuckles turned white around his sword hilt. He grinned. "Protect me from their firebreath, Cyrus. I'll do the rest."

With the dragons sufficiently diverted, Cyrus lowered his sword, cutting off his beacon. Two of the dragons continued toward him while the others returned to the burning town.

The lead dragon dove toward Uriah. As Cyrus had done with the crowd moments before, he summoned a field of protection above his friend. The dragon blew its firebreath and the flames were deflected away.

The dragon landed with a thud and a roar, surprised by Cyrus's magic. While it regained its spent breath, Uriah charged with his spear cocked. The dragon lowered its head and roared at Uriah's advance, but the warrior wouldn't be intimidated. Instead, he hurled his spear at the dragon's open mouth. The spear would have to be perfect in its aim. Perfect in its timing. Perfect in its lethality.

It was.

The spear entered the dragon's mouth and plunged into the soft, unprotected flesh of the creature's palate. The dragon reared back with a screech and helplessly pawed at its mouth. It blew fire into the air to burn away the wooden shaft of the spear, but that did little to remove the embedded stone head.

A second dragon swooped toward Uriah. Cyrus sprinted toward his friend. "Get down," he screamed as the creature lunged.

Uriah hit the ground.

Cyrus leaped over his friend and planted his feet beside him. He launched a blast of air as the dragon loosed its firebreath. His magic burst through the fire to slam against the flying beast with a ground-shaking boom. The blast sent the dragon tumbling over their heads and crashing into the hillside.

Other dragons searched the town with their snouts tracing the torched streets toward the bunkers. Cyrus glanced toward the forest as the last of his countrymen disappeared within.

Uriah screamed, "We have to search for survivors."

Cyrus bit his lip as he looked toward the forest and then toward the burning town. His friend was right. *Damn it.* The two men raced toward the flames. A dragon noticed their advance and swooped in with its firebreath. Cyrus spun and sent those flames back just as he had with the creature before.

The dragon landed between two burning homes to their left. Cyrus and Uriah diverted to the right. The dragon swung its tail through one of the burning homes. Wood and stone exploded. Though Cyrus dove out of the tail's path, Uriah couldn't avoid it. The tail caught him in the chest, sending him through the air to slam face-first into the dirt. He lifted his bloody face and looked around in a daze.

Another dragon landed in the road in front of them, and another one landed to their right. Cyrus raced to his groggy friend's side. There were too many to fight.

The dragons stalked closer. One lunged with its teeth. Cyrus wrapped his arms around Uriah with his back to the creature and braced for impact. He felt its stinking breath on his back only for an instant. He squeezed his eyes shut and prayed to be somewhere else—anywhere else.

The dragon snapped its teeth. Cyrus winced. But instead of pain, an intense wave of nausea grabbed his gut. The constant screech of the circling dragons overhead was muffled suddenly. He opened his eyes and vomited on the stone floor.

Uriah pushed away, his face pale and arms wobbly. "Where are we?"

Cyrus smelled raw meat. He looked around. A dead deer hung from a hook near a familiar countertop. It looked like the butcher's shop he frequented.

Uriah stumbled to his feet with his hands planted on his knees and splattered vomit on the floor. "How'd we get here?" he mumbled as he wiped his mouth with his forearm.

Cyrus fell to his rear, exhausted and disoriented. "I don't know." He rubbed his forehead.

Uriah struggled past him toward a long hallway that led to the front of the shop. "This way, Cyrus. We can still fight them."

"Wait," Cyrus said, stopping his friend.

Uriah turned back. "What do you mean, wait? The dragons will burn this entire town and us in it."

Cyrus struggled to his feet and stumbled to the southern-facing wall. He motioned for Uriah to join him. Then he gently rubbed the wall in small circles until the stone faded and the two men could see outside.

True night had fallen. Only flames reflecting on the bellies of the dragons above broke the darkness. Cyrus couldn't comprehend how so much time had passed in the blink of an eye.

Uriah turned away and scoured the shop. "Help me find a sword or something to use as a weapon."

Cyrus didn't budge from his magic window. Seven dragons soared past the shop overhead. "There's no time, Uriah. They will burn us soon."

Uriah's voice was panicked. "That's why we must go now."

Cyrus bowed his head. For some reason, he didn't want to escape anymore. He felt confused. He heard a voice in his head urge him not to leave and he agreed with it. He felt an unbelievable calm wash over him.

Uriah overturned a table. "Cyrus, help me find something we can use to fight. They'll find us soon."

Cyrus shook his head. "We cannot escape them, my friend. It is too late now."

"I don't want to escape them. I want to fight."

"If you go out there, you will die."

"If we stay in here, we'll die."

Cyrus walked away from the wall and smiled. "Dragons grow greater in numbers each season, my friend. We have been hidden well in this village for many years, but not any longer. Soon, there will be nowhere left for mankind to hide. We as a people on these lands have reached our end."

"That's no reason to stop fighting. In fact, that's why we must fight harder."

Uriah ran toward the hallway. Cyrus waved his hand, slamming the door shut before Uriah could reach it. Uriah turned back, stunned. Confused. "What will you have us do, then? Hang ourselves on hooks like the deer in this very shop?"

Cyrus shook his head. "I see strength in you, Uriah. I always have."

"Are you losing your mind, Cyrus?" Uriah hurried back to the magical window, only half-listening to his friend. "You're rambling. We need to prepare. They're here."

Cyrus's window faded back to stone. He whispered, "The world needs a savior."

Uriah whipped his head around. "A savior? What are you talking about?"

"It is mankind's only hope."

Uriah cocked his head.

Cyrus looked to the ceiling and his body began to tremble. "I am going to give you a gift, my friend."

"A gift?" Uriah snapped the leg of the overturned butcher's table free and tested its strength against his open palm.

Cyrus spoke in the foreign tongue he had used earlier. "Igly ni'eight tammakay." The wood and straw roof parted, revealing thick, choking smoke so dense that it completely hid the night sky. Cyrus split the smoke with his magic to give himself a clear view of the stars above.

Uriah's table leg dropped to his side. "What are you doing, Cyrus? This is unnatural. Stop it."

Cyrus thought about his wife's smile and how he missed her already. He used her dead stare and the knowledge that he would never see her again to fill him with anger and hatred. These dragons needed killing, and the world needed a special warrior to do it.

Cyrus cried to the heavens, "Gods of the stars and the suns and the moons and all that lives on these lands. We did not ask for our people to be at war, but these evil creatures have forced a war upon us. I stand here before you to ask for a gift that will help our people in our struggle. I know I have not shown myself worthy of your power, but if you grant me this wish, I will forfeit my soul to you in return."

"Don't do this, Cyrus," Uriah shouted.

The wind roared around them.

Cyrus ignored Uriah. "I ask you to give this man—this born leader of men—the power to push these dragons from our lands." As he spoke, a single star in the black sky grew brighter. Cyrus shouted, "Star of Epertase, I know you hear my pleas. I ask that you pass your gift, the very light that shines within you, to this righteous man who stands with me."

"No, Cyrus," Uriah screamed. "I do not want this curse."

Cyrus ignored him and cried to the Star of Epertase, "If you give your power to this man, I will remain here between worlds forever. That is my sacrifice to Uriah's bloodline. For all that is right in these lands, I beg of you."

The room buzzed with energy. A focused beam of light brighter than the two suns shot down from the Star of Epertase, between the swarming dragons and through the parted smoke, slamming into Uriah's chest. The dragons circled the beam of light. One of the creatures flew into it as if desperate to stop what had begun. The dragon shrieked, stiffened, and fell to its death somewhere in the town.

Uriah quivered and screamed in agony as Epertase's Light poured into him. His skin glowed beneath his clothes. His gaping mouth and eyes and ears blazed a brilliant white. He wailed as his body lifted from the ground.

Cyrus backed away and watched the greatest magic any wizard had ever crafted. The power entering Uriah pressed Cyrus to his knees. A crack of thunder popped his eardrums. The world exploded in an all-encompassing fire. Cyrus tried to shield his face from the flames, but they didn't burn. And then everything went black.

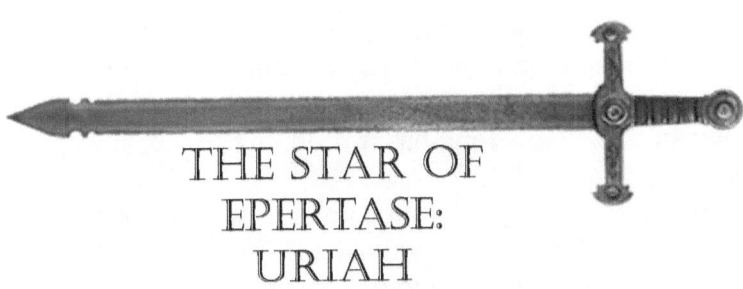

THE STAR OF EPERTASE: URIAH

U riah felt the cold stone floor beneath his cheek. He tried to move his left arm, but it tingled like he had slept on it wrong. His right hand was completely numb, and he pumped his fist to get the blood flowing again. He opened his eyes, but it was just as dark as if he had left them closed. With a groan, he pushed to his knees. The tingling grew into prickling pain as blood returned to his hand.

Where am I?

He remembered the dragons and instinctively felt for his sword at his hip, forgetting he had lost it when he was struck by the dragon's tail. With held breath, he listened for the roars from outside, but only silence returned. He pushed to his feet and staggered into a cold hunk of meat hanging from a hook. *The butcher's shop.* He looked up for the stars, but the straw ceiling had closed, hiding them once again.

From behind, three harmonious voices broke the silence. They sang as one, "Why do you come here?"

Uriah reached for his missing sword again. Three old men stood with their backs against the farthest wall, their faces glowing as if lit from within. Their long, gray hair twisted and ratted with their equally long, gray beards. Their wrinkled and haggard faces seemed somehow familiar.

They tilted their heads in unison and asked as one, "Uriah? Is that you?"

Uriah faintly recognized their voices, though they sounded older and scratchier than he remembered. What he heard didn't match what he saw. He squinted and realized all three men were identical. *Cyrus?* he thought, though he was too stunned to speak his friend's name aloud.

They smiled. "How long has it been, my friend, since we fought the dragons together?"

"I don't know. I've just woken up here on this floor."

"Ahhh, yes. Time moves slower for the living. In the time you have slept, we have traveled to the stars and back."

"What did you do to me, Cyrus?"

"We have given you the Light of the Star of Epertase."

But why?

"So you can fight dragons, of course. The true power the Star has given your bloodline may never fully be realized, but what you now have will protect you as you rid these lands of this dragon infestation."

"I don't understand. If you haven't given me a power I can use, how can I fight?"

"Dear Uriah. The Light we have given you has made you one with all living beings of this land. For any creature to bring unnatural death to you before it is your time means death to all life in your new kingdom."

"So, I am immortal?"

"No, not immortal. Protected."

"And what happens when I die? What then of this Light?"

"Upon the birth of an heir of the Light's choosing, you will pass on your gift. When your life has been lived, the gift within your chosen heir will awaken. Your heir will do the same with his or her offspring, and so forth until time is no more."

"Cyrus, you're a fool. You have ended this world. The dragons will slaughter me without remorse."

The three Cyruses looked to each other and grinned. "The dragons are the wisest of creatures. They already know what lies within you and their fate if you are harmed. You are now the king of these lands. Lead the people against the dragons. Push the beasts to extinction. Lead your people to victory for Epertase."

Though Uriah didn't completely understand, he liked the idea of killing dragons. "Are you coming with me?" he asked.

They bowed and shook their heads. "We are afraid we must forever remain in this …" They paused and looked around the room. "… this lair. That is our sacrifice to the Star. We are Cyrus no more."

Their glow extended throughout the butcher's shop, only it wasn't a butcher's shop any longer. Uriah was in his living room with a fire burning in the fireplace and the table set with his favorite meal of steak and corn. He could smell his wife's cooking.

The Cyrus's smiled. "This is where you most wish to be, we see." Then their faces turned harsh. They looked past him to the blank wall. Uriah followed their eyes. "A dragon has come to confirm that a new slayer has arisen. Go. Meet him. Let him see your face. He will warn his horde of your arrival."

As if on cue, a single dragon roared outside. Uriah walked toward the hallway before turning back. "Cyrus?" he asked.

"Yes?"

"I will build a new world in the name of Epertase. I vow to be a fair and just king to the people."

"We know that you will."

"I will also build a magnificent capital city here in the shadow of the tallest mountain. And I will name this city in honor of your late wife."

The three elderly men lifted their gazes to the ceiling. "Ahhh, Thasula. We have not thought of her in many ages. She was a beautiful woman, was she not?"

"That she was, my friend. That she was."

Good luck to you, the trio mindspoke.

Uriah turned and walked down the long hallway, reinvigorated and determined. As he passed by dried, black torches along the walls, they magically ignited with flames. At the end of the hall, Uriah walked out into the brightness of a fresh day.

The entire village was nothing more than ash for as far as he could see, with the only building still standing being the butcher's shop from which he had just come.

A dragon waited in the street, grunting and snorting and pacing. Uriah stared up into its yellow eyes without fear. The dragon stamped its front foot and roared into Uriah's face. Uriah didn't flinch. The creature snorted and roared again, but Uriah stood firm. *Are you finished?* he whispered into the dragon's mind.

The dragon lifted his head away as though he understood.

Uriah smiled. *I'm going to kill you all.*

The dragon snorted and squatted and looked to the sky. With a beat of its massive wings, it launched toward the suns. Uriah watched until it disappeared beyond the clouds.

The days of hunting dragons have begun. The Dragon-Epertasian War starts today.

Uriah looked back at the butcher's shop and then headed for the southern forest where his people had fled. As he crossed the plains toward the people emerging from the trees, the grass grabbed at his feet. He scanned the plains and saw that the grass danced as if each blade had a mind of its own. He looked to the crowd and saw his pregnant wife. At that same moment, she saw him. He crossed the field to her and squeezed her with all his love.

She pulled her head back and cocked it to the side. "You look different somehow."

He nodded. Then he leaned down to kiss her distended belly and wondered, *Will this be the heir to my Light?*

CHAPTER 1

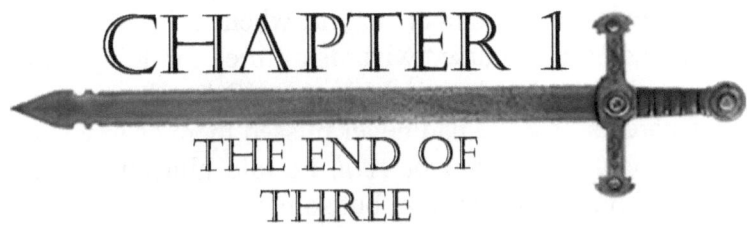

THE END OF
THREE

E pertase had not seen a wizard as powerful as Cyrus in more than fifteen hundred years. But that was before the magic awakened within Tevin the Third. Since true rule of Epertase depended on possessing the Light, capturing Alina was crucial. But Cyn had yet to return with the former queen and Tevin was getting anxious. If anyone knew where Alina hid, it would be the Elder Three.

Tevin walked through the lair's long hallway. As he passed each eternal torch they flared and crackled. Once inside the lair, the walls morphed into the logs of a familiar cabin. The unmistakable scent of pine took Tevin back to his boyhood home. An oil painting of Tevin's mother hung on one wall, identical in every way to the portrait his father had painted many years before. His father's old thinking chair sat next to the fireplace beneath the painting. Tevin half expected to see his father rocking in the chair, though his father was many years dead.

He felt like he was nine years old again. The scent of sweet blueberry tarts lingered over the smell of pine and weakened his knees. It was his mother's favorite treat to make. He braced himself against a wooden stand, the very stand his father had carved when Tevin was five. For a moment, he remembered what it was like to not be consumed by hate and anger, to once more feel childhood innocence and wonder. Though he subconsciously knew what he saw and smelled were simply cruel tricks propagated by wizards, the sound of his mother's voice calling his name from an unseen room sent him to his knees. He let out a groan and clutched the stand.

Some people might enjoy such a magical reminder of a better life, but it was just a game, and knowing that only made Tevin angrier. He didn't want to remember a time when the world seemed so perfect, and damn the cursed wizards of three for doing it to him.

Tevin pulled the stand against his chest. Other than in the months after his parents died, he had never missed them as much as he did at that moment. *This can't be real,* he told himself. He lifted the stand to hurl it across the room, but something caught his eye on its underside. In the center, exactly as his father had carved it in thumb-length letters, were the words "For Tevin."

He felt a tear swell. *For Tevin.* He lowered the stand back to the ground gently and dusted off the top with the back of his hand. What he wouldn't give for his mother to stroll in and lift him from the floor into her loving embrace to make everything all right. But she didn't come from the kitchen. His father wasn't sitting in the chair. And Tevin wasn't home.

He closed his eyes, trying his best to block out the painful reminders, and rose to his feet. "Where are you?" he shouted, his voice echoing as though he were in a canyon. "Enough games. Reveal yourselves."

Faint images of three old men appeared along the wall. They sang as one, "Teeeviiiin? You are not welcome here."

Tevin stepped forward, defiant. He saw a name in his mind that he had never heard before. "I demand to know where Alina is ..." He paused, and his next word dripped with venom. "Cyrus."

The three old wizards looked to each other with surprise and then pulled away from the wall, floating like ghosts. "That name has not been spoken for many centuries. You will not speak it now." A small strip of leather lifted from the floor and shot across the room. It plastered itself over Tevin's mouth, knocking him backward a step.

Tevin ripped the leather away as if the magic behind it was no match for his own. "What did you tell the queen?" he shouted.

"We only told her the answers to what she asked."

"Then I am asking. Where is she now?"

"She is where she needs to be to remain hidden from you."

"Damn it, you must speak the truth to questions asked. The legends say so."

"Yes, we must."

"Then speak the truth or I will tear down this place around you."

"The truth is that we do not wish to tell you where she has gone. Tear away if you must."

"Enough riddles," Tevin screamed, his voice jarring the lair's very foundation.

The three Elders looked curiously at the shaking walls.

"Where is she?" he roared.

The Elder Three floated along the room's perimeter in perfect unison. One of the old wizards reached out invitingly. "Tevin, you are not who you now are. What you hope to achieve has been tried before. You will never possess the Light. The greatest wizards of King Thadius's time found themselves unsuccessful in their attempts, and you will fail as well. The Light is not for you."

"The Light is broken. It has been broken since King Matthew took it from his father."

"That we know."

"I will restore the Light to its greatness. This world has never witnessed the power I now wield." Tevin looked through one of the Elder's transparent bodies to the oil painting of his mother on the farthest wall. His blood boiled at the thought of the wizards besting him with their false images. He pointed at each of them. "Stop your illusory spells or I will stop them for you."

"You see that which you most desire. We have no means to change what you see."

"Then I will end you."

A dull orange glow grew from Tevin's chest, and the painting, along with the wooden walls, melted into the cold stone of the lair. *These wizards will pay for this pain,* he vowed. He began speaking in an ancient tongue unheard by any living soul for many centuries. Even he didn't know where the words came from as he pulled them out of the air.

The Elder Three scowled with concern etched in their hardened faces. "The language you speak is not to be spoken in this world. You violate all natural law."

Tevin broke off his chanting. "Like you did when you cursed this world with the Light in the first place?"

They didn't acknowledge his question. Instead, their eyes glowed red. Tevin felt the heat on his skin an instant before the room exploded into flames. Defiant, he resumed speaking the language of the gods.

In the center of the room, an older woman appeared in a rocking chair untouched by the flames. Tevin didn't recognize her.

"Stop your chanting now," one of the Three shouted, independent of the others.

The woman was older but pretty in a plain sort of way, with shoulder-length curls poking from beneath her teal hood. Tevin wasn't sure what he had accomplished by bringing forth the vision, but planned to watch how it played out.

Another woman entered from a side door. She was younger and prettier. She asked the older woman, "Has Cyrus returned?"

Tevin grinned; now he understood.

The lone Elder who had spoken without the others stepped away from the wall. He exuded sadness that eclipsed any sorrow Tevin had ever beheld.

The Elder floated to the woman in the rocking chair, but she didn't appear to see him. He whispered, "I tried to come home in time." She rocked, oblivious to his presence.

The Elder looked up at Tevin with tear-soaked cheeks, and Tevin saw that the other two Elders wept as well. "Why do you show us such pain?" the Elder asked, again without the harmony of his brethren.

Tevin grinned. "You will feel any pain you inflict on me tenfold."

The Elder reached for the younger woman, but his hand passed through her as she walked by.

The older lady answered, "No, Thasula. He has not returned."

"Well, when he does, let him know that we need fresh water and we—"

Her words were cut short by the blare of a distant horn. Tevin looked over his shoulder toward the sound, but only saw the lair's dark hallway. The older woman stood up and they both looked past Tevin.

The Elders whispered, "Please run. Do not wait for me here."

"Dragons?" the younger woman asked.

The older woman nodded fearfully.

"Should we run?"

The Elders nodded. "Yes. Yes. Run. Please."

But the older woman answered, "Close the shutters. We should wait for Cyrus. We mustn't leave without him."

The lone Elder dropped to his knees. He glared up at Tevin and said through clenched teeth, "No more. End these visions." The flames danced around them.

But Tevin was as curious to see what happened next as he was happy to torture the Three. A roar echoed from outside the illusory room. The flames brightened, and for the first time Tevin felt their heat. Helpless, the Elder Three watched as the women panicked and ran blindly through the smoke to the corner of the room. They huddled together as the flames grew and quickly consumed them. Their screams were ungodly.

The lone Elder whispered repeatedly, "I'm so sorry I wasn't there for you." He clawed at the floor in agony. Anger drew lines on his face and forehead. A low rumble from his gut turned into a roar which shook the room and rivaled the dragons outside. He lunged for Tevin. His face distorted like an abstract painting and his eyes glowed with red hate. His mouth gaped wide enough to swallow Tevin's head. Tevin stood his ground.

A burst of heat hurled Tevin against the wall. His left forearm snapped on impact. He held his wounded arm to his chest and stood up. His fingers went numb. The shattered bones in his forearm crawled beneath his skin. The edges ground together with a sickening din as the deformity righted itself before his eyes.

Impressed, Tevin dusted himself off. When his arm finished mending, he rubbed it and smiled. "I'll ask again. Where is Alina?"

The room changed again into an amalgam of many different rooms. There were boulders and tables intermixed with trees and sand and dirt. Tevin's entire body glowed orange as he fought their illusions with his own. Mental warfare was as much a part of the Elders' arsenal as physical pain. In the center of the illusions, Tevin's grandmother appeared for an instant before Tevin replaced her image with that of a young man he didn't recognize that the Elders called brother.

Tevin stepped away from the wall. He saw Elijah lying in a pool of his own blood in the basement of a factory. He pushed the vision away and an unfamiliar little boy took Elijah's place. Tevin screamed, "You will tell me where Alina hides, one way or another."

The Elders glared at him.

Tevin baited them with a sneer.

One of them charged, but Tevin stood firm. The Elder's skin melted from his ghost-like face, leaving only bone and glowing eyes. He passed through Tevin with a deafening screech, stopped, and turned back.

Tevin dropped to his knees. The hairs on his arms stood on end and his flesh itched deep beneath the skin. He wasn't dead, which meant he was at least as powerful as they were. He pushed back to his feet. His foe tilted his head as his flesh returned to cover his skull.

The Elders realized they had met their match. Together they asked, "What kind of wizard are you?"

Tevin's chest glowed again. The itch below his skin faded. "The kind that ends you."

"If that is to be, then it will be you who replaces us in this lair. It is the Light's will."

Tevin scowled. "No. There is no place that can contain me. As I said, the Light is broken. I can feel it around me in this place, and it is weak. I will make it whole again."

The Elders stood silent.

Tevin glared, one more question burning within. "Before I end you, I must ask. Why is it that you stay in this lair when you are more than powerful enough to break free, especially with the Light so damaged?"

"This lair gives the Light balance. We do not stay because we are unable to leave, Tevin. We stay because it is our sacrifice to the Star of Epertase that allows this kingdom to live. That is also the reason why, if you end us now as you threaten, you will take our place. The Light will never allow you to leave. Epertase's survival depends on it."

"You are fools. I will leave. And when I do, I will take the Light from Alina and restore it to its full power. All will be right again. Only this time, it will be my bloodline who rules forever. Not Uriah's."

The three Elders taunted him with condescending grins. "You are the fool, Tevin. If you kill us, then you must replace us. There is no other way. Even if you find the Light one day, it will matter not. Without you or us here, Epertase will fall within ten of your years. It is the way it must be. It is the deal we made with the Star. Reconsider what you are doing. It cannot end well for you."

Tevin smirked. "Or you. I believe that you lie to save yourselves. With the Light there will be nothing I cannot do, including preventing that which you now falsely prophesize." He sighed in frustration. "Enough talk, old men. Your time has passed."

The Elders lifted their arms, squeezed their fists above their heads, and pulled as though they held ropes fastened to the ceiling. Huge chunks of stone ripped from the straw above and tumbled toward Tevin. He surrounded himself with an invisible bubble, which deflected the chunks of ceiling.

One of the Elders snarled and shot toward him again. Tevin reached out with his footing solid on the floor and grabbed the Elder's throat. The Elder stopped cold within his grasp. Tevin stared into his soulless eyes.

"How do you touch me?" the Elder asked, independent of the others.

Tevin forced the Elder to his knees. With his free hand, he reached for the air beside him and threw an image of a boulder at the other two. They didn't try to escape the boulder's path, no doubt believing it to be harmless. The boulder crashed into them and pinned them against the wall.

The lair was silent. Then the boulder shook and exploded into nothingness.

Tevin hurled the lone Elder at the other two, knocking all three of them to the ground. He waved his hand above his head, grabbing hold of the air and spinning it around the room. The Elders stood up with the winds beating against them. They leaned into it, attempting to remain upright in the wind's increasing force. Tevin stood in the eye of his growing tornado.

The swirling air turned orange with dancing flames.

The Elders screamed in anger, "Teeevin, you disgrace your bloodline."

"You will not judge me," he shouted.

"You are an abomination. It is not too late for you to redeem yourself."

Tevin didn't need redemption; he needed the Light.

The Elder Three released a high-pitched howl that could have been heard throughout Thasula. Their ghost-like flesh pulled away from their bones in concert with the sweet music of their cries.

Unrivaled power coursed hotly through Tevin's veins. He watched as the Elders dropped to their knees in a unified heap within the flaming winds. When they moved no more, he slowed his fiery wind until the lair was as calm and dead as a long-deserted dungeon.

He walked to their bodies and watched as they slowly faded into nothingness at his feet. Knowing they had lived thousands of years in this lair and were no match for his magic made him proud. He was unbeatable. He looked toward the hallway leading out. He walked toward it with a defiant strut. But when he reached the hallway, his nose painfully flattened against an invisible barrier and he stumbled backward. "What kind of desperate spell is this?"

He reached out hesitantly and touched the invisible wall. With both hands, he pushed against it, but the barrier didn't give. Even lowering his shoulder against it didn't help. He stepped back and took a frustrated, angry breath. A blast of magic from his chest only ricocheted and knocked him to his rear. He stood up and dusted himself off. "You will not contain me." He charged the wall again, and again bounced to his butt. "Interesting." He summoned more magic and blasted holes in the surrounding walls, but as quickly as he created them, the stone grew back over them.

This is not possible. No walls can hold me.

He turned back to the blocked hallway and screamed to any gods who were listening, "I demand you free me now." He released another blast and found himself sprawled on the ground once more. He smacked the floor with his hands. His vision blurred from rage. The orange glow grew in his chest until his entire body hid within it. A trickle of blood leaked from his nose.

At the very moment he felt he might burst, the gentle touch of a soft finger brushed his neck and startled him. He spun around, expecting another Elder Three trick. Instead, the image of a woman held his gaze.

"Tevin," she whispered with a soothing voice.

Tevin recognized something about her face, but not enough to call her by name. She was young, in her twenties, and frail. Her high cheekbones made her slightly resemble Tevin's mother.

"Who are you to dare touch me?" he asked.

With the softness of an angel, she whispered, "You are the son to my daughter. You are my blood. I have been watching you." She tilted her head. "The Light has awoken our family's gift within you. With it, you have become more powerful than any person who has ever lived. Use that power to rule these pathetic people. Now, stop playing games and leave this place. Bring glory to our name."

He snapped, "I have tried to leave, but I cannot." He squeezed his fists.

"Yes, you can. You are not trapped. You can free yourself. But you must first control your anger." She ran her fingers down his arm to his wrist and guided his hand to the barrier. With her fingers intertwined with his, she touched the wall. "Use your magic, not your anger. Break through this barrier and free yourself."

"That's what I've been trying to do." He shifted to a more solid stance. His chest began to glow, and that glow ran along his arm to the invisible wall.

She whispered, "Good. Focus your gift."

Tevin pressed his hand against the wall. His muscles tingled with power. His grandmother released his hand and backed away. He closed his eyes. His arms shook and his legs quivered. With a calming breath, he released his magic into the barrier instead of against it. The invisible wall turned orange.

Proudly, Tevin looked back, but his grandmother was gone. With a smirk at where the Elder Three had died and disappeared, he said, "Stuck in here for eternity, huh? Maybe when the Light was stronger it could have contained me, but not now." Tevin followed the long hallway into the streets of Thasula. The torches died behind him.

CHAPTER 2

A FALSE GOD

Rasi ached from his chest through his spine. Heat radiated from his skin as though his bones were on fire. Each troubled breath wheezed from his damaged lungs. He couldn't open his eyes as the throbbing behind them hurt too much. His heels rubbed against something hard like rock, which sent painful needles through his shattered foot. His six living straps tugged at his back.

As the pain in his head subsided, memories of the fishers dragging him into their kingdom flashed through his staticky thoughts. He groaned with each breath, too tired to prevent the sound from passing his lips. Sharp pain shot from his wrist to his elbow. When he finally found the strength to open his eyes, a thick, crusty gunk held his lids closed.

Wherever he was, it reeked of sulfur. He was high off the ground, hanging by his straps. There was someone next to him. A cold, wet cloth pressed against his forehead. He flinched. A female voice whispered into his ear, "Shhhh. Iiee help Rassiiieee." The cold cloth felt like heaven on his feverish forehead and cheeks. She gently wiped his eyes, dragging the gunk away.

After his eyes adjusted to the dim glow around him, he lowered his gaze past his dangling feet. The distant ground was lined with torches, which seemed odd since fishers were blind.

He breathed in short bursts of sulfuric, stale air. The echo of fishers using their high-pitched squeals to guide them told him he was in a cavern of monstrous size.

He squinted and turned his head toward the female beside him. She was a fisher, standing atop a ladder made of bones. Her hair was thin, black, and patchy like chunks had been ripped away in a fight. She was covered in scars and wounds in various stages of healing. Her hanging gut bore tangled maps of stretch marks along both sides, indicating she was a mother. Or had been at one time. Once her cloth was as warm as his flesh, she dropped it. Rasi followed it down until it landed near the torches. He lifted his eyes back to her. She smiled and touched his cheeks with both hands. Her clawed fingers were calloused and cold.

He tried to speak, but she crammed the two stubby, scoop-like claws on her palms into his mouth, almost chipping his front teeth. They tasted like metal and blood.

"Shhhh," she hissed again. "Theyee'll heeear you. You must rest. You are with your peeeople now." She withdrew her claws from his mouth and looked around.

He used the last of his strength to look over his right shoulder. Three of his straps had been stretched flat and nailed with spikes to the rock wall. The other three were nailed on the left side.

"Why?" he struggled to whisper.

She tilted her head and stared for a moment. Then she reached to her waist where a bladder of water hung from a crudely made rope. She held the spout to his dry, cracked lips and dribbled the contents into his mouth. The water was warm, stale, and refreshing.

Rasi hadn't the strength to hold his head up any longer.

She rubbed the back of her finger along his cheek with a gentleness he'd never expected a fisher to possess. Her finger followed the contour of his jaw, under his chin, and across his chest to his mangled forearm. "This is bad. Iieee help you." She gripped his wrist with one hand and his elbow with the other.

Rasi shook his head frantically. He tried to pull his crooked arm away, but he was too weak. Without a hint of remorse, she jerked and twisted, scraping the ends of his bones together until his forearm was straighter. He groaned and winced and turned his head away. She pressed her forearm against his mouth. For a moment, he felt as much pain as he had when Fice's hammer snapped his arm in the first place. And then the pain turned to numbness.

She rubbed the back of his head. "There, there. You beee better now, myee lord."

Lord?

She caressed his cheek again, smiled, and then climbed down the ladder. She passed through the torchlight at the bottom and disappeared into the darkness. Eventually, he fell asleep again. And with sleep, he dreamed.

Rasi's dreams took him back to the mountains near Shadows Peak. Alina had taken a short leave from the kingdom and secretly traveled to his cave home for a weeklong visit. Though hiking through the mountain passes could be extremely dangerous, Alina convinced him to take her on an adventure. Since she seemed to hold a spell over him, he reluctantly agreed.

When they reached Widow's Run, she climbed onto one of the boulders at its base and sat staring while he gathered dead branches for a fire. Feeling her eyes on him, he stopped and looked up at her. At first, he believed she had been merely watching him work, but as he looked closer, he realized she stared at his furry chin.

Why do you stare?

"I think I would like to see you one day with your chin bare."

"Hmph." *It gets pretty cold out here.*

"Can I ask you a question?"

Have you ever not?

"How old are you?"

Well, I must think about that for a moment. What year is it now?

"Matthew 1017."

Then that would mean I have seen thirty-two birthdays.

"That's all?"

He cocked his head and feigned offense. *Yes, that's all. I went to war for your kingdom when I was very young. Sixteen. How many birthdays have you seen, Princess?*

"Twenty-two. Twenty-three in a month. My father says I should have been married by now, and he isn't pleased with my behavior toward the many suitors he has invited to the castle. Blair, the man I was with when you saved me from the ochrid, was the only suitor for whom I felt enough affection to marry."

You don't like the others he has chosen?

"They've all been fine gentlemen and would make wonderful kings, but ..." She shyly bit her lower lip. "I kind of have an eye for another." She climbed down.

Is that so?

"Well," she said and turned away. *Maybe if he would shave his dreadful beard.*

Rasi paused. *Dreadful?*

He knelt by the growing fire as one of the rock formations jutting from the mountain's face caught his eye. In all the times he had been to Widow's Run, he had never paid much attention to how much the jagged, half-circle formation resembled a partial crown. He turned back to tell her.

She met his lips with her own, catching him off guard. He hadn't felt the kiss of a woman in a very long time and he didn't know how to react. She pulled back slightly, her smile hovering just out of reach. He smiled in return and dropped to his rear.

"Now, what did you want to show me?" she asked, and lifted his arm so she could lean against the side of his chest. Still stunned, he lowered his arm around her shoulder and pointed toward the crown.

He didn't have to say anything else. In fact, he probably couldn't have even if he wanted. He held her as the stars filled the sky and she fell asleep in his arms.

A twinge of pain from his broken foot woke him. For a moment he forgot where he was, but the pull of his straps at his back quickly reminded him he was in hell. The times he had spent alone with Alina had been magical, and the mere memory was enough to help him through.

For now.

CHAPTER 3

TEK ISLAND

The shoreline of Torick Island was a high, jagged cliff that overlooked the water. Atticus rowed Alina's boat into a lagoon within the cliff walls. It took all of Alina's strength to hold her head up and see where her friends were staring. The scenery would have been breathtaking if not for the army of Tek soldiers standing in wait along the cliff's edge.

Homer pressed Alina's shoulders back down onto the rolled shirt she had been using as a pillow. The rhythmic bob of the calm ocean had lulled Cridon to sleep in her arms. Atticus and Doctor Eckels argued in intense whispers at the prow.

"We should turn back," Atticus said.

"We can't. Alina's been through too much. She's too weak. She'll never make it."

Irene caressed Alina's forehead while whispering encouraging words into her ear. Reluctantly, Atticus continued rowing until they reached a long pier. Looking up, they could no longer see the Teks beyond the rocky overhang, but they saw an elevated platform hanging from a pulley at the top of the cliff.

"Will they kill us?" Alina whispered.

Homer turned away without answering. Atticus shook his head and said, "I don't think so, Alina," but his tone was less than convincing.

The boat rocked and bumped the cliff wall as small waves beat against the side. Atticus hung over the edge and tied the boat to one of the many posts near the dock.

"Who is there?" someone above shouted in perfect Epertasian.

Atticus stood gingerly in the boat. "I am Captain Atticus of the Epertasian military. We are here in peace. I have need of medical care, food, and shelter." For what seemed like a lifetime, no one answered.

"I don't think we should have come here," Alina whispered.

Atticus's eyes narrowed. "We had no choice. I swear I will protect you to my death."

The wooden planks of the platform swayed above, the chains jangled, and the platform slowly descended. Atticus quietly drew his sword.

The platform stopped on the wooden pier, carrying four Tek soldiers. One of them said, "Captain Atticus, is that really you?"

Atticus nodded.

"It's an honor to see you again."

"Again?"

"Yes. My name is Leander. We met briefly after the war. You were with Queen Alina and ..." As he spoke, he peered past Atticus to where Alina lay in pool of blood. "Queen Alina?"

Atticus stepped into his line of sight. "Yes. It is Alina. She is ill and in need of care."

"By the machine gods, bring her aboard." He motioned two of his companions toward the boat. Atticus tensed his muscles as the Teks climbed from their platform.

Easy, Atticus, Alina said in his mind.

The Teks cautiously maneuvered past Atticus. One of them must have sensed Atticus's tension because he whispered, "Excuse me, sir," in Epertasian. He then nodded politely toward Irene, knelt next to Alina, and said, "Relax, Queen Alina, and let us do the work."

He shoved one hand under her shoulders and another under her knees. The other Tek did the same from the opposite side and they locked their hands together. When the boat swayed, they paused to steady themselves. Then they hoisted her up with Cridon still cradled against her chest. Gently, they carried mother and son to the platform.

Atticus started to climb aboard, but Leander stopped him with a hand on his shoulder. "It isn't strong enough to carry more. I will send the platform back down immediately."

Atticus batted Leander's hand away. "I will not stay behind."

"That's how it has to be, I am afraid. Any added weight and we risk falling into the ocean."

Atticus's face reddened. "Leave one of your men here if you must, but I will not leave her alone with you."

Alina whispered, "Atticus. Let me go with them."

"Your Majesty, I cannot."

"You must. We have to trust them. It's our only chance."

Leander added, "Captain Atticus, you have my word. This platform will immediately return for you and your party. Queen Alina showed us mercy when she spared our lives after the war; we will not let her be harmed." The contraption jerked and began to rise.

At the top of the cliff wall, the Teks carried Alina to a horse-drawn carriage. The last words she heard came from Leander when he said, "Lower the platform and get the others. Bring them to Tek City."

The carriage jerked forward. Alina looked out over a beautiful field of green. In the distance, a herd of wild horses gracefully ran along the edge of a tree line, and she wondered why she had never traveled to the islands to see such beauty before. She rested her head and stared at the cloudless sky until she fell asleep again.

CHAPTER 4

A BROKEN MAN

Masera struggled to hold his water bladder to his lips and empty the last drops into his cotton-dry mouth. Dragging his shattered legs into Homer's house took him an entire afternoon as well as a lot of pain and energy he didn't have. Early during his second day of crawling through the house, he had stopped looking at his grotesque injuries. Seeing his leg bones jutting in such unnatural ways, one even poking through the skin, was almost worse than the unrelenting pain.

The suns had risen four times since Cyn had broken him. At some point, he stopped worrying that she might return to finish the job because there wasn't anything he could do about it if she did. Even if his legs weren't so damaged, he wasn't strong enough to go for help and was relegated to hoping a helpful stranger would happen by. As a soldier, he'd long ago lost faith in hope.

On the fifth afternoon, he pulled himself back to the porch in an attempt to get to the well. He would die of thirst if he didn't. The porch steps were torture. He was half-way to the well when he noticed two horses and riders prancing along the road.

"Hey," he shouted weakly. He waved. They didn't notice at first, but he mustered the strength to yell again and that time they heard.

They rode toward him. It was two women. "Hello?" the younger one said as she approached. "Are you all right?" Then she passed the well and saw his legs. She gasped. "Grandmother," she shouted. "He's hurt badly."

The older lady joined her and also gasped at the sight of his legs. "By the gods, young man. What happened to you?" She didn't give him time to answer. "No matter. We'll get you into the house and take care o—"

"No," Masera snapped. "You've gotta get me far from here."

She dismounted and stepped carefully over his legs. "I suppose we could take you to town and find Doctor Thompson, though he's probably drunk already." Then she mumbled, "Some people take good doctors for granted until they up and move to Thasula." Then she looked into the air and added, "I'm talking to you, Doc Eckels."

Drunk doctor or sober, he didn't care as long as they took him somewhere else.

"Come here, Josephine. Grab under his arm. Be gentle."

The younger woman dismounted and hurried over. Masera groaned as the slightest tug ripped at the mending flesh of his many lacerations. The fractured bones of his lower legs ground against each other as the two women dragged him toward Josephine's horse.

"Find something we can lay him on so we can pull him back to the cottage," the older lady said.

"Yes, ma'am." Josephine disappeared into Homer's barn. The older woman knelt beside Masera and produced a fresh water bladder. She dribbled water onto his lips. Before he was finished, she lifted the bladder away and said, "Slowly, young man. If you drink too much too quickly, it may give you the heaves."

After a few moments, Josephine returned dragging a broken plank of wood. "Will this work?" she asked.

"It'll have to. Help me roll him onto it."

Masera dreaded the move, but he understood the necessity. He held his breath. The pain was excruciating.

The two women placed his back on the wood and tied the plank to the saddle. Josephine walked alongside, keeping her horse at a slow, steady pace. She winced along with him at each bump and jerk.

"I'm so sorry," she said. It was the last thing he heard before darkness swallowed him.

When he opened his eyes again, he was lying in a bed in an unfamiliar room. He pulled the linen away from his bare chest and discovered he wore bandages and little else. As he removed the bedding from atop his legs, he found his lower limbs were bound with wooden splints.

He felt light-headed and strange, almost like he'd imbibed too much ale. His legs didn't hurt nearly as badly as they had before. He held his hand in front of his face and saw that his fingers were also splinted and wrapped in bandages. His little finger was free of the wooden splints and he poked it clumsily at his lips. They felt funny.

Someone knocked on the door and then opened it without waiting for an answer.

"Are you awake, friend?" Josephine asked.

Masera yanked the linen back over him as she entered. She turned away, embarrassed. Now that his vision wasn't so blurry, he saw how pretty she was. He'd always been drawn to darker features, and her hazelnut hair with tight curls that draped over her shoulders was just his type.

"Good morning, sir," she said.

Masera's throat hurt when he spoke. "Are you the one who undressed me?"

She blushed and turned away. "I tried not to look any more than I had to. But my grandmother insisted you get a bath and she was too weak to get you ready on her own."

"It's all right, Josephine. It is Josephine, right?"

She smiled, surprised he remembered her name. "Why, yes," she answered. She poured a mug of water from the bedside stand. "Let me help you."

She cupped the back of his neck and gently lifted his head while holding the mug to his chapped lips. Masera gulped the entire mug down without stopping for a breath. She lowered his head back to the pillow.

"How long have I been asleep?"

"You've been in and out for two days."

"Why do I feel so strange?"

She grinned. "We gave you medicine to help with the pain. Unfortunately, it causes the strange feelings you're now experiencing."

Masera considered arguing about her use of the word "unfortunately."

"We have also been giving you medicine to help with your infection, which I feared was about to do you in as late as yesterday. But your fever broke overnight, and the worst seems to be behind you." Her pleasant smile faded into a frown. "Your legs are very injured, I'm afraid."

"Just need some time to heal, ma'am."

She glanced at his toes as they peeked out from the bottom of the linen. They were an ugly shade of purple. "I don't know if I agree. Are you able to move your toes?"

Of course he was able to move his toes.

"Go ahead," she said. "Move them."

What does she mean? I am *moving them.*

She sadly covered his feet and asked, "Are you hungry?"

Masera nodded. She warmly touched his shoulder before leaving the room.

By the time Josephine came back, the pain had returned a bit. He grimaced when she sat on the bed next to him and hoped she didn't notice. She held bread and a bowl of steaming gravy. "I'm sorry we don't have much to offer, but we were heading to the market when we found you and haven't made it back."

"This will be more than fine." This time he was unable to hide his grimace as he sat up. "I have something I must tell you. You have put yourself and your grandmother in grave danger by helping me. The assassin who did this will track me here, I have no doubt."

"Oh. How will this assassin find us?"

"She's very skilled, maybe the best ever. She's searching for Queen Alina, and she believes I know where to find her."

"Queen Alina? You fight for our queen?"

"With my life."

"Then you have found two new allies, kind sir. I met the queen once while she was still a princess, and I found her generous beyond reproach. I am happy to hear she is alive and remains free."

"For now."

"How can we help you?"

"You can't. You need to take me away from here before the assassin comes for me."

"Well, how 'bout we take you to the queen? Do you know where she is?"

Masera stared into her hazel eyes, searching for any hint of deceit. "I can't let you do that. Anyone who knows where the queen is mustn't return home again. It would be too dangerous."

"Oh. I see." She didn't say anything else, just sat quietly and watched Masera finish the gravy. She took his bowl, tenderly touched his cheek, and then left the room again. When she returned, her grandmother was with her. She said, "We have decided to take you where you need to go."

Masera didn't know how to answer at first. "But you don't even know me. Why would you give up your lives here for a stranger?"

The grandmother spoke. "We recognize the kind of man you are. That's all that's important."

Masera stared, confused.

"You're a soldier, are you not?" she asked.

Masera nodded.

"And your injuries are from defending Queen Alina, yes?"

Masera nodded again.

"We would do anything for our queen. If that means we need to return you to her, then so be it."

"I cannot ask you to put yourselves in any more danger. Just put me on a horse and send me on my—"

"Nonsense. We will not discuss this further. Shall we depart now or in the morning?"

Every moment they waited was a moment closer to Cyn finding them. Masera didn't hesitate. "We should leave now."

"Are you able to travel?"

"I'll manage."

The grandmother immediately left the room. Josephine forced a smile, but the unease in her eyes gave her away.

"What's your grandma's name?"

"Blanche."

"You know you don't have to do this."

Her hand touched her cheek. "We know."

Masera hated bringing two more people into the fray, but he was a soldier first and knew sacrifices had to be made in times of war— sometimes by ordinary people. Besides, Josephine and Blanche were his only chance to get back to Alina and tell her what Cyn had told him. She should know Rasi was dead.

CHAPTER 5

HUNTING GILDONESE

Eldon opened his eyes with a grimace. His face was numb and tight and one of his eyes didn't open all the way. He massaged his sore jaw, wondering why it hurt so badly to open his mouth. The familiar lump in his mattress at the small of his back, along with a look to the ceiling, told him he was home. But how? Daylight shone through his bedroom window.

Sitting up was a chore. His body ached like a belke slug had eaten him and shat him out the other end. His skin stung like he'd kicked a beehive. Pulling back his sticky, blood-soaked sheets revealed the painful reason why. The skin on his sides and back and legs was raw and abraded.

"Rasi?" he called out. "Alina?"

No one answered. Maybe they had gone to town for supplies. As he pressed his sore back against his headboard, he saw more blood on the wall as if someone had been in a fight. With a groan, he threw his legs over the edge of the bed and his feet found the reason for the blood on the walls.

He looked down. "Dog?" He leaned over and scooped his dead friend into his arms. "Who did this to you?" Then he looked to the door. Maybe the killer was still there? He gently laid Dog on the bed and searched the room for his sword. Since he religiously kept it near his bed and it wasn't there, he concluded that someone, perhaps the one who'd killed his dog, must have stolen it.

Cautious, he cracked open his door and swept the living quarters with his eyes. The front door was wide open. A startled squank scurried from behind his chair and through the open door. He followed it onto the porch. The grass around his home was taller than he'd ever let it grow and he wondered how long he'd been asleep. He finished searching his house for intruders. Rasi and Alina's room was empty with the bed made. Eldon crept back outside. He walked his land in search of intruders, but didn't find any signs anyone had been there recently. He returned to his house for a chore he dreaded.

He retrieved Dog and carried him to the field behind the barn. Then he went to the barn for a spade. Inside, two strange horses wandered about, while his horses were gone. They were lean and fit, worthy of the racing scene. *Mighty fine steeds to be hanging around my barn.* Nothing made sense. He left the doors open so his new horses could graze.

Eldon grabbed his spade and spent part of the afternoon digging a deep enough hole that Dog could rest forever in peace. While digging, he kept his eyes alert for anyone who might approach, whether it be an enemy or Rasi and Alina. He said a few kind words about Dog, though there wasn't much one could say about a dog other than, "Thanks for being a friend," and then returned to the house to make dinner. The fruit on his table was rotten so he threw it out for the scavengers. He decided he'd make enough porridge for three people, just in case.

When Alina and Rasi didn't return that evening and he had to throw away half the porridge, he wondered if they had gone to start the war against Fice early without saying goodbye. It seemed rude and not like them, which made him worry. The more he thought about it, the more Rasi leaving for war without him made no sense. He had an important task to accomplish which seemed crucial to Rasi's plans. Was he supposed to leave on his own? Did they change their minds and go home? He wondered when Atticus would show up to set the plan in motion. Maybe Rasi was with him now.

He poured himself a glass of warm water and looked into a piece of reflective glass hanging over his wash sink. "Woah." It was worse than he thought. He poked at his tender eye with a wince. Someone had done quite a number on him.

Before he took his first sip of water, something heavy landed on his roof. He flinched and the water glass shattered on the floor. He barreled into the front yard where he could see his roof.

"Odd," he whispered. It had been more than two centuries since he had seen a hylock, but now, as sure as he was standing in his own yard, one of the Wasteland creatures squatted near his chimney. "And why is it you sit upon my roof, creature?" he asked.

The hylock didn't move. A shadow passed along the ground, drawing Eldon's eyes to the sky. He counted a dozen more hylocks flying overhead. "Odd indeed."

The hylock on his roof finally answered, "You will diiee, Gildoneeese."

"Heh. Is that so?"

"It is Tevin's will."

Tevin? Who's Tevin?

The hylock bounced along the roof to the edge. Eldon had no qualms about killing hylocks, but he did see it as a bit of a challenge when there were so many of them. A glance toward the forest gave him a workable plan. The cover of trees could help against their numbers. It would be quite a run, but Eldon was exceptionally fast.

After a goading wink, he tore off toward the trees. The hylocks gave chase, but their speed was no match for his. He reached the forest with plenty of distance between them. His biggest concern was their legendary venom. He'd be wise to stay away from their nails. He leaped toward a high branch of the closest tree and gracefully scaled it to wait three-quarters of the way up.

Soon, twelve hylocks entered the forest, sweeping the ground with their noses.

Eldon waited.

When three of them strayed from the pack and searched below, Eldon leaned forward. And still he waited. Once they were directly below him, he released the branch. Without a sound, he fell, his arms extended at his sides. He landed on the back of one creature while catching the legs of the other two. He barely grunted on impact. He sprang to his feet.

The hylocks screeched and frantically flapped their wings. He stomped on the neck of the creature beneath him, killing it instantly. Then he pulled the other two closer. They slashed at his chest with their venomous nails, but they were wild and panicked. He danced away with the fluidity of smoke. He slammed one hylock to the ground, stunning it, and then ripped off the head of the other. The stunned hylock scurried away with its wings flailing. Eldon pounced, crushing its skull against the closest tree.

It was no longer a surprise. The other creatures weaved between the trees. It was going to get messy.

The first creature struck like lightning. Eldon sidestepped and ripped off its wings as it lunged past. Another one dove toward his back. Eldon leaped backward, arching his spine just out of reach of the creature's clawed fingers. What he wouldn't give to have his sword. Another one silently stalked from behind, thinking itself sneaky and Eldon too preoccupied to notice. But Eldon had already smelled it. He pretended to stumble behind a thick oak. As the creature pounced, he rounded the other side to the hylock's back. Another hylock, too far away to help, screamed a warning, but it was too late. Eldon snapped a branch free and plunged it through the creature's back. With it convulsing on the ground, he turned to the others. Whoever Tevin was, he had greatly underestimated Eldon by sending pathetic hylocks to do his work.

The rest of the hylocks swarmed. Eldon dodged with spins and bobs and leaps. One by one, they fell to his violent grace until he stood in the center of a dozen dead or dying creatures. He had hardly broken a sweat. He sought out one who hadn't yet succumbed to its injuries. "Why do you creatures hunt me? Does Fice hold sway over you as well?"

"Fiieece is dead. Wee serve Tevin."

"That's the second time one of you has said that name. Who is this Tevin who has sent you to meet your death in this forest so far from your home?"

The creature turned away.

"Very well. This Tevin may send an army if he wishes, and I will end that army just as I did you pathetic creatures." Eldon grabbed its head with both hands. He snapped the creature's neck. After a quick scan of the surrounding bodies, he dusted himself off. Again and again, he repeated the name Tevin as he walked back to his house. Maybe one day he would seek out this "Tevin" and have a few words with him. As soon as he figured out where the hell Rasi had gone.

CHAPTER 6

WORD OF RASI'S DEATH

Alina stretched with a groan. She felt rested for the first time in a long time. While Cridon slumbered in a Tek-built crib beside her bed, she freshened up and dressed for the day. She was no sooner finished than someone knocked on her bedroom door.

"Alina?" She instantly recognized Doc Eckels's voice.

"Come in," she said.

The doctor entered and his eyes widened.

"Why do you look at me so?"

"I'm just amazed at how quickly you improve, my queen."

"Thanks in no small part to you."

"You heal because of your strength."

Cridon cooed from his crib. Doc Eckels glanced at him. "May I hold him?"

"Of course."

He lifted Cridon from the crib and cradled him to his chest.

Cridon squirmed and began to cry. "He must not enjoy my company. Babies are wiser than their years, I suspect."

Alina smiled. "Nonsense. He's just hungry."

Doc Eckels passed Cridon to her. He turned away while Alina lifted her blouse and held Cridon to her bosom. With a blanket covering both her and Cridon, she told the doctor it was safe for him to turn back. "What brings you here this morning, Doc?"

"I have news."

"Oh?" Her eyes blossomed with hope.

"Two women arrived at the island this morning and Masera was with them."

"Masera? That's wonderful. Is he well?"

"I'm afraid not. Cyn injured him quite badly."

Her hand covered her mouth. "Oh my. Will he live?"

"Yes, but I'm afraid he will never walk again."

Alina drew her hand from her mouth down to her breaking heart. "That's awful. I'd like to see him."

"Of course. Though I cannot guarantee he will be awake. He is still recovering."

"I understand. Please send one of the Teks standing guard in the hall for Irene." Doc Eckels complied, and when he returned, she asked, "Who are the women with him?"

"A woman named Blanche and her granddaughter, Josephine. I know them from when I worked near Parsons. Masera said they saved him from certain death. Judging by the state in which he arrived, I don't doubt his words."

By the time the guard returned with Irene, Alina had finished nursing and changing Cridon. The two Tek guards fell in behind them as Doc Eckels escorted Alina through the halls.

They passed from the front door into the street of an incredible Tek town that stole her breath each time she saw it. The Teks who weren't on duty as soldiers wore such fancy suits they must have taken hours to don all the finery. Alina couldn't understand why anyone would want to wear such elaborate outfits simply to go about their everyday lives, but the Teks had their own traditions and culture which she would probably never completely understand.

In the short time she had been there, the Teks had changed the dirt road that ran past the front of her home into a hard, black surface that burned her feet if she didn't wear shoes on a hot day. When she asked Leander why they covered the dirt roads with the new surface that slowed the horses, he answered, "For smoother rides in the wheeled machines we will soon build, of course."

Well, of course.

She hadn't yet seen any of these "wheeled machines," but was quite anxious for the opportunity. Every Tek soldier stopped and respectfully bowed their heads as Alina passed.

Once inside Doc Eckels's new infirmary, Alina searched the room for Masera, quickly finding him in one of the beds. A young woman with hazelnut hair and a longing gaze stood beside his bed. Alina hurried across the room. She could not hide her sadness at the sight of Masera's poorly healing scars and the shape of the blanket that tightly wrapped his crooked legs. His eyes were open and he smiled when she approached.

Alina nodded to the young woman. The lady lowered her gaze and humbly said, "Queen Alina, my name is Josephine. It is an honor to meet you again."

"Again?"

"You once stopped at my village while you were still princess."

"I am afraid I don't remember, Josephine."

"I didn't suppose you would. But you were kind and I have never forgotten." She bowed and stepped backward. "Excuse me, I will leave you two alone."

"Thank you. And thank you for bringing my loyal friend to us. Epertase is grateful."

Josephine smiled, bowed again, and left.

Masera asked, "Why do you look at me with such sadness, my queen? I'm still alive."

"I am just sad that you have suffered so. Doctor Eckels told me about your legs." Her eyes subconsciously went to them again.

"Yes, well, war has costs that every man involved must accept if they are fortunate enough to retain their lives. I see myself as fortunate."

Masera reached out and touched her quivering hand at her side. Two steel plates sandwiched his forearm, and she touched one of them. "You did this for my kingdom and me."

"I did my duty." He winced.

She withdrew her hand. "Where do you hurt most?"

His face relaxed, indicating that the wave of pain had passed. "Everywhere," he answered, followed by a forced chuckle.

Doc Eckels nudged past her. "Excuse me, Alina. Let me give him something for his pain." Alina sat in a bedside chair and waited. Doc Eckels placed a leaf into his palm and wadded it into a ball. "Here," he said as he placed it in Masera's open mouth. "This'll help." Masera chewed on the leaf while Eckels excused himself.

Alina leaned closer. "Your suffering will not be in vain. We will find Rasi and we will regroup. We—"

Masera stopped chewing and sadly turned his head away.

"Masera? What is it?"

Without looking away from the wall, he swallowed and said, "I must tell you something, but I do not know how."

"You have never been one to hold your tongue before. Just say what's troubling you."

"It's something that Cyn told me."

"Yes? What is it?"

He sighed. "Alina, I'm so sorry. She said Rasi was …" He paused. Alina leaned in.

He took a deep breath. "Cyn told me that Rasi was killed. She said she saw his broken body."

Alina stood up, knocking her chair over. His words were like flames and her heart like straw. Her stomach felt suddenly empty and cramped. Her knees went weak and she steadied herself with a hand on the bedside table. She shook her head. "No. That cannot be. Cyn is lying. She is a liar." Her eyes blurred.

Masera didn't respond.

She swallowed hard, denial seemingly the only way to keep from completely breaking down. "It's not true, Masera. I will not believe such. What proof do you have besides the words of a known liar and scoundrel?"

"None, Your Majesty."

"Rasi has been underestimated before."

"That he has. I understand your resolve, Alina, but while you may hold on to hope, we must plan for the worst."

Alina backed away. She wiped her eyes and turned her back to him. She needed to be alone. "Excuse me, Masera. I must go." She hurried from the room, passing Josephine and Doc Eckels without saying a word. Her Tek guards trailed her home.

CHAPTER 7

CRUCIFIED

Rasi had no way of knowing how many days had passed or even whether it was day or night. He continued to fade in and out of consciousness while hanging high above the cavern floor. All he knew was that he could take deeper breaths than before, so perhaps enough time had passed that his lung was actually healing.

His conscious moments were filled with fishers by the dozens entering the room, kneeling in the torch light with their foreheads pressed to the ground, and praying. Then they would leave, only to be replaced by dozens more.

The female fed him raw squank at irregular intervals, and with each meal his strength slowly returned. The pain in his arm and foot had mostly subsided, and he could hold his head up for longer periods of time. During each of the female's visits, he tried to ask why he was there, why he was hanging from his straps and not slaughtered like every other person the creatures had hunted. Instead of answers, she repeatedly shushed him and made sure none of the others had heard.

But he was determined to get answers and wouldn't relent. As she climbed the ladder after another of his naps, he asked again, "Why?"

When she reached him, she shoved her scoop-claw into his mouth with her palm pressed against his lips. "Shhhh," she hissed.

Unwilling to be silenced, Rasi twisted away from her palm, but her scoop-claw was already pressing the inside of his cheek. He considered biting it. Her pale, blind eyes grew wide and she shook her head frantically as he struggled to free his mouth. She bobbed her head toward the other fishers on the ground.

Two of the fishers kneeling below lifted their orange glowing eyes toward him. Glowing eyes meant they had recently eaten and could see better than the others. One of them shouted, "Is heee awake?"

"No," the female lied, but Rasi was done waiting for his fate; he was ready to force their hand. He bit down and she yanked her claw away with a shriek. The other fishers stood up. Their eyes weren't glowing.

Rasi tried to shout, "What do you want with me?" but his words were mostly unintelligible. His straps squirmed and painfully pulled at their restraints.

One of the fishers fled the cavern while another climbed the ladder. The rest of them stood in wait.

"Iiee told you to beee quiiiee-et," the female said. "Iiee must go." She began descending the ladder as the other fisher approached. When they met in the center, he knocked her over the side. She caught one of the lower rungs with a jolt and a grunt. Then she continued down, favoring her shoulder.

When the fisher reached him, Rasi glared hatefully at it. The fisher wore dried blood across its chest and a fresh laceration on its forehead that stretched from ear to ear, a sign that not all sighted creatures gave up their eyes easily. The fisher leaned closer and squinted. It had the same sulfuric stench that all fishers did, but this one exuded the fresh stink of death as well. It snorted and sniffed Rasi's chest.

Rasi pulled as far away from the creature as his restraints would allow. He wanted to grab its head and snap its damn neck, but he didn't feel strong enough for a fight yet. The fisher reached to its waist and drew a pointed, sharpened bone from a crude sheath at its hip. It slowly moved the shank toward Rasi's side.

"You will never leeeave us," it hissed, its voice deep and serious.

Rasi watched the spike as it pressed against the flesh of his ribcage. "No, no, no," he begged.

The fisher looked away, appearing somewhat guilty for what it was about to do. It whispered, "Forgive mee," and then jammed the spike beneath Rasi's ribs.

Rasi groaned and gnashed his teeth.

The fisher withdrew its weapon, allowing the blood to pour from Rasi's side. Then it removed a dirty rag that was tied around a wound on its left arm and shoved it against the new hole in Rasi's gut.

Rasi seethed with hate, his breaths loud and angry. A million ways to slaughter the creature raced through his mind and he was furious at his inability to carry them out.

The fisher held a finger to Rasi's lips and whispered, "Shhhh."

Rasi snapped his teeth at its finger, but the fisher jerked out of reach.

The fisher held the rag to Rasi's wound until it soaked up enough blood to stick. Satisfied, the fisher climbed down the ladder. The female raced back up after he was gone. When she pulled the bloody cloth from Rasi's wound and jammed her own cloth against it, he flinched away from the sting. *Probably salt,* he figured. For that he was grateful.

After the pain faded into numbness, he whispered, "Why?"

She eased some of the pressure on his wound long enough to answer, "You are our god. You will heeal our eyeees."

Rasi used what strength he had left to look down at his fresh wound.

She said, "If you get strong, you will leeave us."

Rasi turned his head away in disgust. She was wrong. If he was strong, he wouldn't leave. He would stay and kill them all.

"Sleeeep now." She lightly dragged her scoop-claw from his forehead to his nose as if to close his eyes for him.

He'd sleep when he wanted to sleep. She climbed down the ladder. Eventually, he did close his eyes.

When he opened them again, the pain in his side had dulled enough to be bearable. He dozed on and off, spending most of his waking moments staring down at the praying fishers with disdain, and most of his sleeping moments dreaming of Alina.

As before, the female fisher continued to bring him food and water and, as sad as it was, company. When a group of worshipping fishers left the room and before a fresh group arrived, he asked her name.

"Meeela," she answered.

Rasi watched the entrance for the next group. In his garbled voice, he asked why the fishers had torches.

"You are the god of the Liieeght. You are the one of whom the legends speeak. You must never bee in the dark liieeke us again."

Rasi shook his head; she couldn't be more wrong.

She gently pushed his arm away from his side to look at his wound. "It is getteeng better."

"Why he'p me?"

"It is myee dutee to keeep you aliieeve."

Rasi didn't fight her touch as she dabbed at his wound with a stinging ointment. He figured whatever it was, it likely helped keep infection at bay, though he was fine with the salt. After she finished feeding him squank meat and quenching his thirst with more stale water, she lightly kissed his shoulder and climbed back down the ladder.

Rasi watched her weave through the fresh group of arriving fishers and move from the cavern into the hall. He understood what they wanted from him now and knew it was something he could never give.

Time passed and Rasi started to feel strong again, or at least stronger than he had in a while. His lung and rib didn't steal his breath with each movement anymore. Nor did his reset arm and slowly healing foot constantly remind him of the hell they had been through. Even the newer wound on his side had mended enough not to pull at itself each time he shifted his weight below his straps. All of that meant another assault to weaken him was coming soon—unless he did something to stop it.

He alerted his straps. *The time is here. We have to free ourselves before they hurt us again.*

The straps were eager. With a subtle flinch, one strap tugged at the spike that held it to the wall. It stung as though the spike was ripping through Rasi's own hand, but that was expected. Below, the fishers continued their daily prayers to their hanging "deity," oblivious of his quiet, painful struggle.

Rasi tugged again, short and steady.

And again.

Though each subtle tug brought more tearing pain, he didn't waver. Fisher groups came and went while he methodically worked. When the strap finally moved slightly on the spike, he grinned. He pulled again, focusing on reuniting with Alina to block out the sting. Little by little, the strap tore away from the spike. It was close. Rasi bit his lower lip and gave a final yank. The strap ripped free and sprang away from the wall, its tip torn into a serpent's forked tongue.

His free strap was furious and thirsty for blood. It couldn't wait to be wrapped around a fisher's neck. Rasi begged it to calm down before they saw. He focused on the enemy while his angry strap danced violently in front of his face as if calling them up the ladder.

Rasi begged his flailing strap, *I swear, if you calm down I will give you your revenge. But you must not let them know you're free. Not yet.*

The strap snapped at the air like a whip. The trailing creature in the line of exiting fishers paused as the others continued through the entrance. It sniffed the air with perked ears.

If they know you're free, they will cut you from me. Please stop.

His strap whipped side to side, daring the creatures to notice. Rasi held his breath. *Please. Trust me. We can't fight until we are all completely free or we will lose.*

Maybe his strap already knew that and was looking for a new host. A fisher would indeed make a vicious one. The trailing fisher tilted its head while Rasi implored his strap to calm down. The strap slithered around his waist and up his neck as if comforting him. *This is our last chance, damn it. Return to the wall now or we're finished.*

The fisher slowly turned its head.

Rasi's strap unraveled and, at the last possible second, shot out to reposition itself around the spike as if it was still pinned. The fisher's eyes glowed orange. Rasi let his head droop, pretending to still be gravely injured. *Thank you,* he told his strap. The fisher snorted, turned, and rejoined the group. Rasi's strap relaxed down his side.

Patience, my friends. Patience. After a brief rest, Rasi started again with a second strap, but that strap didn't immediately obey. Perhaps it wasn't yet convinced of his promises of vengeance, or maybe it just wasn't willing to endure the necessary pain the other had experienced.

Another dozen fishers entered the cavern and Rasi waited for them to kneel before continuing his work. With the creatures praying, Meela arrived. But for the first time, she wasn't alone. A second fisher—the bastard with the shank—followed. At the bottom of the ladder, Meela stopped, moved aside, and allowed her companion to pass. She stood with her head sadly bowed.

Rasi watched with venom as creature climbed up. The orange glow was gone from its eyes, leaving only coated orbs of gray, but the poorly healed scab across its forehead left little doubt that it was him. Meela followed him up.

Wait, Rasi mindspoke to his free strap as the fisher climbed closer. Rasi feigned weakness. The worshippers below finished their prayer, rose, and headed for the exit. *Not yet. Patience.*

Rasi kept one eye on the worshipers and one eye on the climbing fisher. He had to be perfect in his timing. Acting too soon meant the exiting group would hear him. Acting too late meant he would be skewered once again.

The fisher reached the top of the ladder and sniffed the healing wound on Rasi's side. It removed its blood-stained shank from its sheath again. The line of fishers reached the exit.

Still, Rasi waited.

The fisher whispered, "Forgive meee, myee lord," and turned its head away. It pressed the spike against Rasi's healing wound. Rasi grimaced. The fisher slowly and painfully pushed the spike into his flesh. There was no more time.

The last fisher on the ground disappeared into the dark passage beyond the torches. Rasi turned his head to the creature on the ladder. It hesitated, sensing something was different.

Rasi grinned. *Now.* His free strap shot toward the creature's throat while Rasi batted the fisher's hand away from the shank wedged in his side. He ripped it free. The fisher panicked and tried to pull away, but the strap wrapped its neck and yanked it from the ladder. With one fluid motion, the strap whipped the fisher toward the ground and then jerked him to a stop with a bone-cracking snap.

Fearful, Meela fled down the ladder, but Rasi shouted, "Mee'a, wai'." Miraculously, with one foot on the ladder and one on the ground, she stopped.

"He'p me," he said.

The next group of worshippers would be entering at any moment, and when they found the dead fisher it would be over. He staked his entire chance of escaping—his entire chance of living—on Meela's compassion.

She stood, terrified and staring with her blind eyes toward the passage.

Please.

And then she took a step back onto the ladder. *Thank the gods.* She climbed to Rasi again.

"Whyee did you do that to him? They will hurt you worse now."

"Free me."

"They will kill mee."

Rasi's strap slithered around her neck. Unafraid, she sighed and gently dragged the back of her hand along it like she accepted her fate. Rasi begged his angry strap not to harm her.

Heeding his pleas, his strap loosened. She leaned in, kissed Rasi's cheek, and then climbed higher on the ladder to where his top strap was fastened to the wall. She chipped at the rock around the spike with her scoop-claw until it loosened enough that she could wiggle it free. Once released, the strap shot out, ready for battle. She continued to the third and final strap on that side and freed it as well.

Rasi dropped below the other three straps and swung helpless. Although he couldn't see the others yet, he heard the next group of worshipers shuffling their feet in the passage. Meela couldn't reach the other spikes from the ladder and there wasn't time for her to move it. Rasi twisted to face the wall and grabbed a pinned strap in each hand. Despite the pain, he used them to scale the wall until he could touch the spike of the third strap.

He grabbed the head of the spike and wrenched it back and forth until it loosened slightly. He kept working it, the clock in his head screaming at him to hurry. When the spike finally fell to ground, the strap grabbed the top rung of the ladder, just above Meela's head.

Two left and no time. The next group of fishers entered the cavern, though they didn't immediately realize what was happening above their heads. Rasi glanced over his shoulder. This was it—his only shot.

With both feet against the wall, he wrapped the two restrained straps around his forearms and braced himself for the coming pain. He groaned and pulled while pushing against the wall with his legs. Slowly, the straps tore away. Rasi roared, no longer concerned whether the entire fisher kingdom heard him. His thighs quivered. His back screamed in protest. With a final painful yank, both straps ripped free, blood spraying the wall.

Rasi fell, but the strap holding the ladder rung pulled taut and jerked him to a stop. His sudden weight caused the top-heavy ladder to slide along the wall. He used another strap to pull himself against the sliding ladder as Meela toppled from her perch. Two straps caught her left wrist and ankle. The ladder fell toward the ground. Rasi's remaining straps clawed at the wall in a desperate attempt to slow their descent. He pulled the falling ladder close to his chest.

By luck, one of his straps snagged a protruding piece of the jagged wall. There wasn't enough rock for the strap to hold, but it briefly slowed their plunge. Rasi released the ladder.

His straps pulled Meela against his chest and wrapped around the two like a cocoon. Before they struck the ground, the straps flexed and hardened enough to absorb some of the blow. Meela grunted on impact; Rasi didn't make a sound. Rasi uncoiled the straps and bounced to his feet. It felt good to be on solid ground again. His atrophied legs quivered.

The fishers entering the cavern charged and he met them head-on. One of his straps snatched the first fisher's head and flung it face-first against the cavern wall. Three more fishers attacked and Rasi's straps unleashed pent-up anger on their skulls. The others retreated for reinforcements.

Meela hurried to Rasi's side. "Wee cannot fleee. They will fiieend us and kill us. They guard the entrance."

"We mus'."

"Then wee must go deeeeper into the caves."

Rasi turned to grab one of the torches that lined the wall, but Meela pulled his hand. "No tiieeme. Iiee'll leeead you."

Rasi trailed her through the blackest tunnels with only her touch guiding him. She darted one direction and then suddenly veered in another. He was as blind as if he had no eyes, but if he wanted freedom, he had to trust her. When she jerked his hand one way, he followed without hesitation. When he felt her jump, he jumped as well, never knowing what it was that he had hurtled.

He tried to tell her to slow down and she shushed him. The complete darkness played with his mind and he closed his eyes in hopes of fooling his panicking brain. The tunnels led downhill and then back uphill again. His straps weren't as trusting, standing tense above him. Meela jerked his hand downward and, without hesitation, he crouched as he ran. But his straps didn't follow his lead and slammed painfully against the lower tunnel ceiling. For the rest of the run, they cowered close to him. And they were pissed.

Eventually, Meela slowed and stopped. Rasi let loose of her hand, gingerly stood up straight, and stretched. In the distance, a faint glow like a star in the night sky lit the darkness. "There," she said. "Freeedom."

Rasi nudged past her, anxious to see again. He stutter-stepped sideways until he felt the tunnel wall. She moved closer and whispered, "Scaree not to seee, yes?"

And at that moment, Rasi understood the fishers better than many people ever would. He didn't condone their brutality, but now he understood why they did what they did. They craved a reprieve from the blackness that was their lives. Maybe he wouldn't kill them all as he had promised. Maybe he would only kill the ones who tried to stop him.

He felt his way along the tunnel toward the growing brightness. When he saw a fisher shadow dance within the glow, he hesitated.

Meela stopped beside him. "They are the guardeeans of the wall. You must get past them."

Rasi squeezed his fist. This was where his straps would get the revenge he promised. His straps pulled away and snapped at the air—they knew it. He crept forward.

Once he reached the edge of the lighted room, he hid at the side of the entrance. The guardian fishers sniffed the air. They knew he was there. They scrambled in the room.

There was no use hiding anymore. Rasi stepped through the opening. The room had a large hole in the side wall, which allowed the sunlight to shine in. He squinted from the brightness. The fishers hissed and growled as they prepared for battle. Rasi welcomed them with a snarl of his own. His straps flared out from his back.

Meela remained hidden in the tunnel, though the fishers had probably caught her scent as well. They attacked. Rasi's straps engaged them, ripping away arms and heads in unbridled fury. With his eyes adjusting to the brightness, he joined his straps, driving his fists into their blurry faces, one after another. Each blow to their thick skulls sent jolts of pain from his knuckles to his brain, but he didn't relent. The fishers' claws slashed Rasi's straps as they fought, but he ignored the pain, his rage and adrenaline getting the best of him. He was lucky they didn't carry venom like their hylock cousins.

As quickly as the fight began, it was over. Rasi stood covered in both his own blood and the milky-white blood of his enemies. He took in deep, exhausted breaths of stale air as he tried to calm himself and his excited straps. His straps lifted victoriously in the air.

Meela crept into the room, hesitant, as if seeing Rasi's true nature scared her. Rasi saw her trepidation and turned away. Though he didn't like being feared by those who helped him, fear might be all that prevented her from turning on him.

As his eyes focused, he looked for the wall that the fishers guarded. Then, near the opposite end of the room, he saw it—a free-standing wall two men tall stopping short of the ceiling. The sunslight glistened across it. As he moved closer, he noticed that it was covered in drawings and foreign markings that appeared to tell a story.

He glanced back. Meela straightened and lifted her chin, proud of what stood before them. Turning back to the wall, Rasi stared in awe at the primitive artwork and asked what it said.

She touched his shoulder. "It is the storee of your reeturn."

Meela scaled the wall to the top and reached down to caress the symbol beneath the topmost picture. The drawing showed a man standing on a castle balcony. As she dragged her fingers along the symbols, she read, "Keeng Thadeeeus shouted, 'Iiee am immortal. You cannot vanquish mee. Iiee will kill the one who would beee keeeng.'"

Rasi had heard the story of Thadius many times before, but not from the fishers' point of view.

"Keeng Thadeeeus jumped from the tower.'"

The next drawing showed the king jumping to his death. Rasi followed the pictures to the next row of carvings. They depicted a rudimentary wall of flames in front of a circle which appeared to be a sun.

She read the words, "The fiieere in the skyeee took our eyeees."

The pictures showed the flames engulfing an army of kneeling creatures that appeared almost human in shape and size. She continued, explaining that after the loss of their sight, they gained the ability to "see" through sounds. They were soon ostracized by the Epertasians, who began to fear them even though they had been a fringe part of society before the flames. They were eventually forced to flee Epertase to the Wastelands.

The drawings showed Meela's ancestors fighting a civil war. She explained how her people broke into two factions, each with different views on how to respond to the Epertasians who had driven them away. One side wanted to hide from the world and forget what the Epertasians had done while the other group wanted to build an army and one day destroy the kingdom. After seven days of war, the two factions reached a stalemate.

Rasi followed the carvings to the next row while she continued. The next picture was of two armies marching in separate directions. Meela said it was at that point that her ancestors fled to the volcanic regions while the others, the ones Rasi's people called hylocks, disappeared into the Wastelands.

Over many centuries in the dark caves, Meela's people evolved from the nearly human race they had once been. The drawings showed bony protrusions growing from the palms of babies, merely nubs in the first pictures, but evolving into full scoop-like claws in later drawings.

With a smile, Meela told of the gods teaching them how to take the eyes from the very people who had forced them into exile. She said they could use animal eyes, but they liked human sight the best.

Rasi followed the carvings to an elaborate mural that took up the entire bottom third of the wall. The sight stole his breath. His straps lowered to the ground as though they, too, recognized the gravity of its meaning. Meela turned from the painting and smiled. "Seee."

The mural was different from the others in that it was painted instead of carved, indicating it had been created many years after the others. Rasi slowly shook his head. *No. How could this be?*

"Yes," she whispered.

Rasi stumbled backward, his eyes plastered to the painting. The mural showed an army of fishers kneeling before a human figure who stood upon a wall. The figure had a nimbus of bright light surrounding him. But that wasn't what stopped Rasi's heart. Though the figure was very crudely drawn and the body too small in proportion to the rest, it was unmistakable. Six red tentacles extended from his back. Meela climbed down, took his hand, and placed it on the final symbol etched beneath the mural.

"Through him," she said, "the broken Liieeght will bee made whole." She turned back. "You will give us back our eyeees."

Rasi nearly vomited.

CHAPTER 8

THE BLUEFIELDS
OF SORROW

R asi was so absorbed in the fisher story that he had momentarily forgotten he was on the run. At least until Meela sniffed the air and whispered, "They are comeeng."

Rasi grabbed her hand and led her toward the hole in the wall where the sunslight shone through. Behind them, fishers scurried through the tunnels. Meela climbed into the opening. Rasi followed.

The face of the volcano sloped at a treacherous angle and stretched as far down as the bottom of Havens Ravine at least. Meela started down the side, masterfully jamming her claws into crevices as she went. Rasi's straps braced him along the edges of the opening. He looked out over an incredible field of blue that stretched as far as he could see. Even if he survived the climb down the volcano's face and made it to the fields before the fishers caught him, it may all be for naught. To his knowledge, no one had ever defeated the legendary Bluefields of Sorrow, and he wasn't looking forward to trying. Things had gone from bad to worse.

But there was no turning back. Fighting an entire army of fishers was suicide, regardless of how fresh and alive he now felt. He crawled out, his straps clinging to the opening with a death grip.

Rasi searched for his first handhold while one of his straps reluctantly did the same. As he released the ledge, he heard the room fill with fishers. Meela sailed down the wall with incredible speed. In his rush to keep up, Rasi was sloppy. If not for his straps, he would have fallen to his death several times. He picked up his pace, missing a handhold once again, and once again his straps caught him so he could reposition his grip. Meela reached the bottom and waited, pacing on all fours. Rasi was nearly halfway down when a dozen fishers poured from the opening like insects from a hive.

"Wee are trapped," Meela shouted.

Rasi picked up his pace, eventually losing his grip completely and tumbling painfully the rest of the way down. He got to his feet and faced the field.

"No," Meela screamed. "Weee dare not enter the Bluefieeelds. Wee must go to the tunnels that run beelow."

Rasi grabbed her shoulders. "Where?"

She pointed east toward a growing stampede of more fishers rounding the side of the volcano to cut them off. There was no way they would make the tunnels. It was the Bluefields or nothing.

Rasi pulled Meela toward the blue wheat-like stalks that stood higher than he was tall. She fought his pull as though he were leading her into the jaws of a dragon.

She whispered, "Wee're goeeng to diieee."

She was probably right.

The fishers snorted and screeched as they approached from the east, their excitement palpable. The tiny hairs on the back of Rasi's neck stood on end and a tingle ran the length of his body.

He pulled Meela into the first row of blue stalks. She panicked and pulled in the opposite direction. But he refused to let go; he needed her. Besides, they would probably kill her for what she'd done. He spun toward her, grabbed her face with both hands, and pulled her close to him so she could feel his sincerity when he said, "I wi' he'p 'ou."

"Weee will not surviieeve the Bluefieeelds. No one has."

"We have 'o."

She relaxed in his grip, more resigned than trusting. He pulled her farther into the blue. From the moment he entered the field, the weight of the air pressed down on his shoulders. He couldn't have been more than twenty steps in when his legs begged him to stop. His mouth instantly dried. He swallowed hard.

Meela raced past him, pulling his hand. "Wee must keeep goeeng. Come on, Rasiiieeee."

Rasi inhaled deep, choking breaths as the dryness crept down his throat. Meela tugged his arm again. As she tried to get him going faster, he realized she was holding her breath. Rasi slowed. He felt sad.

"It's the fieelds," she cried. She pulled his hand again, digging into his wrist with her scoop-claw. "Wee have to run."

She was right. Rasi pushed forward with a new sense of urgency. His nose poured out snot uncontrollably. He tried to wipe it on his shoulder, but it did no good. The snorts of the few fishers brave enough to challenge the Bluefields closed in around him. Instead of preparing for a fight, Rasi's straps flopped down his back and dragged on the ground. He scowled at them. *What are you doing?* They quivered helpless at his feet. Meela gasped, unable to hold her breath any longer. By her second gasp, she fearfully tucked her head below her shoulders like a punished dog. She yanked her hand free from Rasi's grip and covered her face. Her eyes flowed with tears.

Rasi reached for her, but she flinched away like he was the enemy. Slobber poured from the corners of her mouth. A thousand sorrows painted her face. He froze with his hand out, fearing any sudden movements might scare her farther away. She backed from his outstretched hand, shaking her head. "Weee are goeeeng to diiieee," she said again.

Grab her, he told his dragging straps. They did nothing. Sensing he was about to lose her, he lunged. She pulled out of reach and bolted deeper into the stalks. "Mee'a," he shouted, but she kept running without looking back until she was gone.

He couldn't let her die alone in the fields, not after all she had done for him. His thighs burned with each step, exhausted from both the exertion and the effects of the Bluefields' toxin.

A fisher roared from behind. It sounded like a male, which meant it wasn't Meela, and deathly terrified, which meant it wasn't a threat. Another one yelped nearby, again not her.

The rising suns showed him the way south away from the fishers' lair. His chest tightened and he pressed his forearm across it with a wince. The fields wanted him to quit. He could maybe make it on his own if he pushed on with his tired muscles, but even if he wanted to, he couldn't leave Meela at the mercy of either the fishers or the fields.

His straps quivered behind him. The crushing pain in his chest made him consider joining them on the ground. He plodded forward, almost forgetting the pursuing fishers until their sudden shrill wails of agony reminded him. *Hold on, Meela. Please.*

His breathing grew labored and his chest tighter. He remembered the brutal and miserable times at Shadows Peak and used those lessons of perseverance to take the next step. His stomach turned. Maybe the fields were right. Maybe he should stop and lie down.

He stared through watery eyes at the endless blue stalks surrounding him. As he lost himself in their beauty, they slowly faded into darkness until he couldn't see them anymore. A new sensation met his arms. Though he couldn't see the stalks anymore, they started to sting his flesh whenever he bumped them. Each sting injected more of the deadly toxin directly into his system, making it even more potent. In some ways, it was worse than the hylock's venom; this toxin ate at his mind as well as his body. When he tried to send commands to his muscles, his body lagged behind. He plodded forward as though his feet weighed three times what they should.

Just when he feared he would be lost and alone in the darkness forever, a faint ray of light broke the blackness and highlighted a large maple tree in an open clearing. Rasi felt drawn toward the cone of light as though it was his salvation. The invisible stalks in the darkness still zapped his arms as he walked, but he ignored their sting. A small wooden plank sat at the base of the tree.

Rasi cocked his head as he moved close enough to read what was written on the plank. His lips moved with the words. They were like daggers to his heart.

Here lies a most beautiful and kind woman with her unborn child. Her name was Edonea and she was a friend. She will be missed by all who knew her. The Year of Matthew 988- ...

The last numbers had been gnawed away by wood beetles, but he didn't need to see them to know the year he had lost her. 1012. That was the year that bastard Elijah started all his pain. That was the year Rasi learned what it meant to lose everything a man could lose. That was the year he learned what it was to be truly alone. And today, he was wracked with that same loneliness again.

You died because of me, Edonea. I'm so sorry. Unable to take his eyes from the epitaph, he decided to give in to the murderous pain in his chest. A cool breeze brushed past his hair and tickled his neck, sending a shiver through his body. He plopped to his rear.

The ground rumbled. At the outer edge of the cone of light, a crack opened in the dirt and slowly grew like trails on a map. It threatened to swallow the tree whole. The new fissure called to him, and he wondered if that was where he needed to go to end his suffering.

As he watched through wet, blurry eyes, hoping the hole would swallow him as well, something reached out of the crack near the tree. Rasi dragged his forearm across his eyes and refocused. It was the bones of a decaying hand. A second hand reached up alongside the first and grabbed the edge of the hole. Was he dreaming? Had the blue stalks put a spell on him?

The hands clawed at the dirt as the hole opened wider until a decayed body rose from the depths. Though the body was more bone than flesh, he could tell it was a woman as her beautiful face appeared perfectly preserved. Rasi dropped his shoulders in surrender. An end to his suffering was here.

Edonea.

He looked forward to joining her.

She glanced left and then right as though she wanted to be sure they were alone. Her feet didn't touch the ground as she floated toward him. He shoved his hands over his face and begged the gods to end this torture—to take him and be done with it—but the relentless pain in his chest was his only answer.

A cold but gentle touch pulled his hands away from his face.

Edonea's face floated like a ghost over the decaying flesh of her skull. "Rasi," she said. He had forgotten how her voice sounded.

His tears flowed like rain from a mountain storm. She pointed to the way from which he had come, and he looked back over his shoulder. He was floating with her. Though it was dark where he looked, another cone of light highlighted his own body curled in a fetal position on the ground. He turned back to Edonea. *I don't understand.*

"You cannot give up now, Rasi. You have more to do in this life."

I can't win, Edonea. The Bluefields' toxin is too strong.

"No, my love. That's not true."

It is. I am finished.

"This is not the man I know. You are a fighter, and this is merely another fight."

But I miss you so much. I'm ready to go with you. Rasi bowed his head in shame.

She lifted his chin with one bony finger, but he looked away, afraid to meet her eyes. "These fields are trying to beat you. You cannot let them win. You need to fight the toxins."

How?

"You need to keep moving and not give up. Epertase needs you. Your wife, Alina, needs you. Your newborn son needs you."

He met her eyes. *I have a son, now?*

She smiled lovingly. "They are waiting for you. It will take everything you have to beat these fields, but what you learned on Shadows Peak is the key." She caressed his cheek and he leaned into her hand.

He didn't understand.

"I cannot tell you the answer. It'll only work if you figure it out on your own. Do you remember the night I died?"

He nodded. *Of course.*

"Do you know who killed me?"

Rasi tilted his head. *Yes. It was Tevin.*

"And you're going to let him win now?"

Rasi curled his upper lip and took in a deep, hateful breath through his snotty nose. As Edonea backed away, the darkness faded and the blue stalks began to reappear.

Rasi was no longer floating. He looked up from the ground where he lay with his knees pulled up to his chest. *Please, don't go.* He reached out for her, but she was already gone. His hand trembled. Where Edonea had been was a fresh trail of trampled stalks.

Meela.

There was a desert inside Rasi's soul and death seemed the only thing that would quench his thirst. Why even fight it? Everyone hated him. Dying would be so sweet.

"Use what you learned on Shadows Peak," Edonea had said. But how could Shadows Peak help him now? All it had taught him was a lifetime's worth of loneliness and anger and despair. And why did she bring up Tevin?

Loneliness, anger, and despair.

He was already lonely.

Anger and despair.

Tevin.

Anger.

That was it. That's what had kept him warm for so many nights. That's what had pushed him to hunt when he wanted to sleep another day away. Until now, his life on Shadows Peak had seemed a curse, but as he willfully dredged his sorry ass off the ground, he could finally see that the anger he learned there was a blessing. That pure, raw anger could push his feet forward. He had survived a rashta. He had survived wars with the Teks and a Gildonese king. He had even survived the great Tevin once. Losing everything he had wasn't the end of him. He stood straight and strong. There was no way a bunch of fucking plants were better than him. He took a step, despite his legs not wanting to work. Then another. Each step further solidified his resolve. He had found the secret. Anger and adrenaline could defeat the Bluefields' toxin.

Tevin, I'm coming for you.

He willed two of his straps from the ground. His adrenaline flowed through his veins with dreams of vengeance. He bent over and vomited, but stood right back up and continued walking. He swatted the blue stalks from his path, no longer concerned with their sting. In fact, he welcomed it as it only made him angrier.

The weak part of him told him how the world hated him.

How he deserved all the pain that came his way.

How the very air was wasted on his lungs.

He now knew why they were known as the Bluefields of Sorrow. It was because the pain and misery from the toxin took every bit of hope from a man before killing him completely. But not Rasi. Not that day.

The world didn't hate Meela.

She didn't deserve the pain she was going through.

She did deserve the air she breathed, even if he didn't.

Where are you, Meela? he silently called. *I'm coming. These fields won't beat us.*

He followed the trail of broken stalks until he passed into a small clearing with two fishers in the center. One of them was Meela, squatting on her heels. The other crumpled to the ground and let loose its bladder before convulsing so violently that its teeth shattered.

Meela listened to the creature die as she rocked back and forth, knees pulled against her chest. She lifted her blind eyes toward Rasi as though she smelled him coming. She fell to her side and curled into a ball with one of her scoop-claws in her mouth like a baby sucking its thumb. She had given up, but it wasn't too late. The toxin hadn't yet beaten her either.

Rasi shoved his arms beneath her and lifted. She didn't struggle. He looked for the top of the volcano above the stalks to get his bearings, and then carried her away from it.

The cries of the fishers who had been brave enough to follow them into the fields slowly faded. Rasi stumbled, and a quick glance toward his feet revealed an old fisher skull as the culprit. He didn't falter. His left leg stiffened and stopped working properly, so he dragged it. He thought about Tevin.

Each shuffle-step felt like he was wading through knee-high mud, except his feet were free. Meela twitched in his arms as though her body was about to give in to a fit. Rasi pulled her closer. Painful blisters lifted on his arms. He was running out of time. If his damn straps would only carry their own weight … Meela's legs began to quiver. Her gray eyes rolled back into her head.

The farther Rasi walked, the more the blue stalks thinned and the weight of the heavy air lifted. He saw the end of the fields in the distance. He pushed forward. Nothing could stop him now.

Like a warrior reborn, he burst from the last of the stalks and screamed at the suns. All six of his straps sprang into the air as if reinvigorated and ready for battle. Rasi could only glare at them, disgusted that they celebrated even though they had done nothing to help.

He laid Meela on the cracked desert ground, turned back, and stared at the greatest foe he had ever defeated. The fields seemed to stare back with mutual respect for the only man who had ever bested them. His chest loosened, and his wind slowly returned. His eyes cleared of tears and the blisters on his arms flattened.

Meela sat up, confused. "Rasiiieee?" she asked.

He touched her cheek.

"You saved meee."

"Yeah."

She looked around. "Wee can't rest yet. Iieee feeel the others. They are comeeng through the tunnels beneeath the fieeld."

He turned back for one last victorious look at the Bluefields.

"They will never stop until they have you."

He knew that.

She got up and touched his shoulder. "Thank you."

Without looking at her, he nodded. She took his hand and pulled him into the brutal Wastelands.

In the time since Rasi and Meela had climbed down from the volcano, they had walked for an entire day without water or shelter from the pounding desert heat. Rasi needed water soon. Meela bounced along, the heat and lack of fluids hardly fazing her. A lifetime in the volcanic region had made her strong.

When the suns crossed the horizon and the moon rose, the heat turned to bitter cold. If not for the natural warmth of his straps, he would have frozen to death before he had a chance to die from dehydration.

"Are you thirstee?" Meela whispered.

Rasi nodded.

"Follow mee. Wee are close to water." She continued leading him. "The enemee with the death macheenes made a camp neearby."

The Teks.

"They had ways to get water from deeep in the ground. Wee are close to one of their camps."

They walked until the suns rose again and Rasi caught his first glimpse of where they were headed. Tall cylinders colored like shiny black Tek armor stood in the distance, distorted by heatwaves.

Meela danced from foot to foot. She said, "There. That is where they kept their water."

Rasi willed his exhausted straps to lift over his head and shade him from the blistering suns. At first they refused, since they were as beaten as he, but with the promise of water nearby they obeyed.

Meela nudged her way closer to Rasi, hoping for a bit of relief from the suns as well. Rasi's legs cramped painfully. His lips cracked. He would have licked them if he had a tongue. Or saliva. Or the strength to do so.

The castle-high cylinder was surrounded by an army of the best kind of tents he could possibly find—empty ones. Protruding from the cylinder's side at waist-height was a strange spout. Meela pushed past him and turned a lever as if she'd used it before. The cylinder rumbled and belched before a drop of water fell to the hard ground. That drop was followed by another. Rasi shoved cupped hands out to catch it. And then a steady stream flowed from the spout. He splashed handfuls of warm water into his mouth and over his face. It was heaven.

Frustrated with the small amount of water he was getting with his hands, he shoved his face beneath the spout and gulped like he had never had water so wonderful before. Meela waited patiently. When Rasi realized he was hogging the flow, he pulled away and offered her a drink.

She lapped up a few tonguefuls before backing away. Rasi shoved his mouth back under the spout. After his thirst was finally quenched, he dropped to his rear with his back against the cylinder for a rest. The shade was glorious. The water would give him the strength he needed to finish his journey through the Wastelands and back to Shadows Peak where he could regroup.

Meela disappeared into the sea of tents and then returned with three circular containers hanging from leather straps. Rasi watched with a smile as she filled each container and then plugged their holes with wooden stoppers. He leaned his head beneath the spout again and let the water soak his hair. Once he finished, each of his straps passed below the stream as well.

Meela sat beside him. "Iiee will listen for them if you want to rest."

Rasi couldn't think of anything better. He crawled into one of the tents and closed his eyes.

Rasi found himself falling into a black pit. When he hit the ground, he sat up with a jolt. It was dark again. His breaths floated into the night like small clouds. *Just a dream.*

Meela rushed into the tent. "Rasiiieee?"

He nodded and rubbed his forehead.

"Wee should go."

He nodded again, slung the leather straps of the water containers over his shoulders, and climbed from the tent. He took a piss behind it before joining Meela. As they walked, he asked Meela why her kin hadn't found them yet. He was astonished at how easily she understood his garbled speech.

"They mourn our losses in the Bluefieelds. Wee are a patient peeople. They know they will fiieend you in tiieeme. Wee have waited for our eyeees for manee yeeears. A few more days meeean notheeng."

Rasi and Meela traveled through the torturous Wastelands during the nights while taking shelter behind dunes for the hottest parts of the days. While hunger pangs tore his stomach apart, the containers of water saw him through.

On the fifth morning, farmland finally appeared in the east. Meela tapped Rasi's side and smiled. Rasi smiled back. The hard, cracked ground slowly gave way to greenery. They soon stumbled upon a clear stream where they refilled their Tek water bladders. Though they needed to keep moving, they enjoyed a quick rinse in the refreshing water. When they passed an orchard, they "borrowed" what might have been the best, juiciest apples he'd ever tasted. Each exquisite bite made him crave another and he must have eaten six before they moved on.

At the edge of one farmer's property, three beefy guard dogs with bared teeth blocked their path. While Rasi didn't make a habit of hurting dogs simply for doing their job, his straps prepared to do just that; they didn't always share Rasi's compassion. Meela stepped between the dogs and Rasi and dropped to all fours. The protruding vertebrae of her spine peaked like a hill as her chin brushed the ground. She hissed and growled. The standoff lasted only seconds. The dogs' tails curved between their back legs and their ears flattened against their heads. Meela lunged, sending them yelping toward their master's house. She stood up with a sheepish grin.

They reached Havens Ravine next. Meela sniffed the air and smiled. "Wee are getteeng close to where wee saw you fight the armee of metal deemons. That is when wee knew that you were the god sent to save us."

Rasi scoffed. The fishers were foolish to believe such nonsense. When they reached the edge of the ravine, he noticed the tip of Alina's castle poking through the thin fog that had settled across the plains. From so far away, the castle appeared unmolested and calm, and for the briefest of moments he enjoyed a hopeful image of Alina sitting safely on her throne awaiting his return. But he was wise enough to know that a castle, just like a body, could appear strong from the outside even as disease ate it away from within.

After crossing one of the few remaining bridges that had survived the Tek invasion, Meela shot into the plains as if on a mission. Rasi stood and watched. He enjoyed watching her hunt.

She zigged and zagged with her nose to the dirt until she caught a scent. She dug frantically at the ground as dirt sprayed between her back legs. Her entire head and upper body disappeared into her newly dug hole. After a quick and violent struggle, she emerged with a healthy-sized squank thrashing between her teeth. With a huge grin showing around the squirming rodent, she hurried back to Rasi for approval. He warmly touched her shoulder. She whipped her head to the side and snapped the squank's neck.

After the two cleaned the meat from the bones, a low rumble echoed from the ravine and reminded Rasi of the belke slug below. Meela leaned over the edge. "Don't want to fall down there, do weee?"

Rasi shook his head.

Daylight brought hylocks patrolling the sky near the castle, so Rasi and Meela waited on the bridge for nightfall before continuing their journey. They eventually reached the edge of Concore Forest undetected.

Now it was time for Rasi to show the way. He led Meela through the forest to the rubble at the base of Shadows Peak. Habit pulled his eyes up toward where the cave that had given him shelter for so many nights had once stood. In its place was piled rock. Meela began climbing across the rubble. Rasi followed. He wasn't as fast, but he kept up with the help of his straps.

On the other side they followed a stream that took them to Widows Run. Seeing the crown of stone warmed his heart with the memory of his euphoric first kiss with Alina. But that warmth cooled at the sight of overgrown weeds and cobweb walls. No one had been there in quite some time. While deep down he had hoped Alina would be there waiting, he knew things never went that easily for him.

Meela climbed through the weeds and hopped onto the flat boulder beneath the crown. "Is this where wee will stay?"

Rasi nodded and climbed up beside her.

"Until when?"

He looked away. *Until forever if we must*, he thought.

Rasi dangled his feet over the edge while Meela fell asleep behind him. Though he, too, needed sleep, his racing mind prevented him from closing his eyes.

Morning came with welcomed heat from the two suns. Rasi started the day before Meela woke, gathering branches for a fire and using his straps to catch a few fish. He was cooking them when she surprised him from behind. He was shocked at how close she got before he or his straps noticed. They spent most of the day clearing an area next to the mountain base and creating a shelter with branches and twigs.

Rasi didn't know how long he would wait before he started searching for Alina again, but, as he had learned from years of war, sometimes patience was the best tactic. If she had survived this long without him, she would undoubtedly seek him out at the crown of stone as soon as she was able.

Days passed. If there was anything good about his situation, it was that they appeared to have lost the fishers hunting them. As he looked around the bleak mountain landscape, he wondered how fate could have taken him right back where he'd started.

CHAPTER 9

FALSE SECURITY

Cyn rode the waves near the steep cliff of Tek Island where she could see Tek soldiers lining the ridge above. She had ditched her boat earlier, as she was a skilled swimmer and didn't want to be seen too soon.

Not killing Masera when she'd returned to the farm for him had turned out to be her best decision ever. She was amazed that he was foolish enough to lead her right to Epertase's southern shores. From there their ultimate destination was easily surmised: Tek Island. It was a brilliant place to hide. She'd never have guessed. Unfortunately for them, Masera had made a crucial error. For a ranking member of Alina's Elite Guard, he wasn't too bright. And now she was only a hard climb and a bit of killing away from her goal. Alina didn't stand a chance. Tevin was going to be so proud. She was almost giddy.

For the last leg of her exhausting swim, she spent more time below the surface than above. Two small Tek boats floated alongside a pier. She used them for cover to get close to the cliff where the rocky overhang gave her better cover and time to rest.

She bobbed with the current until she was fresh enough for the climb. The strange platform above the pier would be the easiest way up, but also the most dangerous. Instead, she pulled herself onto a jagged ledge. The shifting metal skin on her arms and legs slithered to her hands and toes, extended to points, and hardened. Slowly, she chipped at the rock and scaled the wall to the top where she waited just below the edge for the patrolling soldiers to move away. Her muscles throbbed and ached and quivered, but it was worth the pain for the fun she was about to have. Once the guards wandered off, she pulled herself over the edge.

There were seven guards close enough to see her if they'd take the time to look away from their current conversations. The complacency of others was an assassin's best friend. She stalked the closest two guards who were engaged in indecipherable chatter away from the others. They were both dead with their throats slit before they even saw her. The darkness of night was her second best friend.

She licked the blood from one of her symbiotic spikes and got an unexpected mouthful of gritty rock dust from her climb. She spat into the dirt.

The other five guards stood in a friendly circle. Cyn brazenly marched toward them. After all, she hadn't swum all that way just to avoid a fight. The first soldier to notice her saw her over his shorter friend's shoulder. He trailed off in mid-sentence and limply pointed in astonishment. The others turned toward her. The moonlight glistened on her metal skin as the silver danced in anticipation.

"Hello, fellas," she said.

One of the soldiers reached over his head for the sword strapped to his back. Cyn bounded into the air and twirled like a dancer. The other soldiers stood in awe. Surprise was an assassin's third best friend. Or maybe it was her first; she always got them mixed up. The soldier slid his sword from the sheath. Cyn landed and struck with a lightning-fast swipe of her arm. The soldier grunted; his eyes went wide. And then he followed his guts to the ground.

The other soldiers panicked. Cyn danced into their midst as they drew their weapons. She lunged, killing another with metal piercing his heart. One of the remaining three swung his sword. She ducked and he killed his charging friend. Then she jammed a metal spike up through his groin.

The lone surviving soldier turned and ran toward his horse. Cyn chuckled. "Where do you think you're going?" She gave chase, quickly catching up and running stride-for-stride with him. He swung his sword blindly backward. She defended with her metal-coated forearm and then grabbed his hair. A backward jerk sent him to his knees. With one brutal swipe, she sliced the flesh along his hairline and pulled. He screamed in agony and then fell to his face. She stood over him, his bloody scalp dangling from her fist.

She dragged him and his fellow guards to the edge of the cliff and fed their bodies to the fish.

Dusting off her hands, she turned toward a distant town. *Now, where's that bitch Alina?*

The Teks' perimeter wall stood as high as a castle and stretched as far as Cyn could see in either direction. The wall wasn't made of wood or stone, but metal, smooth and slippery like her shifting skin. There was no way to scale it. She needed to find another way in. Preferably through the front gate. That would be the most fun and bloodiest way. After all, she doubted they would simply open the gates for her.

She sat with her back to the wall and meditated while watching the sunrise. In the calm quiet of a day not yet started, she often enjoyed the colorful hues as the early suns highlighted the land. The idea of replacing the pleasant interlude with blood and cries excited her. It was such contrasts in violence and beauty that she lived for.

Judging by the large number of guards at the entrance, her chances of surviving seemed about fifty-fifty, but she was excited for the challenge. She was ready to die in the same way she had always lived—violently. She just needed a reason for them to open the gates first.

And then, as if the gods were rooting for her, she saw one. A herd of stampeding wild horses crossed the field, corralled by three Tek soldiers on horseback. She grinned. After a scan of the top of the wall found no attentive guards, she broke toward the horses, confident she could catch them. Her speed was legendary. The three corralling Teks were too preoccupied with the herd to see her coming.

She dove at the nearest Tek. He saw her at the last second, but she was too good for him to do anything about it. She knocked him from his horse. Fluidly, she bounced from the ground, spun away from one stampeding horse, and grabbed the mane of another. The force nearly yanked her arm out of the socket, but she managed to pull herself close to the stallion's neck. Her victim wasn't so lucky and quickly disappeared beneath the stampeding hooves.

Cyn couldn't see past the horses to the other Teks, but that meant they couldn't see her either. She simply rode through the gates, past the army of oblivious Tek guards, and into the town unnoticed. Once the Teks guided the herd into a corral and stepped away, she dropped to the dirt and slipped through a gap in the fence. Commotion was a pretty good friend, as well. A nearby barn made the perfect hideout to plan her next step. The mare in the stall where she hid moved over to make room.

While waiting for nightfall, Cyn ate the mare's oats and drank from the trough. When night finally fell again, she slipped from the barn. Patience was her final best friend.

She scanned the buildings, thinking the Teks would either not appreciate the leader of their enemy paying them a visit or would revere her for showing mercy at the end of the war. It was most likely the latter, so she looked for the finest building around.

Once she moved away from the barn, it wasn't hard to spot such a building. One structure stood higher than the others, with three towering peaks joined by an elaborate, windowless wall. The lack of windows mattered little since she planned to go through the front door, wherever that may be.

CHAPTER 10

A NEW LIFE
BROKEN

Cridon stirred in his crib, waking Alina as he did any time he moved even a little. She stretched, sat up, and whispered, "Good morning," to her little angel. It was already warm, foretelling yet another hot and muggy day—the fifth straight. She would be wise to limit her outdoor activities as best she could.

Since Cridon wasn't yet sleeping through the night, she was extra tired. It was those kinds of mornings that she regretted her stubbornness in not allowing Leander or Atticus or Irene to spend a night with her son so she could get some much-needed rest.

She whispered, "Cridon, when are you going to sleep through the night?" He gazed back with his father's dark eyes. She leaned into his crib and kissed his cheek. "You've soiled yourself. Let me fetch a fresh cloth."

She crossed the room to where a newly laundered dress hung from a hook and changed out of her night clothes. She poured a glass of water from a pitcher on her nightstand and took a sip. Then she gathered a fresh cloth from the drawer, a clean rag, and a pail of lukewarm water.

Cridon groaned and grunted.

"I'm coming, sweetheart."

As she turned back toward him, a thump from the outside hallway startled her. She hesitated, equally curious and nervous. The thump was followed by a brief silence. She looked to Cridon. "Now, what do you think that could have been?"

The door burst open, splintering the frame around the lock. Her hand shot to her chest. Two people stood in the doorway. One was the Tek soldier guarding her door, and the other was the one who had occupied so many of her nightmares. "How?" she whispered.

The soldier whispered, "I'm sorry, Your Majesty. She got the jump on me."

Cyn stood behind the guard, holding a pointed sliver of her shape shifting metal against his throat. She leaned into his ear and whispered, "Shhh." Then she slit his throat and dropped him to the floor.

Alina gasped. Her heart broke knowing he had given his life for her. She whispered, "I'm so sorry."

Cyn cocked her head and smirked. "Empathy," she scoffed, and rolled her eyes. Then she stuck her finger in her mouth and pretended to gag herself. "Don't be sorry for him. You've got far greater problems now."

Since the day Alina had arrived on Tek Island, she'd seen Cyn at every turn, the assassin's jet-black hair and shifting metal skin permanently etched into her subconscious. Her immediate reaction was to look at Cridon, but, fearing that would draw Cyn's attention to him, she quickly turned away.

Cyn cracked her knuckles. "We should stop meeting like this, Alina."

Alina didn't answer, staring in horror as Cyn knelt and wiped her blade on the dead soldier's clothes. Her cold eyes burned through Alina's soul. Alina's prayers that Cridon would stay quiet were cut short by his first big wail of the morning.

Cyn tilted her head and crinkled her brow. She looked from Alina to the crib. "Well, what have we here?"

Alina's pail of water crashed to the floor. "You're here for me, Cyn. Don't go near that crib." She took a step toward the assassin.

Cyn wagged her finger and shook her head. "Tsk, tsk, tsk." She sauntered toward the crib, indifferent to Alina's pleas.

Alina rushed between Cyn and Cridon. "Please, Cyn. Leave him be."

The assassin paused. "Alina, do you really think you will stop me from doing anything I wish? Now, step aside before we regret what happens next. Well, before *one* of us regrets what happens."

A sudden rush of anger washed through Alina and, almost without thought, her open hand smacked Cyn's face. For once, the metal skin didn't try to protect the assassin, letting Alina's hand strike flesh. It was undoubtedly a good slap because Alina's hand immediately stung.

Cyn winked and said, "I allowed you to strike me once. You will not get another chance." Her eyes darkened. She shoved Alina to the floor.

Alina scrambled back to her feet as Cyn leaned over Cridon's crib. She grabbed Cyn's hair, and Cyn drove an elbow into her stomach, doubling her over and sending her back to the floor. Alina tried to get up again, but she couldn't breathe and her legs didn't work. Cyn cradled Cridon in her arms like the loving mother she wasn't.

"No," Alina cried between gasps. "Leave him be."

Cyn looked at Cridon and then glanced at Alina on the floor. "He sure is an ugly bastard," she said. After a pause, she added, "Then again, most babies are."

Alina searched the room for something she could use as a weapon, but there wasn't a weapon invented that could even those odds. She needed help—lots of it.

Leander exploded through the doorway, a narrow Tek sword in his hand.

"She's got Cridon," Alina shouted.

With Cridon cradled in one arm, Cyn closed the gap between her and Leander. In a flash, his sword was on the floor and he was backed against the door frame holding his bleeding arm. He swung a fist and struck metal skin on Cyn's jaw. While still holding Cridon, Cyn sent Leander to the floor with a quick jab to his throat. She turned back to Alina. "Is this man in charge of the people on this island?"

Alina ignored her. Cyn nudged Leander with her foot as he held his throat and struggled for air. "If I let this weakling and your son live, will you come with me without a fight?"

"Go with you?"

"Of course. Why did you think I came? If I wanted you dead, you would not have woken up this morning." The metal on Cyn's middle finger slithered into a point like an extended nail and dented the flesh on Cridon's neck.

Leander coughed and choked on the floor.

Cyn leaned back through the doorway and looked in both directions. Satisfied with the empty hall, she returned to the room. "As long as you and your friend here"—she pointed to Leander— "come with me and keep me company while I return to Epertasian shores, I will leave this pathetic creature you call a son where he can be found by a passing peasant." She paused as if in thought. "Or a hungry wolf, I suppose." And then she grinned, amused by her callousness.

Alina had no other choice. Though she had never truly desired killing a person, seeing Cyn hold her son changed that.

Cyn made a clicking sound like she was calling a dog and kicked Leander's leg. "You too, hero. On your feet. We're going to walk out of this place, out of this town, and off this abomination of an island." Cyn put her lips to Cridon's ear. In a surprisingly gentle and playful tone, she said, "I finally found your whore mother, didn't I?" She rubbed his cheek with her nose. "Yes, I did."

Leander reached for Alina's hand and whispered, "Just give me time. I'll get him back." Alina smiled, thinking Leander both brave and naïve.

Alina glared at Cyn. "If I ever have the opportunity, I'm going to kill you. Somehow, someday, I promise."

Cyn laughed out loud, shook her head, and then slipped into the hall. Alina and Leander hurried to catch up. They passed two dead Tek guards before reaching the stairs. More Tek soldiers stood anxiously at the bottom.

Cyn whispered, "Ah, your friends are here." She paused and glanced over her shoulder. "Perhaps you should tell them to clear the way."

If it was only her life at stake, Alina might have let the pieces fall where they may, but with Cridon's life hanging in the balance she dared not risk it.

Cyn twisted enough that Alina could see Cridon. She pressed her metal nail against the side of his neck again. Cridon made the most awful, pained face, inhaled deeply, and let out a high-pitched wail.

"Stop," Alina cried.

Leander stepped to the landing beside Cyn. "Clear the halls," he shouted. Reluctantly, the Tek soldiers sheathed their swords and stepped aside.

Cyn withdrew her finger, leaving a small, wet, red dot on Cridon's neck. "Shall we continue?"

Alina nodded.

Cyn motioned for Leander to lead the way. He curled his upper lip in defiance, and then did exactly as she ordered. The Teks parted at the bottom of the stairs as Leander led Cyn and Alina out through the main entrance, never taking their eyes off her or their hands off their swords.

Leander shouted, "No one is to come near us. That is an order."

The men stood waiting, itching for a fight. An older man with more scars on his face than teeth in his mouth stepped forward. "Write off the kid, Leander. Let me kill this bitch."

A second Tek shouted, "He's right. The baby is nothing to us. We're not letting an assassin assault our city and then leave with such ease. Especially not with you in tow."

Alina prayed Leander had enough command over them to keep them calm. Leander pointed angrily. "That is exactly what you'll do. If you do not obey, you will hang for insubordination."

Three sword-wielding Teks stepped out from the crowd and turned toward the others. One of them said, "We will do as Leander commands. Is that understood?" The scarred Tek stood firm. Leander stared him down until he finally stepped aside.

Cyn strolled through the crowd behind Leander without a care in the world, even whistling some nomad song at one point and bobbing her shoulders as though she was ready to break into dance. The helpless crowd swelled as Leander led the way.

Cyn stopped at the gate. Cradling Cridon in one arm, she draped her other arm over Leander's shoulders. "We need horses, rope, japsy weed, and enough water for three people to last several days. Can you handle that, sweetie?"

Leander shrugged her arm away and then nodded to someone in the crowd.

Nervous, Alina scanned the Teks, intently aware of how difficult it would be to hold so many hardened soldiers back. The crowd was a coiled spring. And that's when she spotted a single Tek sitting high on a roof beyond the crowd. Her nerves turned to outright terror.

She shook her head and silently begged the young soldier not to do what he was about to do, but he either didn't see or more likely didn't care. He knelt with the butt of a Tek projectile weapon pressed against his shoulder. The long neck of the instrument pointed at Cyn.

Even from that distance, Alina saw him take a deep breath at the same moment she lost hers. *No, no, no.* She fought back the urge to rush Cyn and protect her son for fear Cyn might react by harming him. She could only hope beyond hope that the Tek reconsidered.

She wasn't sure if what she heard was her heart bursting or the weapon discharging. The sound was akin to a crossbow firing an arrow through a steel drum. The world slowed. Alina looked toward Cyn. Whatever projectile the weapon had launched hit the side of Cyn's metal-covered skull, sending her sprawling to the ground. Her eyes blasted wide with shock. Cridon tumbled from her arms and Leander lunged for him.

Alina cried out—too far away to reach her son before Cyn or Leander. As Cyn and Leander both scurried for Cridon, Cyn gave a slight shove which knocked Leander off course. She snatched Cridon's leg, swooped him into the air, and smashed her metal-coated fist into Leander's cheek as he tried to recover his balance.

Alina covered her mouth. "Cyn, please. I didn't know he was going to do that. Please. I'm coming with you. Don't hurt my baby."

Cyn slowly straightened, a trickle of blood oozing from beneath the metal covering her temple. Her face was racked with pain and anger. She rubbed her head. "Bring me that man," she screeched. When none of the Teks moved, she screamed, "Do it now," and shoved a blade against Leander's face.

But they didn't need to go and find the offender because he was already making his way through the crowd. His weapon hung by his hip. "I shot you. And I'd do it again. I do not fear you."

Cyn marched toward the man, Cridon dangling at her side with his head nearly brushing the ground. His face reddened. "Show me that contraption."

The Tek offered his weapon with a scowl. Cyn yanked Cridon up by his leg and secured him against her hip while examining the Tek's weapon.

"Put the end of it in your mouth."

He glared at her.

"Do it, you bastard, or I'll kill everyone here. I've had enough of these games."

Alina cried, "Cyn, no. Let's just leave."

Cyn glowered back. "It either goes in his mouth or this sniveling brat's. You decide."

"I can't trade one life for another, Cyn. That's not fair."

The young man fearlessly grabbed the end of the weapon and shoved it into his mouth.

"Cyn, please don—"

Pop.

The soldier stiffened, his eyes wide. Then he dropped to the ground.

Cyn tossed his weapon aside. "Anyone else?" she shouted.

Though the crowd appeared ready to take up the challenge, no one stepped forward.

Cyn smiled at Leander as he stood up and rubbed his jaw. "Shall we continue?"

Leander's eyes lingered on his dead countryman. He nodded.

A Tek soldier arrived with two horses in tow and the requested supplies strapped to the saddles. Cyn climbed onto one with Cridon clutched to her chest while Alina and Leander climbed onto the other. Then they rode off toward the cliffs.

Once there, Cyn removed the supplies and sent the horses running. She walked to the cliff's edge and leaned over for a better look below. Cridon sat nestled in the crook of her arm, dangerously close to the edge. Alina's stomach turned. "Please, Cyn. Back away from the edge. If he squirms or …"

Cyn glared back. "I'm not going to drop him." She leaned a little farther over the edge and added, "Yet." She nodded toward the Tek platform. "Let's go." She walked close enough to the edge that a single misstep would plunge her and Cridon into the ocean below.

Leander loaded the supplies onto the platform and climbed aboard. Alina followed, the metal lift creaking and swaying with their every movement. Alina held one of the chains for support.

When Cyn reached the platform, she recklessly hopped on. Her momentum, combined with the unstable sway of the platform, carried her and Cridon clumsily over the opposite edge. Alina gasped and lunged for them, but grabbed only air. Cyn snagged one of the four supporting chains with her trailing hand and swung out over the ocean before returning to the safety of the platform. Seeing Alina's terrified face sent uncontrolled laughter from her gut.

Alina wanted to punch her.

With a knife.

In her heart.

Leander pulled a lever and the platform hiccupped and started its descent. Holding on for dear life, Alina peered over the edge and saw one boat close to the dock and two more a short distance away.

The platform jerked and clanked until it stopped on the pier. "All right," Cyn said. "Let's get going." She climbed into the nearest boat.

Alina and Leander followed.

The back of the boat had a small, strange machine half-submerged in the water. Cyn pointed at a lever on its side. "So, how does this thing work?"

"Crank the lever until it catches," Leander answered.

"How will I know when it catches?"

"You'll know. It's loud." Leander settled in for the long ride.

Cyn grabbed the lever and turned it. "What is this, anyway?"

"It's a self-sustaining propeller."

"That means nothing to me."

Leander sighed. "The crank pulls water into the system. The movement of the water causes a device to turn inside, which moves the boat forward. This turning sucks more water into the system, which continues pushing us forward until the device is turned off."

Cyn appeared as lost in Leander's explanation as Alina was. He saw their blank stares and started to explain it again, but Cyn cut him off. "Forget it. I don't care enough, and you bore me."

Cyn cranked the lever until the device rumbled to life and water squirted into the internal workings. Bubbles lifted from below the surface and the boat lurched forward. Cyn smiled. "You Teks are clever shits. You never cease to amaze me." She shook her head. "Such technology, and you were easily bested by a freak with funny tentacles on his back."

After a bit of direction from Leander on how to slow down, she guided their boat to the other two boats. With Cridon still in her arms, she climbed into one, extended a metal spike from her hand, and punched a dozen holes along the bottom. As the water poured in, she climbed into the other boat and did the same. Then she rejoined the others.

As they moved away from the dock, the empty platform lifted again.

"Persistent," she said. Then she steered the boat out into the open sea.

Alina whispered to Leander, "Is that all of the boats you have?"

"We have a few fishing boats on the other side of the island, but not many."

"Why did you not build more?"

"After your army defeated us, we gave our word that we would live out our lives here. The only reason we could see for building more boats was to break that promise."

"You are truly a man of your word."

"If a man doesn't have his word, when everything else is lost, what does he have?"

Cridon whimpered against Cyn's chest, but she ignored him.

"He's hungry," Alina said.

"Then feed him."

Alina held out her arms, but Cyn shook her head. "I think I'll continue to hold him, if you don't mind. You can feed him over here."

"That's ridiculous. There's no harm in letting me hold my son. It's not like there's anywhere I could run."

Cyn regarded the ocean as if pondering what Alina had said. Then she shook her head. "I think I'll continue holding him just the same. Look. I think he likes me."

Alina scoffed. "Trust me. He doesn't."

"Whatever. You can feed him or not, it makes no difference to me. But if he doesn't shut up soon, I'll hold him underwater while you sleep."

Alina didn't plan on sleeping. She climbed across the boat to where Cyn sat beside the contraption that propelled them forward. "Are you really going to make me do this?" she asked.

A sliver of metal extended from Cyn's knuckle and pressed against Cridon's side. With her eyes locked on Alina's, she said, "Go ahead and feed him. But if you have any heroic ideas, like trying to push me from the boat, well …" She jabbed Cridon, causing him to squirm away from her metal touch.

Alina seethed. She unlaced her bodice and leaned over until she could get her breast to Cridon's mouth. Though it was awkward and uncomfortable, Cridon drank her nearly dry. Her face was so close to Cyn's that the assassin's rotten breath nauseated her. While Cridon fed, Alina lifted her eyes to Cyn's and wondered if there was ever any warmth behind them. By the time Cridon finished feeding, she was more convinced than ever that there was none. She laced up her bodice, leaned next to her boy, and kissed his cheek.

"He needs you to pat his back, so he doesn't get a stomachache."

"He will survive a little gas."

Alina imagined how raw and painful Cridon's bottom must be getting in his wet diaper. "May I at least change him, so he doesn't get sores?"

Cyn sighed. "He does stink something awful. Go ahead and change him, but be quick about it."

While Cyn held Cridon out like a bundle of soiled laundry, Alina removed his cloth diaper, leaned over the side of the boat to wash it in the ocean, and then draped it over the edge to dry. "Can I please just hold him until his clothes dry?"

Cyn shook her head. She laid Cridon on the hard wooden planks with her outstretched legs keeping him from rolling with the tide. "You're trying my patience, Alina. Go sit down."

"I hate you."

Cyn chuckled. "Well, I should hope so. If you didn't, I wouldn't know how to take it."

Alina sat next to Leander again. After some time the suns dried Cridon's diaper enough that she could dress him.

Cyn yawned and stretched. Her dark, deep-set eyes and the suns at her back made it hard for Alina to tell if she had fallen asleep or was goading Alina to see what she would do.

Leander leaned close to Alina's ear. "I grow tired of this game, Alina."

"I know you do. But I have an idea. I'll need you to do something for me."

"Name it."

Alina was careful to keep her voice low in case Cyn was indeed awake. "If she's taking me to Thasula, I need you to run into Concore forest. I want you to find Rasi."

Leander pulled back, stunned. "I thought Rasi was dead."

"That's what Cyn told Masera, but I don't believe her."

"How will I find him?"

"There is a mountain called Widows Run. At the base is a rock formation that looks like a crown. If Rasi is still alive, that's where he will go." She went on to describe how to get there.

"It seems like the longest of long shots, Alina."

"That's all we have left. Rasi would have tried to find me. When he couldn't, that's where he'd go. That was our plan."

"It's too dangerous."

"They won't be looking for you."

"I'm not talking about me. I can't leave you with her."

"You have no choice. Rasi is all we have to fight them."

Leander hesitated a while before nodding.

Cyn stretched with a moan and smacked her lips like her mouth tasted sour. "And what are you two whispering about?"

"How to kill you," Alina snapped.

"Heh." She rolled her eyes. Holding Cridon out with his belly exposed, she rubbed her nose back and forth across his stomach. In a playful tone, she said, "Maybe your mommy will tell me what she said if I take off one of your arms. How would that be? You'd like that, wouldn't you? Yes, you would."

"I grow rather tired of your impotent threats, Cyn."

The assassin grinned. "Impotent? Do you really believe I am merely making threats? You haven't been paying attention."

Alina continued to glare at her all the way to Epertase's southern shore.

Cyn gestured to Leander. "Pull us ashore, tough guy."

Leander climbed into the water and pulled the boat onto the sand. Cyn got out and carried Cridon up the beach. Then she had Leander build a fire using wood from the broken boats that littered the shore.

Cridon cried the whole time.

"How do you shut this kid up?" Cyn asked.

"He wants his mother. Something you wouldn't understand."

Though the days were hot that time of year, the nights got a bit chilly so close to the ocean. Cyn laid Cridon on his back in the sand and ignored him while rubbing her hands near the fire. Alina's heart broke to see her baby boy treated so callously.

Cyn poked at the fire with a stick, sending embers to the sky. Her eyes followed them. "I had a child once," she blurted.

Alina's eyes narrowed. She was stunned, not only by what Cyn said, but with her willingness to speak of her past.

"It was a different time, I suppose." She watched the stars with a slight smile, faintly nostalgic. "I named him Ramsey." Quietly, almost to herself, she mumbled, "I haven't thought of him in many years."

"So, you do know what it's like to be a mother."

Cyn turned her soulless eyes back to Alina and, for just a moment, showed a speck of humanity in them. "Yes. I suppose I do."

"Then let me have my son. He needs me."

"Oh, Alina." That brief glimpse of a real person vanished in an instant. Anger creased her forehead. "You're so foolish. If my son couldn't survive me ..." Her voice deepened and slowed. "... what chance at mercy do you think I would give to you?"

Alina gasped. "You killed your own son? How could you?"

Cyn turned away. She didn't say anything else.

Alina didn't think she'd sleep that night. She kept her gaze trained on Cridon as he sucked his thumb and slept alone in the sand. At least the fire kept him warm. With the other symbiots going to whatever gods they ultimately met, her curiosity grew. "Why do you still do this, Cyn? I mean, is it just for money?"

Cyn's face lit up like a young girl with a crush. "Money?" Then it darkened as though she'd realized she had shown too much enthusiasm. "Oh no, not for money. I suppose it was for a while, but not anymore. I would do this for free."

"Why? Just for the sport, then?"

"Maybe at one time. But then I met him. Now, I'll do anything he asks because he is my truest love."

"Do you mean Scorne? I heard he was dead."

Cyn paused with a hint of a frown. "Dead? That I hadn't heard. Sometimes he would disappear for a bit and I just figured he had been hiding out." She gazed off to the side. "That's a shame. Scorne was an interesting fellow." Then she glared back at Alina. "No, I didn't love Scorne, you silly woman." Without a hint of self-awareness, she added, "Scorne was insane. No, I am in love with Tevin the Third."

"Tevin?" Alina almost choked on her own spit. There were few names Cyn could have said that would have stunned her more than Tevin's. "My father's right hand, Tevin?"

"Yes. Tevin."

"Isn't he dead?"

Cyn's eyes widened. "Far from it."

"How does someone like you meet someone like Tevin?"

"Like me?" Cyn asked with her lip curled and her nose wrinkled in annoyance at the question. "You don't know anything about me. After hiring Scorne to kill your grandparents, your father became quite enamored with our ability to carry out his messier tasks.

"Since he couldn't be seen with us, he sent Tevin to the meetings in his stead. And since Scorne was a paranoid psychotic, I sometimes took his place. I rather enjoyed Tevin's company back then, but when he returned to Epertase with such power after the Tek war, my feelings for him grew to unparalleled heights." Cyn breathed deeper and faster as she spoke of him.

"Power?" Alina asked, almost laughing out loud. "Tevin never had any sort of power. He was my father's lackey. In fact, he was afraid to fight in the Heathen War. He had an excuse for missing every battle. My father used to complain all the time about having to defend him from accusations of cowardice."

Cyn snapped, "You lie. Tevin is a warrior. He does not fear anyone, let alone heathens. And now he is the greatest wizard Epertase has ever known."

"Wizard? Are we speaking of the same Tevin?"

"Your father's Light gave him the gift."

Alina shook her head, flabbergasted. "Nothing you say rings true. Why would the Light give Tevin power?"

Cyn shrugged her shoulders. "Well, it did. I have seen his power for myself."

"If what you say is true, then the Light is clearly broken."

Cyn giggled. "Well, of course it is. The Light has been broken for centuries, foolish one. Ever since Matthew took it from his father."

Alina frowned. "Then what does Tevin want with me? I left Epertase. I'm obviously no longer a threat."

"Are you really as naïve as you seem?" Cyn paused, waiting to see if Alina could answer her own question. She groaned. "He wants your Light, you stupid whore," she finally said.

"My Light? Why? It does nothing for me that I can see."

Cyn rolled her eyes and groaned again. "It links your soul to every living creature in Epertase, as it did your father's before you. Tevin says it has untapped power far greater than you or your ancestors have ever wielded. When Tevin has it, he will repair the Light and harness its true power. He will sit alongside the gods."

Alina grinned. "Taking my Light is impossible," she said, almost gloating. "After all this and everything else you have done, Tevin will fail. Have you not heard the tales of Thadius's attempts to take the Light back from his son?"

Cyn raptly listened, as if she hadn't heard the story a thousand times before.

"They all failed, Cyn. The greatest wizards and witches of his time were unable to thwart the Light's will."

"They were not Tevin the Third. The world has never seen such power as he now wields."

Alina couldn't wrap her mind around what Cyn was saying. It seemed impossible that Tevin would have any power at all, let alone enough power to bring down her entire kingdom. "What about Fice and his Gildonese? Where are they?"

"Tevin disposed of those pathetic creatures once they failed him. They were merely pawns in his ultimate plan."

Impossible. They sat in awkward silence for a bit. Though Alina wasn't sure she could believe a word the assassin said, there was one more line of questions she had to ask while Cyn was feeling so chatty. "My friend Masera told me that you claimed Rasi was dead."

"Yes?"

"Did you see Rasi die?"

"Well, he was dying and—"

"No. Did you *see* him dead?"

"Dying. Dead. At that point, there was no difference."

"You're wrong."

"Pfft. It matters little what you believe. Rasi is indeed dead. And you will soon lose your precious Light. Maybe when they write stories of Tevin's rise to power, you and Rasi will find your places as sad footnotes in history." After a pause, she added, "If you make the stories at all. No, you can wish for your lover to be ali—"

"You mean my husband."

Cyn tilted her head. "Is that so? Very well. You can wish for your *husband* to be alive all you like, but in the end, you are still a widow."

"But you didn't see his dead body—that's what you're telling me?"

Cyn gave a frustrated sigh. "No, I suppose I did not see him draw his last breath. But it was imminent."

Alina glanced at Leander and he caught her look. She didn't say another word and neither did Cyn until the suns peeked over the mighty sea. Even when she dozed off, her metal skin woke her if Alina or Leander made the slightest flinch in her direction.

Cyn stood up and dusted herself off. She snatched Cridon from the sand and said, "It's time to go."

They began the long walk to Thasula, travelling the back roads for days. Cyn stole food from homes along the way and they drank from streams. She was as good a thief as she was an assassin. Or maybe she just killed the people inside. Alina prayed it was the former.

What remained of Shadows Peak broke through the fog above the distant Forest of Concore. Alina inched closer to Leander. While Cyn was preoccupied with settling a suddenly squirmy Cridon, Alina whispered, "Be safe, Leander."

Leander nodded. "If Rasi's alive, I'll find him."

"There's no 'if.' Go."

With those words, he touched her shoulder, glanced at Cyn's back, and broke into a sprint for the forest.

Cyn turned to watch him curiously and smirked. "There goes your hero. I'm surprised he stayed as long as he did."

If Cyn had any flaws, it was her inability to understand true loyalty.

"Should I chase him down and kill him?" Cyn mumbled to herself. Then she shook her head. "Not worth the effort." She stopped and waited for Alina to catch up. "Where does he think he's going, anyway? To find Rasi?" She chuckled. "He'd better take a shovel."

We'll see.

They continued walking until they reached the edge of the Concore Forest. There was no sign of Leander. All Alina could do was pray.

CHAPTER 11

RIGHTING WRONGS

Simcane sat alone in the corner of a windowless cell, deemed too dangerous to be in the same cell as other prisoners. Each night he went to sleep with the same scene playing out in his head that he woke to each morning. Surrendering to Jarrah in Lithia was the worse decision he'd ever made, and because of it he was left to rot in a cell forever.

A guard arrived as he had each morning at the same time. He was a skinny young man with tiny acne scars covering his forehead, nose, and cheeks. His upper lip sported a thin line of dark hairs making a desperate attempt to grow a mustache. With a slightly high-pitched voice, he asked, "Hungry?"

Simcane grunted. He was starving, but he refused to grovel for his meals. They only fed him once a day. The kid tossed a partially cooked leg of something big, maybe a horse, between the bars before dragging his wheeled cart to the next cell. Simcane would normally turn away from horse meat, but he needed protein.

Before tearing into the undercooked meat, Simcane went to the iron bars and relieved himself onto the walkway, as he did every day. He hoped one of the guards would open his cell to punish him, but they never did.

Once finished, he sat on the floor and chewed the meat down to the bone. Though it was surprisingly tender and sweet, it still turned his stomach a bit. After the meat was gone, he snapped the bone in half against his knee. Then he sucked down every bit of marrow from within. It tasted like shit, but it was additional nourishment.

After he finished eating, he considered trying his gift against the cell walls again in the unlikely event that Tevin had inadvertently lowered his spell. The faint ripple of purple air hovering across the bars assured he hadn't. That the scrawny guard could pass food through the spell and his own piss could make it outside only added to the oddity that was Tevin's magic.

After the guard was gone, another day of devastating boredom began. Simcane spent the first hour exercising, using the bars in the window for pull-ups and squatting with his bed on his shoulders to work his legs. He had just worked up a sweat when the door at the opposite end of the hall clanged open. Afternoon visitors were rare.

Simcane sat with his back to the wall below the window, facing the bars. He draped a blanket over his head and locked his eye to the floor. Two sets of footsteps clopped to his cell. It was probably a guard showing off Simcane to a new recruit or something. They did that once in a while.

When a key rattled in his cell door's lock, he pinched himself to make sure he wasn't dreaming. Could they possibly be so stupid as to open his door? The lock clanked. *Unbelievable. They are that stupid.* They had no idea the danger they had just put themselves in. Were they new? Suicidal? Beneath the blanket, Simcane subtly shifted his weight to pounce. He'd only get one shot.

The door creaked open. His muscles tensed. Before he could spring, one of the men said, "Simcane? It's me. Andon."

Even better.

He lifted his eye. Andon stood beside a man hiding beneath a shadowy hood. Before pouncing on Andon, he needed to know who his friend was.

The door opened fully. Andon stepped into the cell like a fool. Simcane decided the other man's identity wasn't important after all; he couldn't wait any longer. With the second man still in the doorway, Simcane bounded to his feet and yanked Andon deeper into the cell. Before the hooded stranger could retreat, Simcane lunged and grabbed his shirt.

"Wait, Simcane," the man shouted as he yanked back his hood.

Simcane's fist was already cocked, but one good look at the boy's face made him relax his grip. "Well, I'll be. Hey, kid. How's your mom?"

Bohden nodded. "She's doing well. You nearly scared me to death. I thought you were going to smash me."

Simcane leaned back to check the front of Bohden's pants. "Well, I didn't scare you too much. You didn't wet yourself."

Bohden's face contorted. "Is that common?"

"Heh. More than you'd think."

He looked over his shoulder to Andon. "Why'd you bring him here?"

Bohden answered instead. "He sought me out to help you. He heard how you helped me and my mom."

"Is that so?"

Andon nodded.

Bohden scanned the hall before continuing. "He found me shortly after you were captured. He told me he wanted to help you, but he didn't trust anyone he worked with. He said if I joined the army, he'd get me assigned to the prison."

Andon interrupted, "I didn't want to call in his help just yet, but Alina needs you."

Simcane straightened. "Oh."

"Cyn caught her and is returning with her as we speak. Tevin's hylock scouts just told him. If we have any hope of saving her, we have to act now."

"Where are they?"

"Approaching from the Great Plains. I was ordered to gather soldiers to meet Tevin there."

"And did you?"

Andon shook his head. "I found Bohden and came here instead."

"And why'd you do such a thing?"

"You may not believe me, but I regret turning my back on Alina. I have since the moment I did it. It was the wrong decision and one I can never take back."

"You're right, I don't believe you."

"That's why I'm still in the back of the cell and the door's wide open. You and I both know I can't stop you from leaving."

"I should break your neck for treason."

Andon bowed his head. "And I'd deserve it."

Simcane glared at him and then sighed. He held out his hand. "I'm glad you found your conscience, old friend."

Andon looked at his hand for a few seconds before grabbing hold.

Simcane squeezed a little harder than necessary, which made Andon wince. "I only hope you didn't find it too late."

"We should get going. Alina's going to need you. Bohden will lead the way out of this place."

Simcane nodded and followed Bohden through the door with Andon trailing. But when Andon got to the door, he stepped back into the cell and pulled it shut. Simcane spun around. "What are you doing?"

Andon reached through the bars and jammed a key into the lock. He twisted and then snapped the key off inside. He tossed the rest of the keys to Bohden. "Free everyone," he said.

Simcane reached into the cell to grab Andon's shirt, but Andon backed out of reach. "Go, Sim. Save Alina before it's too late." He stepped onto Simcane's cot and opened his overcoat. A curl of rope hung from his waist.

"Andon, don't." Simcane grabbed the bars and violently shook them. "Andon, stop."

Andon tossed one end of the rope through the window and then pulled it back through. He tied it off and then wrapped the other end around his neck. It was already tied in a noose.

Simcane searched for some other way in. Maybe something to pry the broken key out. "Please, Andon. We can work this out. Stop it. We need you."

Bohden pressed his forehead against the bars. "Don't do it, sir. Please."

In Andon's eyes Simcane saw a deep sadness that his words could never touch. Andon tightened the noose around his neck. "Sim, I have lived with so much guilt lately. This will actually be a relief."

Simcane shook his head. "Alina will forgive you. Let's talk about it."

Andon smiled sadly. "I'm coming, Dru." Then he jumped from the bed. His body stopped with a jolt inches from the ground. Simcane turned away. Seeing Bohden pressed against the bars, he gently turned the kid's head. "Stop watching, kid. Some sights will stick with a man for his entire life. Don't let this be one of them."

Bohden was shaken; it was written in the pain on his face.

"Listen. There's nothing we can do for him now. Go free everyone. When you get to a man named Willum and ..." Bohden's eyes drifted back toward the gurgling in the cell. Simcane shook his shoulders. "Are you listening?"

Bohden snapped back to attention and nodded.

"When you get to a man named Willum and a woman named Gillian, tell them to go to Eldon's land. If Eldon's there, I want them to wait with him until they hear from me again, no matter how long that may be."

"Yes, sir. After that, what do you want me to do?"

"Keep your job as a soldier. Lie low. I may need someone on the inside again one day." Simcane started for the exit.

Bohden shouted, "Simcane. Take my horse. It's a brown and white spotted mare out front."

Simcane appreciated the gesture, but he was taking whatever horse was out there regardless of who gave him permission.

CHAPTER 12

CYN'S FINAL APPROACH

Cyn led Alina along the edge of Concore Forest toward Thasula. They had walked through the night, neither woman speaking, their hatred of each other palpable. Cridon fussed occasionally, but his last feeding had been a good one and he would soon be asleep again.

At the first sight of the city wall, Cyn stopped and smiled. "Not much farther. I've been away from my lover for too long." She sneered at Alina and added, "I will be glad to finally be rid of you and your stupid Light. I can't begin to tell you how much of a headache you have cau—" She froze and lifted her head like prey catching the scent of a predator. She held up her hand and whispered, "Stop." Then she squatted.

Alina started to ask what Cyn had heard, but the assassin shushed her and pulled her down to the ground. *Something is coming,* she mindspoke.

What?

Cyn repositioned Cridon at her waist, less than an arm-length away. Every fiber in Alina's body wanted to snatch him and run. It would be a blessing from the gods just to hold him again. She imagined Cridon in her arms and realized she was subconsciously reaching for him.

Do you smell that? Cyn asked.

Alina smelled a faint sulfurous odor. *Yes. It's horrible. What is it?*

Cyn's metal skin slithered anxiously over her body, some of it forming a point on her free hand. *Back up to the trees.*

Not without my son.

Cyn turned with a scowl. *Do I have to kill this kid for you to listen? I'm your only chance of surviving now.*

Alina slowly backed away, her eyes fixed on her helpless son. Cridon whimpered. Cyn glared at him like she expected him to understand the need to be quiet as well. She followed Alina to the trees, constantly looking over her shoulder. Alina had never seen her so nervous and hesitant for a fight. Whatever was coming must be bad.

"What is it, Cyn?" Alina whispered.

Cyn lifted her finger and pointed toward the west. With a nervous quiver in her voice, she answered, "The fishers are coming." Her words stole Alina's breath.

Alina looked to the city wall. "Can we make it if we run?"

Cyn looked her up and down. She smirked. "Maybe *I* can."

Alina looked to the west. At first, all she saw was the early sunlight settling on an empty field. But then a single hunched-over creature appeared.

Cyn pointed. *That's a scout. There'll be two or three of them.* As soon as she said it, another one poked its head from around a tree farther along at the edge of Concore.

The creatures dropped their heads back and loosed a cackling howl.

Cyn, we have to run. They've caught our scent.

"We'll never make it. We have no choice. I'll have to fight them."

"How many are there?"

Cyn shrugged. "Dozens, if not more."

"Can you win?"

Cyn smirked again and tilted her head. "Of course not."

Alina wilted.

Cyn pointed again. An entire pack of fishers galloped toward them through the Great Plains. Alina's stomach dropped. Her pulse quickened.

Cyn stepped from the tree line into full view of the charging creatures. "Wait here." She was insane.

"Leave Cridon," Alina cried. She reached for Cyn's arm, but Cyn jerked out of reach. Alina lunged for Cridon again and Cyn sank her fist into her gut. Alina doubled over and strained to lift her eyes from her hands and knees. It took all her strength to ask, "Cyn, please leave Cridon with me."

Cyn ignored her as she continued toward the charging horde, Cridon cradled in the crook of her arm. The creatures surrounded her. As if sensing her prowess, they hesitated.

"What do you want, creatures?" Cyn shouted.

"Take her eyees," one of them answered.

Cyn stood defiantly, her metal weapon poised at her side. "What if I take yours first, beast?"

Another fisher, one that the others cowered away from, stepped forward and stood erect. He was as tall as Cyn. "Rasiiieee," he cried. Alina's knees went weak.

Cyn scoffed, "Rasi's dead. The great Tevin the Third has killed him."

"That cannot beee."

Cyn laid Cridon in the grass and closed her fists, metal spikes protruding from her knuckles. "Why do you want Rasi?" she asked.

"Hee is our god."

Cyn slowly turned in a circle, watching intently for any of the creatures to make a move. "Your god? He's no god. He was just a freak with a bunch of goofy strings hanging off his back like a puppet. And he's dead, anyway."

"Shee is a liieear. Kill her." One of them stepped forward.

"Wait," Cyn shouted.

Surprisingly, he paused.

Cyn smiled. "I think we can work something out."

What was she doing? Something didn't feel right. Alina's clenched stomach muscles loosened enough for her to finally stand.

Cyn glanced back when Alina stepped from the tree line. "No fishers need to die here today. If you let me leave, I will give you the next best thing to your god. I will give you his son." Cyn nodded toward the ground where Cridon cooed and kicked in the tall grass.

Alina screamed, "No." She grabbed a stick and charged.

Cyn shouted, "Take him now. Hurry."

They didn't move.

Cyn knelt over Cridon and drew her metal-pointed fist back. "If you don't take him now, I'll slaughter him. I'll kill the son of your god, I swear."

One of the fishers turned toward Alina and sniffed the air. "Who is that?"

Cyn pulled his attention back to her. "You will not harm that woman. She's mine. Now, take the kid. Take him and run. This is your last chance."

The lead fisher tilted his head. Then he nodded and snatched Cridon in a flash. He bolted west. Alina shrieked. The other fishers chased their leader. They galloped with the speed of horses.

Alina dropped her stick and fell to her knees. "Why, Cyn?" she screamed. "You've killed my son." She sobbed into her hands. There was no chance to catch them and nothing she could do if she did.

Cyn quietly walked to her side. "Well, I'd say that was rather easy."

"What have you done?" Alina sobbed.

She sneered down. "I saved your life, you ungrateful wench."

"But you promised."

"No. I promised *you* would live. I said nothing about your pathetic son."

Alina's blood boiled. She wanted to kill Cyn more than she wanted to breathe.

As the fishers raced along the edge of Concore Forest, Cyn smirked. "Fast little bastards, aren't they?"

Alina sprang up from her knees, catching Cyn off guard. She clawed at Cyn's face, but the metal skin defended. Annoyed, Cyn grabbed her hair and yanked her back to the ground. "Fighting me will do you no good, whore. You are going to Tevin, conscious or otherwise."

Alina struggled in Cyn's strong grip. She screamed, "You've sentenced my son to death. You might as well kill me because I'll not willingly go with you any farther."

Cyn leaned in and whispered, "Calm yourself. You will go with me or I'll break your legs and drag you. Tevin wants you alive; he said nothing of you being whole."

With Cridon at the mercy of the fishers, all the fight drained from Alina's broken heart. She pictured what the creatures might do and would have gouged out her own eyes if it would stop the horrible images in her mind.

To further torment her, Cyn added, "Besides, you should be more optimistic. Maybe those creatures have a nursing female and your child won't starve to death. He might have quite the adventure with them. At least, until they run out of meat, that is."

Cyn slowly relaxed her grip. She extended her hand, but Alina spat on it. Cyn pointed to two hylocks circling above. "He knows we're here, now" she said with a grin. She grabbed Alina's ear and pulled her painfully to her feet.

The hylocks landed in front of them. "Tevin is comeeeng," one of them announced.

Alina couldn't stop crying.

CHAPTER 13

HOPE

A s they had each morning, Meela and Rasi climbed onto the boulder beneath the crown of stone for their breakfast of japsy weed and fish. Meela tore into her meat with the same savagery she showed all her prey, forever fearful of losing a meal. She was nearly finished eating when she stopped and perked her ears. She slowly lowered her fish to the rock and sniffed the air.

She lifted her unseeing gray eyes to the path that led from the rubble of Shadows Peak. "Rasiieee. They are neeear," she whispered. The creases deepened in her terrified face. She didn't have to say who was near; he knew she meant her fisher kin.

He stood up, his straps poised for action. "Where?"

"The Plains."

Rasi climbed down from the boulder.

Meela moved to the edge and sniffed the air. "Somebodee else is comeeng." She pointed toward the path just as a stranger stepped around the bend.

Rasi's straps flared out.

The stranger froze when he noticed. Rasi glanced back to where Meela had been standing on the boulder, but she was gone.

"Rasi?" the man shouted.

Rasi's straps snapped the air.

The stranger's face brightened. He took a step forward as sweet little Meela silently rose behind him. She watched Rasi for the signal to take the strangers eyes.

The stranger continued forward, oblivious to the death stalking him from behind. He held up his hands. "I've been searching for you," he said.

Rasi shrugged. A lot of people had searched for him over the years. The man saved his own life by adding, "Alina sent me to find you."

Alina? Rasi raised an empty hand toward Meela and shook his head. She lowered her scoop-claws with an audible sigh.

The stranger stopped and slowly turned his head, seeing Meela for the first time. The color drained from his face. He'd never know how close he had come to losing his eyes. Depending on what he said next, he may yet lose them.

He turned back to Rasi. "I'm not here as an enemy."

Rasi approached. His straps surrounded the stranger, ever wary of a trap.

The man gingerly offered his hand. "My name is Leander. I'm a Tek, sir."

Why Teks? Rasi shook his head. How much worse could things get? He hadn't the time or energy to deal with Teks on top of everything else. He glared at Leander's proffered hand. He didn't have time for pleasantries either. He growled Alina's name.

Leander was quick to answer. "The assassin named Cyn has her. She is taking the queen to the wizard."

"Where?"

"Not far. When I escaped, they were walking toward the edge of the forest."

The air soured between them. Rasi's growing skepticism and mounting anger made him clench his fists. There were few men he hated more than Teks. Fortunately for Leander, Tevin was one of them.

"You have no reason to believe me, sir, but I speak the truth. Alina showed my people mercy by sparing our lives after you defeated us. When she fled to Torick Island, she was very ill. We returned her mercy by nursing her back to health. We have been protecting her ever since."

Hopeful, Rasi listened for anything that would allow him to believe his once sworn enemy.

"Alina told me I would find you here. She said this is where you had your first kiss."

And that was it.

Though it seemed unfathomable that a Tek could ever be his ally, it was all he had. He started past Leander toward the path, but Leander stopped him cold. "Cyn has Cridon, too."

Rasi glanced back. "Who?"

"Your son."

Rasi wobbled. *Cridon?*

Leander tilted his head. "You didn't know?" And then he shook his head and mumbled, "Of course not."

Rasi looked to the path again.

"He's healthy and strong, Rasi."

Rasi's knees nearly buckled.

"Cyn holds him as a hostage. That's why I couldn't do more to free Alina."

Rasi had heard enough. He marched past Leander, roughly knocking the Tek aside. One of his straps waggled in front of Leander's face as if antagonizing him.

Leander reached for Rasi's shoulder, but the strap shoved his hand away. He said, "I'll go with you. I can help."

Rasi broke into a sprint toward Shadows Peak. Meela galloped alongside while Leander, exhausted from his frantic trek, did his best to keep up.

The suns were already hot by the time Rasi had climbed over the rubble at the base of his old home. What he wouldn't give for a horse.

Or a sword.

Or an army.

Meela stayed at his side through Concore Forest to the edge of the plains. There she gasped and grabbed his arm.

Rasi studied her fearful face. "What is it?"

A single tear escaped a pale eye and ran down her cheek. "Iiee'm so sorree. They have your son."

Rasi's heart collapsed. Even after everything he had gone through—after all the physical and mental anguish—he had never known pain like he felt knowing his son was about to face the same horror he had just endured. Or worse.

"Where?" He could barely get the word out.

She turned east and pointed to a horde of fishers racing toward them. Meela tugged his hand toward the trees. "Hiieede. You can't fiieeeght them all. They will kill you."

Rasi would rather die than let them escape with his son. He resisted her pull so he could meet them head-on. He stepped into the open and his straps cracked like whips. "'Ou wan' me," he screamed. When they saw him, they broke off their route across the plains and diverted toward him.

That's it, you bastards. Come get me. I'll show you what your god can do. He ground his teeth in anticipation. He counted at least ten, but they could have numbered twelve or even fourteen. They were coming fast. He concentrated on slowing his anxious breaths, knowing if he went into the fight already winded, he would be quickly spent. He had one chance.

Meela fidgeted. "Bee careful, Rasiieee. Theeese are the hunters. They will bee skilled."

Rasi shrugged. It could be ten of the fiercest fishers in the world or a hundred, it mattered little. He would kill them all to save his son. Leander stumbled from the tree line and hurried to Rasi's side. He braced himself with his hands on his knees before he noticed the coming creatures. "What are we doing?" he asked.

Rasi nodded toward the fishers.

"Oh." Leander straightened and steeled himself for the fight like a good soldier.

Rasi's strap nudged him toward the trees. Leander resisted, but Rasi gave him a look. He would be worthless without any weapons, and there was no use in dying just for dying's sake. Leander reluctantly joined Meela.

There were two scouts at the front of the pack while the rest of the creatures surrounded a single fisher in their center. Rasi knew he would be the one carrying Cridon. Rasi charged them and dove into their mass, straps flailing. They ripped and sliced, but his straps were on point and none of their claws got through. He head-butted the first fisher he reached, opening a gash above his own eye. Finally, a set of claws got through and raked his flesh. He didn't slow. Or even wince. Fishers grunted and strained around him.

The two scouts circled back. As they raced past the tree line, Leander jumped out and collided with one of them. Rasi snapped a neck; his straps snapped a leg. The protected creature drifted within reach.

Rasi grunted and lunged. The creature ducked and dodged and pulled back out of reach as others filled the void. Rasi's straps choked the life out of another creature. Those left swarmed him. Rasi thrashed beneath their weight as the fisher carrying his son disengaged from the pile. They were relentless. Their claws shredded his thigh and back, but he didn't care. Three fishers fell to his straps as three more pounced.

Despite the violent battle he waged, an eerie silence fell over the battlefield. Though he could see the creatures wailing and screeching, he couldn't hear them any longer. Perhaps his rage and strain had blown out his eardrums. He fought against their grips, snot and spit spraying from his silent roar.

And then a single sound broke the silence. Though it was distant at first, there was no mistaking what it was. Perhaps the greatest sound he had ever heard fell on his ears. It was a baby's cry. His son's cry.

And then all the violent sounds of the battle came roaring back. Rasi howled as he searched for his son. A single fisher had broken free and was galloping west. Rasi cried, "Noooo," and killed two more fishers holding him back. As he fought, he kept one eye on his son and one on his opponents. He couldn't break free in time. After he and his straps killed the last of the fishers, Rasi fell to his knees and pressed his hands to his face. He would never forgive himself for failing.

With nearly a dozen dead fishers sprawled out around him, he turned toward Leander. The Tek stood over a dead scout. Though his face was bloody, he had won.

"Where's Cridon?" he shouted.

Rasi pointed west where a couple of fishers had followed Cridon's captor. His strategic mind chased every possible way to get to his son, but none of them ended with Cridon and Alina both safe.

Leander limped to his side. "How 'bout I go for Cridon? You go for—"

Before he finished, Meela exploded from the tree line on all fours and shot past them in pursuit.

"Do you think she'll catch him?" Leander asked.

Rasi nodded, his expression grim. If Meela had any advantage, it was her speed. It was what would happen to her once she caught the fleeing fisher that worried him.

"Rasi, you have to go for Alina."

Rasi looked back toward the eastern hill where the fishers had come from. Then he looked toward Havens Ravine again. Usually, he was decisive and quick to act, but the choice was too painful. He refused to believe he couldn't save them both, and it was his unwillingness to accept the truth that paralyzed him.

Leander grabbed his shoulder. A strap pulled his hand away. "Listen to me. Your fisher friend is going for Cridon. You must trust her to find him. You can't do everything on your own. Your only choice is to go for Alina while there's still a chance she can be rescued. I will find Meela and your son, and then we will find you."

As hard as it was to hear, Leander was right. Rasi knew that if Tevin succeeded, there would be no world left for Cridon to live in. But his heart ached at the thought of his son in the clutches of those vile creatures for even a moment longer.

Rasi's first step east filled him with overwhelming guilt. *Cridon,* he silently prayed. *Be strong, my son. I'll come for you soon.* He sprinted east. The animated grass of the Great Plains grabbed at his feet as the world prepared for another change.

May the gods help us all.

CHAPTER 14

THE STRENGTH OF THE STRONGEST WIZARD

Cyn tied a rope around Alina's wrists and started toward Thasula, two hylocks leading the way. The grass grabbed at their feet. Before they made it very far, a single horse rider burst from the city gate, the sunlight highlighting the long robe that draped over his horse's hind quarters. The rider raced toward them. Alina had no doubt it was Tevin, despite the raggedy beard.

Cyn ordered her to her knees and ran to meet him. She smothered him almost before his feet hit the ground. "My love," she shouted.

Tevin stared over her shoulder at Alina with a kind of breathlessness usually reserved for one's wedding day. He smiled smugly and pushed Cyn to the side.

"I did it, my love," Cyn said.

"I know you did," he answered, never taking his eyes from Alina. Though it was Tevin's voice, she had never heard it carry such confidence and weight.

Before he got to Alina, he stopped cold, a sliver of Cyn's metal skin pressed against his jugular from behind. He didn't break his smile. A subtle orange glow throbbed beneath his robe.

"I don't believe I've received my rightful praise for what I've done for you, my love."

He gently guided her blade away from his neck and looked into her eyes. "Soon. Very soon."

She wilted under his gaze, backed away, and bowed.

Tevin continued toward Alina. "It is good to see you after all this time, young queen."

"Why are you doing this, Tevin? My father was your friend. He would hate you for what you've done to his kingdom. And for what you're doing to me."

Tevin shook his head. "Now, now, Alina. While I'll admit my tactics have been rather crude, it is the results that will be judged by history."

"Why would you ever think my father would approve of your actions?"

"Because you stole his Light."

"No, I didn't. The Light chose to go to me. I didn't even want it. I just wanted my father."

"And your father wanted his Light. So much so, he was willing to sacrifice you for that end. As I see it, your sacrifice here today is long overdue. I cannot bring your father back, but I can rule in his stead."

"You're a fool, Tevin. You are traitorous and undeserving of your newfound power. Your rule will destroy Epertase."

Tevin frowned. "Nonsense. This is all your fault, Alina. You chose Rasi over your own father. It was you and that freak who killed him. The Light has seen what you've done, and that's why it has given me such strength."

"You're wrong. In the end my father couldn't sacrifice me. He turned on Scorne. It was my father and Rasi who saved me, and Scorne who killed him, not us."

"I am disappointed in you, Alina. You've fooled yourself for so long that you believe your own lies. You have twisted the truth to take the throne."

"Ask Cyn about my father's death. She was there, for the gods' sake."

Tevin paused, appearing to weigh her words, but then a scowl washed over his face. "Once I have your father's Light, I will rebuild

Epertase. The people will learn to love me—I will make them if they don't. My rule will be absolute. Sheep need guidance to be truly happy."

"My father would be disgusted with you and your schemes. Keep his name out of your treachery."

"Revolutions can be ugly, but in the end it will be beautiful. I have foreseen it." He drew a knife from his waistband. With evil burning in his cold eyes, he reached for her. She recoiled. A swipe of his blade freed her wrists. He dropped his knife beside her and backed away as if daring her to pick it up.

She couldn't help but look at it.

Tevin smirked. "That's right. Pick it up. Thrust it into my heart."

She looked away, unwilling to ease his conscience by giving him what he wanted.

The corners of his lips curved upward. "Suit yourself, Alina. Your end is near, one way or another."

He planted both feet firmly on the ground and mumbled in a foreign godly language. His eyes glossed over white and his muscles quivered. Dark clouds darted across the sky, plunging the brightness of day into stormy dusk. He lifted his trembling arms above his head.

Cyn watched with her mouth agape, as if she stared upon a god.

The air grew thin like at the top of Shadows Peak. An invisible force pinned Alina's arms to her sides and lifted her body from the ground. The two hylocks cackled beside her. She tried to turn her head away, but Tevin's magic forced her eyes forward.

He lifted his blank eyes to the somber sky. His voice echoed in her ears. "Gods of the stars, I call upon you. This woman you have blessed with your glory has proven unworthy of your gift by her deceit. Your Light has been broken. Give it to me and I will restore it to its rightful glory. I ask you … no, I demand that your Light be stripped from this queen. The corrupt lineage of Thadius will finally end with her death, and I will protect your Light for all eternity."

Cyn cocked her head. "Uh, Tevin?" she called. "Alina has a—"

Tevin flicked his wrist at her, sending her sprawling to the ground.

The tall grass danced around him, as it had in the days before King Elijah's death. The air rumbled as lightning streaked the sky in flashes of brilliance. The clouds parted around a single star which grew brighter as Tevin's thunderous voice boomed. "I feel your greatness," he shouted.

The ground cracked around him and seven perfectly round holes formed near his feet. Snakes of every color of the rainbow slithered from each hole and encircled his legs.

"Colorfuls," Alina whispered.

Tevin ignored them at first, but when they constricted around him, he winced. "What manner of creatures are you to rise up against a god?"

The suffocating air around Alina eased up as Tevin's focus was diverted. Alina could lift her right arm slightly.

The colorfuls entangled his legs and waist. He scowled and his jaw tightened. The dull orange glow in his chest grew brighter and throbbed until a blast of intense heat exploded from his core. The colorfuls squealed and fell to the ground, shattering like crystal on a stone floor.

Tevin smirked and lifted his eyes back to Alina. "Now, where was I? Oh, yes." Her arm was pinned back to her side. He screamed to the skies, "Strike down this former queen and fulfill my destiny. God of Light, grant me the power to rule this land unopposed and I will honor you with that rule."

Thunder crackled over the swaying treetops.

Tevin waved Alina forward and she drifted toward him, stopping within an arm's length. He gently touched her cheek. His voice shook the trees. "With this woman's life, I free her of the Light."

The dancing grass blackened and wilted. The air exploded into flames. Alina closed her eyes as the fire swallowed her. Like the day she'd gained the Light from her father, the flames gyrated beneath her pulsating skin. The cries of a million souls echoed in her ears.

Her eyes shot open with the realization that she was losing everything. Her arms were pried from her sides and flung wide. Her head dropped backward. She could have been inches from the ground or hurtling toward the stars, she couldn't tell. She was enveloped by a deep ache that felt as though her soul was being torn away and sucked out through her pores. The air left her lungs in an uncontrollable scream. A thousand years of pain and death and life and happiness flashed behind her eyes as a blinding light doused the flames.

And as quickly as it had begun, she flopped to the ground.

With her dwindling strength, she lifted her eyes to Tevin. His forearm protected his face as he stumbled backward before collapsing to his knees.

Cyn cackled beside him and rested her hand on the top of his head. "You've done it, my love."

Alina tasted iron as a warm trickle leaked past her lips. She brought a hand toward her mouth, brushing against a cold, hard object in the brittle grass. Tevin's knife. She wrapped her fingers around it.

Tevin swatted Cyn's hand away and slowly shook his head. "The Light …," he panted. His crooked face showed pain and surprise.

Cyn moved to face him and looked into his eyes. "You've won, my love."

"No." He gasped for another breath. "Something is wrong."

"But the Light left Alina. Look at her. She's dying."

Tevin continued shaking his head, stunned. He propped himself up with his hand. "It left Alina, yes, but … but … it didn't come to me."

Alina struggled to her knees, Tevin's knife in hand.

"What do you mean?" Cyn cried.

Tevin wobbled on his knees and reached for Cyn's waist for support. "Somehow, I lost the Light."

Cyn touched his shoulder. "Come, my love. We should get you to the castle to rest." She reached beneath Tevin's arms to help him up, but he shrugged her hands away.

"I'm too weak. Pulling the Light from Alina has made me ill." He looked to the city. "Where are Andon and my soldiers?"

"I don't know," Cyn answered.

Tevin gestured to the hylocks. "Go. Get my men. Bring them here. Hurry."

The hylocks shot into the air.

Strengthened by her anger, Alina pushed to her feet. Cyn didn't see her, preoccupied with Tevin's horse.

Tevin whispered, "I don't understand. If the Light didn't come to me, where did it go? Back to the stars?"

Cyn cocked her head. "Hmm," she said. "I wonder ..."

Tevin regarded her. "What?"

"Well, I don't know. If the Light didn't go to you, do you think it could have gone into Alina's son?"

Tevin froze, his eyes wide. "Son? What do you mean? Alina has no children."

"Sure, she does. She has a son. His name is Cridon. I've held him in my own arms."

Tevin's questioning eyes darkened. "No. That's not possible. How did I not know this?"

"I tried to tell you moments ago, but you silenced me."

Alina staggered toward Cyn's back, the blade hanging at her side. Each slow and painful step took all her strength.

Tevin collapsed to his heels. "Where is her son now?"

"With the fishers, my love. I was forced to give him to the creatures so Alina and I could escape."

"You gave him to the fishers?"

"I had no choice. To fight them would have risked Alina's life." Her shifting metal skin slithered to her back as if to warn her of Alina's advance, but she was too focused on Tevin to notice.

Tevin, however, did see Alina. Instead of warning Cyn, he held her attention for some reason. "I can't believe you gave him to the fishers." He curled his lip.

"I told you, I had no choice. Are you angry with me?"

Tevin's face relaxed and he tilted his head. "No, I'm not angry. Disappointed, but not angry." He turned away sadly. "Though you have failed me."

Having never killed a person before, Alina's conscience argued with what she knew had to be done. If she faltered at that moment, Cridon would never be safe, even if he survived the fishers.

Cyn started to turn as though she sensed Alina's approach, but Tevin grabbed her around the waist. His hand glowed, a subtle threat that drew the metal from Cyn's back.

Alina held her breath, closed her eyes, and struck. The cold steel sank into Cyn's lower back next to her spine.

Cyn's metal skin swarmed from Tevin's touch to the knife, but it was too late. Cyn grunted. She spun toward Alina. She had the same stunned look she had probably caused on many others. "You bitch," she said. Her metal-covered knuckles struck Alina's jaw.

Though it was a glancing blow, it still sent Alina hard to the ground. Cyn staggered backward. She reached back and yanked out the bloody knife and dropped it. She lifted her eyes to Alina. Gore flowed from her wound. She touched it and held her bloody fingers up to see. She smirked. "I didn't think you had it in you." When she coughed, blood spurted and poured down her chin.

Tevin pushed to his feet, still wobbly. Cyn took an angry step toward Alina, but Tevin grabbed her arm. "No, Cyn. Wait."

The assassin turned to face him. Heartbreak etched wrinkles in her face. "Did you let her do this to me?"

Tevin cupped her cheek in his palm, and she leaned into it. "I love you, Cyn. But I'm afraid you have failed me. I cannot tolerate failure of such magnitude. Not now, not with victory so close." He smoothed her hair away from her sweaty face and locked eyes with her. She staggered and her legs gave out. He caught her and pulled her close to his chest.

"I could have helped you find Cridon," she said, her words muffled against his robe.

"I don't need your help."

"I don't feel so well."

"I know." He held her until her hand dropped to her side. Then he gently lowered her to the grass.

"I'm cold," she said. Her metal skin had sealed the wound and slowed the blood loss, but the blade was long and Alina had buried it to the hilt.

"I know," Tevin said again. He knelt beside her. Just out of his view, a section of Cyn's metal skin slithered from her shoulder, down her arm, and over her fist.

Tevin removed his outer robe and covered her. "I'd take you for help, but I'm still too weak. If you stay alive long enough, I'll send someone for you."

While he gazed into her eyes, the metal on her fist grew into a point and hardened. She whispered, "Come closer. I want to feel your lips once more before I die."

Tevin leaned in and pressed his lips to hers. Cyn, always deadly, waited for the right moment. As Tevin slowly pulled away, his face a mere butterfly's breath away, she whispered, "Thank you." She smiled. He smiled back. And then she plunged her weapon toward his neck. His eyes went wide, and he recoiled. Her blade grazed his throat as he swatted her hand. He stood up. A trickle of blood oozed from a small cut on the side of his neck. A hair closer and Cyn would have succeeded in taking him with her into the great darkness.

Tevin touched his superficial wound and looked at his fingers. He nervously chuckled. "You are truly deadly, my love. All the way to the end." He stood over her and watched with sick pleasure as the rise and fall of her chest slowed. Then she gurgled her last breath.

Her metal skin pooled on her stomach before flowing down her side and dripping into a puddle on the ground. As if alive, the liquid metal slithered toward Tevin's feet. He pulled away.

"I'm dying," Alina whispered.

"I know," he answered coldly "But don't fear. You won't be lonely in the next world for long. Your son will soon join you when I take his Light." Tevin retrieved his knife from the grass and wiped Cyn's blood onto his pant leg. "Now, before you die, tell me. Where is it that you and your friends have been hiding?"

No pain he could inflict could make her betray those she loved. She looked toward Cyn and then back to him. "Maybe you should have asked her before she died."

Tevin glanced back. His shoulders slouched. His tongue peeked from the corner of his mouth. "Hm. Perhaps you're right. Though I don't expect your silence will last long once I begin carving you to pieces."

Alina was out of tears.

CHAPTER 15

MEELA

Meela galloped west across the plains toward Havens Ravine, making incredible gains on the fisher carrying Cridon. She caught the fisher's scent and recognized him to be a gatherer-hunter named Reevus. When eyes were needed, Reevus was one of those who went for them. He was the most skilled of the skilled.

In his haste he reached the edge of the ravine before he planned how to cross it, which gave her the chance she needed to catch him. She darted toward the closest bridge, cutting off his route. By the time he made it to the bridge, she was close. There was no way he didn't know she was there. He was halfway across when she reached the bridge.

"Reeevus," she hissed. He stopped.

"Is that you, Meeela? Wee have been lookeeng for you. You are a traitor to your peeeople."

Meela stalked closer, careful to stay out of reach. "The boyee is not whom you seeek."

Reevus lowered Cridon to the wooden bridge. Knowing that meant he planned to fight, Meela pounced. Reevus countered. They slammed into each other, their thrashing claws ripping flesh. As they rolled, they inadvertently bumped Cridon toward the edge. Meela gasped and disengaged enough to lunge with her foot. By some miracle, she caught Cridon's leg. In one fluid swing, she pulled him back onto the bridge. Just then Reevus tackled her over the edge.

They plunged feet-first into the belke slug's slime. A roar in the distance assured them it knew they were there, just like a spider knew when a fly was caught in its web.

Meela tried to swim, but her every movement caused her to sink deeper into the gunk. When her chin met the slime, she took a deep breath and thrashed wildly, which pulled her below. The slime oozed into her ears and nostrils, but she continued to squirm while holding her breath until her feet touched the ground. She thrashed even more to get her scoop-claws against the slimy floor of the ravine.

Then she dug through the mushy ground to the solid dirt beneath. With her claws firm in the ground, she pulled. Then she did it again, each tug moving her closer to the wall. Since fishers were skilled underwater swimmers, holding her breath wasn't a struggle. Again and again, she dug and pulled and dug and pulled until her head bumped the ravine wall. A ripple through the slime announced the belke slug was close by. Using the claws on her feet and the scoops on her hands, she scaled the wall against the downward pull of the slime. Each strenuous lunge higher took her closer to salvation. She wondered if Reevus was as wise or even knew what the belke slug was. With her lungs crying for air, she broke the surface with a gasp.

The belke slug roared again, close enough that her eardrums nearly popped. She looked over her shoulder and released a series of screeches so high-pitched that most living creatures, including men, were unable to hear them. Using the echo from those screeches, she "saw" the giant belke slug inhale a mouthful of slime, along with Reevus, into its mouth. The creature chomped down.

Meela felt no remorse. She didn't much like Reevus anyway. She continued scaling the wall to the top with ease. Once on solid ground again, she wiped the slime from her face and cleared the muck from her arms and legs. Her skin tingled, not from the slime, but from the energy of a sudden and unnatural storm. Fire filled the sky.

As she turned toward Cridon, she sensed him lying dangerously close to the edge. She let out a screech and crossed the bridge in a flash, scooping him against her slimy chest. The sky burned with fire. She shielded him from the all-encompassing blaze, remembering the last time fire had swallowed the land without burning. She heard a few fishers fleeing the fight with Rasi to the north. That there were only three able to flee further solidified in her mind that Rasi was indeed the one. After the flames were sucked back into the sky, she pulled Cridon away from her chest. He cooed up at her. Now to find Rasi. She raced east, careful to keep out of range of the others.

CHAPTER 16

FROM ONE TO ANOTHER

Rasi raced across the Great Plains toward Tevin, who stood straddled over Alina with a knife in hand as she lay motionless on her back. Two hylocks circled above. First Rasi told his straps no mercy. Then he mindspoke to Alina to make sure she still breathed.

Rasi? she answered, and turned her head slightly.

Even within his mind, the loss and despair in her voice was palpable. He made sure Tevin knew he was coming with a battle cry to divert his attention.

Tevin looked up. Seeing Rasi caused his shoulders to slouch. He sighed and rubbed his forehead. "Rasi, you are one durable bastard," he groaned.

He's weak, Alina cried in Rasi's mind. *You must kill him now.* With all her strength, she kicked upward, striking Tevin in the balls and sending him stumbling backward.

Rasi closed in.

Tevin recovered and planted his feet. His fists glowed orange at his sides. Rasi pounced. Tevin unleashed a blast of heated energy from his knuckles.

Rasi's straps shielded him. The impact blasted him to the ground. Though his straps took the brunt of the blow, they didn't take all of it. From his side, he lifted his eyes to Tevin.

Run, Alina, he shouted in her mind.

Alina didn't move.

Tevin drew back his arm for a second, undoubtedly more lethal attack. "Goodbye, Rasi," he growled.

Rasi braced for impact. But before Tevin could strike, a monstrous man charged from behind. In their focus on each other, neither Tevin nor Rasi saw Simcane coming until he was already there. Tevin hesitated and tilted his head slightly. Simcane swung his fist. Tevin jerked away just in time for the blow to glance off his temple. But even a glancing blow from Simcane was enough to do damage. Tevin stumbled and fell to his hands and knees. Simcane reached for his throat.

Rasi bounced up and raced toward them. Tevin's chest glowed orange. Rasi shouted a warning, but he was too late. A concussive blast of Tevin's magic collided with Simcane's chest. Simcane hurtled through the air and slammed to the dirt with such force that his shoulder and face dented the ground.

The city gates opened and a wave of soldiers poured through.

The two hylocks landed between Rasi and Tevin.

"Kill her," Tevin screamed, and pointed at Alina.

Rasi lunged for one of the hylocks, but it pulled just out of reach. The other one leaped next to Alina with its poisonous nails drawn back. Rasi charged. His straps snatched the hylock's wrist an instant before its nails could reach Alina's throat. Rasi tackled the hylock away from her, rose up, and pounded its skull. Eventually, the hylock stopped flailing.

Two straps caught the other hylock as it lunged for Alina and broke its neck. Rasi turned to Tevin, who climbed onto his horse and fled toward the approaching soldiers. Though there were only a dozen, Tevin would be long gone before Rasi could fight his way through them. He turned his attention to Simcane and Alina instead.

Simcane moaned and pushed to his hands and knees. He shook his head and spat a mixture of grass, blood, and dirt. Something slithered through the dead grass toward him.

Rasi screamed his name.

His friend was still too groggy to notice the puddle of silver liquid slithering from Cyn's body toward his feet. The living metal bit into his ankle. He dropped to his side, writhing in pain and clutching his lower leg.

Rasi started for Simcane, shouting in Alina's mind, *Run, Alina.*

I can't, Rasi. Even in his mind, her voice sounded frail.

Rasi slowed and turned toward her. She barely moved. *What's wrong? What did he do to you?*

He stripped my Light from me. I think I'm dying.

Simcane's stolen horse wandered nearby. *Hold on. I'll get you out of here.* The soldiers were closing in. Rasi raced to Simcane and grabbed his shoulder. Simcane looked up through stricken eyes. A veil of determination covered the pain. He growled, "Go to her."

Rasi nodded and thanked him with sincere eyes.

Simcane swallowed hard, pushed through the pain in his leg, and stood up.

Rasi shot toward the horse. In one fluid motion, his straps grabbed the horse's neck and hoisted him onto the saddle. He bolted for Alina. She was pale and drifting from consciousness. *Hold on, my love.* Once at her side, his straps reached down and cradled her. They lifted her to his lap.

"I knew you were still alive," she said with a weak smile. Her eyelids fluttered.

Simcane glanced back at them. "Get her out of here, Rasi. I'll hold 'em off for as long as I can."

As much as Rasi wanted to stay and help his friend, he knew he was right.

Alina's head flopped back against his shoulder. She tried to say something, but her voice was weak and broken. Rasi leaned in. She whispered, "Where's Cridon?"

Rasi kicked his steed into a gallop toward the forest. He glanced back. Simcane rubbed his glistening ankle with a wince and then marched toward the soldiers. They slowed and hesitated, rightfully so. The last sound Rasi heard before disappearing into the trees was the thunderous boom of Simcane's gift.

Good luck, my friend.

Once deep in the woods and confident they hadn't been followed, Rasi turned his attention to finding a wild tornment bush. Maybe the constricting benefits could somehow help her. He had no reason to believe it would, but he had nothing to lose. He propped her against a tree and started his search. Within minutes he found what he was looking for. Tornment bushes were plentiful that time of year. He raced back to Alina.

She smiled weakly, though she was unable to hold up her head for more than a few seconds. Rasi plopped next to her with his back against the thick trunk. He pulled her to his chest, tilted her head back, and squeezed the raw, bittersweet juice into her mouth. *Drink.*

After a second fruit was squeezed dry, she lifted her head and opened her eyes. Rasi held her hand to his prickly chin just so he could feel her touch. She even made a joke. "I'm not terribly happy with the beard, Rasi."

He couldn't help but chuckle. *I know. I've been a bit lazy of late.* He hugged her and kissed her forehead.

"Where's Cridon? We need to find him."

I know. I'm working on it.

"What do we do?"

First, we get you help.

"But they'll kill him."

He shook his head. *I don't think so. I'll get him. We just need to get you help first.*

Her cheek pressed against his chest. Though the stimulating effects of tornment juice typically wore off quickly, the medical benefits lasted a bit longer. That was Alina's best hope.

"Rasi, I lost the Light," she said.

I know. Just rest. He ran his fingers through her long hair. *It'll be all right.*

As night approached, he grew increasingly concerned. He had left Meela a subtle but unmistakable scent trail and expected her to find them long before the suns had set.

With Alina nestled in his arms, he listened to the night creatures begin to stir. Nervous, his straps lifted slightly from the ground. Somewhere in the night, wolves yipped and yelped with their own special type of roll call to keep the pack close to each other. It was going to be a long night. If Meela wasn't there by morning, he didn't know what he would do.

He carefully lowered Alina to the ground and made her a pillow out of leaves. He paced nearby as the night drew on. It was nearly dawn when the wolves suddenly stopped howling. The antsy horse fidgeted from hoof to hoof. The stink of sulfur whisked past his nose. He smiled. "Mee'a?"

She stepped from behind a tree. "Rasiieee? Iieee found you." She was covered in scabbed-over cuts and abrasions. Rasi's eyes shot to the bundle in her arms. His knees went weak. She held his sleeping son. The wispy hair on Cridon's head was as white as snow.

"Iieee'm sorree it took meee so long. Hyeelocks were followeeng you." She grinned. "But they aren't aneemore."

A branch snapped behind them and Rasi's straps flared out. They relaxed when he realized it was Leander. Meela said, "Oh. Iiee brought your friend, too."

Meela held Cridon out to Rasi, but Rasi hesitated, afraid his rough, plodding hands would hurt such a precious and fragile gift.

"Take him, Rasiieee. Hee is your son."

Rasi looked at Cridon, then to Meela, and then back to his son again. He slowly extended his shaky hands and Meela laid Cridon in his arms. His son was so soft and innocent and perfect in every way. Rasi held him close while his tears flowed down his cheeks. He looked to Meela and tapped his heart with his fist.

"You're welcome, Rasiieee."

A strap lovingly brushed her cheek and she leaned into it. With his eyes locked on his perfect son, he went to Alina and knelt beside her. Though he knew she needed to sleep, he also knew she'd want to see her son more than anything. If she was going to die that night, she needed to know Cridon was well before she did. He lightly shook her shoulder. *Alina. Wake up.* When she opened her eyes, he laid Cridon on her chest. Her arm lifted slightly and then fell back to the ground.

It's all right. I'll hold him for you.

"His hair …," she mumbled.

Rasi hugged them both.

She kissed Cridon's forehead. *Thank you, Rasi. You saved our son.*

No. It wasn't me who saved him. Rasi leaned to the side enough that she could see Meela crouched shyly behind him. *It was her.*

Alina flinched. *A fisher?*

Yes. But she's a friend. I trust her.

Cridon cooed and squirmed against Alina's chest as though he were about to wake. Rasi lifted her chin so she could look into his eyes. *Where did you come up with the name Cridon anyway?*

"I named him after your parents."

Criya and Donis?

She nodded.

I love it. Thank you. As Rasi thought about his parents again, an idea struck him like a war hammer to the face. He stood up, Cridon still in his arms. *We must go, Alina. I have an idea, but we must hurry.*

I'm too tired.

I will get you there. But you have to fight.

"Where?"

My parents' farm. He waved Leander over.

"What can I do?" the helpful Tek asked.

"Go wi' Mee'a."

"Where?"

"Somewhere safe."

Though it was undoubtedly hard to make out his words, Leander bobbed his head. "I'll take her to Tek Island."

Rasi nodded. He lifted Alina onto the horse. While two of his straps held her upright and another cradled Cridon, he stuffed several tornment fruits into a saddle bag and then climbed up behind her. He kicked his horse into a full gallop east.

Stay with me, Alina. Please.

CHAPTER 17

LIQUID LIGHT

Though the suns had started to rise, the city had yet to awaken as Simcane staggered along the streets of Thasula. His battle with Tevin's soldiers had been fierce, forcing him to use his gift to its fullest just to escape.

He arrived at Marge's home with only enough energy to collapse on her stoop with his back hard against her door. He hoped she heard him because he was too tired to knock. The handle soon rattled and the door swung open. Simcane fell to his back.

"Simcane," Marge gasped with her hand over her mouth. "By the gods. What happened?" She scanned the street before tugging at his arm as if she had any hope of budging him. "Your face looks like hammered meat."

"You should see the other guy," he chuckled. He dug deep for the strength to crawl inside. He had spent many drunken nights recovering on that same floor in the past. This, however, might have been the first time alcohol wasn't the culprit.

His face stung, but that was minor compared to the deep, throbbing pain in his ankle and calf. What the hell had bitten him? A snake?

Marge fetched a wash basin and wet a cloth before rushing back to his side. She dabbed his split lip and the purple splotches on his cheeks. He winced away from her touch.

"What can I do, Sim?"

He chuckled at the absurdity of her playing the gentle nursemaid. His chuckle turned into a cough that brought blood into his mouth. Marge dabbed his chin again. He gagged and rolled to his side. "I'm sorry about the floor, Marge." He tried to clean it with his sleeve.

"Don't worry about the floor," she said, and swatted his hand away.

"They did a number on me, that's for sure." After another painful cough, he asked, "Can you look at my left leg? It's killing me."

She slid his pant leg up to his knee. "By the gods, Sim. What happened here?"

"I think something bit me. What's it look like to you?"

She looked closer. "I don't see any bite marks, but your leg is covered in sores and blisters. But ... that's not all."

"What is it?"

"It's just that ... well ... the sores are moving."

Her words triggered a memory of Cyn's symbiotic metal skin coming for him. Scorne's had done the same after he had killed him.

"Sim, this looks bad."

It felt bad. He didn't want to worry her. "Ah, I'm sure it's nothing, hon. I've had worse. I'll heal up like I always do. Help me to the bed?"

"Of course." It was a struggle, but the soft mattress was worth the effort. He patted the bed next to him. "Come lie with me for a bit."

Marge lay next to him and pressed against his aching side. Though her weight caused more pain to his ribs, her warmth and her touch made up for it.

"Hey, Sim," she whispered.

"Yeah, hon?"

"When you were last at Arthur's, you did something I've never seen a person do. How did you move the air around you like that?"

Her question caught him off guard. He hadn't realized Marge had witnessed his gift during the attack on him at Arthur's Dive. His eyes uncomfortably traced the outline of the door. Maybe it was time to tell someone his secret; he could think of no one better than Marge. Holding his secret for so many years had weighed on him. He thought back to a time he hadn't thought about for years.

"I've been able to do things others can't since I was eight ..."

Simcane never fully understood what his father did for a living, though he knew he worked for the Lith royal family. When he once asked his mother what his father did, she answered that he sought out new arrangements that would benefit the kingdom. Whether that meant making peace treaties or selling shoes, he didn't know, but he never questioned her any further. Whatever his father did for the king, it gave his family enough gold to go on many vacations, and that was all that mattered to Simcane as a boy.

Each year saw Simcane's family traveling to various destinations within Lithia and Epertase, partially for business, but mostly for fun. Usually, Simcane's father would spend a day or two meeting with a few of the more important members of whatever community they were visiting, but then the rest of the trip would belong to the family. When Simcane was eight years old, the family's summer travel took them to the farmlands of Epertase. Since his father believed young men should be skilled in every possible craft, he often used the trips to educate Simcane in something he had never experienced before. Being a farmhand for a few weeks was that year's lesson.

Arrangements had been made for his family to stay on a large and prosperous farm owned by an odd but friendly fellow named Galloway. Simcane quickly learned that Galloway often liked to complain about how much better things would be if he were anywhere but where he was, yet it quickly became apparent from the farmer's stories that he would be equally disgruntled anywhere else.

Simcane was a hard worker, even if he was rather scrawny for his age. For the first three days of the vacation, his father negotiated some sort of trade agreement with the men who controlled the business end of the farmlands while Galloway taught Simcane the basics of farming. Simcane worked tirelessly, wanting to make his parents proud.

As Simcane and Galloway tended to a japsy weed patch at the edge of the farm, Galloway explained how much better and fuller japsy weed grew if the invasive weeds around them were dug out. It was hard work because Galloway was so particular when it came to getting at the roots. Simcane listened intently; his dad would quiz him at dinner on what he had learned. For a brief bit of the summer, Simcane considered farming as a future.

Once finished with the japsy weed, Galloway took a well-earned break. After wiping the sweat from his brow, he dug into his pocket and pulled out a smoker's pipe. He packed a pinch of tobacco into the pipe and rubbed two pieces of japsy weed together to light it.

Simcane hadn't been around anyone who smoked before and was a bit curious. "Does that taste good?" he asked.

"Hmph. Not as good as the tobacco that grows in the valleys south of here. But lacking that, this this is the easiest tobacco to acquire and it'll do." He took a puff. "You ever seen a tobacco bush?"

"My dad showed me one once."

"What color were the leaves?"

"Brownish, I think."

"Ah. That's the kind I use. At the bottom of the valleys, the tobacco leaves are shaped the same, but they have a reddish tint instead of brown. My mouth waters just thinking about them." After a couple more puffs, he held out the smoldering pipe. "You wanna try it, kid?"

Simcane's curiosity grew. "Really?"

"Sure. Why not." He cast a furtive glance around to make sure no one was watching, which seemed odd. Then he handed the pipe over.

Simcane gingerly held it to his lips.

"Go ahead. Breathe it in."

Simcane took a horrible puff and spent the next few minutes nearly coughing out a lung. Was Galloway crazy? Tobacco tasted like death.

Galloway took back the pipe with a shitty grin. "Remember that feeling the next time you want to try a pipe. It's a nasty habit to take up."

Simcane was quite sure he wouldn't forget.

On his fourth day at the farm, his father gave him free time to "explore and enjoy nature." Simcane wandered a half-day's walk from Farmer Galloway's land to the edge of the southern mountains. He knew he shouldn't have gone so far, but his dad had said to explore. When he came to a narrow pass in a gully, he thought about Galloway's elusive red tobacco and how much of a hero he'd be if he returned with some. And this, the first gully he'd ever seen, was too tempting to pass up. He climbed down. It wasn't the steepest of hills, but it was plenty long enough to be tiring. By the time he reached the bottom, the possibility of finding Galloway's tobacco overtook any concerns he might have about heading back.

He wandered in the small valley until he came upon a reddish bush growing next to a dark cave in the side of a mountain. It couldn't be … Could it? Jagged leaves? Check. Reddish hue? Check again. Smelled like an old man's dirty feet? There was no doubt. Full of zeal, his stuffed his pockets with the prized tobacco leaves until he realized how late it was getting. He turned to leave, but a slight breeze tickled the back of his neck and he turned back. It came from the cave and sounded like when his father had held a shell to his ear on the southern Epertasian beaches two years prior. The wind seemed to speak his name like a ghostly whisper.

"Is someone there?" he asked with a shaky voice. Curiosity mixed with stupidity to push his head inside. Instead of an endless sea of black as he had expected, he saw what looked like a distant star in a night sky. Though the light was nothing more than a speck, it somehow held his stare. Mesmerized, he stepped into the blackness.

Before he realized the entrance was sloped and wet, his back hit the rock floor. As he slid uncontrollably deeper into the cave, he rolled to his stomach and clawed at the slick surface. Unable to slow his descent, he rolled to his back again. It was a terrifying slide. The speck of light grew bigger and brighter as he hurtled toward the end of the tunnel.

With his arms tight against his chest, he burst from the tunnel into a large, bright cavern and plunged into a spring of warm, almost hot, water.

Thankfully, Simcane was a skilled swimmer, again to the credit of his father. He kicked his way to the surface, guided by the blurry light shining above. His first breath free of the water was warm and wonderful and stale.

He treaded water while gathering his wits and adjusting his eyes. The surrounding walls were slick and straight, making them impossible to climb. In the center of the cavern was a single rock column that rose from the water and nearly reached the castle-high ceiling. The light flickered from the top of the column.

Simcane swam to the rocky protrusion and wrapped his frail arms around it to give his legs a rest. He thought of his father; he would be furious when Simcane didn't return home for dinner. Or bedtime, by the looks of things. Though he knew he should try to find a way out to get home as fast as he could, something about the light at the top of the column kept drawing his gaze. He figured it wouldn't hurt to take a quick peek since he was already going to be late.

He felt for a handhold above his head. Once he secured his grip in a crevice, he pulled himself up to the next. The closer he got to the top, the more he could make out a large stone bowl with ancient drawings carved into the brim.

He wondered if returning home with such a treasure would make his father overlook his absence at the dinner table. With his foot secured in another crevice, he reached for the top and hooked two fingers over the edge. It felt solid enough, so he strained and pulled himself high enough to hook his arms.

The water in the bowl glowed brighter than any light Simcane had ever seen, but somehow it didn't blind him. As he looked closer, he could tell that the light didn't shine through the water, but rather appeared to *be* the water. Somewhat spellbound, he inched a finger cautiously toward it.

Before he touched the liquid light, a loud snap echoed through the cavern. He felt instantly weightless. The bowl and its glowing contents chased him to the water below. Panicked, he couldn't get a breath before plunging into the warm spring. The water around him exploded into brightness like he swam inside one of the suns. He swam blindly, unable to determine which way was up. When his hand slammed the rock floor, he realized he had chosen wrong. He needed a breath. With both feet, he pushed off the floor. His brain screamed at him to breathe. He wasn't going to make it. His head nearly burst. As his hand broke the surface, his body forced him to take a breath and he inhaled a lungful of water. He surfaced, choking and gagging and coughing up little drops of white, glowing spittle.

The cavern tingled with hair-raising energy that hadn't been there before. Gasping for breath, he continued coughing up drops of light from his lungs.

As he reached for the column again, thunder echoed through the cavern and the column shattered beneath his touch. A tidal wave of water crashed against the walls. The top of the column tumbled like a felled tree. He inhaled as much air as he could and dove beneath the surface as the avalanche of rock slammed the water above his head. Massive chunks sank all around, threatening to drag him down. Each frantic stroke of his arms in the water sent muffled thunder and waves throughout the spring. There were too many boulders to avoid and one caught his chest, dragging him deeper. When he pushed against it, the boulder shattered like the column. He swam back to the surface and then to the wall beneath the entrance tunnel.

By accident, his hand brushed the wall. Another crackle of thunder turned the face of the wall into rubble. He reached for a handhold, but again the rock exploded beneath his touch.

His exhausted arms and legs felt as if the boulders were now tied to them. His lips repeatedly met the water as he fought to stay afloat. Terror turned his stomach. He made one last desperate reach for the wall as he sank. Though the thunder from his touch was muffled through the water, he still felt the vibration. What was happening to him?

While he was fighting for a breath, his hand swiped the wall again, and again the rock shattered. Only this time, it opened a second tunnel. The water rushed past him like a riptide, pulling him toward the new opening. He was too weak to fight the current.

As he was sucked into the hole, he felt a brief euphoric rush before everything went dark. He couldn't tell if the water had turned black or if he was losing consciousness.

With the water raging around him, he burst from the dank, stale tunnel into fresh air and plunged into another body of water. At least this one was outside. It took all his strength to swim toward land and drag himself onto the bank. He rolled to his back. The air had never tasted so good. Every muscle in his body burned and ached. He tried to lift his arm, but the air was like weights pressing down on him. Bells rang in his ears.

The ground spun like it did in the dizzying game he played sometimes at school. He curled into a ball and waited for the spinning to slow. Trying to move right away made him vomit. His spew glowed briefly.

As he lay there regaining his wind, he thought about how mad his father was going to be. His ass already hurt imagining the beating he was going to get. Eventually, he was able to sit up despite the thick, heavy air. It was a fight to get to his feet, but he made it. With his entire body still tingling, he squeezed a fist in front of his face and saw the air around it ripple. *Weird.*

The cracked ground glowed as if a sun lived underfoot. He used the rising moon as a compass and started for Galloway's farm. His muscles were so tired he dreaded climbing back up the hill. At least the weight of the air had lifted.

The hill was just steep enough that he needed to climb on all fours. When he reached his hand out, an invisible cushion grew between his hand and the rocky ground. The closer his finger came to it, the more resistance he felt. The weeds parted from his touch. He closed his eyes and took a deep breath. Whatever was happening to him couldn't be real. Maybe he had drowned after all and his dead body was dreaming of an afterlife. After much effort and intense concentration, his finger touched the ground and the rippling air dissipated.

Marge quietly listened. He paused and looked to make sure she was still awake since she hadn't said anything for so long. She leaned in expectantly, eager for him to continue.

"And then I climbed out," he said, rather anticlimactically. "When I reached the top, the suns were rising again. Since I knew the farmlands were north, I headed north. By the time I got to the edge of Galloway's farm I had figured out how to control the energy that seemed to push from inside my body."

"That is the most incredible story I've ever heard, Sim. What did your father say when you returned to the farm?"

"He wasn't there. My mother was, but he was out searching for me. She said I had been gone for a week, which seemed impossible. It was only a day at most. I was so scared for my dad to return that night that I couldn't eat. When he got home, I met him and Galloway in the front room. I got ready for a beating as he crossed the room toward me. But he wasn't mad, and he didn't redden my ass. In fact, he nearly broke my ribs hugging me. It was the first and only time I ever saw him cry."

Marge touched his cheek.

"My father was a good man, Marge."

"It sounds like he was."

"I have spent my life trying to be as good a man as he, though I have not always succeeded."

"I don't agree." Marge hesitated and then grinned and turned away.

Simcane cocked his head. "What's so funny?"

"I'm sorry, Sim. I don't mean to make light. It's just that you said you were a scrawny kid, and I'm tryin' ta picture you being anything but as big as a horse."

"Well, I *was* small. I grew a lot after that. The heavy air around me whenever I used my gift made me stronger. It wasn't long before I was the largest child in my school. I got teased as much for that as I ever had for being small."

"Well, I think yer perfect, Sim." She kissed his cheek. "Did you ever give Galloway the red tobacco?"

Simcane paused to think back and then chuckled. "You know, I forgot about that part of the story. Actually, I did."

"What did he say? Was he excited?"

Simcane chuckled again as he remembered Galloway's reaction. "He said it was good, but not as good as the pale tobacco that grew near the underground springs in the west, and if he could have some of that, there would be nothing better."

Her grin matched his.

"Anything else you wanna know?"

"Did ya ever learn what the glowing water was?"

"I did. When I was seventeen, I gathered the courage to travel to Thasula and visit the Elder Three."

"By the gods, you went into their lair?"

"Sure. I had to know what was happening to me. I was terrified, as you can imagine. The Elder Three welcomed me like I was expected. I asked about the bright light in the bowl. They called it liquid light and said I had found a rare, physical manifestation of the actual Light that lives within Alina's soul. They called what I found an aberration—a byproduct of when the Light forced the change from Thadius to Matthew."

"Did you tell them you swam in it and even drank it?"

"They already knew. They asked me how it tasted."

"Amazing. What'd you tell 'em?"

"Like the business end of a dog."

"Did they say anything else?"

"I asked them how the liquid light got into a bowl at the top of a column in a random cavern. They said King Matthew put it there. He found it during one of his famous expeditions and spent the rest of his years searching for the perfect place to hide it. He died two days after finding that cavern."

Simcane looked to the ceiling while Marge digested his story.
"Sim?" she whispered.
"Yeah?"
"Is there somethin' else yer not telling me?"
Simcane wanted to come clean and tell her everything, but many years of quiet guilt held him back. But Marge was special. Maybe she couldn't take away his burden, but just revealing as much as he already had had made him feel better. He finally said, "There was a reason I became a soldier and left Lithia for Epertase many years ago."
"Oh?"
He nodded sadly. "I needed to prove the Elder Three wrong."
"I don't understand."
Simcane took a deep breath that hurt his ribs. Telling the rest of the story was harder than he could have imagined. Marge sat quietly and waited for him to build the courage. He said, "The Elder Three told me I would one day hold the entire fate of Epertase in my hands, and when that day came, I may prove to be unworthy."
"Unworthy? You have defended Epertase with everything you have. There is no way you could ever be unworthy."
"I've told myself the same thing, but I just wish I could believe it. When Epertase joined Lithia in the Heathen War, I joined their cause. I have lived every moment since the day I spoke with the Elder Three in fear that, when the time came, I would fail as they had foreseen. And if they were right and I did indeed fail, Epertase would be lost forever."
"Oh, Sim. If the day ever comes that you hold Epertase's fate in yer hands, I have no doubt you'll save us all." She jabbed his sore ribs and added, "Or at least save me, right?"
Simcane laughed, which hurt his ribs even more than her jab. "I've never told my story to anyone before. I feel better after telling it to you."
Marge snuggled up to him. She whispered, "Thank you." For most of the night, she kept her arm across his chest. A part of him wanted to tell her how much even the slight weight of her arm hurt his ribs, but he didn't want her to move it. He stared at the ceiling in

too much pain to sleep, while she dozed on and off throughout the night.

Eventually, the suns broke through the gap between the shutters and shone directly onto her face. She fidgeted away from the warm ray with a groan.

"Are you awake?" Simcane whispered.

"Um-hm," she answered without opening her eyes. She didn't sound too awake.

"I've been thinking a lot lately."

"What about?" she asked, eyes still closed.

"I've realized over the years that the only times I haven't felt lonely are when I'm with you."

She looked at him with a squint. "I'm glad you feel that way, darlin'. I like havin' you here, too."

Though Simcane was nervous about what he wanted to say next, he knew he didn't have much time and it might be his only chance. Finally, he gathered the courage and asked, "Will you come with me?"

She sat up. His anticipation of her answer nearly put his heartbeat on hold. She looked into his swollen eye and he saw her answer in her sad expression. He forced himself to sit up with a groan. "Epertase belongs to Tevin now," he mumbled, trying to convince her to say yes before she had a chance to say no. "Anyone who wants to keep what freedoms they have must flee."

"And where would we go? It's only a matter of time before Tevin rules all the lands."

"We can find Rasi. Maybe with Rasi we could one day retake Epertase."

"I heard he was dead."

"Well, he's not. I've seen him."

"And what if we can't find him? What will we do then? Hide for the rest of our lives like fugitives?"

"Sure. There are other kingdoms in the world beyond the sea."

"I don't want to leave Epertase, Sim."

"Then I'll find Rasi. I promise. That's what I do best—find people. We can do this. I'm asking you to come with me."

Marge looked away. "Yer asking me to build a new life, but even as you ask, you talk of going to war. I can't love a man who's constantly at war—I won't. My heart couldn't take it. As I look at you now and listen to yer words, I don't believe you will ever be happy until you die trying to prove the Elder Three wrong. If I go with ya, I'd worry every day whether you'd been killed or not. I can't do that. Stay here with me instead. Forget war. Forget what the Elder Three said. Try to enjoy life for a change. I'll make ya happy. We'll make the best of Tevin's kingdom."

"They will come for me, Marge. In fact, they may be on their way now. They've already put me in prison once. I should have fled last night, but while I was in their prison, I realized something more important than my own life; I realized I wanted to be with you. Forever."

He waited for her to say something to break the silence and allow him to take a breath again.

Finally, she whispered, "I can't," and his heart crumbled.

He bowed his head.

"It's not just the worry, Sim. I have family here. My ma is ill. My brothers and cousins have lives in Epertase. I can't … I won't leave them."

Simcane lay back against the headboard with a wince. He considered telling her to bring her family along, but he knew she wouldn't. It was selfish of him to even ask. And he couldn't promise her he wouldn't go to war again either. If Rasi needed him to help take Tevin down, he couldn't sit idly by, no matter who he had promised otherwise.

As he sat beside her, the aching and tingling in his leg crawled up into his groin. He tried to ignore it. Then he whispered, "I understand."

Marge lay against his side.

"I'm sorry, Sim. I—"

"Nothing else needs saying, darlin'."

In the silence that followed, a strange, high-pitched voice spoke in Simcane's mind loud enough that he wondered if Marge could hear. *Kill her,* the voice said. Marge didn't act as though she heard anything. Simcane closed his eye.

CHAPTER 18

WITH THE HELP OF OTHERS

Keep holding on, Alina. It was probably the thousandth time Rasi had implored her to fight in the three days since their battle with Tevin. He found her asleep more than awake and it was getting worse by the day. Rasi feared it wouldn't be long before she wouldn't wake at all. The long journey to Puimia was slow and laborious, but she held on because she was a fighter and knew no other way. *Just a few more days,* he told her.

The road forked ahead where a small campfire burned next to a wagon and a tent. Though Rasi had intentionally avoided people thus far, Alina needed something to eat and he had been unable to leave her and Cridon to hunt for food. Relying on the kindness of strangers wasn't ideal, but under the circumstances he had little choice. The light of the campfire flickered over a young man and woman who hadn't yet noticed his approach.

In hopes of not startling the couple, he called out a garbled, "Hello" before he reached their camp. The man scrambled to his feet, disappeared into the tent, and then returned with a sword. It trembled in his grip. He nudged his frightened female companion behind him.

Rasi held up his hands in surrender even as his straps lifted slightly.

The man's wide eyes followed them. "What do you want?" he asked, bravely standing his ground. Still staring at Rasi's straps, he said, "I've heard of you. Rasi, yes?"

Rasi nodded.

The man lowered his sword. "I heard you were dead."

Rasi nodded again; he got that a lot.

When the man finally looked away from the straps long enough to see Alina in Rasi's arms, he said, "By the gods," and dropped his sword. He stepped forward. Rasi ordered his straps to stay calm.

The man's female companion stood frozen beside the tent. A dark mole beside her nose was the only blemish on her otherwise smooth and delicate face.

"Clara," the man called. "Come here. Hurry." He turned back to Rasi and held out his arms. "May I help you with her?"

Rasi's straps lowered Alina into the man's arms. He was young and strong. Rasi climbed off the horse with Cridon cradled by the other straps.

Clara joined the man as he carried Alina toward the fire. "Do you recognize her?" he asked.

"Should I?"

"It's our queen." He sounded annoyed at her naïveté.

"What's wrong with her?"

He gave Rasi a questioning glance over his shoulder.

Rasi shrugged and shook his head. Having refilled his water bladder at the last stream, he took a swig and then dumped a small splash over the back of his neck.

After being so quiet, Cridon released a wail to let everyone know he was being ignored. Clara blanched. "You have a baby with you?" she asked.

Rasi parted his straps enough for her to see Cridon's face.

The man extended his hand. "I'm Willard. This is my fiancée, Clara."

Rasi shook his hand. It was firm and rough like a farmer's.

"What can we do for you, Rasi?"

Rasi motioned to his mouth.

"Oh. Of course. I was just about to cook a chicken. You are welcome to join us."

Rasi nodded. Then he took a tornment fruit from his saddle bag and went to where Alina was still asleep. He squeezed the juice into her mouth.

Willard retrieved his sword from the ground, grabbed a squawking chicken from a mesh cage near his wagon, and headed behind the tent. Clara tossed a fresh piece of wood on the fire, excused herself, and joined him.

Rasi propped Alina against the tree stump that Willard had been sitting on, and then laid Cridon on her chest. He nudged her shoulder. *Alina? Cridon needs to feed. Are you able?*

She opened her eyes for the first time since Cridon's last feeding and Rasi noticed a pattern emerging. She seemed stronger when nursing, and he wondered if something about their boy gave her the strength to keep fighting.

"How long have I been asleep?" she whispered.

Most of the day.

She nodded.

You just have to hold on for a few more days.

"I'll try." She smiled.

Are you hungry?

She nodded weakly. After looking around, she asked, "Whose tent?"

Friends.

She caressed Cridon's hair as he fed. When he started playing instead of drinking, Rasi took him, burped him, and then played peek-a-boo while Alina watched lovingly. Willard and Clara soon returned and introduced themselves to her. While Willard cooked the chicken, Rasi changed Cridon's soiled diaper for a clean one Clara quickly made from a blanket. She took the dirty diaper to a nearby creak to wash.

Rasi helped Alina eat a few bites of chicken before she was too tired to continue. Her eyelids rapidly lost the battle against sleep again. It was the longest she'd stayed awake since they'd started their travel and he was proud of how hard she fought. *Rest, my love.*

You're doing well. While caressing her hair with one hand, he ate with the other until his own eyelids started to drift shut. He hadn't slept more than a wink for days. Eventually, his head bobbed forward and he jerked it up to see if anyone had noticed.

"Why don't you two go sleep in the tent for the night," Willard said.

Rasi shook his head.

"I insist. We rather like sleeping under the stars anyway."

It was such a tempting offer that Rasi reluctantly accepted. With the help of his straps, he carried Alina and Cridon into the tent. He was asleep almost before his head hit the pillow.

When he next woke, the suns were high and it was hot and muggy. He hadn't slept so well in years. He immediately looked to Alina, who was still out. Then he looked for Cridon, but the blanket where he had been lying was empty. His heart jumped. Had he trusted the wrong people? Had they—

Then he heard a baby coo outside. He hurried from the tent to find Clara next to a fresh fire with Cridon beside her on a blanket. She leaned in and nuzzled Cridon's belly before jerking her head back with a giggle. Cridon seemed to enjoy the game.

Willard made his way over with a plate of cooked eggs. "Good morning. You must have been tired." He handed Rasi the plate.

Clara looked up with a warm smile. Her long, sandy hair stood on end. She carried Cridon over. "He probably should eat. I didn't get a chance to ask last night, but what's his name?"

Rasi concentrated on saying "Cridon" as clearly as he was able.

"Cridon? I like that." She pulled open the tent. "I'd be happy to help the queen feed Cridon if you'd like."

Rasi would like that a lot. He nodded. After eating perhaps the most filling eggs he'd ever had, he announced it was time for them to leave. He felt confident that the couple's generosity had given him the strength to make it the rest of the way. He offered his thanks with a handshake.

Willard swatted his hand away and pulled him in for an awkward hug. Rasi gave a timid, halfhearted hug in return.

"I'm happy just to help you and the queen in any way we're able. I've also refilled your water bladder and left some dried lamb meat and a few tornment fruits in your saddlebag. It's not much, but it's all we could spare."

After feeding Cridon, Alina had the strength again to eat, and this time she didn't leave any food on her plate. Once the three of them were on Rasi's horse, he thanked Clara and Willard again and rode off.

The dried lamb combined with fruit and vegetables scavenged along the way lasted Rasi, Alina, and Cridon the rest of way to Puimia.

Rasi crested the final hill for his first look at his hometown under Tevin's rule. The city appeared blank. Not that Puimia wasn't there, just that the life seemed drained from it. Men and women walked along the same streets as they always had, but their spirits along with their heads were down as though they had been beaten into submission.

As Rasi rode into town, the occasional townsperson would glance at him or his straps with a hint of hope and then just as quickly turn away. This wasn't the Puimia he knew. A teenaged boy with a remarkable likeness to one of Rasi's oldest friends approached.

"Rasi?" the boy asked.

Rasi nodded.

"My father's name is Francis. He told me about you. He said the two of you were friends once."

Rasi nodded again.

"You shouldn't have come back here."

"Why?"

"Tevin the Third has soldiers everywhere. They were here yesterday and they'll no doubt be back soon. They said if you ever returned, we are not to help you in any way or they'll burn our homes with us in them. He also said we must send word if you're seen."

Rasi nodded again.

The kid looked to Rasi's sleeping companion. "Is that the queen?" After studying her for a moment, he added, "Is she all right?"

Rasi shook his head. Then he left the kid standing in the street to continue toward his parents' farm. The kid looked around before shouting, "I'm not going to tell them. Just so you know."

Rasi kicked his horse into a canter.

The first sight of his parents' land filled him with sadness. Sadness and immense anger. The happy memories—playing with his neighbor Annie as a child or helping his father tend the land—were buried so deep that he could no longer find them if he had a shovel and a thousand years. Annie's burned-out house only buried the memories deeper, and he prayed she and her father had moved somewhere safe.

Fearing his heart couldn't take the pain of seeing his parents' graves, he gave them a wide berth. As he, Alina, and Cridon rode through the overgrown field toward the forest, Alina lifted her head to look around. She whispered, "Rasi? Is that you?"

It is.

"Where are we?"

Puimia.

"Oh." She smiled. "That's nice. Are we going to visit your parents?"

Her words hurt, not only because they reminded him that he would never see his parents again, but because they emphasized how badly she was failing.

Yes, my love. We're going to visit them as soon as we're done in the forest. I have something for you to see.

She sighed and whispered, "I look forward to seeing them again."

As do I.

It was night by the time Rasi reached the clearing in the center of the forest where the dragon lived. His horse stopped short of it and refused to go any farther. He had to carry Alina and Cridon the rest of the way. If not for his straps, he'd have needed two trips.

He stared out over the clearing where the dragon rested. Her yellow serpent eyes locked on him from the instant he stepped from the trees, though she'd likely smelled him miles back. Poised at the far end of the scorched field, she watched, curious yet cautious. He assumed she remembered his scent. He marched across the clearing as though he belonged there as much as she. When he reached the halfway point, she grunted and rose to her hind legs, regarding him with a piercing scowl. A small puff of black smoke curled up from one side of her snout.

Rasi gently lowered Alina to the ground and placed Cridon on her chest. The dragon hissed and snorted. The air heated. Rasi didn't falter. He didn't believe she had saved him from the hylocks' poison only to kill him now. She dropped to all fours and paced side to side.

Rasi waited patiently.

Then she stopped and faced him. Rasi started toward her again. She watched cautiously.

When he felt he'd moved close enough for her comfort, he knelt and willed his nervous straps into submission on the ground. *Do you remember me?* he asked.

She snorted.

I am in need of your help once more.

She lowered her snout and opened her mouth aggressively. Then she let loose an ear-piercing roar inches from his face. The charred remains of a large animal's rear leg dangled from between two of her teeth. Her breath smelled of burnt meat.

Rasi didn't cower. She grunted and lifted her head as if suddenly interested in something else. Her eyes went to Alina. Or maybe Cridon. She tilted her head. As though the stars had called her name, she looked curiously up to the night sky and then lowered her gaze back to Rasi. She appeared ready to listen.

Rasi bowed. *Dragon, I am beyond appreciative for the time you're allowing me. I am sure you can feel the cloak of darkness that now suffocates this land. An evil wizard has come to power and drains the life of all he touches. I know that dragons and man have not been allies in the past, but for a reason that I don't yet understand, you helped me before. For that I am thankful. I need to call upon you for help once again. We fight for a common freedom. This wizard is the true threat to both of our species. I'm asking you— for our sake as well as for your own offspring—please help this queen who now lies at your mercy.* He pointed to Alina. *I need you to do for her what you once did for me.*

The dragon's eyes narrowed. She grunted, straightened, and turned away. Her whipping tail almost took off Rasi's head. She crouched, beat her massive wings, and leaped toward the sky.

Rasi watched her nearly touch the clouds. His head fell forward. He went back to Alina, knelt, and took her hand. *I'm so sorry.*

She opened her eyes and turned her head toward the forest. Her eyes brightened.

What is it? He asked.

She smiled and whispered, "It's all right, Rasi. They're calling for me."

Rasi looked to the trees and saw no one. *Who?*

She didn't answer.

Rasi looked back to the dragon circling high above. She appeared to touch the moon before she hovered briefly and then fell back toward the ground with her wings pinned to her sides. Her approach sounded like a tornado's roar. Once near the treetops, she leveled off and soared along the edge of the clearing with such speed that the treetops swayed in her wake. Then she pulled up and flew back to the sky where she circled like a vulture.

Rasi lifted Cridon to Alina's chest in hopes that whatever magic he had done for her earlier he could do again. Instead, her lips turned a bluish hue and her breathing slowed. While Rasi held her head in his lap, one of his straps tugged at his back. Annoyed, he tugged back.

The strap pulled again.

What? he snapped and scowled over his shoulder.

His strap stretched out straight as if pointing toward a trail of bloody puddles along the clearing's edge beneath where the dragon had passed. It took him a moment to process what he saw, but when he did his jaw nearly hit the ground. He snatched Alina in his arms. *Hold on, Alina.* A strap cradled Cridon as Rasi rushed Alina to the closest puddle. *This won't be pleasant,* he warned. He put her down beside the puddle and rolled her onto her stomach, face-down in the blood. *I'm so sorry.*

She was too weak to lift her head and choked and gagged on the blood. Rasi held the back of her head until air bubbles stopped breaking the surface. Then he pulled her free and wiped her face clean with his shirt. She was limp in his arms. He prayed she would take a breath, fearing he had acted too late. *Please, Alina. Wake up.* If there was ever a time for the gods to favor him, it was then. It had to work. He caressed her hair. *I love you, Alina.* He rocked back and forth, silently begging her to breathe.

And then, like a lightning bolt from the sky, she gasped. Her eyes bulged and she sprang up, grabbing her chest. "By the gods, Rasi." Her breaths came too rapidly to control. A look of dread painted her face. She looked around. "Where am I?" she cried. Then she looked at Rasi. "Why are you smiling?"

I'm sorry. I don't mean to smile. I'm just so happy you're all right.

"Do I look all right?" She wiped some of the coagulating gunk from her face and regarded it. "What is this?"

He cringed.

"Rasi?"

It's dragon blood.

Her face distorted. She gagged. "Blood?" She stuck her tongue out. "Is that the awful taste in my mouth? I'm going to vomit." Her breaths continued in rapid bursts.

Rasi pulled her close with his hand on the back of her neck. *Just breathe.*

She pulled away. "Rasi, I can't." She squeezed her hands into fist repeatedly. "My hands are numb."

You're doing fine. Just slow your breathing.

"I can't."

Yes, you can.

"My chest hurts. My fingers tingle."

I know. It's a panic attack. I've seen it in soldiers before battle. It'll pass.

"Are you saying I'm panicking?"

He chortled. *No, no.*

"Stop laughing."

I'm not laughing at you.

He touched her shoulder and she shrugged his hand away, which made him fight the laughter even more. He would rather her be mad at him forever than to have died in his arms.

Since he seemed to be unintentionally escalating her anxiety, he scooted away and played with Cridon. He figured it best to give her space. The worst that could happen was she'd pass out and her breathing would right itself.

Eventually, and no thanks to Rasi, she calmed her breathing enough that her fingers stopped tingling and her chest pains eased. She turned away to keep him from seeing her smile.

He went to her and leaned around her shoulder. *See? Even you're laughing now.*

"No, I'm not."

He playfully poked her side. *Are you sure?*

She squirmed. "Leave me alone. Where's Cridon?"

Rasi's straps lowered Cridon in front of her and she pulled him to her chest. *Friends again?* Rasi asked.

She crinkled her nose. "I suppose. What happened?"

Rasi nodded upward.

Alina squinted toward the sky. "By the gods, Rasi. Is that …?" Her smile grew. "It's beautiful."

It is a she.

"She's beautiful."

She had babies the last time I was here, but it appears they've left the nest.

"I've always dreamed of seeing a dragon."

I know you have. Rasi stood up. *We have to leave.*

"Where will we go?"

Far from here.

"What about Tek Island?"

You trust them? The Teks?

"I do. They saved my life after Cridon was born. They took us in."

So, Leander was telling the truth?

"Yes."

And you think they'll accept me? I killed a lot of their friends.

"They will. They are good people. Reasonable. We can regroup there."

Rasi shook his head. *There's no regrouping.*

Her smile faded. "What do you mean?"

It's over. There's no coming back once we leave.

"What about Epertase?"

Epertase is lost. He hated to be so blunt, but she needed to hear the truth.

"No. I don't believe that."

I'm sorry, Alina. I see no path to victory over Tevin. He is too powerful and his army grows by the day. I fear not even Tek Island will be safe for long.

"What if—?"

Alina. It's over. We lost. We're lucky to be alive.

He kissed her, but she didn't kiss him back.

"I won't give up on my country, Rasi."

I know.

She took his hand and looked into his eyes. "Promise me you won't quit either. There must be a way."

There wasn't, but he relented for the sake ending the argument so they could get going. *I'll tell you what. If something presents itself that I think can work, I'll give it my full weight.*

"That's all I can ask." This time she did kiss him. Together they walked back to the horse to start their long journey to Tek Island.

CHAPTER 19

AN OLD FRIEND

*T*ake him, the voice said. *You know you want to.*

Simcane shook his head. "I don't steal horses."

Yes, we do.

It was early and the streets were still mostly empty. The annoying high-pitched voice he had first heard at Marge's three months back now antagonized him almost daily. Sometimes he even argued with it.

How else will you get to the farmlands? This horse belongs to us as much as it does anyone. This is survival of the fittest, and I see no one as fit as us.

Simcane's head involuntarily jerked to the side. "What do you mean it 'belongs to us'?" He couldn't tell if the voice had started sounding like a higher-pitched version of his own or if he was starting to sound like the voice.

You've fought hard for this kingdom. Now Tevin has stolen the kingdom from us. That means this horse was yours before he took it.

Simcane twitched twice more. Stealing a horse didn't feel right, but the voice made a lot of sense. He smiled. "I suppose you're right."

Think of it as a gift for all our suffering.

Simcane climbed onto the steed.

We should eat. Aren't we hungry?

He nodded, his focus already shifting from the stolen horse. "When we get there, we'll eat."

But we're hungry now.

"There's nothing to eat here."

We can steal something.

"Shut up."

It was no use; neither the voice nor his stomach would shut up all the way through Thasula, into the Great Plains, and across a bridge over Havens Ravine. At the edge of a specific farm in the heart of the farmlands, he took a piss next to his stolen horse while looking over a modest house that brought back fond memories. He doubted Farmer Galloway would still be alive or even remember him if he was, but he needed somewhere to go. Galloway's farm might be just the place to recover from his worsening infection without a bunch of nosey onlookers.

The infection—Cyn's infection—had taken a toll. Tiny sores festered and crawled over his entire body, glistening with specks of metal floating within the pus. He hardly slept because the voice was relentless. Sometimes it loudly counted to ten over and over and over and over for days, killing any chances of restful sleep. Other times it bragged about murders Simcane had no recollection of committing.

He climbed onto his stolen horse again and cantered across Galloway's field toward the farmhouse. Midway across, an old man rode out from the barn to meet him. As the man approached, Simcane recognized his face despite the saggy skin and frail, hunched-over body.

"What can I do for you, big fella?" the man asked wearily.

Simcane stopped. "Do you remember me, sir? I spent a summer here when I was very young. Our name is Simcane."

Galloway tilted his head and squinted. The years had not been kind to his eyesight.

Ask him again. "Do you remember me?"

Galloway twisted his face as if searching the deepest parts of his memory. "I don't know," he finally said. "That depends on whether you brought me some red tobaccy." He shot Simcane a sly grin.

Simcane nodded. *Kill him,* the angry voice whispered. He ignored it.

"Simcane, my boy. You have grown. A lot." He offered his hand. "What can I do for you, old friend?"

"I need a place to stay for a bit."

"I'd love to have you. It gets rather lonely out here since the fever took my dear Claudia."

"I'm sorry to hear. I remember her as being a very kind lady."

"That she was. I can smile, though, 'cause I don't imagine I'm many years from seeing her again." He waved Simcane toward the house. "Come on in."

He fell for it. Like everyone else, he's the enemy. Simcane tried to shake the voice from his ears.

Seeing the twitch, Galloway paused. "Are you all right, big fella?"

We're fine, the voice snapped. Simcane nodded.

Galloway continued to the house. "Are you hungry?" he called back.

Simcane grunted. He was starving.

Inside, Galloway made him a plate of leftover meat and carrots. "I could heat that for you if you let me build a fir—"

Simcane snatched the plate and shoved his face in it. When he finished, he slammed the plate onto the table. "Is that all you have?"

"Uh." Galloway rummaged through a cupboard before returning with three-quarters of a loaf of bread.

Simcane stared at nothing with a drunken, unblinking eye and then released a deep, throaty belch. He ripped the bread from his friend's hand and shoved it into his mouth without breaking his distant gaze.

Galloway pointed a trembling finger toward a hallway door. "You can sleep in there. It's the same room you stayed in as a boy."

The door didn't look familiar. A strange, silent resentment guided Simcane's head back to Galloway. Maybe it was a trap. He tore another chunk of bread away with his teeth. His head uncontrollably jerked to the side. One of the glistening sores crept up his neck from beneath his tattered shirt collar, slithered across his left cheek, past his forehead, and then back down his spine.

Galloway quietly watched. "That's a nasty infection you've got there. Have you salted it?"

"Hmph."

"Whatever happened to your parents, Sim?"

The question made Simcane's head hurt. "I don't remember," he snapped. In truth, he did remember, but the other voice warned him against telling the geezer too much.

Galloway ducked his head and mumbled, "I apologize for asking."

Simcane ignored him, finishing the loaf with the same cold glower. Without a thank you, goodnight, or pleasantry of any kind, he marched to his room. The bed was too small for a grown man, let alone a man as large as he, so he flipped it onto its side and lay on the hard floor.

That night the voice must have been tired because Simcane fell fast asleep. The dreams started immediately. At first, he relived the most violent atrocities he had endured during the Heathen War—the heathens' torturing his back with fire being the worst. But as with most nights, those dreams faded into something far more sinister. He soon found himself hovering over a terrified young woman as she begged for mercy. He wanted to give that mercy to her, but couldn't control where his dream went. Or were they memories? He reached down with hands he didn't recognize and grabbed her throat. Instead of clumsy, bulbous fingers, his hands were petite and feminine with dirt caked under the long, yellowish nails.

"Stop," he begged his dream, but instead of releasing her neck, he squeezed harder until the woman stopped kicking and her soul passed through him with an icy breeze. A shiver ran the length of his body from his toes to the back of his neck.

Wake up, the voice implored.

Simcane bounded up from the floor with tight fists and ragged breaths. Drenched with sweat, he wondered if Galloway had dumped water on his head, but he didn't see the old man or a bucket anywhere. His angle to the open window allowed him to see the moon high in the sky.

You liked killing her, didn't you?

Simcane shook his head.

Then why are you smiling?

He wasn't smil—no, actually, he was.

We should kill Galloway, the voice added.

"Why?"

Why not?

He jerked his head twice toward his left shoulder. "I'm not going to hurt my friend."

Let's just have a look at him, then. What could that hurt?

The voice had a point. What could having a peek hurt?

With aching knees, he stumbled through the small farmhouse to Galloway's bedroom. The bare floor was cold beneath his feverish feet and he imagined how soothing it'd be to lay down in the hall. A rough push banged the door against the wall. Simcane leaned against the doorframe while the old man snored in his bed.

Look at him lying there. This world needs less of the weak and more of the strong, like us.

Simcane hated weakness in men. "Yeah. I suppose you're right."

The top of Simcane's left hand stung suddenly, and a glance down revealed why. At some point, he had subconsciously scratched the skin between his finger and thumb until it was raw and oozing. His glistening infection slithered over the fresh wound.

Wouldn't it be fun to feel his throat in our strong hands?

Simcane shrugged. "I suppose," he said loudly.

Galloway groaned and rolled over. He squinted at first, but then his eyes blew open with a terrified jolt. His back met the headboard and he pulled his covers up to his neck. "Simcane?" he shouted. "Wh-wh-what are you doing?" He fumbled for his spectacles on the bedside table.

Something about Galloway's voice momentarily muffled the evil voice in Simcane's head. Confused, Simcane backed out of the doorway. He was speechless.

Galloway asked again, "What are you doing? Why were you looking at me like that?"

Simcane tried to remember what he was doing in Galloway's room, but the last thing he remembered was killing some young woman with his slender hands. "I ... I don't know, old friend. I'm terribly sorry for startling you. I haven't been myself lately. Please, go back to sleep. I'll go back to my room."

The awful look in Galloway's eyes assured he was done sleeping for the night. Simcane bowed his head and returned to his room, ashamed.

As he lay on his back staring at the ceiling and wondering what he should do next, the voice returned. *You're pathetic. Maybe tomorrow night you won't be so weak.*

"Yeah," he answered. "Maybe tomorrow night."

One. Two. Three. Four. Five. Six. Seven. Eight. Nine. Ten. One. Two ... He fell asleep.

When Simcane woke the next morning, Galloway was already gone, probably tending his fields. Simcane sat at the kitchen table and waited.

And waited.

And waited.

The dim light from the early suns brightened through the window before eventually darkening again while he still sat. The voice had counted to ten 4,227 times. His stomach rumbled.

Where was that old coot? The longer he waited, the angrier he grew. He wished the voice would stop counting. His knuckles turned white around the utensils clenched in each fist.

"Gallowaaaay," he shouted as loud as he could. "Gallowaaaay."

But his old friend didn't come home. After the suns disappeared, Simcane's other voice stopped counting. *How dare he make you wait for so long? You should find him. Find him and make him pay.*

Simcane bounded up, knocking over his chair. He was ready to try anything that might shut the voice up. He threw the utensils against the wall and stormed through the front door, unsure where he was actually going. All he knew was that he was going somewhere.

"Gallowaaaay," he bellowed into the muggy night. His head jerked twice to the left. Only crickets and a distant owl answered his cries. He took in the dusky field. At the far edge of Galloway's property, the silhouette of a horse struggled to stand, fell, and struggled again. Simcane marched toward it. Three vultures circled above. As Simcane approached, he saw that the horse had a broken front leg and was exhausted. It looked at Simcane as if welcoming an end to its pain.

Simcane knew there was no saving it. His voice begged, *Can we watch it suffer?*

Simcane shook his head. He caressed the steed's neck. The glistening infection crawled down his forearm and coated his knuckles. Simcane closed his eye and took a deep breath. He drew back.

Don't to it. We can watch it suffer.

Simcane drove his metal-coated fist into the side of the horse's head. A concussive boom echoed from his gift. It killed the horse instantly.

I can't believe how weak you are. You never let us have any fun.

Simcane smirked. If he could strangle the voice, he would. He was about to say so when an overturned plow in the ditch grabbed his attention. He looked over the steep edge where Galloway stared back with hollow, lifeless eyes from beneath the plow.

"Hmph. That's a shame."

No, it's not.

Simcane walked back to the house and fell fast asleep on the hallway floor.

Simcane sprang up from the floor like he had been shot with an arrow. He staggered against a framed picture on the wall. He recognized Galloway's hallway, but couldn't remember much from the day before. He pressed his palms to his throbbing head. Small flashes of him sitting at Galloway's table crossed his thoughts. He hoped Galloway would have some idea of what had happened. "Hey, Galloway," he shouted.

His friend didn't answer.

He called for him again, and again got no response.

You idiot.

"What?"

Don't you remember what you did?

"What I did?"

How are your knuckles?

Simcane squeezed a fist and his hand ached terribly. An image of Galloway lying helpless beneath a plow flashed in his mind. "Oh my god. Galloway?"

He exploded from the house and into the field. In the distance a horse lay dead on the road. He raced to it. Vultures pecked at it. He shooed them away, but they were stubborn and quickly returned. He kicked one out of anger. Then he leaned over the edge of the ditch.

Look what you did.

"What? I didn't do this." His stomach sank. The dead eyes of his old friend looked up at him.

He was alive when you got here.

"Shut up." He climbed down and yanked the plow from atop his friend. Galloway's skin was cool and blue and rigid. Simcane sat and cradled him. "What have I done?" He sobbed.

You're a murderer.

"No," he cried. "Shut up, damn you."

The merciless pecking of the vultures was more than he could stand, so he stood up. The guilt and self-pity pressing on his shoulders were as heavy as if he had used his gift.

The voice snapped, *Leave him here. He means nothing to you. The birdies are hungry.*

Simcane carried Galloway to the house and laid him on the porch before retrieving a shovel from the barn.

With sweat pouring down his face and mixing with tears, he dug a hole behind Galloway's house next to his wife's headstone. Then he gently lowered his old friend into it and filled the hole. After patting down the dirt, he tossed the shovel aside and bowed his head. "If I had anything to do with your death, my friend, I can never apologize enough. I only hope you are looking down with Claudia now and you see my remorse. You were a friend when I was a boy, and you're still my friend now." He wiped his eye. "I'm so sorry."

No, you're not.

Simcane lowered his head and went to Galloway's stable. "I'm a cancer," he whispered. "I'm a danger to everyone."

His metal-shifting skin crawled from his chest to his thick biceps. He realized something devastating. Despite who he strove to be, he was more like Scorne and Cyn than he wanted to admit. And if he was too much like them, then no one would survive.

CHAPTER 20

TEK LIFE

On Tek Island, word traveled that Leander had injured his arm trying to repair a lift at the wall's main gate. Alina went to check on him at Doc Eckels's, leaving Cridon with Rasi. Leander sat on the edge of a bed in the infirmary. His face brightened when he saw her.

She sat beside him. "Good evening, Leander. How are you feeling?"

"I'll be right soon enough. My pride hurts more than the broken arm. It was a foolish mistake. I know better than to work on that godforsaken lift alone. How are you feeling?"

"Stronger every day."

"That's good. And Cridon and Rasi?"

"They're doing well, too. Though I don't think Rasi has gotten used to the white streak in my hair yet. I catch him looking at it when he doesn't think I see him."

"I think it looks nice. Some might say …" He puffed out his chest in a dignified way and lifted his chin. "… regal, even."

Alina smiled. She noticed a tattoo on Leander's bare shoulder of a Tek symbol with two dots and a vertical curvy line between them.

She pointed. "What's that symbol?"

"That's my Tek marking. When a Tek becomes a soldier, he is permitted one symbol. As he moves up the ranks, he is allowed more if he chooses."

"How many do you have?"

"This is the only one."

"What does it mean?"

He turned so she could see it more clearly. "It's my mother's name. The two dots represent my brothers who are both dead now."

"Oh, I'm sorry."

"That's the life of my people."

"Will you tell me about your home?"

"What do you want to know?"

"I want to know everything. I want to know about your family. What life is like there."

"I suppose. If you think it would be interesting."

"I do." Alina sat quietly and listened.

"What you see here in this city is a tiny glimpse of where I'm from. My country is as large as five Epertases. Imagine buildings taller than the tallest castle and numbering so many that they stretch for as far as a man could travel in a dozen new moons, and you would have some idea of the size.

"The buzz that you hear day and night in this city is magnified a hundredfold. It's hard to sleep without plugs in your ears. The air is thick and dark and sometimes choking because of constantly running machines. It wasn't until I left for war for the first time that I saw the beauty of the two suns without a dark haze blurring them."

Though Alina tried to imagine what he described, she couldn't fathom his world. She asked, "Why do your people take war to so many?"

"The machines require fuel that lives in the ground. Over many years, we have drained our own land of the black blood and we search for more to continue our way of life. My people have become reliant on the comforts those machines provide."

"But that's such a finite solution. Eventually, you'll run out of kingdoms to conquer, will you not?"

"The world is bigger than you could ever imagine. But yes, I agree. We have no other choice, though."

"You could change your lifestyles so you wouldn't rely on those 'comforts' as much."

"Though that sounds reasonable in theory, those comforts are too ingrained in my people and could never be taken away now."

"What kind of comforts are you speaking of?"

"Mostly, moving without horses. Our machines, like the rolling machines you saw during the war, can take us anywhere we choose. My people are inventive, and the black blood fuels many of our inventions. When I left for Epertase, we even had men building contraptions that would one day allow them to fly."

"Fly? That's ridiculous."

"If you could see the things I've seen, you wouldn't doubt what I say."

Alina couldn't imagine any comfort that would be worth destroying other civilizations to have. As far as she was concerned, horses were just fine for travel. "What about the kingdoms you've invaded? What of the people left after you've ravaged their land?"

"I suppose a lot of those people died. And some were taken as slaves."

"And you have no remorse?"

"I never did. We are taught from an early age that outsiders are evil and would kill us if we didn't kill them first. Everyone is an enemy in a Tek's eyes."

"Am I your enemy?"

"Well, no. Of course not. I would never hurt yo—" He paused and looked away as her point sank in. The lines grew deep across his forehead.

"I don't see you as some ruthless soldier, Leander. I see you as a compassionate man who took me in during my time of need. When did you choose to become a soldier?"

"Choose?" His eyes went crooked. "There was no choice. Every male is forced into the military when his voice deepens. The plan for me was no different, but my mother had other ideas. After I had seen thirteen birthdays, she held my funeral."

"I don't understand."

"She hid me beneath our home and reported to the region authority that I had been pinned between a wall and a rolling machine and died. The local doctor was a friend, and she confirmed my mother's story.

"My mother and the other women from my region dug up the body of another recently killed boy and held my funeral with that child in my stead. The authority believed my mother's lies and removed my name from their records. My mother promised me we would one day steal a boat and flee to another land, and I couldn't wait.

"But that day never came. Getting a boat is almost impossible. For several years, the women of my region raised me, constantly on the watch for the authority to return. I don't know why the other women helped my mother, but perhaps it was because their sons had already been taken to the ships and the ones who returned, returned in boxes.

"My mother loved me very much. All the women of my region did. But they couldn't protect me forever. I was finally betrayed by a jealous mother whose son died in battle."

"She turned on you?"

He nodded sadly. "She was filled with such pain that I could only imagine. She gave up my secret to the authority in hopes of sparing her only remaining son from a similar fate. I hold no ill will toward her."

He took a deep breath. "I was seventeen when they came for me. I hid beneath my mother's home as I had so many times before, but they burned our house and forced me out. As punishment, they hanged my mother and most of the other women who had helped her. I was made to watch. And then they took the son of the woman who had turned my family in and brought him with me to the camps."

Alina listened intently. She was horrified yet mesmerized by his story. "What happened to the boy?" she asked.

"Though it was his mother who betrayed me, I felt sorry for him, as any man would. I tried to protect him as best I could while we trained, but the time came for us to begin our first journey across the sea. We reached a land much like Epertase, only smaller, and we invaded. The boy was eleven. Despite my attempts to shield him, he was slaughtered in the first battle."

Alina felt nauseated by his words.

Leander was obviously a hard man; he didn't flinch or hesitate in telling his story. "My people rarely know life without war. It is a hard life."

"So, that's your fate? Servitude until death?"

"No, not entirely. If we survive twenty years of service, we are permitted to retire. Also, we return home between campaigns, sometimes for many moons. That's when we are to take at least one bride and give our country at least one son."

"Have you? Given a son, I mean."

"I have not. I have given the world three daughters."

"And what of them?"

As he spoke, Alina saw the first hint of a smile. "They are well. At least, they were before we left for Epertase. Tek women are treated with respect, maybe because they are often the only good in the life of a soldier."

Doc Eckels entered the room. "Hello, Your Majesty."

"Doctor." Her hand found the top of Leander's. She squeezed and smiled. "Could I ask you one more thing, Leander?"

"Certainly."

"Will your people ever come back to Epertase for vengeance?"

Leander's slight smile curved downward and he looked away. He didn't answer.

"Thank you for your story, Leander. I'll leave you two be."

She started to stand, but he called her back. "Alina?"

She sat down again.

"Do you mind sitting with me while the doc sets my arm? I hear the procedure is none too pleasant."

"Of course I'll stay." While she dreaded witnessing unpleasant medical procedures, she wouldn't dream of leaving now.

Doc Eckels braced Leander's arm with one hand at his wrist and one hand at his elbow. Leander grinned at Alina. She held his gaze and smiled warmly while Eckels counted to three. She didn't watch the doctor straighten the bones, but she heard it. Leander closed his eyes, bit his lip, and grunted. It was the only sign of pain he gave. Well, that and a bead of sweat forming on his forehead. Alina reached for a cloth on the bedside table and dabbed it away. Doc Eckels wrapped Leander's arm in a splint.

Alina stood to leave. "I would love to hear more about your world one day. These rolling machines for everyday travel sound interesting."

"That they are. Just wait until I tell you about the machines that keep our homes warm in the winter without fire and cool in the summer without ice."

"Oh. I look forward to it." She kissed his cheek and started to leave.

"Alina?" he called out.

"Yes?"

"I'm sorry for the pain and suffering that my people have brought you and your kingdom."

"I know you are, Leander. I forgive you." She bowed her head, turned, and left for home.

Later that afternoon, Alina and Rasi took their evening walk along the perimeter fence of the rapidly growing Tek City. It was one of their few routines that they made sure to do religiously. Rasi held her hand. She carried Cridon in a Tek-designed pouch that hung from her shoulder and kept him warm by some kind of technological mystery even as the evening air grew chilly. He fought sleep with a yawn and a stretch.

For weeks Alina had wanted desperately to ask Rasi one nagging question, but the part of her that feared the answer kept her quiet. Until now. She swallowed. "Rasi, we've been here for a while now. Have you devised a plan that would return us to Epertase?"

After a long pause, he answered bluntly, *No.*

"So, the future as you see it has us living out our lives here? What about King Logan and Queen Lona, who are still forced to live in hiding? Or Aidric and the others who have helped us over the years? Or Simcane, Rasi? What about Simcane?"

I don't know where Simcane went after our fight with Tevin, or if he is even still alive. But last night I sent Atticus back to Epertase to find out. I advised him to urge Simcane to come to Tek Island if he locates him.

"Maybe he went back to Homer's," she said hopefully. "Did you tell Atticus to look there?"

Yes.

"What about my loyal servants like Levi and James?"

If they are close to Tevin, I'm afraid we won't be able to get to them.

"I don't accept that."

We have no choice. If James and Levi are still alive, then it means Tevin doesn't see them as threats and they'll continue to be safe.

"My duty is to protect all Epertasians. I cannot simply abandon my people forever."

He tugged her hand. *Come with me. I'd like to show you something.* He led her up a ladder to the top of the wall overlooking the vast fields outside. His straps floated in the fresh air. *Look around. What do you see?*

"A field?"

I see vulnerability. This is where any war with Tevin's army will occur if they discover you're here. I have my hands so full trying to figure out how to fight an army fifty times our numbers out in the open that I can't think of anything else. It's impossible, yet I have no choice but to figure out something. I haven't a moment to plan for anything else, let alone attacking said army at their very stronghold. We wouldn't last the morning.

Alina fidgeted with her fingers. She understood, but it didn't make her any less saddened. She noticed the stress in Rasi's face as he stared toward the northeastern cliff. The best thing she could do at that moment was to support him and not add to his stress. "All right, then," she said. "Let's figure this out together. Do you know for sure they'll come through this field?"

He took a deep, overwhelmed breath. *It's tough. North and east are out because of the cliffs. No army could advance from there.* He pointed back over the city to the west. *The deep and vast western valleys make that direction a poor choice as well. That leaves south. I went to the edge of the island yesterday and the beaches there are easily accessible. That's where any army worth its salt would advance from.*

"Won't Tevin want to surround us and create a siege?"

Rasi pursed his lips. *I don't think so. I'd actually want him to do just that. It takes time to position armies. We wouldn't give them that time and could deal with the smaller forces while they tried to prepare. A straight-on attack will be his only play.*

"That's good that we know it … Right?"

He shook his head solemnly. *It doesn't matter. They number too many. And that's where I'm at. Our best chance is that he never finds us. I think that's a reasonable hope.*

"Why are you so confident?"

Because as far as he knows, the Teks hate us as much as or more than anyone else in the world. As far as he's concerned, there would be no reason for us to come here. He simply sees the Teks as murdering heathens who would kill their enemy—us—if given the chance.

"How do you know that?"

Because I wouldn't have looked for us here. He paused. She hung on his breath, sensing he had more to say. He looked away. *That brings me to something else I need to speak with you about. I'm having difficulty in acquiring the needed weapons for our defense, and I think you can help me with that problem.*

"Oh?"

While I have convinced the Teks of our need for swords, Leander refuses to listen when I speak about the weapons they used when they attacked Epertase. They've got a few here that they use for hunting, but that's it. I've instructed him to start building factories to create more, but he's concerned doing such will break some pact he has with you.

Alina touched his shoulder. "He is a man of his word. I'll release him of his vow to not build weapons at once. I think he's more than earned our trust, don't you?"

And then some.

CHAPTER 21

HIRED HELP

Bohden stood uninvited within a crowd of Epertase's deadliest mercenaries in the Royal Garden of Thasula. He wore a scarf over his head and draped across his face, covering everything but his eyes. Being in the military pretty much forbade him from answering such calls for mercenaries, but he'd gotten curious when he'd heard Simcane's name mentioned in passing.

The captain of his battalion, Casa, oversaw the security detail for the gathering. Bohden kept his head down. None of the attendees spoke to each other, making the garden relatively quiet. Among these types of men, a fight was more likely to break out than a handshake.

Being around men known for their homicidal reputations made Bohden more nervous than he had anticipated. He was an imposter among killers, a fraud hiding in the most dangerous of scenes. An aura of violence permeated the air. He would have left if not for the fear that leaving prematurely would make him stand out. He hid his trembling hands within his baggy sleeves.

Even the twins were there. To see them in public meant a lot of gold must be at stake. They were close enough to Bohden that he could touch them if he really wanted to lose a hand. Horribly disfigured now from their chosen lives of violence, they were said to have once been staggeringly handsome with stunning bright blue eyes. Rumor had it they were very competitive when it came to their scars and took pride in outdoing each other. One brother, Grissum, had intentionally scarred the left side of his own face with acid so people would know which brother he was. Not to be outdone, Turley, the other twin, lopped off the top of his own ear and left it in Grissum's soup as a prank. He also wore an eye patch, though if someone paid close attention they might notice it swapping eyes from time to time. Though Turley's reputation for violence was legendary, it was Grissum people feared the most. He'd killed people for nothing more than bumping into him in a crowd.

Bohden made sure not to make that mistake. As they waited for Tevin to appear, Grissum picked his teeth with the tip of a blood-stained arrow. He slowly turned his head as if sensing Bohden's stare. Bohden quickly looked away, praying he hadn't offended. He felt Grissum's evil grin and it lifted the hairs on his neck.

Thankfully, Tevin stepped onto the balcony above them just in time. Grissum faced forward. Tevin took in the crowd before speaking. "I have called you here because I am in desperate need of your services."

A soldier weaved through the crowd, passing out scrolls.

Tevin loudly cleared his throat before speaking again. "As you may know, I am in search of supporters of the old regime. In addition to my standing offer of more gold than any of you could spend in a lifetime for the capture of the former queen and her son, I am now offering the territory known as Silo for the capture of the mercenary named Simcane."

"Alive?" Grissum shouted.

Tevin pondered the question, and then answered, "Alive is fine; dead is just as good. There will be a place at my side for any man who brings Simcane's head to—"

"Where was he last seen?" Grissum interrupted.

Tevin tilted his head, unaccustomed to being cut off. A slight orange glow showed through the fabric of his robe. He continued through clenched teeth, "As I was about to say, I saw Simcane with my own eyes where the Great Plains meet Concore Forest, but that was a while ago. Since then, I have not—"

Grissum shouted again, "Is there anything else important?"

Tevin took a deep, frustrated breath. "You are trying my patience, Grissum." Tevin's glow grew a little brighter. "I will not be interrupted again. Is that understood?" He waited for acknowledgement, but none came. Finally, he flicked his hand toward the crowd and said, "Be on your way. I have grown weary of your company. Reward is a carriage of gold."

He disappeared into the castle as the crowd of killers filed out through the gates. Bohden's gamble had paid off. He suddenly had a new mission—finding Simcane before these guys did. With his head bowed, Bohden followed the crowd, lost in his own thoughts. Maybe following the brothers would work. He quickly shook his head. That was the most dangerous of stupid ideas. Maybe he—

"Bohden?" someone shouted from behind.

Bohden spun to see Captain Casa hurrying to catch up.

"I thought that was you. What are you doing here?"

"Oh, uh … Sir, I-I was just looking for a little extra work. I'm sure you know that Tevin doesn't pay his soldiers very well. I have my mother to support, you see."

"And you thought mercenary work was the right choice?" Casa snorted. "Son, not only is that forbidden for a soldier, but you don't have the stones for it. Nor the talent."

Bohden wasn't about to argue. "I realize that now."

"You know what? I have an idea. I'll allow you to continue as you were. In return, if you accidentally find someone of interest, you come to me first. I say accidentally because I don't imagine you'll have much deliberate success."

"Probably not, sir."

"If you ever do find a wanted man, I'll help you bring him in and we'll split the reward. Deal?"

"Of course, sir."

"Fine, then. Be on your way."

Bohden considered himself fortunate that Casa placed gold above duty. Now, where had those brothers gone off to? As Casa disappeared into town, Bohden fell back into his thoughts and started to walk away. He didn't get very far before a hand covered his mouth and searing pain pierced his side.

"Shhhh," someone whispered in his ear.

Bohden groaned, winced, and tucked his elbow to his side. He'd never felt such pain. He tried to look down, but the hand over his mouth held his head up. Grissum stepped into view. "Why are you here, boy?" he asked.

Turley twisted his blade in Bohden's side and whispered, "Answer my brother, boy."

"I ... I don't know what you mean." The pain came in waves.

Grissum touched Bohden's wound and then licked the fresh blood from his fingers. "See that blood, boy? It don't taste like no killer blood to me. What are you doing here? Answer me and you may live."

Bohden felt suddenly cold even as warm blood ran down his side. "I've never done this before. My mother and I need money and I thought I could start a new career."

Turley slowly and painfully withdrew his blade.

Grissum smirked. "Oh." He cringed and looked at his brother like he was embarrassed. "My mistake. I thought one of my ex-wives might have sent you. I saw how you were looking at me." He grabbed the back of Bohden's neck and pulled him close. His voice turned deep and grizzled. "You are an amateur among professionals, boy. Go home to your mommy before you really get hurt."

Grissum released Bohden and shoved him away. He and his brother laughed as they melded with the afternoon crowd. Bohden dropped to his knees. Blood poured around his hand. He felt suddenly dizzy. He wobbled and then collapsed to his back.

A concerned woman from a nearby pastry shop shouted, "You all right, boy?" When he didn't answer, she raced over. She pressed her hand against his wound and shouted for a doctor. She leaned close to his ear. "Don't worry, young man. I'll find you help." She ran to her shop and returned with a blanket.

Bohden shivered as she covered him. The blanket didn't seem to help. Another man knelt beside her. "I'm a doctor," he said. "Let me have a look." He lifted the blanket and then lowered it again. "We need to get him to my clinic."

The woman stood up. "I'll get my horse."

The doctor put his hand on Bohden's shoulder. "Rest, young man. I'm confident you'll be all right as soon as we get some new blood into your veins."

Bohden nodded.

The doctor rolled up his sleeve and smacked his own arm until a thick vein lifted. "Ahh. That'll do nicely." He stood up and watched for the woman to return with her horse. Bohden felt like sleeping.

CHAPTER 22

TEVIN'S KILL SQUAD

Christopher ducked into a dark alley on the outskirts of the Epertasian city of Tiffin. He watched as Epertasian soldiers rode into town from the south. There were exactly twenty-one, and they wore a single sleeve of gold fabric on their right arms. That told Christopher they were Tevin's new kill squad, led by a psychopath called Hernon.

Panic bubbled from his gut into his throat. Were they there for him? If they were, how had they found him? He had been so careful since he'd been freed during Simcane's prison break, moving from place to place and never settling down. Regardless of their reason for being in Tiffin, their presence meant it was time for Christopher to move on again.

Christopher watched from behind a rubbish pile as Hernon dismounted from his mare and stood in the center of the street. This was the first time he had ever seen Hernon in person, though the assassin's reputation was well-known. The hand-drawn portraits passed from town to town had conveniently righted his once-broken nose that was so contorted it almost formed an upside-down question mark, and none of the stories mentioned his limp. The rest of his team positioned their horses across the dirt road.

Evening was the busiest time in Tiffin, as it was a social town and most of the townsfolk were already out for their nightly strolls or gathering at the town's famous eateries. A crowd quickly formed around the soldiers to hear Hernon's address.

"People of Tiffin, my name is Hernon. Good day to you."

Hernon's reputation had grown throughout Epertase, and the stories of what he did once he found his prey were as horrible as they were psychotic. He stood with a swagger—an arrogant cuss for sure, though no one would dare say so out loud.

"We have it on good authority that you are harboring a wanted fugitive within your town. If this is so, it is a strict violation of Tevin's law and treason against the new Epertase. You all know of my reputation, yes?" He held up a drawing of what appeared to be a face, though Christopher was too far away to be sure. "You can avoid us burning your town with all of you in it simply by handing over this criminal."

A brave older man in the crowd shouted, "What is this man's name? Your drawing is too crude and looks like many of the young men of this town."

"We do not know what name this man goes by now, but he is Christopher of the Loper family."

Christopher's heart sank. And now this friendly town would suffer for their hospitality.

Hernon continued, "Line up any man who resembles this drawing or everyone in this town will die."

The brave man stepped forward and shouted, "You are not an Epertasian. No Epertasian would treat others in such ways. You're a pawn of the evil wizard, and I will not help you hurt any man of this town."

Hernon flicked his hand with an unimpressed smirk. Even though the man was much older than Christopher and could in no way be mistaken for him, Hernon said, "You fit the description of the criminal rather well." The crowd backed away like the older man had suddenly developed the plague. Two of Hernon's soldiers dismounted, grabbed the man's arms, and forced him to his knees.

An older woman, maybe the man's wife, ran from the crowd and grabbed one of the soldiers' arms. "Please don't hurt him," she cried. "He is sorry for his words."

The soldier smacked her to the ground.

"Do not fear, woman. I will not kill this man. I only plan to … re-educate him." Hernon reached for a small sheath on his belt and drew a long icepick.

Oh no. Christopher had heard about the squad's "re-education" and couldn't in good conscience let any man suffer such a fate when it was meant for him. Though his fear nearly held him back, his honor pushed him into the street. "Wait," he shouted.

Hernon's eyes, along with another hundred eyes, lifted.

"I am the one you're looking for." Christopher untied his sword belt and allowed it to fall, and then lifted his hands in surrender.

Three soldiers drew their swords as they jogged to him. They shoved Christopher to his knees and tied his hands behind his back. The soldiers lifted him to his feet and escorted him through the crowd.

Seeing Hernon up close gave Christopher dreams of a one-on-one fight. Despite the bloated legend of the kill squad, Hernon was a skinny, weaselly fellow with a nasal voice.

"Your name is Christopher?" Hernon asked.

Christopher hesitated and then nodded.

The older man on his knees looked up with relieved, hopeful eyes. Hernon nodded to the soldier standing behind him and the soldier shoved a damp cloth over the man's mouth and nose. The crowd gasped. The man struggled briefly before his body slumped to the ground.

"What are you doing?" Christopher screamed. "I've surrendered."

"If you are indeed who you say you are. This man, however, has spoken with a rebellious tone, and that is unacceptable in the mighty Tevin's kingdom." He straddled the older man's chest. With the icepick in one hand, he used the other to force open the man's left eye. "Is everyone watching?" he shouted. "Bring out the kids. They should bear witness as well."

The older woman, still prone in the dirt, sobbed. Christopher struggled, but the soldiers tightened their grips. Disgusted, he turned away. The soldier beside him forced his head back around and said, "You will watch or this will happen to everyone in this town."

Christopher's stomach turned.

Hernon gently guided the icepick into the old man's eye socket alongside his eyeball. His protruding tongue mimicked his movements as he concentrated. While he held the pick steady, a soldier handed him a mallet. With soft, steady taps, Hernon drove the icepick deeper. When the icepick was where he wanted it, he wiggled it side to side like he was scrambling eggs.

"Do not worry, people of Tiffin," he said as he worked. "I have not damaged this man's eye." He pulled the bloody pick from the socket. "Almost finished." Then he guided the icepick into the man's other eye socket.

People in the crowd sobbed. Some of the men pushed forward, but the soldiers pushed them back with force and threats of being next.

"You are an evil bastard," Christopher shouted.

Hernon wiggled the pick around again, his tongue dancing with each movement of the tool. Satisfied with his work, he removed the pick and wiped it on the old man's pant leg. He stood up. "This man will be fine. He has simply been re-educated. He will be much more subdued in his tone from here on out." He turned to the horrified crowd. "Now then, find me the others who resemble the drawing, just in case."

"No," Christopher shouted. "Why? You have me."

"I cannot trust that you are not, for some odd reason, covering up for the true criminal. Therefore, I must be thorough."

Christopher could only watch as soldiers pushed into the crowd and arrested seven more young men who shared Christopher's dark features. Their mothers, wives, and fathers pleaded for mercy. Then the soldiers mounted their horses and tied their prisoners' bound hands to their saddles with Christopher at the front. Several men slipped from the back of the crowd into a side street.

Hernon addressed the crowd one last time. "Thank you for your cooperation. In return, we will leave you and complete our messy business outside of town. Long live King Tevin." He rode to the front of his men and led them back the way they had come.

They rode to an empty field outside of town where they dismounted and formed a circle around the eight men. With a bubbly, you've-won-a-prize voice, Hernon said, "Now, who's first?" As he climbed down from his mare, the young man next to Christopher dropped to his knees and begged for mercy.

Hernon grabbed the boy's chin and squeezed his cheeks into a forced pucker. "I do not enjoy doing what I have to do, young man, but in the name of Tevin, it is my calling." After a pause he added, "Well, I don't enjoy it *much*." He took out his icepick.

A second soldier dismounted and approached with the same dirty rag he had used on the older man and poured the contents of a water bladder onto it. The air reeked of ether. He stepped behind the young man. "I'd say this coward, sir."

Hernon nodded. "Very well."

The soldier grabbed the back of the young man's head and shoved the rag over his mouth and nose. The man squirmed, but his strength quickly faded. The soldier lowered him to the ground. When he looked up, his eyes drifted past Hernon. "Uh, sir?" he said with a nod across the field.

Hernon casually looked over his shoulder. "Hmm. Now, what do we have here?" He straightened and cocked his head.

Christopher leaned over so he could see past them. At least two dozen men wearing all black rode across the field toward them. When they reached shouting range, they stopped in a single line from left to right. Christopher grinned when he recognized Atticus at the front. His old friend had returned just as he had promised after the war with Fice.

Hernon sheathed his icepick. "Well, this is interesting." After looking to his men, he added, "What are you waiting for? Go see what they want. And bring me the leader's head." With a look to Christopher and a shrug of his shoulders, he asked, "Are these friends of yours?"

If he only knew.

Hernon's men formed a line parallel to the newcomers, drew their swords, and charged. Atticus and his crew waited patiently, swords still at their sides. The kill squad crossed the field. Atticus sat back in his saddle.

Hernon watched with a furrowed brow. He surely realized something was afoot.

The kill squad continued their charge, swords raised. Atticus grinned. Christopher felt anxiety climb up his throat. What was his friend waiting for? He was going to be run down if he didn't do something quick.

And then, within a few horse-lengths of Atticus, the lead soldier's horse stepped awkwardly and tumbled, throwing his rider. Before the others could stop, their horses hit the same hidden pitfall, snapping their legs as well.

Atticus dismounted and pounced, his men following his lead. Before Hernon's men could get back to their feet and gather their wits, Atticus and his men were upon them. They slaughtered Hernon's soldiers within seconds.

Atticus lowered his sword and ordered his men to take care of the horses. His eyes met Hernon's. He winced and shrugged.

Hernon's face blanched. He stumbled backward, suddenly realizing the odds had drastically changed. Atticus calmly climbed back onto his horse and kicked it into a canter, careful to navigate around the shallow trench. His men followed.

Hernon scrambled to his horse, but Christopher, with his hands still bound behind his back, charged and collided with him. The impact bounced Hernon off his horse's flank and he fell to his knees. When he reached for his sword, Christopher kicked him in the teeth.

"Wait, wait, wait," Hernon pleaded through bloody lips.

Christopher stood with a glare, anger and hatred surging through his veins. He looked toward the town. A mob of fathers and brothers approached, weapons in hand.

Hernon noticed, too.

One of the men from town stopped by the unconscious young man and yanked the ether-soaked rag from his face. "Charlie," he cried.

Charlie gasped, though he didn't immediately wake up.

Atticus stepped next to Christopher. "Good to see you, Christopher," he said, as though the two men had seen each other as recently as yesterday.

Christopher smiled. "I can't begin to express how pleased I am to see you today."

Atticus chuckled. "I bet you are." He cut away Christopher's restraints and handed him a knife to do the same for the other prisoners.

"Hey, Atticus, how'd you know where to dig that trench?"

"Heh. Hernon uses the same tactics at every town he visits. I just needed to draw his men in the right direction. I'll admit I didn't expect it to work as well as it did, but ... you know. When you're on the side of good, sometimes you catch a break."

The Tiffin mob surrounded them, eliminating any chance Hernon had to escape. "Kill the bastard," shouted a portly butcher wearing a bloody apron and carrying a cleaver.

"Yeah. Use his icepick," someone else cried from deeper in the crowd.

Hernon shouted, "No. Wait." He turned in a circle while still on his knees. "If you kill these men and help me, I'll tell Tevin the good you have done. You'll be heroes in his kingdom. Tiffin will be forever safe."

Christopher leaned into Atticus's ear. "Should we let the townspeople have him?"

Atticus thought for a moment and then shook his head. "These are regular people. They don't need something like this on their conscience. I'll do it." He drew his sword.

Hernon's eyes widened. His pleas fell on deaf ears as Atticus moved closer with a murderous purpose. The fear in his eyes shifted to defiance. He shouted, "If you allow this, Tevin's men will come and rape your wives and daughters and kill you all. He'll burn this city to ashes."

Atticus advanced without a word.

"You're a coward," Hernon shouted, and pulled out his icepick. He plunged it toward Atticus's gut. Atticus took the pick and

Hernon's hand with an upward slash of his sword. Before Hernon's severed hand hit the ground, Atticus rammed the point of his blade through Hernon's left eye. Hernon grunted. And then, with a foot planted on Hernon's forehead, Atticus pulled his blade free.

As Hernon quivered on the ground, Atticus wiped his blade on the bastard's golden sleeve. He turned to the townspeople. "I guess this man has been re-educated."

The butcher stepped forward, his arm around the shoulders of his son, who had been one of Hernon's captives. "Thank you."

"No thanks needed. Listen to me. This is critical. Bury them all. Leave no trace that they were ever here. Tell everyone in town to never to speak of this day again. If anyone comes asking about Hernon and his kill squad, you know nothing. You must all make a pact with one another. If anyone slips, Tevin will come, and he will kill you all."

The butcher nodded.

"Now, go. Hurry." Atticus turned to Christopher. "You're not safe anywhere you go. They know you helped us in the war." Atticus leaned close to his ear and whispered, "We are living on the Island of Torick with the Teks."

Christopher pulled back with a grin. "Very sneaky. I never considered you might go there."

"Well, neither would Tevin, which is why we hide there. After you led our surrender to Jarrah's men, I made a promise that I would come back for you. I know it has taken a while, but today I have kept that promise. Are you with us?"

"To my death, sir."

"If you have anyone you'd like to bring along, gather them now. Just be sure they don't know our destination and understand that if they join us, they may never return home. Is that understood?"

"Yes, sir."

"By the way, have you heard any word on where Simcane is hiding? We can't find him anywhere."

"I'm afraid not. I've heard finding him is a top priority for Tevin, and a great reward has been offered for his head. But where he has gone, I don't know."

"That Simcane sure has a talent for not being found. Homer thinks he may return to his farm one day. We'll stop there on our way back to Tek Island. I wish we had more time to search for him. I hope wherever he is he's well. Once we leave Epertasian shores this time, we will not be coming back for a long time, if ever."

Atticus looked around and then said, "You'll need a horse." He nodded toward Hernon's. "I think his will do."

"Are we going to Tek Island now?"

"Soon. We have a few people to locate beforehand. We came for you first because my contact in Tevin's military told me you were scheduled for re-education."

"So, where are we headed?"

"I've heard King Logan and Queen Lona are preparing to attack Jarrah in Lithia. I'm hoping to catch them before they do and convince them to reconsider." He grinned as he removed a blue crystal from a bag at his hip. "Tell me, Christopher, have you ever been to the Tunnels of Eiger?"

CHAPTER 23

MISSED OPPORTUNITY

After Simcane left Galloway's farm, he wandered aimlessly for the next few months, sleeping in gutters and abandoned homes and eating rotten food from garbage heaps throughout Epertase. Most of his waking moments were spent trying to ignore the nasty voice. *Let's kill the world,* became its favorite prod. Arguing was pointless.

Perhaps subconsciously, his travels took him to the edge of Homer's farm. He stood in an overgrown field that used to be meticulously cared for. He knew because he had tended to it himself for a while. Homer's front door was wide open.

The evil voice whispered, *Let's go kill him.*

"Shut up."

A raindrop splashed onto his hand. He looked to the dark, bulbous clouds. He hated rain. By the time he made it through the overgrown field to Homer's front door, the clouds had opened and he was drenched.

"Homer?" he called out. A squank scurried from the empty fireplace to behind the couch. "Are you here?"

Yes, Homer, come out so we can kill you.

"Shut up ... Irene?"

Only silence answered. He swiped his hand through a spider web and stepped inside. He removed his drenched scarf and dropped it on the floor. After two involuntary sideways jerks of his head, he plodded through more cobwebs in the hallway to Homer's bedroom. No one was there. He checked the empty guestroom next. Then he returned to the dining room. He dragged his fingers along the top of the table, drawing clean lines through the thick dust. A single scroll lay in the center with Simcane's name written on the side. He recognized the design pressed into the wax seal as Homer's family crest. Simcane tilted his head.

What is it?

"I don't know yet. Shut up." He picked up the scroll, looked around for a trap, and then blew the dust from it. He slid his finger under the outer flap and broke the wax seal. It read:

Simcane, if you find this scroll, know that we came here looking for you. We are glad you are safe and hope you will remain so. Rasi and Alina send their best and want you to know you are in their thoughts each and every day. We cannot tell you where we hide in this missive, but someday we hope to find you and show you. If we never meet again, please remain safe.

The scroll was signed by Atticus, followed by another brief message addressed to Tevin.

False King Tevin, if it is you who reads this scroll, know that we are waiting for our revenge. Sleep well knowing Rasi will one day come for you.

Simcane dropped the scroll to the floor. *We don't need them,* the voice said.

"No, I don't suppose we do."

Maybe your other friends will be home soon.

"Yes, maybe."

And then we can kill them.

Simcane plopped into the chair with his fists clenched on the tabletop and waited for Homer and Irene to return. The longer he waited, the angrier he grew. He squeezed his fists until his knuckles turned white.

Maybe your friends are hiding. You should call out for Homer.

The voice was right. Simcane drew in a deep breath and bellowed, "Hooomerrr," as loud as he could. "Hooomerrr," he shouted again. He continued shouting for most of the dreary night.

Once his throat was sore from shouting, he lowered his head onto the table and fell asleep. When he opened his eye again, it was daylight and the rain had stopped.

The angry voice returned. *How dare he make you wait? When he returns, you should make him pay.*

"Yes. I think I should."

The angry voice turned soft. *It could be a while, though. You wanna find something to eat?*

He grunted. That meant yes. He overturned the couch, sending the hiding squank scurrying for the door. He snatched its tail and bit off its head. Each crunchy, bitter bite gave him the protein he needed to push on.

We should go to town.

"We're not going to town."

But we can kill everyone.

"We're not killing anyone."

One... Two ... Three ... Four ...

"Aaarrrrggghh." Pressing his palms over his ears did nothing to quiet the sounds. "Hoomerrr," he bellowed over the incessant counting.

For nearly six long years, Simcane lived alone in Homer's house. During the days he hunted and ate, while during the nights he tried, often unsuccessfully, to sleep. And during every evening of those six long years, he sat at the table and bellowed for Homer.

CHAPTER 24

SEEING BLIND

Cridon celebrated his sixth birthday on Tek Island with many friends from a place called Epertase. He'd asked about Epertase a few times, but his mother had always insisted it wasn't important. Cridon heard his father getting ready to leave, so he grabbed his wooden sword from his bedroom and met Rasi at the front door. "Can I go with you, Dad?"

Rasi nodded. *Tell your mother.* Though he had learned to speak fairly well without his tongue, he still used mindspeak whenever possible because he said he didn't like the sound of his words. Cridon didn't think his father sounded odd, but being able to hear mindspeak made him feel special.

Cridon excitedly bobbed his head as he raced through the house, shouting for Alina.

"What's the emergency, Cridon?" she asked from the hall.

"I'm going with Dad." He didn't wait for an answer and raced past Rasi through the front door. "Come on, Dad." He waited out front for Rasi to kiss Alina goodbye and then catch up.

As they walked, Cridon asked, "Hey, Dad, who's Thasula?"

Rasi stopped and tilted his head. *Where'd you hear that name?*

"I heard Mom tell you she missed Thasula last night."

You mean when you were supposed to be in bed?

Cridon grinned.

Thasula is a city far away from here.

"Why's Mom miss it?"

She grew up in Thasula.

"Oh. Can we go there so Mom doesn't miss it anymore?"

Rasi playfully rubbed Cridon's hair. *You know, you ask a lot of questions.*

They walked past one of Leander's factories. Already forgetting Thasula, Cridon asked, "What do they make in there?"

Weapons.

"For what?"

Protection.

"Why?"

Same reason I teach you how to use your sword.

Cridon held up his wooden sword and examined it. He liked the noisemaking weapons the soldiers sometimes practiced with better, and said so.

Swords are important.

"Why? You don't even have to be close to the bad guys with the Tek weapons."

What would you do if your Tek weapon didn't work and the bad man you were fighting had a sword?

"I'd … Well … Hmph." Rasi was right. When Cridon saw Leander at the front of the Tek army, he started running and shouted, "Race you, Dad."

One of Rasi's straps grabbed him from behind and pulled him back as Rasi blew past. Every time Cridon tried to pass his father, Rasi's straps pulled the same maneuver. Rasi was the first to reach Leander's side. Cridon smacked Rasi's hip. "You cheated."

Rasi laughed. *No, I used my advantages.*

Cridon groaned. Then he looked toward the massive Tek army standing in formation, quickly forgetting his defeat. Leander tapped his shoulder. "Good morning, Cridon."

Cridon answered without looking back, "Good morning, sir."

Leander addressed Rasi. "Shall we?"

Rasi nodded. Christopher soon joined them and they started walking along the front line of soldiers. Cridon mimicked them from behind, but it was hard for his little legs to keep up while marching.

Eventually, Rasi, Leander, and Christopher stopped and faced the men. Cridon did the same, regarding his father to be sure he had copied his posture perfectly.

Rasi glanced down with a subtle grin. He raised his hand. Cridon did the same. The deafening screech of a thousand swords leaving a thousand sheaths made Cridon flinch, as it did every time. Early on, he'd stopped trying to cover his ears after he saw that his father never covered his.

Leander shouted, "On my command …" He paused and surveyed the men. "Begin."

As if strung together like puppets, the men began their rhythmic morning exercises. They plunged their swords forward, spun with their swords drawn back to their bodies, and then slashed imaginary targets behind them. They were so close to each other that a single mistake by one soldier could be fatal to another, but they were skilled and precise. They were, as Leander liked to say, "well-oiled machines," whatever that meant.

Though he tried to be still, Cridon grimaced at the noise. When a whole army grunted at once, the sound was thunderous. Rasi nudged him with a strap and then pointed back toward the factory where Meela crouched in a field of flowers. *You've done well today, son. Now go play with Meela.*

Meela wasn't paying attention. With a mischievous grin, Cridon formed a devious plan. He'd never successfully sneaked up on her without getting caught, but he was confident he could this time. He ran half the way before dropping into a crawl. He felt like a predator. Like a fisher.

Meela sat with her back toward him and sniffed a flower she'd picked. Cridon glanced back at Rasi, who watched with a skeptical grin. Cridon continued forward, slow and silent. It was the closest he'd ever gotten undetected. He was ready to pounce when Meela's ears perked. He held his breath and leaped.

Meela spun like lightning and snatched him from the air. Startled by her speed, he squealed. She laughed and laid him on his back in the flowers. Her high-pitched laugh always made him giggle. She turned and ran. He scrambled to his feet and gave chase. She slowed just enough for him to catch her. He dove at her legs. She feigned injury and flopped forward into the grass. He landed beside her, still giggling so uncontrollably that he couldn't catch his breath.

She snorted and tickled his side, not giving him a break from his laughter. He covered his eyes and begged, "Meela, stop. I can't breathe."

And then she stopped. He peeked past his fingers. Suddenly preoccupied, Meela sniffed the ground, maybe for a tasty worm or something. She was easily distracted by food, which gave him a fresh advantage. He got up and ran.

She abandoned her potential snack and gave chase. She shot past him and spun around. Cridon's momentum carried him into her outstretched arms. He laughed even harder as she tickled him again. With no other choice, he shouted her magic words: "I love you, Meela." Once he said that, she had to stop no matter what. It was their rule.

She plopped down in the grass beside him. "Iieee love you, too, Criieedon."

He rested his cheek on her arm.

"Are you still haveeng bad dreeams?" she asked.

Cridon nodded.

"What are they showeeeng you now?"

Cridon stared at the ground. "They show me another place that I don't recognize. A dark wizard is looking for me. No matter where I hide, he always finds me. I'm afraid he's looking at me right now. He says I have something he needs to fix the world. I know the world is dying for some reason, but I don't feel like he can fix it."

"Iiee am sorree you have theese dreeams."

He lifted his eyes. "Are they real, Meela? Is a dark wizard coming for me?"

Meela lowered her head. "Have you asked your father?"

"Uh-hm."

"And what does hee say?"

"He says I shouldn't worry."

"Then Iiee beelieeve you should listen to him." She smiled, and her smile was comforting.

He leaned forward and looked into her milky eyes. "Why can't you see, Meela?"

She appeared to stare over his head. "Myee peeople have not been able to seee since the days of Keeng Matthew."

Cridon stood up and put his face closer to hers, cocking his head and gazing into her blank eyes. "I don't like that you can't see. It doesn't seem fair."

Meela grinned. "It is what it is."

"Well, I don't like it." He leaned in and kissed her cheek. As he pulled away, he hesitated and touched her shoulder. Almost in a trance, he whispered, "I wish you could see."

A flash of lightning crackled across the clear sky. He flinched. Meela tilted her head curiously. The air tickled his neck.

She gently pushed him away.

"What's wrong, Meela?"

She turned. "Notheeng. Notheeng is wrong. Wee neeed to get you back home."

She scooped him in her arms and galloped toward the Tek city without another word spoken.

CHAPTER 25

RECURRING NIGHTMARES

Rasi lay awake as the dawn suns rose. He didn't have much use for sleep anymore and, even if he had, his racing mind rarely slowed enough for him to enjoy it. Alina was sound asleep beneath the covers at his side. Careful not to disturb her, he slid his feet off the bed and sat up. His straps carefully untangled from around her. She stretched and rolled over, but didn't wake.

Rasi sneaked from the room. As he pushed the door closed and turned toward the stairs to the kitchen, he heard a soft moan from Cridon's room at the other end of the hallway. He listened carefully.

Cridon moaned again, this time a little louder. It was likely another nightmare. The bad dreams had grown more frequent over the last year, and it tore Rasi apart that he couldn't help his son stop them. He walked down the hall and peeked into Cridon's room.

Cridon tossed and turned beneath the covers, his hair and pillow drenched with sweat. He stretched and moaned, then curled into a shivering ball. Rasi sat on the bed next to him and pulled down the sweat-soaked blanket. He reached for a cloth on the nightstand and dipped it into a pitcher of water they kept by Cridon's bed.

While dabbing Cridon's forehead, he whispered into his mind, *You're all right, son. Nothing will hurt you.*

Cridon didn't open his eyes, but mumbled, "I have to go back."

Back to where, son?

Cridon rolled onto his other side with his back toward Rasi. He mumbled again. "The Star's Light needs me."

Rasi froze. *What light, son?* How could Cridon know about the Light? He and Alina had vowed to keep it and most everything about Epertase secret until he was old enough to understand.

Cridon answered without opening his eyes, "It is broken." He rolled back toward Rasi. "It is broken," he mumbled again. "It is broken." He shivered.

Rasi retrieved a folded sheet from the foot of the bed, scooted Cridon to the dry side, and covered his boy with the fresh sheet. Cridon repeated, "It is broken," until he finally drifted into a deeper, more peaceful sleep.

Rasi rubbed his back for a bit before kissing his cheek and heading back to his own room. Though he was careful and quiet, Alina sat up when he closed the door. *I'm sorry I woke you.*

"It's all right. Did Cridon have another nightmare?"

He nodded.

She patted the bed beside her and whispered, "That isn't the only thing on your mind lately, is it?"

He shook his head.

"Sit down. Tell me what's bothering you."

Rasi sat, his straps sprawling across the bed like they owned it. One even nudged Alina out of its way. *Did you tell Cridon about the Light?*

"Of course not. We swore not to tell him until he was older. Why?"

His nightmares are getting worse. Tonight, he asked about the Light. Though he called it the Star's Light, whatever that means.

"How could he know about the Light? Who could have told him? Atticus would never. Meela?"

I don't believe anyone told him. That's not all he said. He told me something else, something Meela once said when I was in the fisher caves. He said the Light is broken.

Alina sighed.

Alina?

"It's just that … well … Cyn said the same to me. She said the Light had been broken for a long time and that Tevin was going to fix it. Do you think the Light is calling Cridon to Tevin?"

I don't know. He paused, and she leaned forward to look into his eyes.

"What is it, Rasi? I know you too well. Is there something else you're not telling me?"

He nodded. *It's something Meela told me last night.*

"Go on."

She said for the first time in her life she could see the brightness of the suns. She said it hurt her eyes.

The lines deepened on Alina's forehead. "I don't understand."

She can see. Unsure he wanted to finish the story, he paused and studied the wall. Finally, he said, *Meela said Cridon gave her sight.*

"Cridon? What do you mean, he 'gave her sight'? How could that be? Where is Meela? I wish to speak with her."

He dropped his head. *She's gone.*

"Gone? Where?"

She said she needed to be with her people.

"But you said they would kill her if she ever returned. Why didn't you stop her?"

I tried. But she was resolute. She said they would forgive her when they learned she had sight. I tried to convince her to stay, but she said she had to leave immediately.

"Oh no. Cridon will be crushed."

I know.

"How do we tell him?"

"Tell me what, Mommy?" Cridon stood in the doorway and rubbed his eyes.

Alina leaned past Rasi to see him. "Come here, buddy."

He climbed up next to her, maneuvering around Rasi's rude straps.

She held his hand. "Honey, I'm afraid Meela needed to leave for a while."

"What do you mean?"

"She had to go home to see her family. She's been away from them for a long time. And they miss her."

Rasi rubbed his back. *She told me to tell you that she loves you very much and will see you again soon.*

Cridon's lower lip puffed out. "Is it because of what I did?"

Alina hugged him. "No, no, honey. You didn't do anything wrong. She just needed to be with her family."

"But I'll miss her."

"I know you will. We all will. But you have to have faith in her parting words and know you'll see her again." She pulled him close and looked sadly at Rasi.

Rasi lowered his head and looked away. *We should go see Doc Eckels.*

Alina agreed.

Doc Eckels was just opening his doors when Rasi, Alina, and Cridon arrived. His eyes brightened at the sight of his friends. "Come on in." He escorted them into his clinic and handed Cridon a wooden lap game to keep him occupied. While Cridon played, the adults walked out of earshot.

"What brings you out this early morning?" Eckels asked.

Rasi looked to Alina to answer. "Meela, actually," she said.

"Meela? Is she all right?"

"Yes, she's fine. Actually, she's better than fine, and that's why we've come to see you."

"Oh?"

"Meela said Cridon somehow gave her sight."

The doctor tapped his chin. "Interesting."

Alina cocked her head. She looked at Rasi, confused, and then back to Doc Eckels. "You don't seem very surprised. Why is that?"

Doc Eckels paced with his hands behind his back. When he stopped, he said, "Your son is quite special. I've known since the night I delivered him on the boat. I can't explain what happened that night, but Cridon was born without life, and then, suddenly, he lived. I've never seen anything like it. I know you two are trying to pretend the Light doesn't exist within him, but it does. And I think it's more powerful than anyone could have imagined." He shook his head in amazement. "It makes sense, actually."

Alina's eyebrows went crooked. "How so?"

"Alina, you received the Light from your father when you were much older. Cridon was just a baby when Tevin unintentionally passed it to him. He's growing up with it. Everything he learns, he's learning with the Light already active inside him. I believe there's no telling what that boy can one day achieve."

Cridon sat playing, oblivious to being the center of their conversation a few feet away. Alina watched him lovingly. She didn't want him to be special; she just wanted him to be a boy like all other boys.

Eckels rubbed the back of his neck. "I wonder ..." He studied Cridon. "Do you think he could do it again? I mean, heal someone else's affliction?"

Rasi shrugged.

"Before now I didn't think he could do it once. What do you have in mind?" Alina asked.

"Masera will be here soon. He brings me breakfast each day. Maybe we could see if Cridon could help his legs."

Alina shrugged. "I don't see why we couldn't try." She called Cridon over.

He set the game on his chair and ran to them.

Doc Eckels knelt with a smile. "Hello, Cridon."

"Hello, sir."

"Do you know who Masera is?"

Cridon giggled. "Of course I know who Masera is. He has the broken legs."

"Yes, that's him. I was wondering, would you do something for me?"

"Sure."

"Do you think you could talk to Masera about his legs?"

Cridon looked to Rasi for approval and Rasi nodded. "What should I talk to him about?"

"I don't know. Maybe help him with his legs like you helped Meela."

"Oh, like with her eyes?"

"Yes. Exactly."

Alina glanced at Rasi.

Cridon picked at a thread hanging from his shorts. "I can try, I guess. But I don't feel like it'll help much."

"No?"

He shook his head. "I don't feel it."

"Did you feel it with Meela?"

He bobbed his head. "Um-hm."

"Will you try with Masera anyway?"

"I guess."

"That would be wonderful. Thank you."

As Doc Eckels grunted with the effort to get up with his old knees, Josephine helped Masera through the door. Masera sat in a wheeled chair the Teks had designed for him.

Doc Eckels clapped his hands together. "Masera. We were just talking about you."

"Is that so? Discussing my staggering good looks, I assume."

"No. Well, only Rasi." Eckels shot Rasi an ornery smile.

Masera rolled his chair to them and shook Rasi's hand. He bowed his head to Alina. She smiled. "Masera. Josephine. How are the newlyweds this morning?"

Josephine blushed. "We are as happy as ever, thank you for asking."

"Masera, would you do me a favor?" Eckels asked.

"I suppose."

"Would you talk to Cridon about your legs?"

Masera wrinkled his forehead.

"I know it's a strange request, but I'll explain later."

"Sure." He lightly smacked Cridon's shoulder. "Come on, kid." He wheeled himself to where Cridon's game sat. Cridon climbed onto the chair.

Doc Eckels, Josephine, Alina, and Rasi watched from across the room. Cridon listened intently while Masera talked. After Masera finished, Cridon leaned forward, said something, and then put his hand on Masera's knee. After he was finished, he grabbed his game and started playing again. Masera wheeled back to Doc Eckels and the others.

"Well?" Eckels asked, wide-eyed.

"It was a good talk. I told him a bad person hurt my legs."

"What did he say when he touched you?"

"He said he wished I could walk. I thought it was sweet and told him, 'you and me both, kid.'"

"Did you feel anything when he said it?"

"You mean besides general unease about how strange you three are acting?"

"Yes, yes. Anything else?"

"I can't say I did. What was I supposed to feel?"

The doctor's shoulders slouched. "Nothing. We were just testing a theory."

Alina touched Masera's shoulder. "Thank you all. We're going to head out now. It was good seeing you." She and Rasi gathered Cridon and left.

That night, Rasi opted to sleep in Cridon's room in case the nightmares returned. The chair was uncomfortable, with a wooden slat pressing against his lower spine, but he'd slept in worse places.

For the third time that night, Cridon tossed and turned and moaned, waking Rasi shortly after he had fallen asleep following the last nightmare.

"I don't know," Cridon mumbled, still clinging to sleep. "A lot of water."

Rasi sat on the bed and gently shook Cridon's shoulder. "No, Tevin," Cridon shouted, and sat up with bulging eyes. His stare burned through Rasi's chest, making Rasi turn to look at the empty doorway.

Hey, buddy. Wake up. It's all right. It's your dad. You're safe.

Cridon's eyes slowly softened, the blankness replaced with life. "Dad?" he whispered.

I'm here, son.

"Something's wrong."

What do you mean?

"I don't think I belong here anymore."

Why do you say that?

"There's a dark wizard searching for me. I saw him."

Rasi listened quietly as each word struck him in the soul. If there had been any doubt previously about what was happening, it couldn't be ignored any longer. The Light was pulling his boy back to Epertase and their days of hiding were over. A different plan was needed.

It was close enough to morning that Rasi allowed Cridon to get up to play. *Maybe we can make your mother breakfast before she wakes.*

Cridon nodded enthusiastically.

Rasi started to stand, but Cridon grabbed his hand. "Dad?"

What is it?

"Do you know a man named Simcane?"

Rasi sighed; his son was seeing too much. *What about him?*

"I saw him in my dreams last night. He scares me."

There's no reason to fear Simcane. He's our friend.

"If he's our friend, then we should help him."

Help him? Why? What's wrong?

"He's sick. And the dark wizard is going to find him soon."

Rasi's straps rose slightly and he called them back down. *Where is he, son?*

"He's in a house that I've never seen before."

You must think hard. Is there anything in your dream that you recognize? Anything that might give me an idea of where he is?

"I saw a barn outside the window."

A lot of people have barns. Anything else? Anything inside the house?

"Well … There's an open scroll on the table. That's how I knew the mean man's name. It said 'Simcane.'"

That's good, son. A million thoughts raced through Rasi's head. *Don't worry about Simcane. I'll take care of it. Come on. Let's make your mother breakfast in bed.*

Cridon's glee at the prospect of surprising his mother put the bad dreams back on the shelf. He and Rasi made Alina a bowl of oatmeal with fresh blueberries mixed in. A glass of tornment juice and a piece of toast smeared with strawberry jam completed the meal. Cridon crawled into bed with her as she started to stir. Rasi set the tray on the stand beside her. As Cridon revealed the surprise, Rasi dressed for the day. For the first time in years, he strapped his sword belt around his waist. He hated how it felt.

With most of Tek City either still sleeping or working the night shift in the factories or guard towers, Rasi rode his horse to Atticus and Celia's home. He knocked softly on the door.

It took a bit, but Atticus eventually came to the door with bloodshot eyes. He held a sword in one hand and his loose britches in the other. When he saw Rasi, he had to decide whether to drop his sword or his britches to shake Rasi's hand, and Rasi was relieved that he chose to drop the sword.

"What brings you here at this ungodly hour, Rasi?"

"Simcane."

"You've found him?"

"He's at Homer's old farm. Go get him."

"I'll gather a team and leave first thing."

Rasi nodded. "Gather Eldon and the others. Bring them all back here."

A smile touched Atticus's lips. "It's time, isn't it? We're finally gonna fight?"

Rasi nodded again. He didn't return Atticus's smile.

Atticus bobbed his head. "Perfect. I've grown tired of hiding. I'll have them here within two full moons." Atticus turned to go back into his house, but Rasi grabbed his shoulder. Glancing back, Atticus said, "I know, I know. Don't let them see me."

"That's not what I was going to say."

Atticus's hand fell to his waist. "You *want* them to see me?"

Rasi nodded.

"If they see me, they'll follow me here."

Rasi nodded again.

He shrugged. "If that's what you want. What kind of crazy plan is running through that strategic mind of yours?"

One that wasn't ready to be revealed yet. He said, "Patience."

"That's good enough for me."

Part of the reason Rasi hadn't told his friend everything was indeed that the details were still bouncing around in his head, but also in case Atticus was captured and Tevin had some type of interrogation magic. Like a good soldier, Atticus understood and didn't press.

Before Atticus ducked back into his house, he added, "I'd follow you into the gates of Hell, Rasi, because I know with you at our lead, we would walk out the victors with the devil's head on a pike."

Rasi appreciated the words.

When he returned home, he found Alina in her favorite outside chair reading a Tek book. She couldn't get enough of anything they wrote.

What are you reading today? he asked.

"It's about their machine gods and the different gods of all the cultures they've encountered."

Oh.

"You know, it says that in some parts of the world, people have personal gods that give them special powers."

Rasi rolled his eyes. *Yeah, right.* He sat in the chair beside her and reached for the book. *Besides a bunch of nonsense, how is it?*

She handed it over and shrugged. "Eh. Not the best one I've read."

The text was hand-written, the pages bound together with three curls of twine. The cover showed a crude drawing of clouds with angry eyes peering through. Rasi absently riffled through it. *Where's Cridon?*

She pointed toward the field beside the house. "Slaying ochrids again with his wooden sword. I don't know why you ever told him about those horrid creatures. By the way, where were you off to so early this morning?"

To see Atticus. We may have found Simcane.

Her eyes lit up. "That's wonderful."

Rasi set the book on the ground and then picked at a thumbnail.

Alina leaned over and rubbed his back between the straps. "What is it?"

Just saying the words was sure to set a new plan into motion, regardless of whether he was ready or not. *It's time to go back to Epertase,* he finally answered.

Alina's hand stopped on his back. Angst carved creases in her forehead. "Why?"

You don't want to?

"Of course I want to. But why now?"

We can't fight it any longer. The Light needs Cridon to go home. That's what his nightmares are about.

"But what about Tevin?"

I'm going to kill the bastard.

"And his army? I don't wish to kill Epertasians. My people may have accepted Tevin as their leader, but they're still my people."

Rasi didn't agree. *The men who draw swords against us are no longer your people. They must be seen as the enemy if we have any chance for victory. If we win, I promise to show them mercy, but that's the best I can do.*

"Do you really think we can win?"

He didn't answer.

"I'm ready to fight, Rasi. I've been ready. This place is nice, but it's not my home."

I know. Understand, though, this will be the final battle one way or another; there will be nowhere to go if we lose.

He stood up.

Her hand slid down his arm to his wrist. She kissed his hand. "I'm with you until the end of time."

He walked to the field where Cridon slashed at imaginary creatures from every angle. His boy was apparently surrounded and could really use some help. Rasi grabbed a stick and joined the fight.

"You get them over there, Dad."

Rasi danced and dodged and fought to the bitter imaginary end. Cridon giggled, and it was the greatest sound in the world. Rasi spent the rest of the morning playing with his son, knowing it was perhaps his last chance before the coming war. By the next day, planning would surely consume him. The future was as scary as it had ever been.

CHAPTER 26
TWINS

The surface of the pond near the edge of Homer's farm reflected a haggard face Simcane no longer recognized. His greasy hair kept falling over his eyes no matter how often he tucked it behind his ears.

Hungry today, yes?

Simcane nodded.

We should go to town today, yes?

Simcane shook his head, though he no longer knew why he refused to go to town.

But it would be so fun. You haven't let us kill anyone.

Simcane paused. They were right. He squeezed his empty hand. "Why did you forget my fishing spear?" he asked out loud.

You're the one who forgot it.

Simcane splashed mossy water onto his face and let it drip from his bird's nest of a beard. He wiped his eye and lifted his gaze across the pond.

A young man stared back. Seeing a stranger for the first time in years almost stole his breath. The angry voice said, *We should kill him.*

It wasn't a bad idea. Simcane rose to his feet, wondering if he could get around the pond before the man could flee. He locked gazes with the man for what felt like an eternity.

Go get him, the angry voice whispered.

"We won't reach him in time."

We'll never know unless we try.

The voice had a point. "Yes, I don't suppose we would." Simcane tested the stranger by taking a step to his left.

The young man mimicked him with a step backward. When Simcane froze, the man froze as well.

Get him. Now.

Simcane broke into a sprint along the water's edge. The man turned and fled toward the trees. When Simcane reached the final turn along the edge of the pond, the man reached his waiting horse, leaped onto it, and sped off down the road.

With the chase obviously futile, Simcane stopped.

You're too slow, his voice chided. *Pathetic, even.*

"You didn't tell me he had a horse."

I didn't know.

He groaned and turned back to Homer's house. "Do you think he'll tell anyone we're here?"

Why would he? No one even knows who we are anymore.

"I suppose you're right. We should eat something."

Maybe your fat ass could catch us a sloth.

Simcane drank from the pond, even though the same water had given him the runs only two nights before.

Simcane returned to the pond every night for the next week in hopes of seeing the stranger again. He sat on a tree stump next to a bucket holding the last trout he'd caught that afternoon. When he reached for it, the slippery bastard squirmed out of his grasp. Annoyed, he chased the fish around the bottom until he caught it. With his glower fixed on the other side of the pond, he bit a chunk out of the fish's side. While he chewed, he continued his vigil until it was too dark to see across the pond.

With another long day ended, he kicked the bucket over and stood up. His stomach rumbled, threatening another bout of the runs. He hunched over and waited for the cramping to pass. Once his stomach settled again, he headed back to Homer's house. Those long walks made him wish he still had the stolen horse, but the stupid voice had convinced him that horses made great meals. The voice turned out to be right. Stupid, but right.

Once inside Homer's bedroom, he lay on the dirty floor next to the bed. He hadn't slept for two nights and was exhausted. Whenever he had tried to close his eyes, the angry voice would whisper like a ticking clock, *Kill, kill, kill, kill, kill, kill, kill, kill,* until he couldn't stand it any longer. Tonight was no different. After a couple hours counting the cracks in the ceiling, he groaned and sat up. His eyelid weighed a ton.

"Why won't you just let me sleep?" he asked.

When you let us kill, then you sleep.

Simcane pissed in the corner before walking down the hall to the dining room. The scent of pine stopped him cold at the end of the hallway. He tried to remember if he had spilled pine resin earlier in the day, but then quickly remembered he hadn't used pine resin to start a fire in years.

His shoulders slumped. "Damn," he whispered. There was someone else there.

The angry voice whispered back, *Let's kill them.*

He just might.

A shadow shot across the open front door before the doorframe burst into flames. The heat quickly crawled across the floor and surrounded him. He turned to an open window that was filled with fire as well. Smoke thickened within the room, burning his throat and lungs.

Holding his breath, he buried his face in his forearm and rushed through the flaming front doorway. Despite his speed, the flesh on his legs and arms blistered from the heat. He tumbled from the porch, the unmistakable smell of burning hair polluting his nostrils.

The smell only preceded the pain by a second. He slapped his scalp until the flames were smothered. He started to get up, but an arrow plunged into his thigh and sent him back to the ground. "I though you protected me," he shouted to his swarming metal skin.

We didn't see it.

A man darted behind Simcane and cold steel opened his flesh. He instinctively arched his back to get away from the blade "And that one?"

Sorry. We're out of practice.

Another arrow whizzed past Simcane's neck and embedded in the porch frame. Pissed, Simcane pushed to his feet and limped around the house to get out of sight of the archer. As he rounded the corner, he came face to face with the man who had sliced his back. The man licked the blood from his blade.

"Turley," Simcane sneered. He hated the twins. "I guess your brother's the one with the arrows.

Turley grinned and lunged at Simcane's chest. The shifting metal skin finally deflected a blow. Turley's eyes went wide. Overconfident, he had fully committed to his attack, unaware of Simcane's metal friends. Simcane grabbed Turley's arm and pulled him close. Turley wrestled against his powerful grip, but he might as well try to push over an oak.

"Since when did Grissum become such a coward fighting with arrows from afar?" Simcane snarled.

Turley spat in his face.

Kill him.

"I'm working on it." Simcane smelled pine resin on Turley's clothes and smiled. With his scalp still throbbing, he heaved Turley against the side of the burning house. Turley's clothes burst into flames. He hit the ground and fled toward the field, ripping at his burning shirt.

Another arrow was deflected by the metal skin on Simcane's arm and plowed into his chest below his left collarbone.

Oops.

Simcane groaned and grabbed the fletching. "Yeah. Oops." He yanked the arrow out. Plenty of meat came with the barbed tip. A patch of metal skin sealed the wound. Simcane's head twitched twice to the side. He cursed under his breath and then hobbled toward Homer's barn with his eye fixed on the regrouping twins. Turley had stripped down to his skivvies. Smoke rose from his bright-red chest and shoulders.

Grissum dropped his bow and pulled out a knife the size of his forearm. The brothers gave chase. It was no secret that the twins were skilled and methodical in their hunts—their opening salvo proved as much—but their mistake was in letting Simcane gather himself.

As Simcane limped into the barn, he mentally prepared for the twins' next assault, despite the unfocused angry voice. *One ... Two ... Three ... Four ...*

"Stop it."

Oh, sorry.

He waited in the center of the barn next to the loft's wooden support column. He heard laughter that he first believed came from one of the twins, but as he concentrated harder, he realized it came from the voice.

"Shut up," he whispered.

Grissum ripped open the barn door. Turley stepped through first. Blisters had already risen across his chest. A blister near his left armpit had popped and fluid seeped down his side, leaving a glistening trail. His smile was full of hate as he drew a sword with a curved blade. "I'm going to kill you, Simcane. Slowly."

Grissum followed him and moved toward Simcane's left side while Turley stalked to the right.

Now can we kill someone? the angry voice asked.

"Yes," Simcane answered.

Grissum lunged. Simcane blocked with his forearm and the blade slid off the metal skin. With a punch at the air, Simcane used his gift to blast Grissum's chest, knocking him into the loft's support column. Debris rained from the loft. Simcane spun toward Turley as the assassin swung his curved blade. With a metal-coated palm, Simcane grabbed the blade and yanked it from Turley's hand and tossed it aside. The momentum pulled Turley closer. Simcane kicked him in the chest.

In his bloodlust, he had already forgotten the other twin. Grissum jumped on his back, stabbing at Simcane's neck over and over in hopes of getting past the ever-shifting metal.

Simcane staggered under the sudden weight. He reached over his head and grabbed Grissum's hair. Grissum hugged him tight. Simcane ripped out a fistful of hair in his attempt to dislodge the killer.

Turley retrieved his sword and charged.

Grissum whispered into Simcane's ear, "I've wanted to do this for a long time." He reached around and pressed the edge of his weapon against the side of Simcane's neck. Simcane's metal swarmed his throat and hardened just as Grissum dragged the blade across.

With the metal skin preoccupied, Turley drove his curved blade toward Simcane's exposed stomach. The metal shot from Simcane's neck as he grabbed Grissum's hand. Turley's blade plunged into his flesh as the metal arrived a split second too late. Simcane snapped Grissum's forearm and then grabbed Turley's hands around the sword hilt. Grissum's knife dropped to the dirt. Turley drove forward, his thrust pushing his curved sword through Simcane and into his brother's hip.

Simcane pulled Turley closer. With the blade lodged in his gut and Grissum still clinging to his back, he grabbed the back of Turley's head, knelt, and drove the assassin's face as hard as he could into the dirt floor. His fingers met the ground. Then he reached back, grabbed Grissum's shirt collar, and yanked him over his shoulder. From his back, Grissum grabbed the hilt protruding from Simcane's gut. Simcane winced and threw his weight backward, sliding free of the blade. He stumbled against the support column of the loft and Grissum bounced to his feet.

Simcane's metal skin swarmed over the wounds on his stomach and back and hardened. Blood filled his mouth. Grissum raised the sword over his shoulder.

Despite the tearing pain in his stomach, Simcane lifted a fist above his head. As Grissum grunted and swung his blade, Simcane drove his fist to the ground. His gift blasted the loft's support column, snapping it like a twig.

Grissum looked up and froze. The loft crashed down on them both.

A thick piece of timber, probably one of the very timbers Simcane had used to rebuild Homer's loft years ago, slammed into his chest, pinning him to the ground. Though his wounds were making it difficult to breathe already, if not for the timber across his chest coming to rest on another piece of wood, he wouldn't be able to breathe at all. He couldn't move.

The following silence told him Grissum wasn't moving either. For the first time since he could remember, the voice in his head wasn't telling him to kill. He closed his eye.

"Simcane," someone shouted through the fog of sleep. "Simcane."

He opened his eye. A familiar face stared down at him.

"It's me. Atticus. We're going to get you out of here." He turned and shouted, "Get the ropes, men. Start digging."

Though Simcane couldn't see the men Atticus spoke to, he could hear them clearing wood from the wreckage. Two of them secured ropes around the beam pinning Simcane's chest.

"Tie this to the horses," one of them shouted.

Within a few seconds, the beam shifted. When it was pulled completely free of Simcane's chest, he took the deepest breath he could. Atticus leaned over him again. "We're going to take you to Doc Eckels and get you patched up, buddy."

The soldier beside him spoke as if Simcane couldn't hear. "I don't think he'll make it, sir."

"Just get him back to the island. He's one of the strongest men I've ever met. Leave three men with me and leave one of the boats for us. Tell Rasi I'll gather Eldon and the others and return as soon as I'm able."

It took four men to get Simcane onto a plank tied to a horse. Simcane studied the strange faces dragging him away. *That was fun. Let's kill them too.*

"Shut up." For the first time in days, Simcane fell asleep.

CHAPTER 27

WHEN FRIENDS ARE STRANGERS

Alina and Irene were spending a pleasant afternoon doing laundry behind Irene and Homer's home. Leander kept insisting they take the clothes to the laundry-washing machines recently built near the center of town, but neither Alina nor Irene were convinced they would do as good a job as old-fashioned hard work.

Cridon was playing by himself in the yard while Rasi was in the spare-bedroom-turned-war-room with King Logan, Aidric, Leander, and a few other Tek commanders, where he had been strategizing almost nonstop since Atticus had left for Epertase. Christopher was the only one missing.

"By the way, how is Rasi doing?" Irene asked as she took one of Rasi's dry shirts off a clothesline.

"Oh, Irene, I worry about him. He only eats when I practically force-feed him, and he barely sleeps anymore. When I look into his eyes, they're always so dark and tired. He spends every waking moment trying to figure out a way to win against Tevin, but I know he doesn't believe there is one."

A palpable silence settled over them as Irene quietly went back to emptying the clotheslines. After Alina's wicker basket was full, she carried it to her horse tethered in the side yard to exchange it for an empty basket. Movement in the street caught her eye. Someone was riding in a full gallop toward her. The rider shouted her name. It was Christopher.

"Come quick," he yelled.

She set the empty basket next to the full one. "What is it, Christopher?"

"Atticus has found Simcane. They're taking him to Doc Eckels's clinic now. He's terribly injured."

She left the baskets and climbed onto her horse. Before she could ask, Irene shouted, "I'll stay with Cridon. He'll be fine."

Alina and Christopher raced to town.

At the clinic, a crowd of curious onlookers had formed. Several Teks stood guard at the door, keeping the gawkers outside. As Alina approached, they parted and one of the guards said, "Go on in, Queen Alina."

Inside, several Teks huddled around a curtained-off bed at the back of the clinic. "Doc?" she called as she crossed the room.

Doc Eckels stepped from behind the curtain. He solemnly looked at Alina and shook his head.

"Oh no," she gasped.

He pressed his lips tightly together and the corners drifted downward. "He has been run through by a sword."

Alina covered her mouth—she knew what that meant.

"He also has a bad infection and a collapsed lung."

"Is he awake?"

"No. He's been unconscious since he arrived."

"Will he live?" Part of her didn't want to hear the answer.

"Quite honestly, it could go either way. Anyone but Simcane wouldn't have survived the trip. If he beats the infection, which I'm treating as best I can, he will have a chance. But it's difficult to determine how much damage has been done without cutting into his belly."

"You're going to operate?"

He shook his head. "I think his best chance is to wait and hope. It could be a while before we know anything, though." He paused as if he wanted to say something else. Alina encouraged him to continue.

"There's something you should see."

"Oh?"

Doc Eckels parted the curtains and then ushered Alina to Simcane's bedside. Simcane didn't look like the same man she had known. Aside from the full beard and long, dirty hair, his face was gaunt and sickly, and he must have lost at least three stone since last they met. She felt the heat of his fever without even touching him. She sat on a chair beside his bed and held his hand while Christopher's cousin, who had trained in Tiffin as a nurse, dripped water onto his forehead.

Alina turned to Eckels. "He's so hot. Won't his brain cook from the fever?"

"Maybe. That's why we're keeping him as cool as we can. In fact, it's almost time for another soaking."

She leaned close to Simcane's ear and whispered, "You have to fight, my friend."

A Tek soldier brought a fresh bucket of cool water from one of their amazing ice machines and set it next to the nurse. Alina touched Simcane's cheek. "I'll leave you now so you can concentrate on getting better." When she caressed the side of his face, a silver blotch swarmed up his neck from beneath the sheet and hardened beneath her touch. She jerked her hand away and stood up. She turned her frightened eyes to Eckels. "What is …?"

"That's what I thought you should see."

"How? I mean …"

"I don't know."

Images of Cyn and Scorne and the other symbiots flashed past her eyes and she staggered.

Eckels gently grabbed her arm to steady her. "Are you all right?"

Her hand covered her chest. "Yes … Um … Just let me know when he wakes, please."

"Of course. Do you need a drink or something?"

"No. I … I just need to get back to Cridon. Thank you, Doc. Take care of our friend."

She backed through the curtain as the nurse pulled the sheet down from Simcane's chest. More of the metal skin covered a festering wound on his gut. He had another rotten hole the size of an arrowhead near his collarbone.

She pulled the curtain closed, wondering how she could have possibly lived such a peaceful life for so many years while her dear friend fought the world in her stead. As she stood helpless outside the curtain, she said a prayer to her gods, the machine gods, and any other gods who might be listening for his speedy recovery.

The ride home was full of guilt and worry. If someone as strong as Simcane had faced such torment, what had happened to everyone else she had known and loved who couldn't be with her on the island? One thing she did know was that Rasi was right—the time to return was long overdue.

CHAPTER 28

PEPPERBUGS

A tticus and his three Tek companions, Ulery, Wheaten, and Slone, led their horses through the forest that bordered Eldon's land. In each city they had passed through, no one had paid them much attention, more concerned with keeping to themselves than the affairs of others. He wondered how many other Hernon-type kill squads Tevin employed to keep everyone living in such fear.

Atticus examined the trail. "If I remember correctly, we haven't much farther to go," he said. He hacked through some particularly dense brush. "In fact, I'd say we—" He stopped, his forehead creased.

Beyond the brush was an ocean of strange bushes that stretched in both directions for as far as he could see. He didn't remember seeing such bushes when he'd traveled to Eldon's home for Rasi's wedding, but that had been years ago. Something about the bright purple leaves heightened his nerves, though he couldn't remember why.

He lifted his hand, stopping his companions. What was it about those leaves that bothered him so?

He glanced back at the others. Wheaton shrugged. A low buzz like that from a hornet's nest, accompanied the foul odor of curdled milk. Before Atticus could turn back to the bushes, Ulery flinched and smacked the back of his neck as though he had been touched by a lightning bolt. "Ouch," he shouted.

Then Slone twitched his nose and made a pained face before sneezing. Atticus's nose began to tickle as well, as if he had sniffed pepper. His eyes widened. The buried memory that had caused his apprehension surfaced, filling him with dread. *Oh no.* A long-forgotten nursery rhyme came vividly to mind as though he had heard it only the day before.

> *If wandering through the forest,*
> *A purple bush you see.*
> *Rub your skin with leafoil,*
> *'Ere the pepperbugs come for thee.*
> *But if a scout doth bite you,*
> *Great illness will be known,*
> *And pepperbugs will swarm you,*
> *To tear skin from bone.*

He spun back to the nearest bush and grabbed a handful of purple leaves. Ulery staggered and then dropped to his rear. Atticus's stomach sank. Racing back to the others, he shouted, "Ulery's been bitten by a pepperbug scout." That meant nothing to them. He handed leaves to the other two men. "Rub the oil on your flesh. Hurry. Don't miss any exposed skin."

"What about Ulery?" Wheaton asked.

"We have to get him away from here. The bite from the scout will draw the others to him." The buzzing from the waking pepperbugs grew louder. Though they were infinitely slow to stir, they were infinitely deadly once they did. "There'll be more scouts nearby," he shouted. "We don't have much—" One of the horses neighed and bucked as though it had been smacked in its hindquarters. It wobbled and staggered off the trail. Atticus shouted, "When you're done covering yourselves with the leaf oil, cover the horses as well. Hurry." Atticus squatted next to Ulery and rubbed the leaves on him as the stricken man vomited. One bite from a scout was torturous, but more bites would be devastating. After Ulery's skin was colored a purplish tint from the leaves, Atticus began covering himself with the oil.

Before he finished, a stinging pinch exploded in his left wrist, stopping him cold. He squashed the violet mosquito-like bug, but the damage had already been done. Ignoring the agonizing burning that raced up his arm, he continued rubbing the oil over the rest of his exposed flesh while the buzzing grew louder from the bushes.

Atticus turned to the horse that had been bitten. His vision swam with a double image of identical horses staggering drunkenly. A sudden wave of nausea washed over him and he, too, staggered.

Slone ran to his side. "Come on, sir. We gotta go."

Atticus pointed to the stricken horse as a black cloud of insects lifted from one of the bushes and descended on it. The horse bucked for a moment and then flopped to its side. Atticus had never heard a horse scream like that before, and he hoped never to hear such a sound again.

Slone and Wheaton hoisted Ulery onto Wheaton's horse and then helped Atticus onto his horse.

"You have to hold on," Slone shouted. Atticus grabbed a handful of mane and squeezed as tightly as he could. Wheaton climbed up behind Ulery, and Slone mounted his own horse and grabbed the reins of Atticus's. They tore off at a gallop.

Atticus fought desperately to hold on as the blur of purple plants zipped past. His wrist festered with white, bubbling pus. The buzz of the pepperbugs grew louder as the insects gave chase.

"Where do we go?" Wheaten screamed.

Atticus was too weak to answer, even if he knew. Slone and Wheaton led Atticus's horse through the trees, darting left and then right, the ever-constant buzz of insects behind.

"Where do we go?" Wheaton shouted again, panic growing thicker in his voice.

Atticus wanted to tell Wheaton he was safe because of the leaf oil, but he couldn't make the words. Holding on to his horse was taking all he had. He wouldn't make it much farther.

With Atticus's strength fading fast, the men burst from the tree line into an overgrown field. He saw a house in the distance. It was Eldon's. As they rode toward the front, a single figure bolted from the door and shot across the field toward them. Even from such a distance and with such blurry eyes, Atticus recognized the smooth, lanky stride of his towering Gildonese friend.

No, Eldon. Run the other way.

Eldon stopped and waited at the center of the field directly in their path. Slone was the first to ride past. Then Wheaton, with Ulery draped over his saddle. Eldon shouted, "Keep going. I'll catch you next."

As Atticus's horse galloped by, Eldon snagged the saddle and, with the fluidity of a water snake, hoisted himself up.

"Where did the scout bite you?" he shouted.

Atticus struggled to hold up his wrist while Eldon supported him. Eldon grabbed his hand and shoved the wound into his mouth. He sucked the white pus with such strength that he nearly swallowed Atticus's hand whole, or so it seemed. After spitting out the pus, he shouted, "They shouldn't follow you anymore. Now let me help your friends."

Eldon steered Atticus's horse toward Wheaton and Ulery and raced to catch up. "Can you hold on?" he asked.

Atticus felt his strength already returning. He nodded weakly.

Eldon stood up on the saddle, balancing with apparent ease. Wheaton glanced back.

"Are you completely covered with leafoil?" Eldon shouted.

"Yes," Wheaton shouted back.

"Then fall from your horse. If you haven't been stung by a scout, you'll be safe from the pepperbugs."

Wheaton hurled himself to the grass. He tumbled along the ground as Eldon leaped from Atticus's horse to Wheaton's. As Ulery started to slide from the saddle, Eldon grabbed him with one hand and pulled him back up.

Atticus slowed his horse to a stop as the pepperbug cloud blazed past. Exhausted as though he had been in a days-long battle, he couldn't keep his eyes open and slumped over the horse's neck.

The suns seemed extra bright through the open shades of Eldon's window as Atticus squinted and slowly focused his eyes. The room hadn't changed a bit since last he'd visited. He sat up and stretched with a groan. He felt rested and strong. His wrist was sore beneath a moist bandage. "Eldon?" he called.

His Gildonese friend peeked into the room. "Ah. My friend Atticus. You are awake."

"I suspect it's only because of you."

Eldon humbly shook his head. "Nonsense. I just happened to be here. I would thank your gods before thanking me."

Atticus's next thoughts went to his three Tek friends. "What about the others?"

"They're all fine, including the man named Ulery who had a nasty case of pepper-sickness. They're waiting for you in the other room. I have prepared a feast as a welcome."

"How long have I been asleep?"

"Only since yesterday. It takes nearly a day for my healing salve to counter the toxins from the sting. Your friend Ulery woke up just before you did. We will have plenty of time to talk over dinner, but for now, I must get back to my cooking and the hilarious stories I'm telling your friends. Go ahead and get dressed and come out whenever you feel up to it." He pointed to Atticus's clothes—clean and neatly pressed—draped over the back of a chair.

After dressing, Atticus joined the others in the main room. Gillian and Willum were the first to greet him. He imagined his own smile at seeing them likely eclipsed theirs combined. Gillian gave him a hug and Willum enthusiastically shook his hand.

"You two look well," Atticus said with relief.

"That we are," Gillian replied. "We've been waiting years now to hear from Rasi. Is he alive?"

Eldon lifted his eyes from his cooking pot at the mention of Rasi's name.

"Very much so," Atticus answered. "And he's eager to return."

"Where have you been hiding all these years? There hasn't even been whispers of where you could be."

"We hide on Torick Island with the Teks. They took us in and have pledged their small army to Rasi and Queen Alina."

"Queen Alina is alive as well? Thank the heavens."

"We wanted to come for you sooner, but we worried it would be too risky. Now Rasi feels it is time to take that risk. He is going to need a lot of help if he is to have any hopes of winning the coming war."

Gillian blurted, "But of course. We have been waiting for this day."

Eldon's feast of vegetables, deer meat, and wine was a welcomed treat for Atticus and the Teks after so many days of travel. Next to the meat on Atticus's plate was a dead, tiny, winged bug.

"And what's this?" Atticus asked, pointing with his fork. There was one on everyone's plates.

Eldon grinned. "I took the liberty of catching a few pepperbugs for your pleasure."

"You eat these?" Atticus asked.

"Oh, yes. They are quite complimentary to meat. Smoosh it in and give it a taste."

Atticus did as recommended. The first bite lit his taste buds with a salty sweetness he had never tasted before. The others had waited to see his reaction before digging in themselves. There was something oddly satisfying about feasting on the very insect that had nearly taken his life.

He studied the others as he ate. Everyone seemed in good spirits. Gillian sat so close to Willum that she was almost in his lap.

"I see married life is treating you both well," Atticus said.

Willum rolled his eyes. Gillian's stern glare sent him frantically searching for a way out of the hole he had just dug. "No ... I mean, everything is wonderful. How could it not be with such a beautiful angel at my side?"

With a half-scowl she answered, "That's what you'd better say." She leaned in as if for a kiss, but when Willum puckered up, she jabbed him in the gut instead. Then she smiled and resumed eating.

Atticus shoved the last bite of deer into his mouth while wishing for more despite his full belly. "So, you live nearby?" he asked Willum.

"Yep. Eldon has been kind enough to share his property. We built a house together."

"And are there any little ones sharing that home with you?"

Gillian grinned from dimple to dimple. She looked at her belly and answered, "Not yet."

After everyone had eaten, Eldon shoved his plate away, leaned back, and crossed his arms. "Well, let's get to it. What's Rasi's plan for Epertase?"

Atticus wiped his mouth with a napkin before answering. "Actually, I don't know. My orders are to send you to Tek Island with these soldiers. After that, I'm to go to Thasula and give Tevin a show."

"I don't understand," Eldon said. "What do you mean by a show?"

"You know, let him know that we're still alive and well."

"He'll kill you. Actually, he won't kill you. He'll have you followed to find out where Rasi and Alina hide. If Tevin is as powerful as these two have said, why would you go to Thasula and, as you put it, give him a show?"

"That's what Rasi wants me to do. I learned long ago to trust him when he has a plan."

"It is too dangerous for you to do this alone. I shall go with you."

Atticus shook his head. "I'm afraid not, my friend. Rasi was very clear that he needs you at Tek Island as soon as possible. Besides, I'm not planning on being captured, just noticed."

Eldon was a good enough soldier not to argue, though his skeptical eyes spoke volumes. After that, everyone went out onto the porch for more wine and conversation until night fell. Willum and Gillian made room in their home for Ulery, Wheaton, and Slone. Atticus stayed with Eldon.

When morning came, Atticus said his goodbyes, mounted his horse, and headed toward Thasula while the others prepared for the long journey to Tek Island.

CHAPTER 29

INSTIGATING A STORM

Atticus approached Thasula on foot with his horse in tow. Though it had been many years since he had been in Tevin's Epertase, he understood that being seen on horseback within the city limits would likely get him arrested on the spot. His sword was wedged under his saddle and well-hidden by an old, frayed blanket. He wore his hood drooped over his forehead and his scarf hid most of his face. By all appearances, he was nothing more than a weary traveler.

At the edge of the city, a couple of patrolling hylocks flew overhead. He waited beneath a tree for them to move on, which they quickly did. He entered Thasula's main drag, his head low and his eyes to the ground.

Three Epertasian soldiers rode toward him on what appeared to be a routine patrol. Atticus was careful not to make eye contact. When the people on the sidewalks stopped and bowed as the soldiers rode past, Atticus mimicked them. Then he turned away and brushed his horse's mane with his fingers.

One of the soldiers spoke as they passed. "Fine nag you have there," he said.

Atticus lifted his hand politely, turned with his eyes to the ground and his head bowed, and answered, "Thank you, sir."

When the soldier turned away, Atticus lifted his head. He didn't recognize the soldier who had spoken to him or the one at that man's side, but when he caught the profile of the third soldier, he winced. The man's name was Kessel and he was an asshole.

Atticus watched as Kessel crossed the road to an elderly lady standing in front of a blacksmith's shop. He pointed and snapped, "You, there."

"Me, sir?" she asked, trying to look up despite the hunch in her upper back. She moved with slow, careful movements.

Kessel shouted, "Everyone, gather 'round." A crowd formed. Atticus led his horse to the outer edge of the circle.

A little boy, probably nine or ten years old, stood on his tip-toes for a better view.

Atticus tapped his shoulder. "Hey, kid."

The boy looked up. Atticus handed him the reins of his horse. "Will you wait with my horse for a moment?" He handed him a piece of silver.

"Sure, mister."

Atticus mussed the boy's hair. Then he weaved through the crowd toward one of the mounted soldiers who watched the developing show. He faked a stumble and crowded against the soldier's leg. The soldier glanced down, annoyed.

Atticus bowed. "I'm terribly sorry, sir." He did his best to appear intoxicated.

"Drunkard," the soldier mumbled, and turned his attention back to Kessel. Atticus deftly reached beneath the horse's belly and unfastened the saddle's flank cinch.

When he turned back to the crowd, he met the eyes of an observant young lady. He put a finger to his lips. "Shhh."

She grinned and looked away.

Kessel continued addressing the crowd about "proper etiquette around Tevin's soldiers" or some such garbage while Atticus worked his way back to his horse and the young boy. "Thanks, kid," he said as he took back the reins. "You should probably run home now. It's gonna get a bit chaotic."

The boy lowered his head and walked away as instructed.

Kessel dismounted and continued, strutting around with his chest puffed out. "This rebel doesn't feel the need to bow when soldiers pass her by." He pointed at the old woman and circled her as he spoke. She cowered.

"I did not see you, sir," she said. "My mind was elsewhere."

"Get on your knees." Kessel moved behind her. She grimaced as she struggled to her knees while a man from the crowd rushed over to help.

Kessel put the sole of his boot on the back of the poor woman's shoulder and violently shoved her face to the dirt. She lay there motionless, too afraid to move. Or maybe too injured. Kessel spat on her for emphasis. The other two soldiers laughed.

Kessel shouted, "All of you can go home now. Just remember your manners from now on."

What Atticus was about to do was going to be a pleasure. Though Kessel had always been a bit insufferable, a little power had really emboldened his dickishness. Atticus waited for the crowd to disperse. After a glance to the sky to assure that the patrolling hylocks hadn't returned, he climbed onto his horse in clear defiance of the law.

It wasn't long before Kessel took notice. "You there," he shouted. "On the horse. Why are you on your horse?"

Atticus lowered the scarf from his mouth, pulled his hood back, and glanced over his shoulder. Then he lifted his middle finger.

Kessel's mouth dropped open. "Atticus?"

Perfect. "Kessel?" Atticus raised his hands in surrender. Kessel's two soldiers rode to each side of him with their hands on their swords.

Kessel stared in disbelief, unable to fathom that it was actually Atticus before him. "Atticus?" he asked again, only louder.

Atticus continued the game, eyes on Kessel's two soldiers. "Kessel, I'm just going to ride off. Please, pretend you never saw me."

"You know I can't do that. You're a wanted man. There's a reward for your capture. King Tevin would have my head if he knew

I let you flee. You must come with me. If you don't resist, I'll take you in personally so no one will harm you."

Or so no one else will get the reward, Atticus thought as he slowly lowered his hands to his reins.

Kessel shook his head. "What are you doing? Put your hands back up. There's nowhere you can go now."

Atticus shook his head. "I cannot do that." After another glance at the other two soldiers, he added, "You know, Kessel, I never did like you much."

"Yeah?" Kessel spat tobacco juice. "Well, I never much liked you either." He nodded to the soldier at Atticus's right.

When the soldier reached for Atticus's reins, Atticus punched him square in the jaw and sent him tumbling from his saddle.

The other soldier reached out. Atticus pulled the reins beyond the soldier's reach. As Kessel climbed onto his own horse, Atticus spun, gave his nag a kick and a lash, and raced down the street. The crowd watched, quietly rooting for Atticus's escape.

Kessel and the other soldier gave chase, but the soldier's saddle shifted and dumped him on the street. That left only Kessel, which was exactly what Atticus wanted. Once outside the city, Atticus circled around and slowed his horse.

Kessel stopped and looked around as if suddenly realizing he was alone with a most dangerous man. But even assholes could be brave. "You're coming with me one way or the other." His bravery made him stupid, though. He drew his sword.

Atticus lifted his saddle blanket and drew his own blade. "I'm not going back with you, Kessel."

"It's over, Atticus. Even if you escape me, Tevin will send his hylocks to track you. There'll be nowhere to hide."

Atticus shrugged. That's what he was counting on.

Kessel sighed. "Very well." He grunted and whipped his horse into a charge. Atticus met his advance. Kessel lifted his sword above his head; Atticus draped his blade across his body. The two men blazed past each other close enough that their knees brushed. Their swords clanged.

Atticus released his sword as though Kessel had won the exchange. The two men circled around for another pass. Atticus charged, despite being swordless. Kessel's blade swung toward his head. Atticus bent backward over his steed's hindquarters as the sword swung past his face. He plunged a knife from his waistband into Kessel's gut. The momentum threw him from his saddle to land hard. He quickly lifted his eyes as Kessel's horse slowed to a stop. Kessel gawked at the knife still lodged in his gut. He turned to look at Atticus with sad confusion in his eyes. Then he wobbled and fell from his horse.

Atticus wiped a clump of dirt from his forehead and retrieved his sword. Kessel groaned and rolled to his back. Blood leaked from the corner of his mouth. He stared at the sky.

"Atticus?" he whispered, and then coughed.

Atticus stood over him. "What is it?"

Despite the obvious pain, he got to his knees. "It's a mortal wound."

"I know."

"Will you give me a warrior's death before all the blood leaves me?"

Atticus nodded, not that the bastard deserved it. He circled around to Kessel's rear. Kessel bowed his head and closed his eyes. With both hands, Atticus grasped his sword hilt and rested the tip against the back of Kessel's neck. He placed one hand on the pommel and said, "I hope you choose the right path in the next world." Then he drove his sword into Kessel's spine.

Kessel's body went limp. Atticus cleaned his blade in the grass and retrieved his horse as the other two soldiers bolted from the city. Atticus had a good enough head start to lose them. If he didn't he'd kill them instead.

After he lost them in the woods, he slowed for a rest. As he rode, he tore off small pieces of his horse blanket and dropped them for the hylock trackers. He figured he didn't need to hit the creatures over the head with clues, but he also figured it wouldn't hurt to be sure.

He smiled. *And now it begins.*

CHAPTER 30

A SLEEPING
GIANT AWAKENS

*W*ake up.

Simcane groaned.

We've been sleeping long enough. There are plenty of people around here to kill.

Simcane opened his eye and took a few seconds to focus. He was in an unfamiliar bed, beneath an unfamiliar ceiling, surrounded by unfamiliar curtains. People talked just beyond the curtain, but fuzzy static in his ears prevented him from hearing what they said. He tried to sit up. Pain stabbed his stomach like he had swallowed acid. Each movement sent needles through the left side of his chest. His skin crawled as his metal slithered up the right side of his neck, over his chin, cheek, and forehead, and then back down the other side.

"Where are we?" he whispered.

In the enemy's den. We need to escape or we're dead.

"What if we—"

No. Listen.

"But …"

One … Two … Three … Four …

"All right. Stop."

Get up.

"I can't. It hurts too bad."

You're weak. We need to flee or they'll come back for us.

Simcane didn't know who "they" were and he didn't want to find out, either. He held his breath and yanked the covers from his bare chest with a grimace.

That's it. Push through the pain.

He winced and swung his legs over the side of the bed. The room spun, but the longer he focused the more the spinning slowed.

Hurry.

His feet touched the cold floor. With his first wobbly step he fell against a nightstand, knocking it over with a bang.

You're so stupid and loud.

The curtain at the foot of his bed yanked open and a man rushed to his side. "Simcane?" the man said as he grabbed Simcane's arm. "You need to lie back down."

Simcane glared at the man. "Who is he?" he asked the voice.

I don't know. Kill him.

The man's forehead wrinkled. "Simcane, it's Doctor Eckels. Don't you recognize me?"

Simcane shrugged his arm out of the doctor's grip.

"Easy, big fella. Let me help you back into bed." He tried to grab Simcane's arm again.

It's a trap. Kill him.

Ignoring the pain in his stomach, Simcane snatched the doctor's wrist and twisted. The doctor cried out nearly as loud as the snap of his breaking bone. Simcane released his crooked arm.

Doc Eckels pulled his hand against his chest and backed away, his eyes as wide as gold coins. "Simcane?"

Simcane used his gift to send a small push against the doctor, knocking him over the bed and to the floor. Even such a small use of his gift caused too much strain, and he fell to his knees.

Get up. They'll send more. Soldiers next time. You're too pathetic to fight them now.

Simcane pulled himself up with the edge of the bed. His stomach knotted and tore at itself. A wave of nausea had him vomiting blood onto the white bedsheet.

Doc Eckels rolled to his rear and fearfully scooted away. He shouted, "Simcane, you need to rest. I don't know what's happening to you, but I just want to help."

Liar.

Simcane steadied himself with his hand in the puddle of vomit. With his eye trained on his enemy, he staggered to the open curtain, pain hunching him over. He scanned the room for the next threat. It was a large room with beds lining both sides. A few of the beds were occupied by men who stared at him as he passed.

Let's kill them all before we leave.

"Soon," Simcane said. He continued through a door at the other end of the room and into a lobby. The street outside had a strange, hard, black surface stretching in both directions. Beyond one of the shorter buildings across the street he could see the tips of trees.

"Sir?" someone asked from behind, startling him.

Simcane spun with weak fists raised.

The man backed away and held his palms out in surrender. "Calm down, friend."

Though Simcane didn't recognize his uniform, he had been in enough battles to know the man was a soldier.

Kill him. Hurry.

The soldier extended his open hand. "Simcane, right? Does Doctor Eckels know you're out here?"

Simcane looked down at the man's outstretched hand and then back up to his eyes.

I told you. They're all in this together.

Simcane grabbed the soldier's hand and squeezed. The man's legs weakened, and his face contorted. As he writhed in Simcane's powerful grip, he pried at Simcane's fingers with his free hand. Metal swarmed Simcane's forehead. He lunged forward and bashed his skull against the soldier's brow. The soldier dropped. Simcane released his suddenly limp hand.

A crowd had gathered. Simcane's eye shot back to the treetops. A forest was the only place to hide until he could gather his thoughts.

Don't leave. Not without killing them first.

Simcane jerked his head twice to the side. With other soldiers calmly telling him to "Relax," Simcane backed across the street.

They'll get you if you don't run.

Simcane looked around and then sprinted between two buildings toward the forest. Since the soldiers didn't give chase, only a wall stood in his way. He easily scaled it. His adrenaline held back the pain.

At least until he got to the forest.

CHAPTER 31

A VIOLENT
BETRAYAL

Rasi stood atop the city wall and watched the working Teks line the perimeter with wooden spikes. He spent most mornings walking alone atop the wall to clear his head, but even the beauty of a new day couldn't dispel the constant worry gnawing at his gut. He'd never faced such odds, even against the Teks, and his current plan required a lot of imagination and untested tactics.

Someone climbed the ladder behind him. He didn't turn, even when Alina touched his shoulder. His straps lay draped over the edge of the wall.

"Hi," she said.

He leaned his cheek against her hand. *How is Simcane today?*

"Doctor Eckels says his fever finally broke last night, which is positive news."

But he isn't awake yet?

"Not last I checked."

I hope he wakes up soon. I could use a healthy Simcane for the coming fight.

Alina walked to the edge of the wall and looked down at the working Teks. "How's the preparation coming along?"

"Heh." *As good as it could, I suppose.*

She turned to face him and brushed his hair from his face. "You look terrible." She touched the bags under his eyes. "You need a break."

He looked away.

She guided his chin back. "I'm serious, Rasi. This is killing you before the fighting even starts. Come home and see Cridon. He's been asking about you."

You don't understand.

"What don't I understand? You've been through many battles."

It's not the battle that troubles me.

"Then what is it?"

Rasi bowed his head, ashamed. In every fight he had been in, he at least thought he had a chance. This time was different. *I can't beat him, Alina. Tevin is too powerful. Even if I can lead our army to victory, it will be for naught because no matter how hard I try, I cannot devise a way to defeat a wizard as powerful as he has become.*

Alina hugged him and whispered into his ear, "We will find a way. I have faith in you. Just come home." She leaned back and stared into his eyes. "Come home, Rasi."

Rasi weighed her words while she coaxed him with pleading eyes. He didn't want to leave, but she was right—or maybe he just wanted her to be right.

She took his hand. "You've wanted to take Cridon out and teach him how to hunt. Why don't you do that today? Spend a few hours with him, take an afternoon nap, and then come back out here refreshed."

It's too late in the morning to find any game. We can hunt tomorrow.

"Rasi. Just take him out and teach him. It doesn't matter if you actually find anything. Just spend some time with him."

I really should monitor the men this morning.

"Leander can do it today." She pulled his hand toward the ladder.

He resisted her pull for a moment before reluctantly giving in. *Maybe for just a little while.*

"Perfect. Irene's making Cridon lunch and getting him ready."

You didn't even know I would agree.

She cocked her head with a look that said there was only one answer he could have given. He sighed and followed her down the ladder.

Cridon was ready and waiting on the front porch with a smile as big as a rashta's. Rasi gathered a water bladder, his bow with a quiver of arrows, and a wooden ladder that he slung over his shoulder.

Together they walked southwest to the outer wall, Cridon playing a game of tag with Rasi's straps. They used the ladder to scale the wall and continued into the forest where Rasi quickly found Cridon's first lesson. *Do you see that?* he asked, pointing to a tree with bark missing from its trunk.

Cridon nodded.

A buck has left his mark by scraping his antlers against that tree.

"Why do they do that?"

A bunch of reasons. Mainly to let other bucks know he's around. He wants to have babies and is leaving his scent for the doe.

Rasi knelt next to a pile of droppings and smashed a pellet between his fingers. Then he wiped his hand on his pant leg. *This is pretty fresh. There might be a buck nearby. Now we hide and wait.*

As the morning passed, he expected Cridon to grow restless and fidgety, but his boy didn't waver. He watched patiently over a nearby clearing. Rasi was proud. It might have been the longest Cridon had ever remained quiet aside from when he slept.

Fighting heavy eyelids, Rasi was about to call it a morning when Cridon tugged on his pant leg and pointed. Rasi followed his finger across the clearing to where a buck grazed.

"That's a big one," Cridon whispered.

Old, Rasi answered.

"How do you know?"

It has too big of a rack to be young.

The buck wandered across the clearing as Rasi and Cridon waited patiently. When the buck strolled within range, Rasi slowly lifted his bow and removed an arrow from his quiver. He took aim.

Cridon turned his head toward the buck and then back to Rasi with sudden concern.

Rasi concentrated. Though he wasn't an archer by trade, he was passable, mostly hitting his target when needed. He took a deep breath and held it.

Cridon looked to the deer again and then back to Rasi. He wrinkled his forehead. *Cridon, you're making it hard to concentrate. Sit still.*

"But I don't want you to shoot it, Dad."

His voice spooked the buck and it darted in a zigzag from the clearing.

Rasi sighed and relaxed the tension on his bowstring. *Son, why did you do that? We're hunting. This is how we gather food.*

"I didn't want you to hurt it."

Rasi lowered his bow and stood up. His straps sulked along the ground. *Why do you think we came out here if not to shoot a deer?*

"To teach me how to hunt. And you've taught me."

Rasi was torn. He was angry that such a fine prize was lost, but seeing Alina's compassion in his son made him proud.

"I'm sorry, Dad."

Rasi smiled. *It's all right, son. Did you learn anything, at least?*

"Um-hm."

Me too. Ready to head home?

"Are you angry with me?"

I've never been angry with you. I will always ... He trailed off as Cridon's gaze shifted to a spot behind Rasi and his eyes widened. Fear filled his face like he had seen Tevin himself. A branch snapped. Rasi's straps shot up as he spun to a find someone leaning against a nearby tree.

Sim? He almost didn't recognize his hunched-over friend beneath the beard and sickly physique.

Simcane glared through Rasi as though he didn't recognize his old friend. Rapid, shallow breaths fluttered his chest like he'd just run a marathon. He mumbled something that Rasi strained to make out. It sounded like, "Yes, I will kill them," but that couldn't be right. Rasi's straps snapped in the air as if they had heard as well.

Simcane pushed away from the tree and staggered toward them. He mumbled again, only louder. This time there was no mistaking his words. He said, "You're right. If we kill the boy with the Light, that'll kill them all." Drool dripped from his chin.

Rasi's eyes darted to Cridon. Simcane charged, a distant, crazed look in his eyes. Time froze. Rasi gave Cridon a shove. *Run.* Then two straps lunged at his old friend to slow him long enough that they could talk.

Simcane caught one strap in his powerful grip. Despite lacking his customary girth, he was still as strong as an ox. Crazy strong. The other strap wrapped around his forearm. Simcane yanked it toward him, jerking Rasi forward. Rasi dropped his bow and shifted his grip on the arrow.

Whoever this man was, it wasn't Simcane. As Rasi's momentum pulled him against Simcane's chest, he struck with the arrow, seeking to wound, not kill. Shifting metal skin like Cyn's hardened beneath the arrowhead, deflecting it. Panic filled Rasi. Simcane's fist connected with Rasi's cheek. The blow spun Rasi into a tree before he dropped hard to the ground. With the help of his straps, he bounced to his feet. He just needed to hold Simcane back long enough for Cridon to get away. A glance at his son froze his heart with dread. Not only had Cridon not fled, he was approaching Simcane fearlessly from behind.

"Mister?" he whispered with a soft and innocent voice.

An evil grin contorted Simcane's face. He slowly turned his head. "I know," he said. "I see him."

Rasi clenched his fists. *Oh, Cridon, why didn't you run?* A strap ripped a tree branch free and swung it, striking the back of Simcane's head. Simcane barely flinched. *Cridon,* Rasi shouted in his boy's mind. *Listen to me. You need to run now and don't stop until you find Leander.*

Simcane glanced over his shoulder. "We are going to kill you all," he said.

We?

Simcane twitched his head to the side. His metal blotches danced across his back, exposing a scabbing, festering wound. A trickle of blood leaked from it. He took a step toward Cridon and doubled over with a grimace. He lifted his head toward Rasi. It was the first time the real Simcane showed in his eyes.

"Rasi?" he groaned. "Kill me before it's too late. I can't control it anymore." After another violent twitch of his head, his eyes went blank again. He looked to the heavens and roared like a beast. Then he stood up straight, winced, and sneered. "It all ends today."

"What ends today?" Cridon asked.

Simcane answered, "Epertase."

That's all Rasi needed to hear. Old friend or not, Cridon's safety was all that mattered. Rasi pounced. *Cridon, run.*

Wait, Dad. I can help you.

Rasi landed on Simcane's back. *Damn it, boy. Get away from here now.* He hooked a strap around Simcane's waist and another around his metal-covered throat. With all his strength, he squeezed. Simcane staggered and dropped to his knees.

Rasi silently apologized before pounding his fists into the back of Simcane's head. He landed two powerful blows before some of Simcane's metal skin shifted from his neck to defend his skull.

Simcane roared and pushed to his feet. Rasi held on for the ride as Simcane reared back against a tree. The impact jarred Rasi loose, and he and his straps went momentarily limp. Simcane stepped forward, leaving Rasi to slide down the tree to his rear. Simcane grabbed his gut and fell to his knees. He gasped for air. Rasi struggled for breath as well.

"Shut up," Simcane shouted. "I'm trying. It's those damn tentacles." He pushed back to his feet and faced Rasi again. Rasi started to get up, but his chest seized, paralyzing him. Simcane lifted his foot. Rasi grabbed his ankle with two straps, but Simcane's foot still drove at his head. Rasi ducked to the side, but not fast enough to completely avoid the impact. Simcane's heel met his face.

The world flashed black. It could have lasted for a second or a week, he couldn't tell. He lifted his throbbing head and tried to focus, but the world was a blur. Simcane backed away as if satisfied. Rasi tried to push himself up with the tree at his back, but the ground whirled and tossed him to his side. He blinked away the blurriness enough to see Simcane stomp toward Cridon. Cridon stared up at him with innocent eyes.

Simcane fell to his knees, his palms pressed to his temples. "No," he screamed. "I won't do it. You can't make me hurt this boy." He pounded a palm against his head while Cridon looked on.

Why didn't you run, Cridon? Rasi used his straps and a tree branch to pull himself back to his feet. The spinning ground shoved him sideways once more and he hit the dirt again. His stomach turned and he vomited. The pressure built in his brain until he feared his head was going to explode. He lifted his spinning eyes back to Simcane. He wanted more than anything to get to his feet and buy his son time to escape, but his body failed him over and over. He started to crawl.

Simcane buried his face in his hands and openly sobbed. Cridon touched his shoulder.

No, no, no. Rasi reached out with his straps, but his son was too far away.

"I'm sorry, son of Alina," Simcane said coldly. "The Elder Three were right. I wish I had been stronger." Then he scooped the boy against his chest and roared to the gods.

Rasi screamed for him to stop.

The forest flashed bright white as if lightning had swallowed the world.

Rasi's palms fell from his eyes. He couldn't save his son. He would never forgive himself for being so weak. He begged the gods to give his body enough strength to get revenge on his one-time friend before Simcane killed him as well.

Simcane stood with his back to him and his head bowed. He seemed calm and at peace with what he had just done.

As if the gods heard Rasi's pleas, his legs finally answered his call and he pushed to his feet. He wobbled and steadied himself against a tree with an outstretched strap. He charged.

I will kill you for this, Simcane. His straps smacked the ground on each side like walking sticks to keep him steady and on course. Simcane turned with empty arms. "Where is he?" Rasi screamed. He wrapped a strap around Simcane's throat and pulled himself face to face with the murderer. Rage burned within his murderous glare. Beneath his strap he felt soft, fragile flesh instead of cold metal, so he squeezed tighter.

Simcane choked and gagged. His eyes bulged and his face turned cherry-red. A high-pitched wheeze escaped his mouth. As Rasi squeezed tighter, even the wheezes were muffled. As he waited for the proof of Simcane's soul leaving his body, he wondered why Simcane didn't fight back.

Simcane dropped to his rear and Rasi followed him down, never breaking his gaze. When Simcane flopped to his back, Rasi straddled him. If he'd had enough strength, he would have snapped the bastard's head clean from his body, but the fight had taken too much out of him.

As Simcane went limp, a hand touched Rasi's leg. Rasi ordered one of his straps to strike at the newest threat, but the strap refused.

The pink of Simcane's lips turned a bluish-white. His eyelid slowly closed. Breaking through Rasi's rage was the tiniest of voices.

"Dad?"

It must have been an angel.

"Dad. Stop hurting him."

The strap around Simcane's throat relaxed despite Rasi's demands that it finished what it had started. Stunned by his strap's defiance, he turned toward the angel's voice. But it wasn't an angel. It was Cridon. And he appeared alive and healthy.

As Simcane rolled to his side, coughing and hacking, Rasi scooped up his son and carried him out of Simcane's reach. He couldn't believe he really held his son. He quickly looked him over for injuries. Finding none, he set him down and ordered him to wait there. He turned back, standing between Simcane and Cridon, ready for the second round.

Cridon grabbed his leg. "Dad, stop. He isn't sick anymore."

Simcane sat up with a wince. "Rasi?" His voice was scratchy and damaged. "It's all right. It's me now."

Rasi glowered at him.

Simcane shook his head and rubbed his neck. "It was Cyn's metal skin. I couldn't fight it. I don't even know how I got here." He looked around. "Or where here is, for that matter."

Rasi listened, but didn't lower his guard.

Simcane looked to Cridon. "Thank you for helping me, kid." Then he looked back to Rasi.

"See, Dad. He's better now. You don't have to fight him anymore."

"He's telling the truth, Rasi." Simcane rubbed a hand over his face. "It was Cyn's metal. It got me that day on the Great Plains. I think it drove me mad. You know, the Elder Three once told me I would prove unworthy when I held Epertase's fate in my hands. I'm ashamed to say they were right. I'm so sorry, Rasi. I really was going to kill your son." He slowly stood up.

Rasi still refused to lower his guard. "Then why didn't you?"

Simcane looked to Cridon.

Cridon smiled. "I took away his monsters."

I don't understand, son. How?

Simcane shrugged. "When the boy touched me and whispered, 'I wish you weren't sick,' it was like the fog of a long, violent dream lifted and I could see clearly for the first time in years. Cyn's metal fell off and slithered away." He searched the ground as if looking for any remnants of liquid metal.

Simcane seemed sincere, but Rasi wasn't taking any chances. He kept a cautious watch as he knelt by his son. *Cridon, how did you help Simcane?*

"I just helped him."

I don't understand.

"It's the Star's Light, Dad. It lets me help people."

But you didn't heal Masera's legs.

"Because the broken Light didn't hurt him."

A thousand questions pounded Rasi's already aching brain. *But the Light didn't cause Simcane's infection either.*

Cridon looked cross at him. "Sure it did. A long time ago when King Thadius broke the Light, the metal that was on Simcane's skin was born. It is very old. And very angry."

How do you know any of this?

"My dreams show me."

Knowing the world as Rasi did, he could only imagine the other terrible things Cridon had seen in his dreams. After everything he had done to protect his son from the horrors of the world, something more powerful was at work thwarting his efforts. *I don't know what else you've seen in your sleep, son, but I'm sorry you've had to see any of it.*

Cridon fidgeted for a moment before saying, "The black wizard wants to kill me."

Rasi put his hand on the back of Cridon's neck. *I won't let him.*

"You can't stop him, Dad. He'll kill you if you try."

A strap snapped the air. *I'm working on that.*

Cridon smiled, ever trusting of his father.

Rasi turned away. *We should go now.*

But Cridon didn't move. He said, "Dad?"

Rasi glanced over his shoulder. *What is it?*

He pointed to one of the straps as it floated by. "Do you want me to fix your back?"

Rasi's knees weakened. *My back? What do you mean?*

"Do you want me to take away your straps?"

Cridon's question sliced through his soul like a knife. He lost his breath.

How? I mean, it's not possible.

"The broken Light gave your straps life, just like Mr. Simcane's metal."

No, that cannot be. When I visited the Elder Three, they told me "none that is broken can be so here." Yet while I was in their lair, I still had the straps.

"That was true. Just because the Light gave your straps life when it was broken by Matthew doesn't mean your straps themselves are broken. They are a part of you, but I can take them away now if you want."

Cridon had stunned Rasi in a way he had seldom been stunned. Rasi had spent years living in the mountains and dreaming of being normal again. He would have done anything to be rid of his violent appendages back then. He looked to Cridon. Doc Eckels was right— the Light was more powerful than anyone could have imagined.

As much as Rasi had hated his straps when they'd forced themselves onto his back in the rashta pit, he had grown to accept them, even appreciate them. Now they were as much a part of him as his arms or his legs. He thought about Tevin and how evil the world had become. With visions of being normal again still playing out in his mind, he answered in the only way he could. *No, son. I still need them.*

"All right, Dad."

Rasi pulled him in for a hug.

Simcane kept his distance. "What now, Rasi?" he asked.

Rasi said, "Tevin is coming. We prepare for war."

Simcane held out his hand. Rasi regarded it. Then he nudged Cridon behind him and shook Simcane's hand. Together, the three headed back toward the city wall where Rasi's ladder stood.

By the time they neared Rasi's home, his head throbbed and he struggled to keep going. Simcane struggled too, the wounds on his stomach and back red and inflamed. When Alina saw them approach, she set her book beside her chair and raced out to meet them. She wrapped her arms around Simcane and squeezed. "I'm so happy to see you," she cried. She stepped back when she noticed Simcane's grimace. "My god, Sim. You should be lying down. We need to get you back to the clinic right away."

Simcane nodded.

Rasi wobbled behind her and caught himself with a strap on the ground so she wouldn't see. He needed to lie down, too. *Hey, Cridon.*

Cridon hurried to him.

Run and get Homer. Tell him to come help Simcane back to Doc's.
Cridon sprinted toward Homer's house.

Alina said, "I can go with Sim."

Rasi shook his head. *I'd rather you and Cridon stay behind.* He gave Simcane a look. While he accepted Simcane's story, he wasn't confident enough to send Alina with him just yet.

Alina caught the way he was side-eyeing Simcane. "What's going on?"

Simcane answered, "He's right, Your Majesty. You should stay behind. I'll be all right. Homer can help me."

"I don't understand."

Rasi wobbled on his feet again.

This time she saw and grabbed his arm. "What's wrong, Rasi?"

I'll explain everything in the house. Just get me to a bed. He started to fall. Alina caught him with the help of his straps. She helped him to the house, peppering him with questions along the way. He managed to tell her everything that had happened before he got to a bed and fell asleep.

Sometime later, Atticus's voice woke him. He sat up, his head still throbbing a bit, but not as bad as before. He swung his feet off the bed and rested his face in his hands for a few minutes. At least the floor wasn't spinning anymore. He took the glass of water on the table and downed it in one swig.

Alina appeared in the doorway with Doc Eckels. She smiled. "Hi, Rasi. How are you feeling?"

Better. How long have I been out?

"Since yesterday."

Doc Eckels went to his side. He listened to his lungs and then watched his eyes as he had him follow his finger back and forth. He wore a splint on his forearm.

What happened to you, Doc?

"I'd say the same big fella that happened to you."

Rasi straightened, filled with anxiety.

Doc Eckels rested his hand on his shoulder and said, "Don't worry. It was before Cridon helped him. We've worked everything out. I think Simcane is more upset over my arm than I am."

Atticus entered next. "Good to see you awake for a change. I thought you might sleep through the whole war."

Rasi blew off his joke with an annoyed wave.

"It's done," Atticus continued. "Tevin should know where we are by now. I hope you're confident in your plans."

He wasn't, but there was no going back now.

Doc Eckels excused himself and left, comfortable with Rasi's progress. Atticus sat in a chair. Alina returned with a plate of apple slices.

Rasi took a bite. *Pull up a seat, Alina. It's time you two heard the plan.*

Rasi laid out his defense against Tevin's army and how the Teks were to begin rationing the food they'd been storing for the siege immediately. He told them he would lead the attack himself, to which Alina responded by demanding to be at his side. He wasn't keen on the idea, but he wasn't up for arguing at that point. Though he told them almost every part of the plan, he held a couple of pieces back, feeling it best to not reveal them just yet.

Alina hung on his every word. When Rasi finished, Atticus shook his head as if amazed.

"If there was any plan that could possibly succeed, you may have found it, you old devil."

Alina grinned. "This just might work."

Rasi lowered his head as Alina and Atticus continued discussing the plan. He hoped they were right.

CHAPTER 32

JARRAH'S MARCH TO WAR

In response a summons from Tevin, Jarrah made the long trip from Lithia back to Thasula. When he reached Tevin's castle, he left his entourage in the courtyard and met James, Alina's former aide, in the foyer. James directed him to the trophy room on the second floor. The door was open. Tevin stood at the farthest window facing outside.

"Your Majesty?" Jarrah called.

Tevin turned. He held up a Tek helmet from the war for Jarrah's inspection. "Fine piece of work these Teks created, wouldn't you say?"

"I suppose. I didn't have much time to admire them as they were coming at me with their noise-making weapons."

Tevin chuckled and set the helmet back in the trophy case next to a full set of Tek armor. "No, I don't suppose you did." He closed the glass lid and walked to another display mounted on the wall. "Have you seen this before, Jarrah?" He dragged his finger along the glass that housed a thin sword with a blue blade.

Jarrah shook his head.

"This was the Tek commander's weapon. As the story goes, Rasi used it to kill him."

"What's so special about it?"

"They say it will slice through virtually any armor without strain."

"They say? You haven't given it a try?"

Tevin turned away from the display. "No, no. I've never been much of a swordsman. Though, I do marvel at the technology that created such a weapon." He motioned to a set of high-backed chairs. The chairs slid into the middle of the room as if pulled by an unseen rope. "Have a seat, my loyal friend."

Jarrah couldn't remember the last time he had heard Tevin speak with such warmth and pleasantness. "You sound well today, Tevin."

"I am well."

"Why have you called me here? I'm quite busy in Lithia."

"I know you are, but this is important. Over the years I have searched every corner of Epertase for that bastard child with the Light, to no avail. Even my sorcery hasn't yielded the boy's location, and I have long suspected that the Light may be shielding him from me. I've tried repeatedly to force him out of hiding, also with no luck." Tevin walked to a refreshment table and poured Jarrah a glass of whiskey. Then he poured himself a glass and sat across from him.

Jarrah took a sip and hid the wince. Tevin had always liked the harsher stuff.

"Too strong?"

Jarrah shook his head. "Not at all, my king."

Tevin smirked. Jarrah took a larger swig just to show his mettle.

"I found the boy," Tevin finally blurted.

Jarrah nearly choked. He let the liquid drain back into his glass and wiped his chin with his forearm. "You've found him? How?"

"You remember that fool Atticus?"

"Of course."

"He was spotted in Thasula. Though he tried to hide after killing one of my more promising soldiers, he underestimated the tracking abilities of my hylocks."

Jarrah leaned forward. "Where is he? I'll go after him right away."

Tevin held up his free hand. "Calm down, my friend. It won't be as easy as you might think. The boy hides with his mother and Rasi on the Island of Torick." After a pause to allow his words to sink in, he added, "We believe he is sheltering with the Teks."

Jarrah was glad he was sitting else his knees might have given way. Knowing that recovering the Light would complete Tevin's quest and permanently secure his own rule of Lithia, he said, "What can I do to help?"

"I want you to lead my army and bring the boy back to me. I want you to exterminate the Teks once and for all. And I want you to kill Rasi."

"I will do anything you ask, my king, but how do we know Rasi and Alina won't flee with the boy before we ever get near?"

"Simple. He doesn't know Atticus was followed."

Jarrah smiled. Surprise was perhaps the greatest weapon an army could have. "I suspect I won't need much more than a couple battalions. After all, how many Teks could there be?"

"Twelve thousand. That's the number Alina banished after the Tek War. We have to assume that is how many still remain."

"I see. Well, maybe I'll need a few more than a couple battalions."

"Jarrah, I want you to take as many men as you need to succeed. Take the entire army if you must. I will not accept failure."

Jarrah nodded confidently. "I assure you, I will bring you the boy."

"I don't want to leave any chance for him to escape. Rasi will not surrender easily. You must beat him, and you must do it with such an overwhelming force that he has no chance. The Teks have had many years to prepare a defense. They will have the advantage of being dug in. That is why you must have superior numbers."

"Understood, sir. A move this large across the sea will take time to prepare. We will need a fleet of ships."

"We have the Tek ships that Alina used to transport the prisoners to the island after the war. They have not been tended to in years, but with work they can be used as part of our fleet."

"Oh yes. I forgot about those. Are they still on the east coast?"

"They are. You have full rein to use any and all Epertasian shipwrights and carpenters to help you build the rest of the fleet."

Jarrah grinned. "I can't wait to see Rasi's face."

"Me neither. In fact, maybe you should just bring me his head so I can see it myself."

Jarrah nodded. "Of course."

For the next four months, Jarrah oversaw the creation of a powerful fleet of ships large enough to take his army to the Island of Torick. Combined with the Tek ships, the fleet stretched from the southern shores as far into the ocean as he could see. One hundred ships, to be precise, each carrying over three hundred soldiers and enough food, water, and weapons for the campaign.

For the next five days, Jarrah and his second-in-command, Pierce, oversaw the loading of supplies while additional battalions of Epertasian soldiers continued to arrive from as far north as New Arc and as far east as Parsons. Once the supplies were loaded, Jarrah sent word to Tevin that the largest sea deployment in the history of Epertase was ready to proceed.

Tevin arrived to see them off, a convoy of wagons trailing him. Jarrah smiled, already knowing what surprise those wagons carried. After the Tek War, Alina had gathered the leftover Tek projectile weapons and stored them in Parsons's warehouse district. Thanks to Tevin, his soldiers would be armed with weapons more advanced and powerful than mere swords and arrows. A new era in Epertasian warfare was about to begin.

Tevin ordered Jarrah to have his soldiers gather one weapon for every ten men before boarding their ships. Hundreds of smaller vessels ferried the soldiers from the beach to the larger vessels.

Confident, Jarrah surveyed his fleet and thought, *There is nothing an Epertasian army cannot achieve.* Once the fleet was ready to sail, Jarrah said goodbye to Tevin, shook his hand, and climbed into the last ferry.

As they pulled away from shore, Jarrah shouted, "Send word to my wife in Lithia that I love her. Tell her I have left for the greater good of our kingdoms, and I will return when the battle is over and not a day later."

Tevin bowed politely and agreed with a wave.

Once on the flagship, Jarrah stared out over the empty sea. They would sail east and approach from the south. Anyone who had studied the Island of Torick knew the cliffs prevented any other practical access.

Pierce joined him at the bow. "You seem distracted, Jarrah. You can't possibly be nervous about the inevitable outcome of this campaign."

"No, I don't suppose I can. I have thought long and hard to find some way the Teks could pose any threat to us, but I cannot imagine anything to be wary of. Is that wrong? I mean, to be so confident?"

"Not at all, sir. I share your confidence. That is why we're taking an overwhelming force—so the end comes as quickly and permanently as possible."

That pronouncement didn't sit well with Jarrah. He added, "We have to remember, they still have Rasi. He should never be underestimated."

"He is one man, sir. While I respect Rasi's skills in battle, I am confident we will easily overcome whatever he rustles up as a defense." He snickered.

"What's so funny?" Jarrah asked.

"I was just imagining the look on Rasi's face when he realizes we are coming. He might even loose his bladder."

Jarrah smirked. "He will definitely need to make a decision in a hurry, and, if I know Rasi, I expect that decision to be a fight to the death."

"Then he will die."

"As if there was any doubt."

Making landfall on the southern beaches was uneventful. Jarrah stood at the edge of a sprawling field. The Tek city stood in the distance. It didn't look too imposing. The wall protecting it promised to be the largest hurdle. But it was nothing a good old-fashioned siege wouldn't take care of. That his forces hadn't yet encountered resistance of any kind during their approach meant their advantage of surprise was intact. Even if Rasi knew they were coming, it was a numbers game at that point, and Rasi didn't have them. It was all going as planned.

Pierce joined him. "Do you hear that?" he asked. A strange, faint buzzing sound emanated from within the city.

"I do."

"What do you think it is?"

"I have no idea. These Teks are strange creatures. It could be anything."

Billowing smokestacks beyond the wall suggested the city was alive and prosperous. A sea of protruding wooden spikes cluttered the space between the wall and a single row of Tek rolling machines. Though Jarrah secretly admitted that the war machines concerned him, he understood his army's sheer numbers would quickly overrun them. He would take losses on his approach, but what war didn't incur losses?

Looking through a monocular, he saw that the top of the wall was lined with Tek soldiers in their legendary suits of armor. They were disciplined and motionless as if goading Jarrah's men forward. He passed his monocular to Pierce.

"Do you think they have some kind of secret weapon we don't know about?" Pierce asked quietly so as not to be heard by the men.

Jarrah thought before answering. "It's hard to know. But I don't foresee any weapon that could match the force we've brought." He playfully tapped Pierce's shoulder. "Buck up, friend. You never know, the Teks might not even plan to fight for Rasi's cause. After all, how loyal could they be to their conqueror? With Tevin the Third on our side, we cannot lose. He has blessed this campaign."

"Yes, I suppose you're right, sir."

Sweat soaked the back of Jarrah's shirt. He looked to the blistering morning suns; it was going to be a long afternoon.

Pierce whispered into his ear, "Should we advance? They're obviously going to make us make the first move."

"I know."

"Staying out here in the suns is just going to take an increasingly harsh toll on the men. We should probably force the action sooner rather than later."

Jarrah nodded.

"Besides, waiting any longer now that they have surely seen us will only give Rasi more time to flee."

"Rasi won't go anywhere. You can call him a lot of things, but coward isn't one of them."

"Is loser?"

Jarrah snorted. "Soon." He pointed to the main gate which remarkably sat open. "The one thing I don't get. It's like they're inviting us inside."

"Maybe to dump hot tar from above?"

"Maybe. But what would that do? Kill a hundred of our men?"

"Urban warfare can benefit the defenders if done right."

"Yeah. I don't know. That would only work if we didn't have so many soldiers and if we cared about civilian casualties. There are no innocents here. If someone hides in a house, we'll simply burn them out. Rasi knows that."

Pierce pondered the situation for a moment. "Even if they have explosion-making weapons inside, is that really a threat?"

Jarrah subtly shook his head. "It just doesn't feel right."

"Well, we won't know until we get in there and see."

Pierce was right. Jarrah nodded once. "Very well. Send the first wave."

"Yes, sir." He turned to the Epertasian commander on his left. "You heard the man. Order the advance." The signal callers lifted their flags along the front line. As one, the army marched forward in practiced unison. Jarrah led next to Pierce. Each step increased his nervous anticipation. Once the rolling machines got going, the casualties would be immense. The machines continued to sit quietly as Jarrah's men moved closer. It was even more nerve-wracking than if they'd roared to life and launched an assault.

Once they reached the midpoint of the battlefield, Jarrah's instinct was to deploy the archers, but he had witnessed first-hand how useless arrows were against Tek armor. Since his men had little practice with the Tek weapons, he decided to get closer before using them. He didn't want to waste a single shot.

He lifted his sword and his men stopped advancing. He faced them. The air grew thick with nervous energy. He screamed, "Men, we haven't traveled this far to lie down and die. You've known this battle has been coming for some time now, and today it is here. Once we start, we will not stop until we are alone in the center of this Tek city with only dead Teks surrounding us." His men roared their approval. He waited until they quieted down. Then he screamed, "Do not stop until we have our victory." He pointed his sword at the wall. "Chaaaarge," he cried, his voice cracking from the strain.

The ground rumbled. His army's battle cry let anyone who didn't know they were coming in on the secret. The more fit and enthusiastic soldiers raced past Jarrah and Pierce until the two men were well behind the front line. As they ran, the ones carrying Tek weapons braced them against their shoulders and pulled the levers. Thunderous projectiles sailed toward the armored Teks along the top of the wall. The ones that struck their marks sent some of the armored Teks backward over the edge, while others absorbed the projectiles with little more than flinches.

Why don't they attack? What are they waiting for? Even the Tek machines at the base of the wall still sat idle as if abandoned. Jarrah slowed. A sudden dread filled his gut. He stopped as the soldiers continued to charge past him. *Abandoned?*

Pierce glanced back at him and slowed as well. As the army raced toward the open gate, Jarrah realized a new possibility.

"What is it?" Pierce shouted.

Jarrah shook his head.

Pierce ran to his side. "Sir?"

"Don't you see it, Pierce? We might have made a terrible mistake."

Pierce looked to the motionless machines and his shoulders drooped. "They're not here, are they, sir?"

The first of the forces swarmed the impotent war machines as others raced through the open gate. And all Jarrah could do was watch. A soldier on one of the machines struggled with the hatch until it opened. He jammed his sword inside. Then he stood up and signaled to Jarrah. "It's empty, sir."

Of course it's empty.

The soldiers continued pouring through the gates, unaware of what Jarrah and some of the others had just realized. He had prepared for every possible defense.

Except one.

He and Pierce walked through the gate into the city. Those of his men who hadn't yet figured out they'd been horribly duped stormed the closest buildings, still expecting some sort of counterattack. One by one, they stopped and looked around in stunned silence. They parted for Jarrah and Pierce.

"What's going on, sir?" one of the soldiers asked.

Jarrah looked above the buildings to the smokestacks still spewing black smoke. The enemy's deception had been meticulously planned.

Pierce didn't have words.

Jarrah shook his head, ignoring the question. He walked to one of the armored Tek soldiers who had fallen from the top of the wall and rolled him to his back. With an army watching, he unlatched the helmet and pulled it free. The armor was stuffed with straw. Jarrah lifted his eyes to the top of the wall. From the back, he could see the metal stands that held the empty suits of armor in position.

How could this be? Where could twelve thousand men hide without being seen? One of the other islands? That wasn't likely. His scouts would have found them.

He addressed his confused men. "Search the city for stragglers. If you find any, bring them to me." He knew they wouldn't. He turned to Pierce. "We must get back to Epertase at once."

"That'll take weeks."

"I know."

"And Rasi?"

Jarrah lowered his head and turned away. "He's probably already there."

"Oh, shit. King Tevin will not be pleased."

"Yes. I realize that."

CHAPTER 33

CHRISTOPHER

The waves gently rocked Christopher's small boat as he approached the southern shores of Tek Island where Jarrah's armada of ships awaited. He stared in awe, having never seen even a single ship of such size, let alone nearly one hundred of them. Their towering masts and sprawling decks were a sight to behold. It seemed a shame to do what he was about to do to them. His twelve Tek companions were unmoved.

He stood and looked over his own fleet of fifty small Tek boats, each one also crowded with thirteen soldiers and propelled by mechanical devices. Their speed and maneuverability were unmatched in the water. It was their only advantage. Well, that and surprise. Along with the soldiers, each boat carried a dozen bows and countless fire arrows, japsy weed, a barrel of the Tek's black blood, and a single iron ball that took two men to move. Something the Teks called a fuse poked from its end.

Christopher nodded to the lead Tek in the boat beside him. "Remember," he shouted to his fleet. "Two ships each. That is your goal."

A Tek shouted from another boat, "We're taking three."

Once the suns conceded the sky to the moon, it was time to move forward. Christopher waved a small lantern over his head. The Tek soldier at the stern started the propulsion machine and the boat lunged forward. Christopher held the rim for balance. Another machine rumbled from the boat beside his. And then another, and another, until the night air filled with a deep growl from fifty vessels.

As they approached the first line of Jarrah's ships, a Tek in Christopher's boat rubbed japsy weed together and ignited a cloth that had been soaked in black blood. He dropped the flaming cloth into a metal drum, setting it alight.

If the skeleton crew of Epertasians tasked with maintaining their ships didn't hear the engines, they surely saw the glow from so many tiny fires flickering on the dark sea. Distant shouting soon indicated that they had.

The first arrow splashed into the water alongside Christopher's boat. And then a hail of arrows plunged around them. Tek soldiers fell into the water. Christopher shouted, "Aim for the sails."

The engines whined as the boats separated and sped toward different parts of the fleet. The dark sky erupted with tiny flames as though hundreds of fireflies had taken flight. Christopher stood fearlessly at the prow amid the continuing barrage of arrows.

The deflated main sail of the closest ship ignited. The clamorous cheers of the Teks likely woke any Epertasians who had still been sleeping below deck. A second flaming assault, along with the falling pieces of burning sail, lit the deck. Epertasians scrambled to extinguish the flames with pails of seawater, but the fires grew too fast. More sails on other boats caught fire next.

The Epertasians in the burning boats had choices to make: burn alive or jump into the murky sea. They mostly chose the sea despite likely not knowing how to swim. Hell, Christopher couldn't swim either, for that matter.

The flames tickled the sky—their heat blazing as Christopher weaved between the ships. It was an awesome sight as chunks of burning wood fell to the water with stunning flickers of orange reflecting off the black surface within the dull, pale reflection of the moon. The smoke soon even blotted that out.

As Christopher and the others snaked between the burning ships, crewmembers who hadn't yet abandoned their vessels hurled debris at the speeding Tek boats, including heavy chunks of burning deck. Christopher saw at least two Tek boats sink under the assault. Other nearby Teks pulled survivors to safety, but they had surely lost men despite their efforts.

Christopher maneuvered around the first burning line of ships toward more dangerous targets. The repurposed metal Tek ships wouldn't be sunk so easily. That's what the iron balls were for. As they approached the first metal beast, slats along the hull opened and dozens of arrows poked through.

Oh no. Christopher's boat was right in the line of fire. "Get down," Christopher shouted.

The wave of arrows plowed into him and his men. He fell back with an arrow through his biceps and another in the side of his chest. Another bunch of arrows poked from the hull.

Christopher shielded a Tek soldier who hadn't yet been struck and took another arrow clean through his cheek as his reward. It plowed into the boat. Christopher pressed his palm against the bleeding hole and his tongue found the gap in his shattered teeth. He tasted blood and fell back against a dead Tek with an arrow through his ear.

With a wince, Christopher snapped off the arrow in his chest, leaving the point perhaps permanently in his lung. More arrows plowed into the dead and dying bodies around him, only sparing him more pain by luck. The Tek he had previously shielded now had an arrow lodged in the side of his neck with blood spurting from between his fingers as he tried to cover the wound.

The Epertasians turned their arrows on another boat. A look around told Christopher everything he needed to know as water slowly covered his feet. There were too many holes to plug. Just like his men. He looked to the Tek with the arrow lodged in his neck and the only other man still alive and gave them a defeated nod. They nodded back, their resignation written in their eyes. Christopher climbed across the bodies and rolled the iron ball to the prow. The Tek without the mortal wound to his neck climbed to the stern and directed the boat toward the metal ship.

Christopher coughed and wheezed. His every movement was painful.

The wounded Tek reached for an arrow lying on the planks and dunked it into the fire barrel. He had grown pale from loss of blood and barely had the strength to lift the flaming arrow to the iron ball's fuse. He smiled sadly. The fuse sizzled as the flame took hold. He wobbled and fell atop the other bodies. Christopher's boat bumped against the metal ship's hull.

The last living Tek at the rear asked, "Should we jump, sir?"

Christopher climbed over the bodies to him. He hadn't the strength to swim even if he knew how. "I can't swim," he said.

"Heh, heh." The Tek coughed blood. "Me neither." He offered his bloody hand. "Sir, it has been an honor to serve wi—"

A flash rippled the air, followed by a heated blast that popped Christopher's ears and rattled what was left of his teeth. The boat shattered around him. He went weightless before slamming into the water amid a floating field of wooden debris.

His ears rang. He reached for a piece of wood and saw blackened skin sloughing from his left arm. With his last bit of strength, he looked to the metal ship where water poured into an enormous hole in its hull. Christopher smiled a bloody smile. Though he knew it was unlikely his men would destroy every ship in the fleet, he was happy to see they had destroyed enough to meet their goal.

Men jumped from the metal ship, landing all around him.

As the hypnotic bobbing of the waves urged him to close his eyes, he wondered what would get him first—his injuries or the sharks. He hoped it wouldn't be the sharks. He wondered how Rasi was doing and if he and the rest of the Teks had made it to the Forest of Concore yet. Then he saw an image of his mother in the flame of a floating timber and it made him smile again. He was proud of how his life had ended. She would be, too. His tired hands slid from the piece of wood and his head slipped beneath the surface.

CHAPTER 34

THE CALM

Rasi stood at the edge of the Great Plains with his army of Tek soldiers waiting in the Forest of Concore behind him. The trek through the mountain region had been long and difficult.

An army of Epertasian soldiers amassed at the northern edge of the plains, revealing their scouts had spotted Rasi's approach at some point. It was expected. A few hylocks circled overhead. Perhaps they had been the scouts.

Leander stood beside him. "You did it, Rasi. You got us here."

"Yeah." Though getting there without Jarrah's fleet seeing them leave Tek Island was no mean feat, they hadn't accomplished anything yet. In fact, that was the easy part since Jarrah was so predictable. Had Jarrah possessed even a speck of imagination and chosen a different approach instead of the obvious one, the fight would have been over before it started.

As Rasi surveyed his army of Teks making camp within the trees, he wondered if Jarrah had figured it out yet. The thought of his surprised face gave Rasi his first chuckle in quite some time.

Alina approached from behind. "Leander, did Logan and the others get started?"

Leander bowed. "Yes, Your Majesty. Though Gillian and Willum were not very happy with your orders to escort the noncombatants to Muél."

"What did they expect?"

"Gillian insisted on staying to fight."

"She's with child, for the gods' sake."

Leander dipped his head in quiet acknowledgement. "I'm simply telling you what she said, Your Majesty. King Logan resisted leaving also, but even he knew his cough has gotten too bad for him to stay. It must be hard for a former fighter to realize he has become a liability."

While Rasi knew the trip to Muél could be difficult, he also knew it was the only place they would be safe if the war went south. Homer, Irene, Celia, Josephine and her grandmother, Masera, Logan, and Lona were in safe hands with Gillian and Willum leading the way.

Alina touched Rasi's shoulder as Leander took his leave. "So, it looks like they know we're coming." She didn't sound as upset as Rasi expected her to be.

I knew they would. We have too large a force to hide once we made landfall. But that's fine. He no longer has the time to round up soldiers from afar. When we attack, he will be stuck with only what he has already guarding Thasula.

"How many is that?"

Normally, not enough. But since Tevin is rightfully paranoid, he has likely dug in. I'd say he has roughly twice our numbers, if not a bit more.

"How are you so sure he didn't go to Tek Island himself?"

I hope he did. Strategically, I'd much rather defend your castle than attack it. But Tevin has never joined a battle he could avoid, and I doubt he would now. During the Heathen War, he stayed as far from the fighting as he could. She didn't appear completely satisfied with his answer, so he asked, *What else is bothering you?*

"I know we've talked about this before, but it still pains me. The soldiers we face were once our people. If we are victorious, it'll be because we killed them. Does that not concern you?"

He coldly shook his head. *I will have plenty of guilt when this is over, as I always do after war. But for now, guilt will only make me weak and hesitant. I have done all I can to spare as many Epertasian lives as possible. We must accept that when kings and queens make war, innocent men die. It doesn't make it right; it just makes it so.*

"Do you think they might rejoin us instead of fighting? They can't possibly like Tevin's Epertase more than ours."

That's what he loved about her—undying hope no matter how misplaced. *I will make every effort to give them that chance.* He didn't have the heart to tell her the truth. He kissed her and looked into her emerald eyes. *It starts tomorrow. We should spend tonight with Cridon before he leaves with Simcane.*

"Yes." She took his hand and they walked into the woods.

The smell of cooked pig wafted through the air near the command tent. Cridon hid behind Simcane's leg near the fire as if playing a game.

"Simcane," Alina called and waved him over.

He hurried to her with Cridon clinging to his leg and taking a ride with each step. "What is it, Your Majesty?"

"Are you prepared to go?"

"First thing in the morning, right?"

"Yes. You understand we are trusting you with our most precious treasure?"

"Of course."

She took his hands in hers and looked into his eye. "I am so afraid, Simcane. But if there's anyone Rasi and I trust to protect Cridon, it's you."

Simcane stood a little straighter. "I would give my life for this boy and—"

Cridon, oblivious to the weight of the conversation, tackled Simcane's left arm with a giggle. Simcane lifted his arm as Cridon held on tightly. "What are you doing, little man?" he asked.

Rasi smirked.

Cridon giggled even more. "I am going to defeat you," he declared as he dangled from Simcane's tree-trunk biceps.

"You are, are you?" Simcane grabbed Cridon and tickled him until he warned that he was about to wet his pants. Simcane set him down so Cridon could catch his breath. Then he looked up at Alina and asked, "What was I saying?"

She tilted her head and smiled. "It's all right, Sim. We understand."

Rasi couldn't help but grin as Cridon tried to recreate his favorite game with Meela by sneaking up on Simcane from behind. Without looking back, Simcane said, "I wouldn't do that if I were you, kid."

"Cridon," Alina snapped, wanting to get the conversation back on track. "Knock it off."

Cridon stood up straight and stepped around Simcane's leg to see his mother. She smiled and said, "There'll be time for playing later, son. We have important business to discuss." She motioned Cridon to her and knelt in front of him. "When you and Simcane leave for your adventure, I need you to listen to him and do everything he says. Do you understand?"

Cridon bobbed his head. "Um-hm."

"Excuse me?" she said.

"Oh, I mean, yes, Mother."

"Tell Simcane goodnight."

He did as ordered. Simcane mussed his hair. Alina started into the tent, but paused. "Are you coming, Rasi?"

Not right now.

She and Cridon disappeared inside.

Leander made his way over to join Simcane and Rasi. He looked around to make sure no one was watching and handed Simcane a small key which Simcane shoved into his waistband. "Alina's going to kill me for this, Rasi," Simcane whispered. "I hope you're sure about this plan."

"It's our only chance to win," he struggled to say.

"I hope you're right. I'm not taking the heat when she finds out."

Rasi had no doubt she'd be furious. She may never speak to him again.

In the distance behind Simcane, Eldon lumbered through the meandering soldiers toward the pig roast. Rasi excused himself to catch up to his gangly friend.

Eldon.

Eldon straightened and looked around until his eyes found his summoner. "Ah. Rasi."

Rasi jogged to him.

"What can I do for you, my friend?"

I have an important request.

"Of course. What is it?"

As you know, we're starting the battle tomorrow morning and—

"I'm rather looking forward to it."

Yes, I'm sure you are. But I need you to promise me something.

"I can't promise until I know what I'm promising."

If at any time during the course of this battle you encounter Tevin, you are to retreat without delay. You are not to engage the wizard, no matter what happens.

"Well, that seems rather silly. If I see Tevin, I plan to kill him."

No.

Eldon tilted his head. "You don't want him dead?"

No ... Yes ... I mean ... Just listen. I watched Tevin kill Fice with merely a touch. You hear me? A touch. I don't want you anywhere near him.

"Men die in war, Rasi. How they die is irrelevant, and I have no interest in fleeing from a murdering wiz—"

Eldon. Please. This is important.

Eldon bit his lower lip and then answered, "You should understand that I am as afraid of this Tevin fellow as I am of an ant, and I would enjoy squashing him if ever I was fortunate enough to get such an opportunity."

I know. But this is one fight I'm begging you to avoid.

"I'll tell you what, Rasi. I give you my word that I will be as careful as I can, and I hope that is enough for your conscience."

Rasi sighed. *I guess that's all I can ask.*

"I do appreciate your concern. Now, if you'll excuse me, I am quite hungry, and I think I smell pig."

As he started to walk away, Rasi grabbed his shoulder with a strap. *Remember, just don't let him touch you.*

Eldon glanced back with a sly grin. "Sounds simple enough." Rasi's strap let go and Eldon joined the party at the fire.

Rasi returned to his tent and crawled inside.

Alina sat across from Cridon. "You're getting so big," she said with a sad smile. She held up her hand with her palm out and Cridon pressed his open hand against it. She shook her head. "Before long, your hand will be as big as mine."

"And Dad's," he answered with a hopeful glance at Rasi.

Before you know it, son.

A plate of meat waited next to Rasi's bedroll. *Is this for me?*

I knew you wouldn't eat if I didn't practically feed it to you.

He smiled and grabbed the plate; he was indeed hungry.

Cridon grinned and pulled his hand away from his mother's. He turned and wriggled onto her lap with his back against her chest. She kissed the top of his head and then ran her hand through his thick, white hair. "You're going to be brave for Simcane, aren't you?"

Rasi tore a piece of meat from the bone and looked up.

Cridon glanced at him before answering. "Um-hm."

"I know you will," she said.

"Mommy, my eyes are tired."

She wiped her own wet eyes with her free hand. "Just rest."

"Will you tell me a story?"

"Of course. Have I ever told you about how King Matthew became the most special king?"

Cridon shook his head. "Do you mean King Matthew from my dreams?"

She smiled. "I think probably."

Cridon yawned and stretched as Alina began the tale of Matthew. She told of his compassion and his father's selfishness, how the Light chose Matthew, and how he gained the fate of the kingdom when his father died. She explained how that very magical Light had been passed down through the generations to him.

Half asleep, he mumbled, "I'll help you fix the Light, Mommy."

She kissed his head again. "I know, honey. But you let Mommy and Daddy worry about that." He was asleep before she finished the sentence. She settled him on his blankets and lay beside him with her arm draped over him. Soon, she fell asleep too. Rasi went over and knelt next to them, kissed them both, and then left the tent to join his commanders huddled around the fire.

"Are you ready for tomorrow?" Leander asked when he saw Rasi approach.

Rasi curled his upper lip and looked away. It was time to be angry. He nodded, grabbed another chunk of meat, and sat against a tree to be alone with his thoughts.

Simcane was waiting outside Rasi's tent when he returned just before dawn. Rasi hadn't slept a wink. He slipped past Simcane and crawled in.

Alina was already awake and stirring inside. Her eyes were puffy and red. "Where have you been?" she asked, and wiped her tears with the back of her hand.

Just reviewing the plans.

"I can't do it, Rasi. I can't let him go."

Then go with him.

She snapped her head around. "I told you, I'm fighting for my throne."

He lifted his hands in surrender and then gently pulled her close. *I love you.*

"Do you think he'll be all right?"

I trust Simcane.

"I know. I do too, but it's just so hard."

This will be the last time we will ever be separated from him. I promise.

Her head nodded even as her eyes protested.

Come out when you're ready. He rejoined Simcane outside to wait.

Simcane's gaze was warm and gentle. "This is going to be a tough one, huh?"

Rasi wiped his own eyes and then gave his friend a wet glare. He nodded.

It wasn't long before Alina and Cridon joined them.

"Hi, Simcane," Cridon said with a bubbly smile.

Simcane playfully pinched his shoulder. "Hey, kid."

Alina knelt in front of Cridon. She straightened his shirt. "I'm going to miss you so much, but be strong. We'll be together again soon. I love you more than the distance to the two suns."

"I know. I love you, too, Mom."

Alina wrapped her arms around him so tightly that he squeaked out, "You're hurting me." She must have kissed him a hundred times before loosening her embrace. She turned away to hide the tears.

Rasi knelt. His straps floated around Cridon, seemingly wanting to hug him as well. *You be good.*

"I will, Dad."

Do everything Simcane says to do.

"I will, Dad."

I love you.

Cridon huffed, "I *know*. You tell me all the time."

Rasi hugged him and allowed his straps to wrap around them both. He never wanted to let go. Eventually, however, he had to unravel his straps and step back. He put a firm hand on Simcane's shoulder. He didn't need to say a word.

"I know, my friend. I'll protect him with my life."

Alina hugged Simcane and then turned away. Rasi draped his arm around her shoulders.

Simcane ruffled Cridon's hair. "Come on, kid."

Then they left, taking most of Alina's heart with them.

THE FINAL WAR

CHAPTER 35
NEGOTIATIONS

A s always, Rasi had planned meticulously. His Tek soldiers
had been well fed and rested before they faced their enemy
with their backs to Concore Forest. Rasi sat astride his horse
next to Alina's and held a tall shield at his side that covered him
from knees to nose. His straps carried a second shield for Alina
against his back.

Waiting across the plains was the very Epertasian army he had
once commanded. Even at a small fraction of its full size, the force
left to defend Thasula, the castle, and the evil wizard residing within,
was awe-inspiring. It was difficult to see the many Epertasian flags
fluttering in the breeze and not wonder how fate could have led him
to the opposing side. The world was upside-down.

As Alina looked upon her former people, Rasi saw regret in her
eyes. He needed to keep her focused. *Remember, they're now our
enemy. They choose to follow Tevin. They want to kill you and take
Cridon.*

"I know." Her voice weighed a thousand stone.

Are you ready?

She nodded.

He lifted two straps in the air and kicked his horse into a canter.
The straps wore flexible metal armor created by the Teks that glinted

in the suns. Though Rasi liked the added protection the armor gave, he liked the sharp edges even more.

Formalities of war dictated that a parley take place in the center of the battlefield before the bloodshed began. To Rasi's knowledge, never in Epertase's rich military history had any prewar parley yielded peace, but the exchange was still expected. At least, by Epertasian armies.

He and Alina began the long ride to meet the enemy leaders. Only the two of them made the journey, which seemed risky, but in reality was expertly calculated. Two Epertasian commanders led a delegation of a half dozen soldiers out to meet them.

One of the two commanders, a middle-aged soldier with a round face and a belly to match, greeted them. He looked familiar. "Rasi. Alina," he said. His shirt was only half-tucked into his pants and hung out below his armored chest plate, which was dull enough to be disgraceful. The man sniffled and wiped his bare forearm across his nose, leaving a streak of matted hair.

Rasi stared with venomous eyes.

"You may not remember me," the man continued, "but my name is Captain Zenner. I fought alongside you against the Teks before I was promoted."

Rasi remembered him vaguely. As he recalled, Zenner was a lazy oaf who never should have made it to the rank of captain.

Zenner wiped his nose again. "Damn allergies," he mumbled. "I do not enjoy the opposing positions we now find ourselves in."

Considering that Zenner weighed quite a bit more than Rasi remembered him weighing, he had no doubt the captain enjoyed his new position a little too much.

Zenner pressed one of his nostrils with a finger, leaned to the side of his horse, and blew snot into the grass. He pinched his fingers along the bottom of his nose and then wiped them on his pants. "Apologies. The grass makes my nose run something awful."

Alina disgustedly looked ahead.

"Anyway, I apologize for my rudeness, but I think we should proceed with our demands."

Whatever the slob said next would be a waste of breath, but Rasi had promised Alina to hear him out.

Zenner removed a scroll from his saddlebag and unrolled it. He held spectacles to his eyes and cleared his throat. "Rasi and Alina ..." He lowered the scroll, looked over the top of his spectacles, and added, "That would be you." Then he lifted the scroll again. "... are considered criminals under Tevin's law, and are to be arrested on sight. In addition to their arrest, their soldiers must surrender and face punishment for harboring them for all these years. The Epertasian army realizes you have not brought this army here today in order to surrender, but we are asking you to do just that. If you do, you will save your friends a lot of death and misery." He looked up again with a proud smile. "I added the misery part."

Rasi continued glaring. His straps subtly shifted, anxious for a fight. He struggled to keep them from lashing out and breaking Zenner's fat neck.

Rasi mindspoke to Alina, *I am growing annoyed with this man. This is your opportunity, as I promised, to convince him to join his men with ours and return Epertase to its rightful ruler. But my patience is thin.*

Alina moved her horse forward. "Captain Zenner?"

"Ma'am."

"It wasn't long ago that you fought for me and my kingdom—"

"I still fight for the same kingdom. Only the one giving the orders has changed."

"Please, hear me out."

"My apologies." He hocked and spat next to his horse.

"We are here to end Tevin's madness. The only obstacles in our way are you and your men. It doesn't have to be that way. Do you remember my Epertase? My father's? My grandfather's? Do you remember the freedoms you had? Don't you want to be free like that again?"

"I am still free, ma'am."

"Maybe you are, but your neighbors—probably even members of your own family, if you were to be honest—have lost the very freedoms you profess to enjoy. Tell me, can your wife ride a horse within Thasula today? Can your mother or father still speak freely without threat of punishment, or travel the streets at any time of the night without being jailed or worse? Tevin is as much a threat to Epertase as the invading Teks or the heathens before them."

"And yet you align yourself with those very Teks now. You insist that Tevin is a tyrant, except it is you who brings foreigners to fight your own people."

The other captain, a man Rasi didn't recognize, sighed and slouched as if bored. *Patience,* Rasi thought. *I'll bring war to you soon enough.*

Zenner continued. "What you do not understand is that Tevin is more powerful than you could ever imagine. Even if I trusted these Teks who stand with you, joining you would only doom us all. I have a wife and child, and betraying Tevin would not bode well for any of us. For the last time, I am begging you. Alina, Rasi, give up this fantasy of ruling Epertase again. Lay down your arms and come with us. If you choose war instead, you will be killing the very people you claim to want to protect. If you truly want to protect them, you can end this without a single Epertasian life sacrificed. Simply come with us and give Tevin what he needs."

"How could I do that when what he needs is my son's death?"

Zenner shrugged.

The other captain crowded his horse against Zenner's and said, "Enough talk. They can surrender or they can die; it makes no difference to me." Despite his brave words, he never took his nervous eyes from Rasi's hovering straps.

Zenner held up his hand to quiet his fellow captain. "You will have your chance to fight in a moment. Be patient. If nothing else, you owe it to our former queen."

Rasi whispered into Alina's mind, *We could use their horses. And I'm done negotiating. Have you finished?*

Alina bowed her head. "Zenner, is there nothing I can say to change your heart?"

"My heart was never against you, Alina."

Rasi shook his head. He subtly moved his horse closer to the two captains. *No more talk, Alina. Back away.* She tugged at her reins.

The smug captain grinned, and Rasi couldn't wait to knock it from his face.

Are we finished, Alina?

Reluctantly, she nodded.

Now, it was Rasi's turn to grin. He lunged, his straps grabbing both men and yanking them from their horses. They both hit the ground before they knew what was happening. Zenner scurried to his knees, his eyes full of terror as Rasi rode past and kicked him in the teeth, sending him unconscious to the ground. He wished he had killed him.

The other soldier scooted away on his rear, not as brave as he was moments before. The half-dozen soldiers reached for their swords and Rasi's straps flared out, knocking one of them to the ground. Rasi grabbed the captain's neck with a strap and hoisted the man in the air. Then he slammed him to the ground. The strap recoiled from the motionless captain's throat.

Rasi felt Alina's glare on his back.

"Was that necessary?" she asked.

I thought so. Tell them to take their leaders and leave.

She relayed his message.

Rasi took possession of the two riderless horses as the soldiers gathered their unconscious captains and fled toward the safety of their numbers.

"We really should go," Alina said as she turned her horse toward the Teks.

Rasi studied the Epertasian front line briefly before following. *Their arrow barrage will be epic,* he warned once they reached their soldiers. He nudged his horse close to hers.

Leander faced his men. "The battle begins. Raise your shields." The Teks knelt and held their tall shields over their heads, forming a nearly impenetrable ceiling of sorts. They were skilled and well-rehearsed, each of their shields held in perfect coordination to leave no unintended gaps.

Leander turned back to Rasi. "Let them send their arrows. We are ready."

Alina, when the arrows come, it will get very loud and chaotic. Be sure to control your horse and keep him beneath our shields. Rasi used his straps to hold her shield in front of her horse's head as she leaned against its neck. He did the same on his horse.

He took a slow, calming breath. It was that briefest of moments that his fears and doubts gave way to the inevitability of what was coming, and he somehow felt at peace. As much as he hated war, he belonged on the battlefield.

A nervous silence stretched through his men.

"After each wave of arrows, we all move forward as one." Leander commanded.

The suns hid behind a blanket of Epertasian arrows.

It begins.

CHAPTER 36

THE SECOND
TEK WAR

The first arrow bounced with a dull thud off the shield above Alina's head, causing her to flinch. Rasi closed his eyes in calm meditation as the arrow was followed by a thousand more clanging against the shields around him. His horse jostled and danced, and he fought to keep close to Alina. After the arrow barrage, silence fell, only to be broken by sporadic moans throughout the Teks' ranks. As good as their defense was, some arrows were bound to sneak through.

As one, the army lurched forward and reset. Another benefit of Rasi's surprise advance was that it prevented the Epertasian army from setting up their legendary catapults.

Have you been struck? Rasi shouted in Alina's mind. He lowered the shields briefly to check.

She shook her head. *I'm fine.*

The ground appeared to have sprouted a thousand rigid blades of grass adorned with purple fletching. A strap snatched up an arrow and held it above Rasi's head. A second strap grabbed hold, and they snapped it in two and dropped the pieces.

Every eye across the field watched to see how Rasi's army would counter. The front line of Teks dropped their arrow-riddled shields and lifted their long, cylindrical weapons to their shoulders. Alina glanced back nervously.

Face forward, Alina. Have faith in their aim. They will not hit us.

The Epertasians lifted their own shields and crouched behind them. Their commanders sat on horseback along the front line, unprotected. It was a tactic Rasi had used in the past to show his men strength and fearlessness.

Leander sat on his saddle facing his men. Farther down the line, Atticus and Eldon and every other commander did the same. They looked to each other and lifted their swords in concert. Then their swords dropped to their sides.

The cylindrical weapons popped with deafening din along the front line. Projectiles slammed into Epertasian shields with the distant sound of gravel hurled against tin. Some Epertasian soldiers fell forward on their hole-riddled shields. By the sheer luck of the gods, most of the commanders avoided the first Tek assault, although two riderless horses cantered into the field. One other horse lay dead. The remaining commanders steadied their steeds and held their ground.

The Teks lowered their weapons and lifted their shields again as the second volley of Epertasian arrows chased the sky. Rasi lifted Alina's shield over her with his straps, but he laid his own at his horse's feet. Sometimes demonstrations of fearlessness from commanders were as important as sound tactics. The men would fight harder knowing their leaders would never falter.

Leander shouted from behind his shield, "Rasi, what are you doing? Take cover."

Alina's terrified eyes burned through the side of his face, but he ignored her.

He sat straight and defiant as the arrows peppered the ground and shields around him. He didn't cower. He didn't flinch. Exposing himself as he had was risky, but his enemy as well as his own men needed to see that he was as fearless as the Epertasian commanders.

During the second volley of arrows, the Tek front line reloaded their cylindrical weapons. After a second hurried advance, their second explosion of thunder felled another row of Epertasians. This time their commanders hid behind shields, their show of bravery accomplished. And again, the Teks lifted their shields in anticipation of the forthcoming counter. Rasi also lifted his shield.

More Teks fell as arrows slipped past their defenses, but overall the shields did their jobs. The men marched forward again. It would be a long day. Some would question Rasi's tactics, opting instead for a full-on advance, but his reasons were sound and would be revealed in due time. He looked east, hopeful the revelation would come sooner rather than later.

The relentless suns pounded the battlefield throughout the afternoon and into the evening, seemingly adding weight to the Teks' oversized shields. At the end of the first day, Rasi rode along the Tek front taking stock of his forces, pleased they had held up relatively well. The Epertasians' first day hadn't been as fruitful as they had undoubtedly expected. Refilled water bladders passed from the rear supply cache throughout the ranks. One of the reasons Rasi had chosen the Great Plains as his battlefield was because of the fresh water supply from the streams near Shadows Peak.

Night fell. Everyone was exhausted. Rasi studied Alina's weary face. *Alina?*

Without looking at him, she snapped, "Don't even say it, Rasi. I'm staying here."

I was just thinking how much the wounded might benefit from your sparkling smile at the tents.

Her eyes narrowed. "Are you being facetious?"

He held his first finger close to his thumb and grinned. *Maybe a little.*

"It's not helpful."

Apologies.

"I'll fall back and help with the wounded once we advance, as promised. But for now, I should be seen at the front."

That she was right didn't alleviate any of his worry.

Beneath the cover of their shields, the Teks prepared their secret weapon. Leander spread the word to, "Release the rolling thunders."

Tek soldiers hurried to the front with what looked like metal tortoises with beefy, thick-treaded wheels strapped to their backs.

They set the rolling thunders along the front line. If all went as planned, the shin-high grass combined with the darkening skies would provide sufficient cover so the Epertasians wouldn't see what was coming until it was too late. They set the thunder machines in the grass and backed away. The machines drudged forward like real tortoises, taking most of the night to reach the Epertasian side.

The Epertasians launched occasional arrow volleys which were deflected by the Tek shields while the soldiers got their rest. But for the most part both sides waited for morning. When the rolling thunders reached the Epertasian front line, the confused Epertasians panicked and scrambled to get out of their paths. But there was nowhere to go.

The first rolling machine flashed with a great fireball, trailed by a distant rumble. Epertasian soldiers and their newly detached limbs hurtled through the air. Then the rest of the rolling machines detonated with equally horrific results. Cries and moans followed explosions and chaos. The commanders galloped along the front, screaming frantically for their men to stand strong.

Capitalizing on the chaos, the Teks fired their weapons again, this time dropping Epertasians by the hundreds. Leander gave Rasi a confident nod. "Small victories, Rasi. Small victories."

And then the army moved forward and reset. Rasi looked east again. He couldn't wait much longer to attack.

Eventually, the Epertasian commanders restored order among their men, but not their nerves. They continued scanning the field for more rolling thunders.

Morning brought a single fireball soaring over the wall from within the castle grounds. Rasi watched it fly overhead and slam into his forces with devastating results. He bowed his head. *Damn.* The catapults had arrived. Though he knew it wouldn't be a full catapult assault, he also knew even the few they could gather in a hurry could be extremely damaging. And there was nothing he could do to avoid the first wave. A dozen more fireballs trailed the first.

"Rasi, what do we do?" Alina screamed, her face blanching with terror.

We stay calm, Alina. We lead. We endure. And then we attack.

Rasi's eyes tracked the fireballs over his head. The Teks near the rear of his forces scrambled as explosions sent burning bodies into the air. It was only a matter of time before the Epertasians dialed down their range. The only escape from a catapult assault was advance beyond their shallowest range. But that meant starting the battle before Rasi was ready. He looked east again just in case.

Leander shouted. "Maybe she's not coming."

It had been a long shot. Leander was right.

The Epertasians quickly followed the catapult assault with another volley of arrows. Leander rode fearlessly along the front line, screaming for his men to hold their ground. An arrow pinned his foot to his horse. He snapped the fletching off and ripped his foot free.

The next catapult attack fell closer in the midpoint of his forces. It was as disastrous as the first. Rasi sighed. He had no other choice. *Order the charge, Alina.*

Alina nodded to Leander. "He says it's time."

Leander sent the word to the commanders down the line. "On Rasi's command," he shouted.

Another wave of fireballs ravaged his men, followed by another blanket of arrows.

Rasi captured Alina's gaze. *You've done what you needed to do. Your people have seen your strength. Now, for Cridon's sake, it is time for you to return to the forest. You will do more good helping the wounded.*

"But …"

Alina, you promised.

She nodded in reluctant agreement. *Be careful, my love.*

He inhaled deep through his nose, envisioning his sword ripping through his enemy. He winked and then kicked his steed into a gallop.

As Alina rode through the Tek army, they slung their shields over their shoulders and drew their swords. Their unified war cry could wake the dead.

While greatly outnumbered, facing a powerful wizard, and with the hylocks from the Wastelands sure to join the fight, the brave Teks began their charge behind Rasi.

The Epertasians drew their swords. Fireballs soared overhead.

Rasi collided with the front line of Epertasian foot soldiers a split second before the Tek front line. Weapons met shields, flesh, and bone with a shrill clamor. Rasi swung and hacked and killed with skill and determination while his straps sliced and ripped with equal fervor. He was a living weapon, his eyes focused, his sword unyielding.

He plunged his sword without mercy into the mass of soldiers that swarmed him and his men. His straps defended his horse, knowing the horse was a great advantage. This was where Rasi belonged. This was where he did his best work. He howled as he massacred men by the handfuls. His straps deflected strikes again and again, while delivering their own blows with razor-edged steel.

The Epertasians were suffocating in their sheer numbers, but the Teks battled forward, one man to every three. These weren't the same Teks Rasi had defeated years ago, though; these were Teks trained under his watch, and they had become as skilled in the use of a blade as any Epertasian. Maybe more so.

As his initial wave tired, they fell back to be immediately replaced by their fresher brothers in a coordinated attempt at attrition. The Epertasians were less disciplined, every man fighting as if the battle would be short and he was alone. The years under Tevin and Jarrah's command had hurt their preparation. Not just anyone could lead an army.

Tek soldiers crowded around Rasi, giving him a chance to back off and catch his breath. He surveyed the Tek push. Though they held up well, they weren't making any headway. There were just too many Epertasians.

"We'll never break through like this," Atticus screamed, suddenly beside him. He could see Eldon towering above his foes as he sliced through them. He was the only one of Rasi's commanders to never drop back for a breather. Rasi studied the battle lines, desperately searching for a single surge that pushed deeper than the rest of the front. The entirety of his plan hinged on penetrating to the castle wall in one V-shaped formation. The results of their initial thrust proved that goal was going to take some time to accomplish.

Like with most battles, when the actual face-to-face combat began, it was brief and violent and shocking. Few soldiers, despite their training and endurance, could keep up such a violent pace for long. Several times, both armies mutually pulled back enough to regroup and regain their wind.

Well into the evening, the armies fought these short, brutal battles again and again with neither side giving much ground. Teks and Epertasians alike used the brief lulls to drag their wounded from the battlefield.

Night fell, and with it a pause in the fighting. The two armies rested so close to each other that they could hear each other's whispers. More arrows rained from the top of the wall throughout the night, but the Tek's still had their shields. Brief skirmishes broke out here and there, but overall the two sides used the time to recuperate.

Rasi downed an entire bladder of water and then closed his eyes for the better part of an hour. When he woke, he felt refreshed. He passed word through the ranks that the next advance would begin at sunrise.

He led the morning charge. The Epertasians were ready.

By the afternoon of the next day, the Teks had pushed the front line of Epertasians back just enough to show progress, but not enough to mean much. Rasi did ongoing assessments of the numbers. It was painfully obvious the current tactic was unsustainable. There were just too many of them.

Atticus rode nearby, shouting orders to his men and engaging the Epertasians whenever the opportunity arose.

Rasi was exhausted, as were all his men. His upper arms burned with fatigue, and even his straps took breaks to drag behind his horse whenever they could.

Eldon finally took his first breather of the day and joined Rasi and Atticus just out of the fray. "Rasi, do you want me to make you a hole to advance now? This current plan doesn't seem to be working."

As good as Eldon was, there were simply too many Epertasian soldiers to take his boasts seriously. Rasi shook his head. *We just have to hold them, Eldon. Somewhere along the front, we'll break through.* He looked to the empty eastern skies again. Any hope that she was coming had faded by now.

Eldon, however, called Rasi's attention westward where the sky filled with a dark cloud of winged beasts. Rasi had hoped their absence had meant they weren't coming at all. The hylocks' arrival was about to tip the pendulum so greatly in Tevin's favor that the Teks may never recover.

The focus inevitably turned from the battle on the ground to the approaching swarm in the sky. Atticus rode through the battlefield shouting, "Keep fighting the man in front of you. Focus."

The hylocks dove toward them with a unified cackling squeal. They snatched Tek soldiers and carried them high into the air before dropping them to their deaths. The Teks who turned to fight off the beasts died by Epertasian blades. It was quickly becoming a massacre. Leander called the Tek archers forward, but there weren't enough arrows in the world to fend off such an onslaught. After the first volley, the hylocks turned their attention to the archers. They tried to retreat, but there was no escape. The hylocks slashed with their venomous nails.

Rasi's straps caught one swooping creature, ripped its leg off, and left it flopping on the ground to be skewered by a passing Tek. Eldon fought valiantly, killing hylocks and Epertasian soldiers alike. He leaped, snatched another passing hylock's foot, and left its windpipe dangling outside its neck. Rasi needed a dozen more soldiers like him.

The hylocks had the unique advantage of being able to attack deep within Rasi's reserves with far more precision than the catapults. If this kept up, Rasi wouldn't be able to replenish the front lines.

To Rasi's dread, the hylocks were attacking closer and closer to the forest where Alina and the medical tents waited. Killing the doctors and medics was a brutal yet effective strategy. Unable to abandon his position, he said a silent prayer that the soldiers could hold them off and that the creatures were too naïve to recognize the opportunity.

As Rasi rode forward, countless Tek soldiers retreated with bleeding gashes in their flesh, already feeling the effects of the venom. He pitied them for the agony they were about to endure.

He ordered another charge, swinging his sword and lashing out with his armored straps along the way.

"Keep fighting," Eldon shouted with glee. "These creatures cannot stay in the air forever—no creature can. When they land, we will gain the advantage." As he screamed the words, he plucked another hylock from the air and slaughtered it.

Soldiers fell by the hundreds without making a dent in the Epertasian lines. Rasi looked east again. He had one fleeting hope left.

Aidric, we're counting on you. May the gods be on your side.

CHAPTER 37

CHOOSING A SIDE

Aidric stood at the edge of a clearing in the center of a forest he had never been in before. The ground was scorched bare of any vegetation and the dirt was hard and cracked like that of the deepest parts of the Wastelands. The trees lining the clearing were dead and burnt. He was as scared as he'd ever been. As the reality of what he was doing settled in, he wondered why he had even considered—let alone accepted—Rasi's request to take on the mission. He must have suffered a temporary loss of sanity.

Aidric sat down and waited for most of the afternoon and into the evening. It was a rare moon rising. Its center remained hidden in darkness while its edges shone bright, reflecting the two setting suns like an hourglass.

Aidric's journey had taken longer than planned because his horse had stumbled and broken its leg on some uneven terrain. It took him an entire afternoon to acquire another without drawing attention. Being caught stealing a horse wouldn't bode well for his mission. Another half-day was wasted when he had to hide after encountering a group of soldiers who had happened to make their camp near his on their way to Thasula. He worried Rasi's fight would be over before he ever joined him.

He snacked on jerky he'd picked up at the Puimia market as he waited. When the moon reached the stars a single muffled *whoosh* cut through the calm night air. With suddenly trembling hands, Aidric stood up. This was why he had come, he told himself. There was no turning back. Who could have ever dreamed that his death would come by way of a dragon? No other creature's wings could make such a noise. He slowly turned south toward the sound. The whooshing sound came again, and again, closer and more rhythmic. A magnificent beast crossed the face of the moon.

Aidric's breathing rivaled a hummingbird's. His heart danced nervously in his chest.

Instinctively, he reached for his sword, forgetting he had left it outside the clearing per Rasi's instructions, further proof of his insanity. Though he wanted to flee, he waited and whispered silent prayers that the gods would protect him from the fiercest creature ever given life.

The dragon eyed him from the sky and then dove with a roar. When she reached the treetops, she pulled up and circled the clearing. She tilted her head as she flew, keeping her hypnotizing yellow eyes on the intruder in her nest. Why she didn't simply fry him and be done with it, he would never know. He knelt in wait with his head bowed.

When she reached the far edge of the clearing, she pulled up and landed with a ground-shaking thud. Then she paced side to side, never taking her serpent eyes off him. It's what Rasi had said she would do. So far, so good. He lifted his hands in surrender.

She roared, the heat from her breath nearly singing the hair on his forearms. He spoke respectfully. "I'm not here as your enemy. Please do not bring me harm."

She continued to pace, grunting and snorting as he spoke. Her eyes crossed at him. That he wasn't already dead meant she was at least willing to listen. "I have been sent by Rasi. He said you have helped him in the past. He needs your help once again."

She slowed her pacing. A trickle of smoke lifted from her snout. He wondered how many people in her centuries-long life had witnessed such a sight before she'd cooked them in her flames.

Emboldened by the fact that he still breathed, he stepped forward. "I don't know why you helped Rasi and Alina before, but you must have seen something good in them."

She stopped his cautious advance with a low, rumbling growl.

He swallowed hard. "The wizard that now rules these lands seeks to steal the Light from Queen Alina's son. If he succeeds, he will become unstoppable. Tevin the Third will not rest until every person … every creature in this world is either enslaved or destroyed."

She lifted her head above the trees and looked to the west as though she already knew where the battle waged.

"Rasi sent me here with no weapons so you could see that we are not your enemy. We want peace. Unless Tevin the Third is stopped, that can never be. Rasi said you had children. He believes they should remain as free as every other creature of these lands. You once saw something in him. Please, help him … help us … save this kingdom." He started walking again. This time she didn't stop him. The air near her felt like he'd lowered his head too close to a blacksmith's forge.

She looked to the sky as if pondering his words. Then she moved her snout close to him again and roared into his face. His ears popped. He cringed away. Instead of turning him to ash, she squatted, flapped her mighty wings, and shot toward the moon again. With no way of knowing whether he'd gotten through to her or not, he dropped to his rear and focused on calming his nerves. He would stay there for the rest of the night.

CHAPTER 38

PERSEVERE

The initial hylock attack had been brutal and effective, but by nightfall the Teks had adjusted. Though the soldiers weren't pushing forward, they had stopped giving back their hard-fought gains.

The night was filled with cries and moans from both sides of the battlefield. The front lines had calmed as an unspoken temporary truce had formed so both sides could attend to their wounded. The hylocks, however, continued swooping in and picking at the Teks throughout the night.

Eldon, Atticus, Leander, and Rasi met to discuss the next day's strategy. Rasi laid it out in simple terms. "If Aidric doesn't send the dragon soon, we will have to make a final push with everything we have."

Leander, with resignation thick in his voice, said, "We cannot win." He was tired—they all were.

"We must keep fighting," Eldon said when Rasi didn't respond. "We must fight with every breath we still have, for this war is our last chance. Failure means death. Each new day brings a new opportunity, and I have faith that tomorrow will bring another. We just have to be ready to seize it."

A hylock swooped down behind him as he spoke. Eldon ducked, caught the creature, and then drove its head into the ground. With a grin he looked up and said, "Keep your eyes open. These creatures are becoming quite the nuisance."

When the suns rose the Epertasians were ready and waiting. The hylocks had stopped attacking just before dawn, though their rest would undoubtedly be short. Rasi ordered another advance. His weary soldiers answered his call without hesitation.

From the rear of the Epertasian lines, the hylock army took to the air again. Within moments, the battle was in full swing.

The hylocks were devastating and ruthless. By midmorning, the Teks had given back their previous gains completely. Rasi repeatedly looked to the empty eastern sky, still hopeful for Aidric's success, though his hope was dwindling fast. As he watched his men falling in waves, for the first time in his life he contemplated surrendering. Tevin's army—an army Rasi had helped build—was still too powerful, even with its reduced size. If they didn't break through soon, by tomorrow surrender would be inevitable.

Atticus rode to Rasi's side. "We cannot break through. Do you think Aidric has failed?"

Rasi looked east again, wishing he knew. Though he had tried to plan the battle with the expectation that the dragon would never arrive, deep down he knew their chances of victory were nil without her. But that was the hand he'd been dealt, and he needed to fight as hard as he could regardless.

He told Atticus to order the final push and not to let up until it was over one way or the other. Atticus nodded and rode away. It was time for Rasi to honor his last promise to Alina. He hurried across the plains to the forest where the medical tents were. Alina was working outside. Her weary eyes matched her slouching shoulders and rumpled clothes. Blood stained her dress and forehead. She stood over a soldier on a gurney and shoved her hands over one bleeding wound only to find a second one spurting. She unfastened the soldier's sword belt and cinched it around his upper leg, just above the second wound. Then she wrapped the belt around the hilt of his sword and twisted until the spurting slowed and stopped. Then she wedged the sword between his side and the ground so it wouldn't unravel. "Be strong," she said with a light touch to his cheek. After wiping her hands on her blood-stained blouse, she moved to her next patient. His neck wound was obviously fatal. Some of the Teks writhed in agony and cried that their veins were burning, and it broke Rasi's heart. He'd felt their pain.

The dead lay piled around the tents. The living waited patiently for treatment, some with missing limbs, and others with limbs so mangled and wounds so dirty that they may yet need to be severed.

If he could protect Alina from witnessing such horrors, he would move mountains to do so. She pushed her disheveled hair back with a bloody hand, wiped the sweat from her brow, and looked toward Rasi by chance.

Though exhausted, her eyes brightened when she saw him. He dismounted, an eye still watching the treetops for hylocks.

She raced to Rasi. "Thank the gods you're still alive," she cried. She looked him up and down. "Are you injured?"

This blood is not mine. He stretched with a wince and added, *Well, not all of it.* He hugged her. *Are you getting by?*

"Barely. It's awful here. I've seen too many men die. Even young Randell. He was just a kid when I met him." Her eyes blurred with tears. "I can't imagine telling his father when this is over. If *he's* even still alive."

Rasi hadn't the heart to tell her he wasn't. She looked into his eyes sadly. "Is it time?"

He nodded.

"All right. I'm ready."

He lowered his head. *Before we go, I need you to promise me something.*

"Anything."

You must promise you'll forgive me for anything you see today, no matter what it is.

Her head cocked and her brow wrinkled. "Of course I'll forgive you. I'm not some naïve little girl. I know what needs to be done."

He longed to tell her the rest of the plan, the part that had gnawed at his gut ever since he had first envisioned it on Tek Island. But he knew the secret would break her heart—that she would never accept it. His plan was as risky as they came. If it worked, she may not speak to him for a long time. But if it failed, there wouldn't be enough time in the world for her to forgive him.

Or for him to forgive himself.

She leaned up and kissed his cheek. "I love you."

He nodded and helped her onto her horse.

A Tek soldier carrying a rolling thunder strapped to his back approached. "Here, sir. It's our last one." He helped Rasi fasten it to his saddle.

Together, Rasi and Alina started back toward the battle at the wall.

CHAPTER 39

THE SECRET
PART

Simcane scanned the fronts of the buildings to make sure no one was watching before sneaking into an abandoned house near Thasula's main drag. He'd been staying there with Marge and Cridon while the battle waged. He hurried upstairs.

"What have you heard?" Marge asked from her fixed perch at the window.

Simcane shut the door and wedged the back of a chair under the handle. "The war's still waging. Have you seen any sign of her?"

Marge looked through the window toward the eastern sky again and then shook her head.

"Damn. We should have seen her by now."

"What'd Rasi tell you to do if the dragon didn't come?"

"He told me to flee the city."

"Then we should leave."

Simcane sighed. "Maybe. I think we need to give it a bit longer, though."

Marge turned from the window. "Did you find your friend?"

"I did."

"And did he agree to help?"

"Of course."

"Are ya sure you can trust him? You said he's an Epertasian soldier, after all."

"Oh, yes, I trust him completely. His name's Bohden, and I helped him and his mom out of a pinch several years ago."

"Then we just need the dragon?"

He nodded, and the corners of his mouth drifted downward. He stepped beside Marge and touched her shoulder. Her eyelids appeared heavy. "Why don't you rest? I can watch for a while."

She leaned into his hand. "I guess I could use a little nap before Cridon wakes."

Simcane's eye darted to a blanket by the farthest wall where Cridon slept. Though it ate at him to not be with Rasi for the battle, one look at Cridon reminded him why he wasn't.

Marge no sooner crawled under a blanket near Cridon than he sat up and rubbed his eyes. "Mr. Simcane?" he said with a scratchy, tired voice.

Simcane held his finger in front of his lips and bobbed his head toward where Marge lay, her eyes already plastered shut. "Come 'ere."

Cridon sat on a chair beside him. "Are we going to see my mom and dad today?"

Simcane gently slid Cridon's chair so he couldn't be seen through the window. "Soon, kid."

"I'm bored, Mr. Simcane."

Simcane studied the street outside and then said, "All right. Let's play a game. I see something red. What is it?"

Cridon climbed from his chair and peeked through the window. There was a red sign across the street, a red scarf stuck around a horse post where the wind must have carried it, and red stained glass in the church window down the road. "How many guesses?"

"Two."

Cridon groaned. Then he studied the outside as though the entire world depended on him getting it right. He struggled for the answer before confidently saying, "The sign."

Simcane shook his head.

Cridon pumped his fists in disappointment.

"One more guess."

"The scarf by the post."

It was actually the stained glass, but Simcane nodded.

"Yes. I knew it." Victorious, Cridon asked for some deer jerky and Simcane pointed him to Marge's bag.

Simcane settled in for a long watch, but he had been awake just as long as Marge, if not longer, and his forehead soon rested on the window pane.

"Simcane," Marge whispered loudly with a firm shake of his arm. "Simcane."

He sprang to his feet, hand already on his sword. Before he could ask what she wanted, he heard a faint whoosh of air unlike any sound he'd ever heard.

"I think I saw her." Marge pointed east.

Though he couldn't see the dragon in the sky at first, he saw her shadow trace the street toward them. And then he saw her. He stood up in awe. He'd seen a lot in his life, but never anything as impressive and intimidating as the creature that flew with her enormous wings just above the rooftops. She was magnificent. If she were a painting by the most legendary Epertasian artist, he wouldn't believe such a beautiful creature could exist. As she soared close to the street, he beckoned Cridon over to see. Her scales glistened in the sunslight.

Cridon gazed through the window as the dragon shot past close enough Simcane could have almost touched her had the window been open. Cridon's eyes widened; Simcane's eye probably did as well. Then she let out a blood-curdling roar that shook the windows and made Cridon covered his ears. Once she reached the end of the street, she darted skyward and streaked toward the Great Plains.

"She's coming, Rasi," Simcane whispered. "Aidric did it. Hold strong."

Marge stood on her tiptoes to see past Simcane's shoulder. She playfully mussed Cridon's hair. "Can you believe what you just saw?"

He shook his head without looking away from the window.

Simcane watched the street fill with onlookers, which would give them all the perfect cover. "Let's go," he snapped, and grabbed Cridon's hand. "Bohden will be here soon." He led Cridon down the stairs to the front door where Bohden was already waiting outside.

"Did you see that, Sim?" he said with the exuberance of a child.

"I saw." Simcane stepped from the porch and froze. Hurried whispers from the alley told Simcane of a trap before he saw the soldiers. He reached for his sword and turned to Bohden as soldiers pounced from both sides of the house and surrounded them. There were four.

Bohden backed away. "I'm so sorry, Sim."

One of the soldiers grabbed Marge before Simcane could get to her and pressed a knife to her throat. Simcane pulled Cridon close to his leg.

A soldier in captain's garb rode a horse out of the alley and stopped behind Bohden.

"Captain Casa," Bohden said.

The captain nodded. "You've done well, Bohden. You even managed not to get stabbed this time." With a glance to Cridon, he added, "You may have single-handedly ended this war, kid. And made me ... er ... us rich in the process."

Simcane started to draw his sword, but the soldier holding Marge cleared his throat.

Captain Casa relaxed in his saddle, wearing a half-cocked smile. "There's no use fighting us, Simcane. I won't hesitate to kill this woman and you if you resist."

Cridon looked up with fearful eyes.

Simcane didn't look down, but reassured him with mindspeak. *You have to be strong now. Trust me. I won't let them hurt you.*

I trust you, Mr. Simcane.

While Casa droned on about how Tevin would reward him and his men, Simcane nudged Cridon in front of him. With Cridon shielding his actions, he fished through a bag tied to his sword belt for Leander's tiny gift. Once in hand, he faked a cough and shoved the key into his mouth. He pushed it with his tongue between his upper teeth and cheek. Then he nudged Cridon behind his leg.

Casa's speech finally wound down, and he stretched and yawned. "Why in the world would you be so foolish as to bring the boy into the city?"

Simcane shook his head. He felt Cridon's grip tighten on his leg. The soldiers had the numbers, but they also had respect for him as a legendary warrior, and that made them hesitate. Simcane held up his hand and said, "I won't fight you. But I won't be separated from this boy, either."

Casa rolled his eyes.

Simcane added, "All I ask are two things. First, you release the woman since she has nothing to do with this war. And second, you do not try to separate me from this boy. Do those two things and I'll surrender willingly."

After weighing Simcane's words, Casa finally answered, "No deal. The woman goes with us. Without her, my leverage on you is cut in half. However, as far as you and the boy, well, I don't care how you go to Tevin as long as you go." He addressed his men. "Bring all three." Then he turned his horse away.

A fifth soldier led horses from the alley. The soldier next to Casa retrieved shackles from a saddlebag and approached Simcane.

Simcane shook his head, stopping the soldier in his tracks. "Toss them here. I'll put them on myself. You can watch, but you're not getting close to us."

With the soldier hesitant to advance and Simcane clearly resolute, Casa relented. "Simcane, you truly are a thorn. Very well. Leave your sword on the ground, though. I'll not budge on that." He nodded to his soldier. "Give him the shackles."

"Fair enough." Simcane dropped his sword and knelt. *Climb onto my back and hold on, Cridon.* With his help, Cridon climbed onto his back and wrapped his skinny arms around Simcane's broad shoulders.

Simcane fastened the shackles around his wrists and tossed the chain back to the soldier, who then fastened it to his saddle. The five soldiers, Bohden, and Captain Casa led Marge, Cridon, and Simcane toward the castle gates.

CHAPTER 40

A CHANCE

The front lines had blurred enough that there was no longer a clear separation of Epertasian and Tek soldiers as Rasi approached from the medical tents with Alina sharing his saddle.

"How will we get through?" she asked.

We must fight our way in.

She squeezed him. "I'm with you, Rasi, till the end."

Rasi scanned the fighting men until he saw Atticus and Atticus saw him. They gave each other slight nods. Rasi pointed him out to Alina. *We follow Atticus.* He kicked his horse into a gallop and readied his sword. Hylocks continued lifting Tek soldiers and dropping them throughout the battlefield. Alina gasped as one swooped close by, but Rasi's straps snatched it from the air and snapped its neck with a violent jerk. Another one dove for Atticus, who blindly whipped his sword over his head. The creature's guts spilled to the ground.

While Atticus was distracted by that creature, an Epertasian soldier jammed a spear through his horse's chest plate. The horse reared back, throwing Atticus from the saddle. The impact jolted his sword from his hand and his helmet from his head. His horse fell on his right leg, pinning him. A hylock landed nearby, licking its lips and circling its now helpless prey.

Atticus pushed against his dying horse with his free leg, but it was too heavy. The hylock approached. Rasi downed several soldiers to get to his friend. He finally had a clear path and raced toward Atticus.

Atticus reached for his sword, but his outstretched fingers barely brushed the hilt. A hylock straddled him, drool leaking past its lips. It lunged for Atticus's throat, too far away for Rasi to reach in time. He tossed his sword and a strap caught it, stretched out, and swung. The blade struck flesh and took the hylock's head an instant before its teeth met Atticus's throat. Milky blood painted Atticus's face. He winced away from the spurting gore.

Stay near, Rasi told Alina, and handed her the reins. He jumped from his horse and raced to Atticus's side, killing another soldier who intercepted him. His straps wrapped around the dead horse while he planted his feet. They strained. The horse shifted slightly. Atticus wiggled his leg free.

Leander came to their side. Atticus wiped his face and struggled to his feet, clearly favoring his right leg.

"Is your leg broken?" Leander asked.

Atticus shook his head and worked out the kink. By the time he retrieved his sword, his gait was already improving.

Leander looked to Rasi. "Time for the push, sir?"

Rasi nodded before climbing back onto his horse behind Alina. Leander had brought fresh soldiers from the rear. They plowed forward, joining their already fighting men for a fresh push toward the wall. The tired Epertasians seemed to wilt at the sight of enemy reinforcements. The Teks fought with renewed vigor, pushing forward. Rasi and his straps were at the height of their talent as they sliced through soldiers with ease. The wall was within sight. This was it. This was their best chance.

"Puuush," Atticus cried, his sword dancing in front of him.

For that one small part of the offensive, that one small section, Rasi had a shot. *Just get me to the wall,* he thought.

And then, only a few hundred feet away to the east, the main gate opened and what appeared to be a thousand Epertasian Elite Guardsmen poured out. Rasi froze. His shoulders slouched. He slowly shook his head. For the first time in his fighting career, he didn't know how to proceed.

Leander saw it at the same time. "Should we retreat?" he screamed.

Though Rasi didn't know what to do, he knew retreating wasn't it. The reality was this was their last chance to break through.

What are you thinking, Rasi? Alina asked.

Have Atticus take you and flee. He killed another two soldiers with his straps.

What? I'm not going anywhere.

Alina, you must. Think about Cridon.

She shot a scowl over her shoulder. *And what about you?*

Rasi was tired of fighting. He was tired of always having bad odds. He was tired of hylocks and wizards and killing. As he watched his overwhelmed men around him, he was tired of seeing friends die. And he was just plain tired. *I've always been destined to die on a battlefield. This one looks as good as any.*

"That will never be the answer. I'm not leaving your side."

You must. This is it, Alina. This is the way it has to b—

A distant roar beyond the city wall interrupted him. He slowly lifted his eyes. Though he didn't see anything at first, he knew the sound. Anyone who had ever heard that roar could never forget it. The fighting halted as everyone's heads turned east.

And then, with seemingly the entire world waiting in silence, the most magnificent beast shot up from behind the buildings of Thasula. She would be beautiful if she wasn't so deadly. She appeared to taste the clouds before twisting in the air and diving as though in freefall.

The hylocks were the first to disengage and turn their attention to the newest threat. Tek arrows chased them as they flew to meet her head-on.

As she plummeted, they swarmed her like bees whose hive had been shaken by a mischievous boy. She devoured three of them in a single chomp and then set fire to another dozen. They scratched at her scales with their worthless venomous nails as she hurtled toward the ground. She ignored them like one might ignore a swarm of gnats.

Soldiers scattered beneath her. With her wings pinned to her sides, the hylocks couldn't keep up and she pulled away, leveling off just before reaching the ground. She soared over the soldiers' heads with such speed that the wind nearly blew them over. Two thin trails of smoke drew a line from the hylocks she had scorched to her nostrils. After reaching the outer edge of the battlefield, she banked and started back.

Leander rode through his men, screaming over and over, "Pull back. Pull back." His voice cracked from the strain. The Teks retreated as the Epertasians struggled with whether to stop them, prepare for the impossible task of fighting a dragon, or retreat, though the wall at their backs prevented them from going anywhere fast.

The dragon's first streak of firebreath torched dozens of screaming Epertasians in the center of their forces. Catapulted fireballs sailed at her from within the wall, but they were sloppy tools and easily avoided. While she inhaled for another firebreath, she snatched handfuls of men and tossed them aside. The Epertasians panicked, trampling their own brothers in their fervor to escape the next blast of fire. As men engulfed in flames ran blindly from the scorched ground, Alina turned away.

The dragon righted herself and landed on a crowd of scrambling men between Rasi and the wall. She looked back as if she'd known where he had been all along.

He pointed his straps to the wall. *I need to get there.*

She narrowed her eyes. Then she breathed in deep and seared a path through everyone and everything between her and the wall. She lowered her head and roared, rattling the very stones of the distant castle and telling Tevin his time was near.

Alina shouted to the Teks, "Bring the archers. Protect the dragon."

Tek soldiers charged past her and formed lines along the scorched path. Rasi kicked his steed into a gallop and charged the wall.

More hylocks attacked the dragon, harassing her sides as she lunged at them. She caught a few in her mouth, but not enough. For the first time, she winced, indicating her tolerance for their venom was finite. Rasi pointed to the hylocks and the archers took aim. The hylocks continued their attack, seeing her as more of a threat than the arrows. Some of them fell, but still not enough.

Eldon joined Rasi's advance, running stride-for-stride with his horse.

The Tek formation had already started to falter. Rasi glanced back at his dragon ally, but she was overwhelmed. She snagged two more hylocks in her mouth and chewed them into mush. The rest continued to pounce. For every ten she killed, twenty more took their place. She unleashed another explosion of fire as she spun. It looked like a tornado of flames. Burnt hylock carcasses fell by the dozens. She squatted and then shot toward the sky as another hundred hylocks gave chase. More fireballs launched from the catapults. She led the hylocks over Rasi's head and past the wall to where the catapults waited. The roar of her firebreath was music to Rasi's ears. Epertasian soldiers cried out as they, along with the catapults, went up in flames.

As the catapults burned, she rose above the battlefield. The sky filled with arrows from the Epertasian archers atop the wall, but they bounced harmlessly off her scales.

Eldon fought off soldiers as they broke through the Tek defenses. The crease was about to give way. At the wall, Rasi vaulted from his horse. Eldon, Leander, Atticus and a couple dozen Tek soldiers defended his back as he removed the rolling thunder from the saddle and shoved it against the wall. After activating it with a switch, he joined the others and climbed back into his saddle behind Alina. *You might want to plug your ears.*

Alina barely had time to lift her hands before a magnificent explosion rocked the wall. Stone and archers flew through the air. A large hole opened at its base. Rasi, Eldon, and Alina ran through it and headed for the castle. As Eldon passed through, he turned back and shouted to Leander, "Get to safety. We'll take it from here."

Still dogged by the hylocks, the dragon swooped by and laid waste to another mass of Epertasian soldiers, giving Atticus, Leander, and their men a path to return to their side of the battlefield.

Inside the wall, more Epertasian soldiers lay strewn among the debris. Soldiers formed a bucket brigade in a futile attempt to save what was left of their burning catapults. Others were too preoccupied tending to the wounded to notice Rasi, Alina, and Eldon in the smoke. The ones who did notice were easily dispatched.

Beyond the Epertasian army's chaotic staging area, the streets were mostly deserted until they neared the castle gates. Eldon raced ahead and slaughtered the gate guards, but not before they could give the alarm. Half a dozen disbelieving soldiers poured out of the gatehouse.

Rasi dismounted and helped Alina down. He smacked his horse's hindquarters to send him running through the courtyard. *Hold them off, Eldon,* he shouted in his friend's mind. He grabbed Alina's hand and pulled her around the side of the castle toward the servants' entrance. Eldon defended their backs as he trailed them. They slipped inside.

CHAPTER 41

BATTLE OF LEGENDS

Tevin climbed onto the wall alongside his archers and surveyed the battlefield as a dragon laid waste to large swaths of his army. Why hadn't anyone told him that Rasi had a dragon? They'd been doing so well before she showed up. And where the hell were Jarrah and the bulk of his army? Surely, Rasi hadn't beaten them on Tek Island. Unless the dragon …

As he stood watching the magnificent beast, he couldn't help but marvel. *What raw power,* he thought. She landed, scorched another flock of pursuing hylocks, and then sprang into the air again. As the hylocks attacked, she spun in a spiral to elude their pestering attacks.

The dragon made another pass through his soldiers, her firebreath annihilating all in her path. Something needed to be done before she ended the war by herself. He would have preferred to stay in the castle until the battle was ended, but she had already decimated a chunk of his army. He stood tall, his purple-lined black robe fluttering in the calm breeze, and watched until he'd had enough.

"Come to me," he whispered. Though she was too far away to hear, she turned her head slightly. He grinned. "Face me, dragon." He dropped his head back and pointed his chest toward the sky with his arms outstretched at his sides. An orange beam blasted from his chest through the clouds. The men on the battlefield went silent, all eyes turning to Tevin's beam. The dragon banked and shot toward the beam as if drawn to his power. Tevin lifted his head and let the beacon fade. "That's it, beast. Come to me." He ground his teeth. His eyes glowed orange.

The dragon pinned her wings back as she sped toward him.

He waited.

The yellow of her reptilian eyes contrasted the red and purple hues of her jagged face. Trails of smoke leaked from her nostrils as she stoked her firebreath for another burst.

The archers realized they were too close and backed away. Still, he waited.

She answered his call with a low growl that pervaded the space between them as she sucked in all the air around her.

Tevin's quivering feet caused pieces of the wall to crumble from its face. When she opened her mouth, she was close enough that Tevin saw the fire twisting and turning in the back of her throat. He smiled. *Silly beast.*

Before she released her firebreath, he sent a blast of his own heated air at her face. The force twisted her head to the side and sent her tumbling head over heels. Tevin dove out of the way as her back slammed into the wall where he had stood. The stone shattered like a mirror struck with a hammer. The impact flipped her onto her chest next to the burning catapults in the staging area. Her snout dug into the dirt, leaving a divot as long as seven or eight carriages.

She didn't move. Tevin wondered if killing a dragon could possibly be that easy. An Epertasian archer helped him to his feet and stood slack-jawed with his bow hanging loosely from his fingers. Tevin nudged him with his elbow. "You think that's all a dragon has to offer?" He chuckled as he dusted himself off. Then he shouted, "Who wants dragon meat for dinner?"

The archer nervously shared his laugh. Tevin climbed down the ladder and walked into the courtyard to have a better look at his prize. Several soldiers followed. He marveled at her. His fingers traced her scaly ribs as her chest lifted and fell. Each of her breaths heated the air with thick, moist, suffocating heat.

When Tevin reached her snout, she opened her eyes. He planted his feet again and a faint orange glow lifted from his fists. "You may want to step back," he said to the soldiers.

They nearly trampled each other in their retreat.

"Are you ready for more?" he asked.

She snorted and pushed to all fours.

Tevin could think of no better challenge to test his power than a battle with a dragon, and was slightly pleased it hadn't yet ended. Her roar shook his bones. Her fury was palpable.

"You, my dear, will make a fine trophy," Tevin whispered.

She reared back on her hind legs and then slammed her front feet to the dirt like a bluffing bear. Tevin stood firm and fearless. He smiled as her rotten breath beat against his face. She curled her snout, bared her teeth, and stalked side to side, her eyes never leaving Tevin's. He wondered why she hesitated. Maybe a lifetime of having no equal had made her soft.

Tevin slammed her with another blast from his chest. She shielded herself with a wing. Some of her scales blackened. She yelped, probably more from shock than from actual pain, but either way Tevin had gotten her attention.

Again.

She inhaled so powerfully that she nearly sucked him into her mouth. Tevin pressed his palms together in front of his face as if praying. She unleashed a blast of fire. The flames struck Tevin's hands, parted, and blew past him along each side. The walls blackened. Even within his magical cocoon, smoke lifted from his clothes and his skin started to sting. She was powerful, and the sheer impact of her sustained attack pushed Tevin backward, his heels digging furrows in the ground. To add to the pressure, she lowered her snout toward him. His legs trembled. His skin reddened. His muscles threatened to give way.

And then she recoiled to take another breath. It was the break Tevin needed. He lowered his hands. The ground smoked. Though he wasn't much of a swordsman, he drew his blade. "Now, dragon, the fight really begins."

She glared at him. Tevin charged, sword in hand. She swung her mighty claws at him, but he ducked and avoided the certainly fatal blow. He darted to the side. She wanted to use her fire again—he saw it in her eyes—but she had given too much on her last one. She roared, trying to slow him with intimidation. At the same time, she shuffled backward. Tevin used his magic to propel his leap toward her snout. She flapped her wings a single time and a tornado-like wind slammed him against the wall. Only his magic kept his bones from breaking. The impact sent his sword spinning away. He crumpled to his knees. With a grin, he dragged his forearm across his bloody mouth and pushed back to his feet. "Impressive," he said. "I'll not make that mistake again."

After dusting himself off, he casually retrieved his sword and stepped back into the open. She charged, the ground quaking beneath her feet. She smelled his blood.

Tevin led her on a merry chase through the city, heedless of how much destruction she wrought in her pursuit. What did he care if a few dozen buildings got flattened? When they reached the castle, he propelled himself over the wall into the courtyard, and then turned to wait for her. He had an idea.

As soon as the dragon crashed through the wall, Tevin twirled and hurled his sword at her. Then he planted his feet and sent a blast of magic behind it. She tried to avoid the weapon, but the magic had pushed it too fast and the blade plunged between two scales in her neck. She wailed and recoiled, the hilt protruding from her flesh. Blood poured from the wound, puddling in divots her feet had made in the ground.

She reared back, angry. Dark smoke lifted from her snout.

Tevin stood strong, his power growing. She drew back with another deep breath and blew fire. Tevin unleashed his own wave of heat. He felt strong. Invulnerable.

The impact of their blasts colliding kicked him in the gut like an angry mule, depositing him on his knees. But his magic continued meeting her flames. She held her ground, blowing with all she had. The stones of the courtyard glowed orange. Anything made of wood ignited. Neither combatant gave ground.

Tevin's eyes watered. Snot mixed with blood and poured from his nose. If he let up, she'd burn him alive. She dropped to all fours, adding increased vigor to her firebreath. Tevin's lips quivered. It would all come down to who would falter first. For the first time of the fight, Tevin feared it would be him. But then a subtle contraction of the muscles between her ribs gave him a glimmer of hope. She was waning.

If he had any chance of winning, the time was now. With a violent jerk sideways, Tevin shifted his blast just enough to deflect her flames. The air exploded between them. Tevin's body slammed against the wall; hers against the castle. The corner crumbled beneath her weight. While Tevin tried to shake away the cobwebs, she scurried to her feet and searched the sky for an escape. She stumbled and then leapt over the wall, but was unable to take flight. Her left wing was bent unnaturally.

Tevin pushed to his knees. She flapped her good wing, the other one gyrating clumsily. Archers who had followed them from the wall surrounded Tevin and unleashed a wave of arrows as she fled through the city. Tevin could only watch, too weak to give chase.

When she stumbled through the breach in the wall, Epertasian soldiers ran at her with swords. The Teks intercepted them to give her room to flee. She ran gracelessly through the battlefield, whipping her tail against swarming hylocks and Epertasians alike. Howling and shrieking as the hylocks continued picking at her back, she fled east.

An archer helped Tevin to his feet. With his arm still around the archer's shoulder, he pointed to a puddle of her blood. "Get me over there," he ordered.

The archer helped him to the puddle. He pulled away from the archer and dropped to his knees. His body ached like he had slept beneath a boulder and his jaw throbbed like his teeth had rotted.

"What are you doing, Your Majesty?" the archer asked.

He plunged cupped hands into the blood. "Have you not heard of the magic of dragon blood?"

The archer shook his head.

"Hmph." The blood was warm on his lips. His tongue sizzled and then went numb. The pain in his jaw faded. After he drank all he could stomach, he stood up and smeared the gore from his lips across his cheek. He felt suddenly strong as if the fight had never happened. Even the aching shoulder that had been bothering him for weeks felt strong as a teenager's.

He grabbed his archer's arm. "Come and tell me when they're all dead and you have Rasi and Alina in custody."

"Yes, Your Majesty."

Confident that the battle was as good as over, Tevin headed back to the castle.

CHAPTER 42

FEELINGS OF BETRAYAL

R asi stood with Alina and Eldon inside the servants' entrance. As further evidence of Tevin's overconfidence, only three soldiers stood guard. Eldon quickly disposed of them. Rasi tugged Alina's hand, but she pulled back. He spun toward her. *What is it?*

"I did what you asked. Now will you tell me where we're going?"

The throne room.

"Why the throne room?"

Preoccupied with wondering why it sounded like the dragon was rampaging right outside the castle, he blurted, *Because that's where we're meeting th—* If he'd had a tongue, he'd have bitten it.

She scowled, confused. "Meeting who, Rasi?"

He hesitated. Eldon slipped farther down the hall to stand guard. Or to not be a part of what he knew was coming.

"Rasi?" she asked.

He breathed deep. *You're not going to like the answer.*

She cocked her head. "How is it you plan to stop Tevin?"

He clenched his teeth, his every fiber afraid to answer.

"Rasi?"

I just need you to trust me.

"I do trust you, but I need to know."

He sighed and looked into her eyes. *You must understand that everything I do, I do for you and Cridon and your kingdom.*

"I know, but you're scaring me. Who are we meeting in the throne room?"

Rasi looked away. There was no use fighting it any longer. *Simcane,* he answered. Telling her was even harder than he expected.

She didn't say anything at first. He reached for her hand. Confusion filled her face. "Why would Simcane be here? He's protecting Cridon. He should be far away by now."

Alina, please hear me out before you get upset. Tevin is too powerful for me—for any of us—to defeat. I came up with a plan. It's risky, but—

"Rasi." She pulled her hand away. "Where's Cridon?"

Rasi could barely answer. *In the throne room with Simcane, if all went according to plan.*

He saw her heartbreak in her anguished eyes. Her knees wobbled and she stumbled. He reached for her arm, but she jerked away. Her hand lifted to her chest. "I don't even know what to say."

Alina ...

"You've brought Cridon into the wolf's den? I can't even ..."

With a piercing glare at him, she backed away. Then she looked down the hall at Eldon, who turned away. She looked back at Rasi. "He's in the throne room now?"

I hope.

"But why?"

It's complicated. We don't have time to explain. Please, if you've ever trusted me, trust me now. It's our only chance.

She slowly shook her head. With her searing eyes lingering on him, she backed farther down the hall. Then she turned and marched with a purpose toward Eldon.

As she approached him, he said, "I'm terribly sorry to have kept this from you. Rasi said it was the only way. I—"

The door beside him swung open. Eldon's eyes widened and he lunged for whoever had opened it. He drew back his fist and pulled James from the room.

Alina shouted, "Wait, Eldon."

Eldon loosened his grip.

James lifted his eyes, seeing her for the first time. "Alina?"

"James." She ran to him and wrapped her arms around him. "You are well, thank the gods."

"I should say the same to you, Your Majesty. I've lived with terrible worry over your safety for many years."

Rasi joined Eldon, hardly acknowledging the reunion. *Is he with us or not, Alina? We need to move.*

She glared back. "Of course he's with us."

Rasi peeked around the corner before stepping into the foyer. Alina, Eldon, and James followed. The entrance to the throne room was on the other side. Alina pushed past him and ran to the throne room door.

Alina, wait. Rasi's straps reached for her, but she was already out of reach.

She disappeared inside.

Rasi started across the foyer, but stopped when Alina reappeared in the doorway. Her face was racked with fear. "He's not here."

Eldon turned back, unable to hide his concern.

Rasi grabbed Alina's shoulders. There was no more time for gentleness. *Listen to me, Alina. You must run now.* He waved Eldon over. *Take her. Get her and James to safety as fast as you can. Find Cridon and Simcane, if Simcane's still alive, and leave these lands forever. My plan has failed.*

Alina gasped. "What does this mean, Rasi?"

His straps lifted, sensing his growing anxiety. *It means we've lost. I'll try to hold Tevin off as long as I can so you can escape.* He looked to Eldon again with a dark and serious scowl. *If she won't go willingly, you make her.*

Her eyes widened. "Rasi?"

A dull orange glow emanated from the servants' hallway where they had just been. He looked to the main doors, but they'd never get to them in time. He turned to the others in a panic. *He's coming. Hide.*

Tevin stepped from the hallway. Seeing Rasi and Alina, he grinned. "Rasi? I thought I smelled fear in here."

CHAPTER 43

ALL PART OF
THE PLAN

Captain Casa stopped at the castle gates and spoke to the guards who were clearing up after some recent carnage. Cridon's fingernails dug into Simcane's chest as he clung tight to Simcane's back. The sounds of battle beyond the wall assured him the war was still ongoing. Simcane figured that was a good thing. The soldiers at the castle gates parted to allow Captain Casa and his prisoners to pass through.

"Good work, sir," one of them said. "Tevin will be pleased."

Casa was all smiles.

"Did you see that dragon?"

Casa shook his head. "I missed it. Looks like it did quite a number on the courtyard."

Simcane mindspoke to Cridon. *I'm gonna need you to walk now, kid.*

All right, Mr. Simcane. Are we going to see my parents now?

Soon. He squatted enough that Cridon could climb down, spitting Leander's key into his hand with another fake cough. *Walk in front of me, kid.*

Cridon did as he was told, shielding Simcane's wrists from the soldiers' line of sight. Simcane maneuvered the key into the lock of his shackles. It was a perfect fit. Those Teks were geniuses. Simcane held the loose shackles closed to keep up appearance.

Casa glanced back with a cocky smirk. "I must say, Simcane, I'm surprised you surrendered so easily. I don't know what you were thinking, but Tevin will simply take this boy from you and probably kill you in the process. There's no stopping him, you know. Especially not for some tired, washed-up mercenary. No offense."

He was right about Simcane being tired, but washed-up was something else altogether. Simcane mindspoke to Cridon again. *Stay out of the fray, kid. Understood?*

What's a fray? Cridon asked with big, innocent eyes.

A fight.

Cridon nodded. *Oh.*

Bohden steered his horse closer to Casa without making it obvious. The captain asked him, "How did you know Simcane was in that house, anyway?"

"I saw him while on my patrol, so I followed him." Bohden's head was on a swivel as he spoke, and only Simcane knew why.

Once shielded from the guards at the front gate by the corner of an outbuilding, Bohden discreetly drew his sword and held it by the blade. "We're still going to share the reward, right?" he asked.

Casa laughed and grabbed his belly. "Sure, Bohden. Whatever."

Bohden looked to the five other soldiers who seemed preoccupied with trying to get a glimpse of the damage the dragon had done. He lifted his sword by the blade.

"You know what else, Bohden?" Casa asked as he started to turn back. "I—"

Bohden smashed the hilt into Casa's temple. The captain never knew what hit him. Simcane dug in his feet and jerked the chain that attached his shackles to his captor's horse. The horse stopped with violent suddenness, throwing its rider over its neck to the ground. Simcane dropped the shackles and pounced on the soldier holding Marge. He quickly removed him from his horse and broke his jaw. Bohden dispatched the soldier who had fallen from his horse with a swipe of his blade.

Two of the remaining three soldiers fled toward the main gate. Simcane reached for the downed soldier's horse. Before he could climb on, Bohden raced past him in pursuit.

"Go get 'em, kid," he whispered, and turned to the last soldier. "Your move."

Wisely, the soldier tossed his sword away and lifted his hands in surrender. Simcane nodded for him to dismount.

"You're not going to hurt me, are you, Simcane?"

"Nah. But I can't have you telling anyone we're here, now, can I?" He lifted his shackles and nodded toward a well alongside an outbuilding. Then he tossed the shackles to the soldier, who carried them to the well and fastened himself to it.

Simcane scooped Cridon up, grabbed Marge's hand, and ran toward a small alleyway beyond the well. By nothing less than shitty luck, they turned into the path of four more men who were having a smoke.

"Well, well, well," one soldier said as he flicked his weed stick away. "Imagine the great Simcane stumbling into our path. You know there's a helluva reward out for you?"

Simcane sneered. "Good luck cashing in."

The four men peeled away from the wall and cautiously surrounded them.

Simcane whispered to Marge, "I'll tell ya, babe. I grow tired of these young kids thinking they should test me all the time."

"Well, teach them that it's not a good idea, Simmy."

Simcane twisted his face. "Simmy?"

She shrugged. "No good?"

He pulled Cridon close to his chest and knelt, grabbing Marge's hand. "Hug me tight, Marge. It's the only way I can protect you from my gift." Then he whispered, "Plug your ears, kid."

The soldiers crept closer. Marge buried her face against his shoulder. Cridon shoved his fingers in his ears so hard that Simcane worried he might poke his brain.

The soldiers pounced.

Simcane drove his fist to the ground. The air rippled around him. His ears popped. He felt Marge and Cridon flinch. He'd done something similar back in the Heathen War, but it took every bit of his concentration to keep his gift from catching Marge and Cridon. Two of the soldiers bounced off the wall they had been leaning against, while the other two hit the outbuilding.

Simcane stood up against the weight of his gift.

Cridon's legs quivered. "Why don't my legs wanna work, Mr. Simcane?"

Marge struggled to stand as well. "Yeah, Sim. Why's the air so heavy?"

"It's just from my gift. It'll go away soon." By the time they reached the side of the castle, the heavy air had lifted.

Bohden caught up to them. He had blood smeared across his cheek and his uniform was disheveled, but he wore a winner's grin.

Simcane shook his hand. "Good work."

He handed Simcane a sword. "Thought you might need one of these."

"That I will."

"You know I'd do anything for you, Sim. No matter how insane it sounds."

"Good. I need you to do one more thing."

"Name it."

"Take Marge, get your mother, and flee Thasula until this war is over. If we lose, you'll need to go into hiding, maybe forever."

"I understand."

"Thank you for everything, Bohden. If we never meet again, I have been fortunate to call you my friend." Simcane kissed Marge's cheek. "I love you, Marge. I always have. Now, go." Marge reluctantly joined Bohden, her gaze lingering until they rounded a corner. Simcane grabbed Cridon's hand. "Let's go find your mom and dad, kid."

"How do we get in?" Cridon asked.

"Easy. We're going through the front door."

CHAPTER 44

UNBEATABLE

Rasi stood frozen, anger churning through his blood. His greatest enemy stood not more than a stone's throw away. He had dreamed of his straps around the bastard's neck every night for years.

Tevin's haggard face and singed clothing evidenced a difficult battle. He still drew himself up and bowed like a courtier. "Greetings, Alina."

Every door within earshot slammed shut, making everyone in the room jump. James grabbed Alina's arm and pulled her slowly toward the staircase in the center of the foyer.

Tevin watched with an uninterested chuckle. "And where are you taking her, James?" Unconcerned with the possibility she might escape, he turned his attention back to Rasi. "You never cease to amaze me, Rasi. You're like a persistent cough that all the medicine in Epertase can't seem to cure." He inspected Eldon from his feet to his face. "And you've brought me a new Gildonese pet. How kind."

Few times in Rasi's life had he wanted to kill a man as much as he did at that moment, but the distance between him and Tevin gave the wizard the advantage. He had to play it smart and calm. An orange glow grew from beneath Tevin's sleeve and told Rasi who was going to make the first move.

Rasi panicked. He shouted, "Move," and pushed Eldon aside as Tevin unleashed a blast of heated air. Rasi tossed his sword and dove out of the way of the blast. A strap snagged the sword from the air and slung it at Tevin's head as the wizard's magic blew a hole in the stone wall behind Rasi. Tevin contorted out of the sword's path. It clanged harmlessly to the floor.

Tevin planted his feet and fired off another blast before Rasi could get up. Rasi turned away, the force striking the side of his chest. He hit the floor with a grunt. As his skin sizzled beneath his red-hot chest plate, he fumbled with the buckles until he was free. His chest blistered. Alina cried out from the top of the stairs.

Eager for a fight, Eldon leaped between Rasi and Tevin.

Tevin laughed. Eldon rushed him. Rasi knew Eldon's tactics well enough to recognize that he was lulling Tevin into slowness as he charged. Tevin unleashed another blast that Eldon easily side-stepped.

Rasi pushed to his knees, the pain of his burned flesh cinching the muscles between his ribs with each breath. He lifted his head in time to see Eldon, with sword in hand, leap toward Tevin. He screamed in Eldon's mind, *Don't get close.*

The Gildonese swung his sword at Tevin's neck. Tevin twirled and snatched the Gildonese warrior in mid-air with a spell. Eldon strained against Tevin's magic, but he seemed frozen in place.

With a side-eye to Rasi, Tevin said casually, "You saw how easily I killed the greatest Gildonese of them all. Why, then, would you bring me one as young as this warrior?" He addressed Eldon with a murderous grin. "Tell me, young warrior, have you ever heard of the Gildonese Syndrome?" Tevin lowered Eldon to his knees and held him paralyzed within his spell.

Rasi blocked out his pain, pushed to his feet, and raced across the room.

Without taking his eyes from Eldon, Tevin whispered, "I see you, Rasi," and hurtled a blast at Rasi's legs. Rasi grunted, his face plowing into the floor. His straps clawed at the stone to drag him closer to his foe. Tevin's finger glowed orange as he reached for Eldon's jaw.

Rasi asked his straps to forgive him for what had to be done. Despite the memory of Tevin killing his strap in Lithia, he lunged at Tevin's legs. He hoped to snap them before Tevin could react like he'd done to Fice. He strained. A femur didn't snap easily.

Tevin grabbed the strap around his left leg and sent an immediate jolt into Rasi's back. The strap around his right leg fell free. And then all six straps stiffened before dropping limply to the floor.

Tevin tilted his head. "You know what?" he said, He gave the strap a good yank. "I'll take those." Another jolt shot through Rasi's core as though he had been struck by lightning. Rasi rolled to his side and pulled his knees to his chest. The pain felt like someone was tearing his arm from his shoulder, only in seven different places along his back. His muscles and flesh popped and ripped as he writhed on the floor. He could no longer see Tevin through the haze of pain, but he heard the wizard laughing. Somewhere in the distance, beyond the pain and Tevin's laughter, he also heard Alina cry.

And then, with a final agonizing rip, all seven straps—the six living ones and the shriveled, dead stub—pulled free of his flesh. Rasi cried out. Blood squirted around him, quickly pooling and settling into the cracks in the floor. He shivered hard enough that his teeth nearly shattered. He lifted his head to look at the unbeatable wizard.

Distracted by the straps, Tevin had loosened his grip on Eldon's invisible restrains just enough to give the Gildonese a chance. Eldon pounced. Tevin spun. Rasi's straps scurried across the floor to the wall near the main doors as if they feared Tevin. Eldon grabbed for Tevin's throat with the same speed he had used to best Rasi many times.

Tevin's glowing fist hit his jaw.

It didn't appear to be the hardest of blows, but Eldon stumbled backward, wide-eyed, and grabbed his chin. He looked up to Alina and James, and then to Rasi, dread darkening his eyes. Alina stared back in horror.

Rasi reached out, despite there being nothing he could do. *I'm so sorry, Eldon.*

Eldon turned and fled through the servants' hall. James looked to Alina and she cried, "Go help him." James sprinted down the stairs like a man half his age and disappeared down the hall. Though he was a capable man, Rasi knew there was no helping his Gildonese friend.

Tevin grabbed his gut and nearly fell over laughing.

Rage replaced Rasi's pain. He bounced to his feet and grabbed a small table from beside the stairs. He growled like an animal as he heaved the table at Tevin's head. Tevin brushed his hand at it and the table exploded. Using the distraction, Rasi charged. He dove at Tevin's legs and tackled him to the ground. If there was one thing he knew about Tevin, it was that he couldn't fist fight worth a shit. Before Tevin could react, Rasi rained down two vicious punches. The first splatter of blood from Tevin's nose sent a wave of euphoria through Rasi's pain-racked body. Tevin impotently flailed at Rasi's chest, but Rasi swatted his arms away and drove an elbow at Tevin's brow. A gash opened over the wizard's left eye. It was as if in Tevin's panic he had forgotten he was a wizard.

Rasi couldn't give him time to remember. His left knuckle shattered against Tevin's defending forearm. He ignored the pain and punched again. Terror filled Tevin's eyes. He wouldn't survive Rasi's rage if he didn't do something fast. Rasi had no intention of stopping until Tevin's head was mush.

When a slight orange glow appeared beneath Tevin's blood-soaked shirt, Rasi realized he had taken his best shot and it wasn't enough. He punched Tevin again with his broken knuckles.

And then he felt it—Tevin's soft touch on his thigh. A muffled pop sent a chunk of Rasi's flesh and muscle into the air. Tevin released a second, weaker blast from his core, which threw Rasi from his chest. He pushed to his feet and wobbled.

Rasi grabbed his gushing thigh. He heard Alina descend the stairs and his eyes shot toward her. "Stop," he screamed.

Tevin launched a blast that knocked her down. He pressed his hand against the gash above his eye and stumbled, his back to the main doors. They slowly creaked open, Tevin's spell holding them closed broken.

"Rasi," Tevin said with a suddenly nasal voice. Blood poured from his nose. "You broke my nose."

Rasi subtly looked past him at the opening double doors.

Tevin struggled to catch his breath. He shouted between gasps, "Do you feel that, Rasi?"

Rasi didn't feel anything but pain.

Tevin straightened. "It is the Light. It is near. Where are you hiding that bastard son of yours?"

Rasi returned a hate-filled glare.

Tevin planted his feet. His chest glowed orange.

Rasi looked around for something—anything—to defend against the coming blast. There was nothing.

Tevin raised his fist for the killing blow. A shadow darkened the doorway. Tevin paused. His head cocked. His face paled and he slowly lowered his fist. As he turned toward the doorway, Simcane barreled through, a sword poised above his head. He drove the blade at Tevin's neck.

Tevin's eyes blazed. With no time to focus his defense, he released an all-encompassing blast from his core. His magic slammed Simcane back through the doorway and knocked his sword against the wall.

Tevin staggered toward Alina, still lying on the stairs. He passed Rasi as if he was inconsequential. But then Simcane plowed through the doorway again like a charging bull. Tevin turned and planted his feet for another blast, but Simcane stopped short and clapped his hands together, sending his own gift at Tevin's magic with a boom. Their gifts collided with such violence that it sent Tevin hard against the stairs next to Alina.

Simcane snatched his sword from the ground and leaped forward, the sword held over his head. His war cry could deafen the gods. Tevin's chest glowed orange.

Simcane landed straddling Tevin and drove the blade downward. Tevin flinched and unleashed his most powerful burst yet. The walls rattled. Simcane grunted. The force crashed Simcane through the ceiling to the second floor. Chunks of stone and plaster rained down from the new hole.

Tevin reached for the bannister and pulled himself to his feet. There was nothing Rasi could do but watch.

And then the world changed for the worst with a single word.

"Dad?" Cridon called from the doorway.

Oh no.

CHAPTER 45

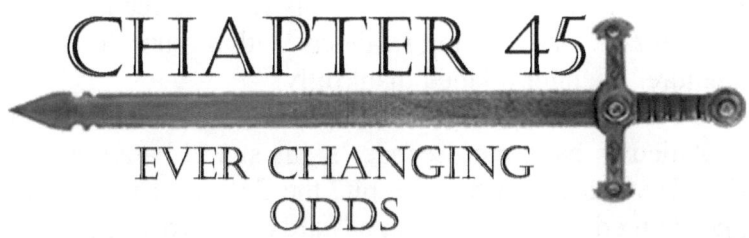

EVER CHANGING ODDS

The Teks had fought valiantly, but they were too vastly outnumbered. Though they had understood from the start that victory was unlikely, they had vowed to give Rasi everything they had. They might have had a shot against the Epertasians, but the damn hylock army made winning an impossibility. No matter how many hylocks they killed, the bastards kept coming.

Tek soldiers dragged their wounded out of the fray. Atticus saw the death of their morale in their slouching shoulders and searched for anything to give them a boost. The wounded still breathed despite the hylock venom, which he hoped meant the hylocks were running out. Atticus shouted, "Keep fighting, men. Their poison is losing its strength." It was probably more wishful thinking than reality, but he needed something to push them through the fatigue and hopelessness. Their only chance was to keep fighting until Rasi killed the wizard. After seeing Tevin defeat the dragon, that plan seemed overwhelmingly unrealistic.

And the hylocks kept coming. Atticus barely had time to catch his breath before the next creature or enemy soldier attacked.

Leander screamed, "We're not going to hold much longer, sir."

Atticus slashed another Epertasian and glanced back, enemy blood hiding his face. "I know. But what else would you have us do?

Retreat? We're dead no matter what. We—" A hylock shot out of the sky and barreled into his chest, knocking him over. When Leander tried to help, another hylock intercepted him, barely missing with a swipe of its nails. Atticus struggled beneath the creature, shifting just out of reach of the hylocks nails. The hylock's weight shifted to the side. Atticus used its momentum to roll the creature to its back. He jammed a knife from his waistband into the hylock's throat and then bounced to his feet. He readied his sword and went for the one stalking Leander. With a grunt, he decapitated the creature. Leander nodded thankfully.

More hylocks surrounded them, bloodthirsty scowls on their ugly faces. Atticus's back met Leander's, his sword hanging weakly at his side. He was exhausted. Despite the fight nearing its inevitable end, he shouted, "Come on, you bastards." He vowed to give all he had till the end.

The hylocks drooled as they stalked closer, their prey trapped. Leander said, "It was an honor fighting alongside you, sir."

"And you as well, Leander. I never dreamed that a Tek could become my friend."

Atticus lifted his weary sword arm. The lead hylock coiled for the attack. But instead of striking, its nose lifted and it sniffed the air. The others immediately mimicked him, their focus already shifted from Leander and Atticus. They turned west. As if every other dirty hylock throughout the battlefield had smelled the same thing, they all disengaged and sprang into the air.

Leander's sword lowered. "What the hell is that about?"

A strong scent of sulfur caught Atticus's nose. A look west turned his stomach. As bad as the battle had been going, the fishers arriving could only make it worse. What better place to harvest eyes than a battlefield?

Leander tapped his shoulder. "So, we have to fight fishers now too?"

Atticus scanned his exhausted army. "I don't think it's going to be much of a fight."

The hylocks dove at their mortal enemies. There must have been thousands of fishers. The first of them leaped at the swooping hylocks and pulled them to the ground where the fight was more even. Some of the hylocks lifted the fishers instead and dropped them to their deaths.

Roars and wails and high-pitched screeches like dogs fighting amplified by a thousand traveled the battlefield. Atticus turned to his stunned men. "Use the distraction to push to the wall. Ignore the fishers. Focus on the Epertasians." The break from the hylock assault reinvigorated his tired arms and lessened the crushing weight of his sword. He held it over his head and charged headlong into the Epertasian forces. His men followed his lead.

For the first time he saw fear in his Epertasian opponents as they backed away. They were just as tired as he. Without the hylock advantage, they wanted no part of the battle, especially if fishers awaited the victor.

As Atticus fought his way forward, Leander caught his attention and nodded toward a single fisher galloping their way, weaving through his men. A smile curved Atticus's lips. "Meela," he whispered.

Meela raced toward him as if locked onto his scent. She stopped short and smiled. Her eyes followed his movements, their once pale irises now colored a dull brownish hue. Atticus pulled her in for a hug and lifted her from the ground. After he lowered her back to her feet, he stared into her eyes. She stared back, proud and focused.

"Meela, you came back for us."

Meela shyly looked away.

"How? I mean, how did you convince your people to help us?"

"They fiieeght for their god."

"But Rasi's not your god. You know that."

"Not Rasiieee. Criieeedon."

Cridon? Any more questions would have to wait. He turned to his men. "The fishers are on our side," he shouted in hopes of giving them their seventh or even eighth wind of the long day. "We must take the wall." He looked to the hylock-fisher battle as the surviving hylocks retreated to the west. The victorious fisher army turned their attention to Meela and Atticus and galloped toward them. The Teks parted to let them pass. They didn't slow as if they already knew the mission. They were as violent as any creatures alive, effortlessly laying waste to any Epertasian soldiers brave enough, or stupid enough, to not immediately lay down their swords. The ones who did lay down their weapons dropped to their knees in surrender. The fishers showed them mercy as they bolted past, en route to the wall. The Epertasians disengaged and retreated toward the wall.

Atticus looked to the castle towers. "Rasi, it's all up to you, my friend."

CHAPTER 46

THE LIGHT
ARRIVES

Cridon stood alone in the open doorway. Rasi's head bowed; it wasn't supposed to be like this. *Son, you must run.*

Alina looked to Cridon with horror stealing her breath. She froze.

At the base of the stairs next to her, Tevin followed her stunned gaze. His lips formed a sick smile. "Well now, what do we have here?"

With eyes locked on Tevin, Rasi limped across the foyer to his son.

Cridon sadly looked up at him, his eyes as bright and innocent as ever. "You're not mad at me, are you, Dad?"

Rasi shook his head and pulled Cridon against his hip. Alina wobbled to her feet and staggered to them while Tevin stood and watched.

Alina rested a hand on Cridon's shoulder and her anguished eyes met Rasi's. *Should we run?*

Rasi looked back through the open door where soldiers loitered outside. He shook his head. *There's nowhere left to run.*

As if sensing Rasi's thoughts, Tevin slammed the doors shut with his magic.

Rasi told her, *I'm sorry.*

The devastation on her face hurt worse than any anger she could have shown. She answered with tired resignation, *I know you are, Rasi.*

Tevin whistled as he sauntered toward them. Rasi hobbled forward and nudged Alina and Cridon behind him.

Tevin stopped just out of reach.

Rasi would not plead for his life. He started to tell Tevin what a bastard the wizard was, but Tevin flicked his hand and sent Rasi sliding face-first across the stone floor to slam hard against the side wall. Rasi groaned and rolled to his aching back. His thigh that had gone numb after Tevin had blasted away a chunk of it seemed like the only part of his body that didn't hurt. Blood continued to ooze from his strapless back.

Alina stepped between Tevin and Cridon. "Tevin. For all that you once were in my father's eyes, please, don't hurt my son."

Tevin sneered. He lifted his hand and pulled the air between them, ripping Alina from Cridon's grip and throwing her to the floor. Tevin looked down at Cridon. "Well, hello there, young man."

Cridon looked past him to Rasi.

Tevin pointed two fingers at his eyes and made a clicking sound. "Eyes here, young man. I'm speaking to you."

Cridon did as ordered.

"Good. Now, as much as I'd like to tell you what is going to happen next won't hurt, I'd rather not lie."

Cridon lifted his hand toward Tevin, but the wizard's magic pinned his arms back to his sides. His feet left the ground. Tevin slowly pulled him closer with a lazy hand gesture.

Rasi fought to his weary feet, his love for his son willing him forward.

Tevin ignored him. He tilted his head back and his eyes rolled into his head. The air rippled into a tinted bubble around him and Cridon.

Rasi reached out. When his finger touched Tevin's magic dome, a sharp bite sent him back to his rear.

Tevin chanted in an ancient tongue.

From his seat on the cold floor, Rasi searched the foyer for something—anything—he could use to break the spell. He found Simcane's sword nearby.

Tevin's ancient chant flowed into Epertasian words. "Gods of the stars and the suns and the moons and all that lives within these lands, I call upon you. This boy whom you have blessed with your glory has proven unworthy of your gift. Your Light is still broken within him. I will restore it to its rightful glory, as it was before Matthew stole it from his father.

"I ask … No, I demand that your Light be stripped from this boy and given to me, for I will protect it for all eternity." He shook in his stance. The air grew as thin as it was high on Shadow's Peak. Thunder rumbled outside.

Rasi gathered the last of his strength and pushed to his feet. He charged and drove the sword at the rippling air of Tevin's magic cocoon. A deafening boom shattered the blade. The recoil threw Rasi back onto the stairs. He coughed and choked on his own blood. Though his body was broken, he begged the gods for the strength to help his son, though he couldn't even lift his head any longer.

And then, with all hope lost, a thick boot stepped next to his head. Simcane leaned over him. His broad smile revealed two of his teeth were missing. Blood flowed down his face from a gash on his forehead. He held his crooked left arm close to his body, a jagged piece of bone protruding near his shoulder. "Hey, Rasi. We're taking quite the beating, huh?" Blood leaked from his mouth. "You think maybe this could help? I found it upstairs." He lifted a thin sword with a glowing blue blade. "Didn't you kill the Tek commander with this?"

Rasi nodded weakly.

"I found it in the trophy room upstairs. They say it cuts through anything, right?"

Rasi nodded again.

"Maybe even magic?" Simcane staggered down the stairs toward Tevin's back. He drew back the blade, closed his eye, and swung with all his strength, his gift, and his rage. The blue blade sliced into the rippled air like it was belke slug slime. The foyer flashed a blinding white. The air was sucked from the room and then returned with explosive fury.

Simcane struck the western wall. Cridon slid toward the throne room. Tevin hit the front doors.

The castle shook. Large chunks of stone fell from the ceiling. Rasi turned his head toward Cridon. Cridon sat up.

Rasi's eyes went wide. *Cridon, look out.* But he was too late. The very creatures that had lived as an angry part of him for so long slithered toward his son's back. Like violent leeches, Rasi's straps swarmed Cridon.

Cridon's little chest jutted outward and he yowled in pain. Alina scrambled across the foyer to him. She grabbed one of the straps and pulled with all her strength, but it was too strong and determined to find a new host.

Rasi bellowed in Cridon's mind, *Cridon, tell them you don't want them. You said you could take them from my back; remove them from yourself. Please.*

But Cridon either didn't hear or was in too much pain to act.

Alina cradled Cridon and rocked him, helpless to stop his pain as the straps brutally merged with him. She sobbed and cursed them while Cridon twisted in her arms. She spoke with the same soothing voice that had helped him through his many nightmares. "I've got you, my baby boy. I love you. It'll be over soon."

A falling chunk of ceiling shattered next to Rasi's legs. *Alina,* Rasi screamed in her mind. *Get him out of here.*

The ceiling roared and crumbled. Another chunk of stone fell toward him. He tried to shield himself with his forearm, but the boulder bashed his forehead before rolling down the stairs. A flash of light blinded him briefly. Blood poured down his face. He wondered where he was for a moment. When he remembered, he saw himself standing up and fighting for his family, but he found himself still lying broken on the stairs.

"Rasi," Alina cried.

He looked toward her. She was blurry.

More of the ceiling crashed around him. *Alina, you must go while you can.*

She reached out, too far away to actually touch him.

And then Tevin stepped beside her.

"Noooo," Rasi screamed.

Tevin grabbed Allina's hair and yanked her away from Cridon. With deep, hateful breaths, he threw her down and straddled her chest. "I've had my fill of you and your family." His fist glowed orange.

Just as Tevin was about to strike with his glowing fist, Cridon stepped behind him, Rasi's straps dancing on his bloody back.

Now, son. Do it.

Cridon grabbed Tevin's other hand. Tevin glare down at it.

Rasi mouthed the words as Cridon spoke them. "I return to the world what the broken Light has given you." And then Cridon added a word not part of Rasi's script. "Meanie."

Tevin jerked his hand free, knocking Cridon down. He stood and backed away, looked to Rasi, and then back to Cridon, dread painted across his face. Stunned, he collapsed to his rear with his hands held in front of his face. The orange glow was gone. He slurred his words when he said, "Somethingiswrong." His right hand dropped to the floor. The right side of his mouth drooped downward. He dropped his head back and howled in pain as rippling air exploded from his chest and blasted through the crumbling ceiling.

Rasi watched until his sight grew too blurry and he couldn't see Tevin anymore. He heard Alina say, "Simcane, grab Rasi. Bring him with us."

A powerful hand gripped Rasi's arm. He felt suddenly weightless. Crushing pain seized his chest. He closed his eyes for the last time. He heard Alina crying.

CHAPTER 47

THE OTHER SIDE

Rasi opened his eyes to a bright, picturesque summer day. He knelt in the high grass of the Great Plains. There was no one around. No soldiers. No hylocks. No evil wizards. Even the city and the Forest of Concore were gone, replaced by an ocean of grass for as far as he could see. He pushed to his feet, amazed that he could stand, and even more amazed that he felt no pain. He took a step. The hole in his thigh was gone, not even a scar to hint that it had ever been there. He squeezed a fist just to see if he could. Where was he?

He tried to remember what had happened after Tevin had beaten him, but his memories were foggy like they were from a thousand years ago.

Realizing he couldn't just stand in the field forever, he started walking. Images of Cridon and Alina and Simcane danced in his mind, and he wondered if they had made it out of the castle before it crumbled. The suns didn't move as he walked, and no matter how far he went he couldn't see an end to the grass. Lost in his thoughts, he almost didn't see the three blurry figures that had appeared in the distance. He wondered if they might know where he was.

He continued walking toward them. As he got closer, he noticed one of them was a strapping young man. The other two were young women, one of whom held a baby. Slowly their faces became clearer and he recognized them. He should have been shocked or excited or even confused, but seeing them felt perfectly natural somehow.

His mother smiled. She held his father's hand as they walked. They were young and vibrant and happy—it was written across their warm faces. His father no longer trembled with the shaking disease. Walking slightly behind them was Edonea, as beautiful as they day he had married her. She held his son. They stopped before him. His mother tilted her head.

"Mother?" he whispered, his speech smooth and clear.

She caressed his cheek. He closed his eyes.

His father patted his shoulder. He was as strong as an ox.

Edonea's eyes met his and his mother stepped aside.

"Hi, Edonea," he said.

"Hi, Rasi."

"I've missed you so much."

"We've missed you."

Rasi looked around. "Where are we?"

His mother answered, "Right where you need to be." She pointed behind him. "Come with us, son. You've had enough pain in that world. It is time."

He looked over his shoulder to where a magnificent castle now sat on the horizon.

Donis nodded. "There's no more pain and suffering here. I'm proud of you, son."

Rasi longed for such a place. "I don't know if I'm ready, Dad."

"We're never ready."

"What about Alina and Cridon? Are they safe?"

He pursed his lips. "You've fought well. They are for the living now."

Rasi bowed his head. Maybe his father was right. He studied his mother's outstretched hand and looked to Edonea. She nodded. When Rasi lifted his hand to take Criya's, she hesitated and withdrew her hand slightly.

"What is it, Mom?"

She frowned and looked at Donis.

Donis's forehead creased and his head tilted. "Maybe we were wrong, son. We love you." He turned away.

"Dad? What's going on?"

Edonea and Criya turned to follow.

"No, wait," Rasi whispered. "Don't leave me again."

Edonea glanced back with a loving smile and a gentle wave.

Rasi wanted to follow, but his legs didn't work. He could do nothing but watch them fade into the distance. He started crying.

The once-frozen suns darted across the sky toward the horizon. When they disappeared, blackness as dark as the deepest pit covered the land. A frigid streak raced up Rasi's spine, sending shivers deep into his bones. Cold stone pressed against his back. A breath choked its way out of his mouth. He rolled to his side, coughing and gagging like he had been held underwater.

"It's all right, Rasi," Alina whispered.

His eyes jolted open. He was in a dimly lit room with dank stone walls and the stink of mildew. Alina's soft hand traced his back. He instinctively reached for the wound on his forehead, but there was nothing there. His mouth felt full and dry like it had been stuffed with cotton. He touched his tongue. "Where am I," he asked.

"You're in the lair of the Elder Three."

Her words filled him with fright. "No, Alina. This cannot be. What did you do?"

"I had to bring you here. You were losing too much blood. You were dying. I—"

"You should have let me die."

Alina caressed his cheek with her knuckle and then dragged her finger to his forehead as if tracing an invisible wound. "I'm sorry, Rasi. You can't leave us. Cridon needs you in his life. I need you."

He cupped her cheek. "My wounds were mortal, Alina. When I leave this lair, they'll only return and I'll die again."

She shook her head. "It doesn't have to be that way."

"I don't understand."

Before she could answer, someone coughed in the dark behind him. He twisted his head to see. It was Tevin, sitting with his back to the wall and his head drooping forward. Slobber hung from his lower lip.

Rasi almost choked on his own breath. He sprang to his feet and shoved Alina behind him. His hand grabbed for a sword that wasn't at his waist. "Why is he still alive?" he shouted, and charged his enemy.

Tevin didn't react. Rasi grabbed his hair and yanked his head back. He needed a blade to open the bastard's neck. Tevin gazed back with blank, dead eyes.

Alina grabbed Rasi's arm. "Stop. The fight is over. Your plan worked. Cridon removed Tevin's magic. He's harmless now."

Rasi growled, "As long as he has his snake tongue, he's not harmless. He should be executed. He's too dangerous to draw breath even for another moment." Rasi shrugged Alina's hand away and grabbed Tevin's collar. He twisted the fabric in his fist until it cut the air from Tevin's lungs.

Alina grabbed his shoulder. "I said stop. You will not kill him."

"He must be punished."

"I agree. But not like this." Her hand slid down Rasi's arm and stopped at his wrist.

He loosened his grip. "He's caused the deaths of thousands. He should meet the gallows, if not my own justice."

She gently removed his hand from Tevin's robe.

Rasi couldn't understand how Alina could have such misguided mercy. Sparing Tevin should be unthinkable, even for her.

Alina ran her finger along Rasi's shoulder and across his cheek. She guided his head around so his eyes met hers. "What you have done for Epertase cannot be repaid. But now Cridon has the Light and the kingdom has a chance to be born anew. That rebirth should not be tainted with cold-blooded murder, no matter how deserving of it Tevin may be."

"But he's responsible for the most heinous atrocities throughout the kingdom. He's killed our friends. He tried to kill our son.

Because of him, how many Epertasians will not sleep tonight because their loved ones are in the ground? I cannot breathe another breath while he still does."

"Epertase has seen enough death, my love. Because of you, the war is over. You've won. We've won."

"But what of him?" Rasi glared back at Tevin.

"Because Tevin killed the Elder Three, it is his destiny to replace them here in their lair. That prophecy must be upheld or, despite everything we have been through, the Light will be destroyed. Tevin's punishment is this prison for all eternity. He will never be free again."

Rasi shook his head. He feared Alina would never be safe as long as Tevin lived. He wondered if the gods had let him come back just to save his wonderful wife from her own kindness once more.

When he looked back at Tevin, he saw his parents burning in their home in Puimia. He saw all the dead Epertasian and Tek soldiers lying on the Great Plains. He saw Zaffka and remembered how right it had felt killing him. It was his purpose in life to protect those he loved, regardless of the penance he would pay for it.

He looked into Alina's pleading emerald eyes and remembered how hard it was to be away from her. For the first time, he wondered if killing Zaffka might have been wrong. He thought about Leander's friendship and how he couldn't have kept his family safe without it. If he had had his way after the Tek War, he would have sent all the Teks, Leander included, to the gallows. Alina was right to show them mercy then, and maybe she was right in showing Tevin mercy now. He felt nothing but anger and hate when he looked at the wizard.

Alina squeezed his hand. "Please, Rasi. Don't start this new world with death."

He scowled at Tevin and whispered the wizard's name.

Tevin lifted his head slightly.

"I knew you could hear me."

A faint glimmer of recognition twinkled in Tevin's glazed eyes.

Rasi squatted closer. "I want you to listen to me. For your crimes, you deserve death. But I will spare you. You should live out your days thankful to Alina, for she is the one who has saved your worthless life."

A tear spilled from Tevin's eye and leaked down his cheek.

Rasi smiled. "You will spend your life and many more lifetimes here, Tevin. You understand me, don't you?"

Rasi stepped away. It felt good to leave the anger behind. He turned and hugged Alina. "The years I spent with you and Cridon on Tek Island were the greatest years of my life. They made everything else, even my mortal wounds, worth the pain. We should leave. I'm ready to die now."

He started toward the door, but she held him back. "What if I said I can help you stay with us, if you'll let me?"

"It's not possible."

"It is." As she backed away, she whispered, "Wait here." She looked him in the eye to make sure he agreed.

He nodded.

She disappeared into the hallway before returning with Cridon, his straps—Rasi's straps—floating behind him. Seeing them embedded in his son's back hurt his heart. He fought back tears. He said, "Cridon can't help my injuries. Just like the injuries to Masera's legs, they weren't caused by the Light."

"I know."

Rasi dropped to his knees and Cridon dove into his arms. The straps wrapped around them both, surely recognizing their former host and friend.

"Show him what you have, Cridon," Alina said.

Cridon smiled. He pulled away and held out a tiny corked bottle full of thick, red liquid.

"What is this?" Rasi asked.

"It's dragon blood, Dad."

Rasi looked up at Alina. "But how?"

"Eldon found it in the courtyard where Tevin wounded her. He knew of the blood's healing powers and used it to save himself from the Syndrome."

"So, he is well?"

She nodded with happy tears welling up in her eyes. "I had Simcane bring you here while Eldon retrieved more dragon blood for you. Being inside the lair has sustained you until he could get here."

"But it's not natural."

"Too much in this world isn't natural. Living a full and happy life with you and Cridon feels as natural as anything to me. You just have to drink this."

If Rasi had learned anything after all he had been through, it was that he needed to trust those he loved. As he saw it, Cridon deserved to have his father. Alina deserved to have her husband. And he deserved to be happy. He closed his eyes and nodded a single time. She made a sound that was half-laugh, half-sob.

Rasi mussed Cridon's hair and stood up. Before he could use the dragon blood, he would need to leave the lair so his injuries could return. "Cridon shouldn't see this," he said.

Alina agreed.

He wiped a tear from her cheek and then headed to the hallway.

Before he stepped out, she grabbed his hand. "If this doesn't work, I want you to know I have always loved you with all my heart."

He kissed her cheek. "I know." Then he stepped into the hallway. His thigh started to throb. Another step caused the skin on his forehead to tear open again, spilling fresh blood down his face. It hurt as badly as when the ceiling stone first struck him. Then his throbbing thigh ripped open and a chunk of flesh disintegrated. He started to limp. Another step and his tongue turned to ash that floated from his mouth. He doubled over and vomited. He needed to get a little farther before he used the dragon blood just to be safe.

He glanced back at Alina as she stood in the doorway with her hand over Cridon's eyes. *I love you both and always will.* He fell to his knees, then to his side. The bottle of dragon blood rolled out of reach and he was too weak to fetch it. His eyes went blurry. He heard Alina's footsteps before he felt her touch.

"I'm here, Rasi," she said. She sat on the floor and cradled his head on her lap. "I will always be with you." She rocked him back and forth.

Rasi gasped for breath.

"It's time. Drink this." She poured the dragon blood into his mouth. It was bitter and warm, despite how long it had been out of the dragon's veins. He gagged and choked it into his lungs.

He closed his eyes.

CHAPTER 48

A BALANCE
RETURNED

It could have been moments or even years, but eventually Tevin lifted his drooping head as he sat against the stone wall. Though his senses weren't yet clear, they were returning. He faintly remembered Rasi kneeling over him and telling him some of the most awful things. He hated Rasi.

Though he didn't know why, he mumbled, "Look what you did."

Someone else answered, "No. Look what *you* did."

He turned toward the voice to see an image of himself staring back at him.

"You both did this," said another voice on his other side. It, too, came from someone who looked just like him.

"Who are you?" Tevin shouted. They shouted back the same question. Tevin used the wall to push himself to his feet. The other two Tevins mimicked him and backed against opposite walls. Bugs crawled under his skin. "I said, who are you?" he cried.

The other two Tevins answered as one, "We are Tevin the Three, of course."

Tevin's hands went numb and he held them in front of his face. They slowly faded until he could see through them. "I'm not staying here," he said. He pulled away from the wall and walked toward the hallway. The other two Tevins watched as if amused. When Tevin reached the hall, he smashed against an invisible barrier, like when he had first tried to leave after killing the Elder Three.

"We aren't going anywhere, are we?" the other two Tevins said with a chuckle.

Tevin sneered back, "This lair could not keep me after I killed the Elder Three. It won't keep me now."

Their next words sent a chill to his core. "But that was when we had our magic."

Tevin made fists and gritted his teeth. "We shall see." He pounded on the barrier over and over. The invisible wall didn't falter. Then he remembered how he had left the first time. He pressed his hand against the barrier, closed his eyes, and concentrated. The other Tevins continued laughing.

"Shut up," he screamed.

But they didn't.

His hand fell from the barrier and his head drooped forward. It wasn't fair. He looked back. "But ... I don't want to be here forever." He shivered and rubbed his arms. "It's so cold."

"Yes. We are cold as well."

"I don't feel well. My stomach hurts. When will that feeling end?"

They laughed. "End? Why would it ever end?"

"But I was powerful. I won't accept this."

The other Tevins couldn't stop laughing. The echo pounded his ears and shook the walls.

"Stop it," he screamed. "I hate you. Why are you doing this? You are me, damn it."

"Yes, we are."

Tevin felt pulled back to the wall where he had awakened. He took a deep, resigned breath. Filled with eternal despair, he pressed his back against the wall and melded into the stone. "Please, somebody help me," he whispered.

There was no answer, only laughter. A tear leaked from his eye.

CHAPTER 49

A PROPHECY
FULFILLED

While Rasi recovered in Doc Eckels's old clinic, Alina left him to take Cridon to the city wall. The Tek soldiers, led by Atticus, had secured the city and the Epertasians had completely surrendered. Alina led Cridon to a ladder that leaned against the wall. "Go on," she said.

He climbed to the top and she followed. They looked over what had been a battlefield only a day before. The chewed-up ground of the Great Plains was covered with bodies. Both Tek and Epertasian soldiers gathered their dead, laying them out in rows for the grim task of identification. While just a day before they were mortal enemies, with Tevin defeated and Epertase on its way back to accepting its rightful ruler, the two armies worked together out of respect for the dead. Since Alina knew Epertase couldn't move forward without its army, she had ordered Atticus to offer peace and a way forward. With a few exceptions, she promised no retaliation to anyone who accepted her return to the throne and vowed their allegiance.

Her close friends Levi and James joined her and Cridon at the top of the wall. As much as Alina wanted to shield Cridon from such horrors, she knew that in his reign as king he would be a better leader for having witnessed the damage war did to his people.

Though she loved Rasi immensely, she didn't want her son to have the same penchant for war that he had developed as a young man. The sooner Cridon learned that war should only be used as a last resort, the better.

Hundreds of tents had been erected throughout the plains to shelter the wounded, and it was in those tents earlier in the day that Alina had learned of her friend Christopher's fate at sea, breaking her heart yet again. She vowed to honor him along with the many others who had sacrificed everything for Epertase in the days and years that followed.

The fishers stalked the battlefield, searching for hylocks who still drew breath. They were relentless in their hunt. Cridon started fidgeting when he recognized what they were doing. His straps drooped sadly behind him.

"Cridon?" Alina asked.

"Yes, Mother?"

She touched his back between the straps. "Couldn't you remove your father's straps?"

He tilted his head like it was a silly question. "Of course. The Light gave them their life."

"Then why do you keep them?"

"I don't understand."

"Well, if you don't have to bear such a burden, why would you?"

"Because they live, Mom. Just like us. If I remove them, they will either die or give the pain they gave me to some other person or creature. I don't want them to die. And I don't want anyone else to suffer."

"But you once asked your father if he wanted you to remove them from his back."

"I didn't know how they felt until they joined with me. Now I know that they're afraid. I don't know why I feel this way, but I don't think any creature should have to be afraid."

Alina smiled, proud of her son who was wise beyond his years. "You feel that way because you're a caring boy. This kingdom ... your kingdom ... will be better with you as its king."

Cridon's attention diverted back to the field where a fisher raced toward the wall. "There's Meela," he said, and pointed excitedly. "Meela," he shouted, waving his hands and straps frantically over his head.

Alina tapped his shoulder. "She sees you, honey. Calm down."

When Meela reached the bottom of the wall, Alina directed her through the gates and up one of the ladders. Meela charged up to them and scooped Cridon in her arms and spun around.

Cridon giggled. "Let me down. I'm dizzy."

"What's the magic words?"

"I love you, Meela."

She grinned and set him down. He wobbled and she held his arm until he recovered.

"You're so handsome, Criieedon," she said as she looked him over with her brown eyes.

Cridon smiled and then turned back to the field. "Meela, why is your family still killing the hylocks?"

Meela stared over the battlefield, surprised by his question.

"I don't like it," he added.

"Would you liieeke to tell them to stop?"

Cridon nodded.

Meela bowed and stepped to the edge of the wall. She opened her mouth wide enough that her jaw popped and dislocated. Her head bobbed as she loosed a high-pitch staccato screech that carried across the field. Everyone paused and looked up, including the fishers. Slowly the army of fishers made their way to the base of the wall and pressed their foreheads to the ground.

Meela turned back to Cridon. "Tell them what you want."

Cridon looked up at Alina.

"Well, what is it you want, honey?"

"I want to help them like I helped Meela, but I don't want them to kill anymore."

"Then you must tell them that."

"Will they listen?"

"They will. They believe you to be their savior. Look at how they wait for your words."

"Will you tell them for me?"

She playfully mussed his hair. "Yes, honey, I'll tell them." She cleared her throat. "Fisher kingdom," she shouted. "My son, Cridon, King of Epertase, demands that you cease your killing immediately. In exchange for your vow to live your lives in peace from this day forward, my son will give you the sight you so desperately desire. From this day forward, fishers and Epertasians will no longer be a divided race, but symbiotic in our lives on this land."

Cridon tugged at her pants. "What's symbiotic mean?"

Alina shushed him. "I'll explain later." She looked to Meela. "Do they accept?"

Meela stepped to the edge of the wall. After a few seconds she turned back and nodded.

Alina knelt before Cridon. "They are ready for you, son."

"I need to be down there with them."

She nodded.

Meela got down on all fours. Cridon climbed onto her back like he used to on Tek Island. She zipped down the ladder and carried him through the gates. She stopped next to the closest fisher. Alina soon joined them.

Cridon climbed down and then hesitated, so she nudged him forward. He took the nearest creature's hand in his. That creature reached for the hand of the one beside him. Soon, every fisher there that day were joined hand in hand.

Cridon closed his eyes. "I ask you, Light of the star, please return to this race that which you took many years ago. I wish for these fishers to regain their sight."

Cridon's straps floated above him as the clouds rumbled. Light shot from the sky, striking the Great Plains like a bolt of lightning and toppling every fisher at once.

One by one they got back to their feet and looked westward. The one closest to Cridon turned back, his eyes focusing on the young king. He smiled. Then, as one, every fisher dropped to all fours and galloped toward Havens Ravine.

Meela hugged Cridon from behind. "Thank you, Criieedon."

He grinned.

"Iiee must leeave now. Iiee must bee with myee familee."

His smile faded. "I don't want you to go, Meela."

"Iiee must. Iiee will reeturn one day. Iiee promise." She rubbed her belly. "Iiee will have a son."

Alina tilted her head with a smile. "Oh, Meela. I'm so happy for you."

Cridon took her three fingers into his hand. "But I'll miss you."

She leaned in and licked his cheek. He giggled and pulled away. She whispered, "Iiee knew you were the one." Then she turned and chased her fisher family on their long run back to the Volcanic Region.

Alina led Cridon back through the gates where Leander stood talking with Atticus. "And what are we talking about, my friends?" she asked.

Atticus answered, "Well, Leander here is talking about leaving Epertase and I'm trying to talk him out of it."

"Oh?"

Leander bowed. "Only if my queen grants us a reprieve from our promise to live out our lives on Tek Island, that is."

"Of course I release you from our earlier agreement, Leander. You and your people are not only free, but free with our deepest gratitude. However, I must ask why you want to leave."

"Because of you, Alina."

"Me?"

"Yes. Over the years, my people have left a lot of kingdoms in ruins. I never saw what we did as being wrong, simply believing we deserved the spoils for being the most powerful army in all the lands. I've thought a lot about what you said when you came to visit me after I broke my arm. For the first time, I truly saw how wrong my people have been. In the time since, I have grown to love you as I would love my own sister, and I have wished every day that I could go back and save you from the suffering my people caused. Sadly, I know I cannot. But we can try to help others whose land my people have laid to waste. I now believe I have an obligation to do everything in my power to repair some of that damage. I cannot live with myself if I don't at least try. If you would allow us some of the ships used during the war, we would be grateful."

"You may take anything you need, though I ask that you reconsider. We would love for you to stay."

"And we would love to stay, but I believe we have more yet to do. Perhaps one day we will even free our own people and return here—not as warriors, but as friends."

"Is there anything we can do to help?"

"Your people have seen enough tragedy because of us. You have a kingdom to rebuild."

"We will miss you. My heart will always be with you."

Leander held out his hand. Alina looked at it and, instead of shaking it, embraced her Tek friend.

Surprised, Leander returned the embrace and then stepped back. "Enough about us. What are your plans, my queen?"

She looked past her two friends to her mostly demolished castle and said, "I think it's time for a new home—a new symbol for Epertase. What do you think, Atticus?"

"I think it's long overdue."

"Any word on Jarrah's forces?"

Atticus shook his head. "Not yet. This morning we sent a delegation to Tek Island to inform Jarrah of our victory. We will take him into custody immediately and return him to face your punishment. I will inform you when I hear more."

"That is good to hear. And King Logan and the others?"

"Eldon has gone to retrieve them. We have sent word to Lithia about King Logan and Queen Lona's impending return. I will personally keep you abreast of any news on that front as well."

"Very good, Atticus."

CHAPTER 50

SHE SAID YES

A few weeks had passed by the time Simcane found his way back to Arthur's Dive in search of Marge. She must have been worried sick after he didn't immediately return from the battle. He stepped through the door. His arm rested in a sling and he hadn't gotten used to his missing teeth yet, but he was feeling better.

Marge looked up from cleaning a table and her face brightened. She hurried over and hugged him hard enough to nearly unset his still-healing bones. Then she pulled back and swatted his arm. "I was worried sick. Where have you been?"

"Well, let's see. First, I had to recover after a wizard beat the shit out of me. Then I had some business in Lithia. I just got back. Can you step out front with me for a moment?"

Her eyes narrowed.

He took her hand. "Come on."

Eldon, Willum, and Gillian were waiting outside.

Marge hesitated on the stoop. "What's going on here, Sim?"

Simcane struggled to get down on one knee and took her hand. "I'm quite tired of fighting, Marge. I think I should settle down and rest for, say, the next hundred years or so. And I want to settle down with you."

Marge whispered, "Oh, Sim. I'm sorry I didn't go with ya a few years ago when you asked. I—"

"Don't say anything else, Marge. You're here now, and that's all that matters. Just say yes."

"You haven't asked anything yet."

"Marge, will you marry me?"

She guided him back to his feet and buried her face in his chest. He wrapped his good arm around her.

"I don't wanna be away from ya ever again, Sim."

"So, it's a yes?"

She blubbered, "Yes."

"You'll never have to wait tables in some dive bar again," he vowed. "But I promise you'll never be bored." He nodded toward Willum and Gillian. "If nothing else, I imagine these two are going to need someone to help watch after the little one from time to time."

Willum nodded. Gillian held up two fingers with a sly grin.

Simcane's eyebrows flew up his forehead. "Twins?"

Her grin widened. "That's what the good doctor thinks."

Willum rubbed his forehead as if the thought of it had already given him a headache.

Bohden approached on horseback and quickly dismounted. "Am I late?" he asked.

"Just missed it, kid."

"Damn it. Well, congratulations, pal. I know you two will be happy for many years to come. Do I still get to be the best man?"

Eldon's eyes lifted. "Him?"

Simcane cringed. "Maybe I could have two best men."

Eldon shook his head. "Oh no. Don't do me any favors. I see how it is."

Marge held out her hand and wiggled her fingers. "So, where's my ring?"

Simcane nervously rubbed the back of his neck. "I … uh … have been a bit busy."

She smacked his good shoulder. "You should remedy that as soon as you're able."

Eldon started for the door to Arthur's Dive. "Should we celebrate?"

Willum nodded. "I could definitely use a few drinks." The group of friends went inside where Arthur himself was cleaning Marge's table. Simcane hadn't even known he was a real person. After hearing the happy news, he made the drinks on the house. They celebrated late into the night.

EPILOGUE

THE NEW KING
OF EPERTASE

C ridon turned seven years old without a care in the world. The
fact that he was king of a mighty and prosperous civilization
was mostly lost on him. He was more concerned with play
dates, sweat treats, and running in the open fields of the Great Plains
than he was with the fate of the world.

That's where Alina came in. Since the Light had been forced into
Cridon at such a young age, she would serve as Queen Regent until
he grew old enough to rule.

As she watched him play, she felt sad for him for many reasons.
She knew his childhood would be abbreviated and tough. While he
wanted to be like other boys, the simple truth was that he was
anything but. He would be expected to rule Epertase by his
thirteenth birthday—fourteenth if she could hold off the people long
enough—and that would be a heavy weight on his young shoulders.

She looked over the hill at some of the most beautiful landscape
ever created by the gods, and instead of feeling pleasure as she once
had, she saw danger everywhere. As she had painfully learned, the
world wasn't as small or peaceful as she had believed for most of
her life. Cridon would undoubtedly have plenty of heartache.

But then she looked toward the construction site of their new
castle beyond where her ancestors' castle had stood for so many

generations, and it gave her renewed hope. She watched Cridon laugh as he played, oblivious to her fears, and she tried to soak in his every giggle. With his long, white hair and Rasi's oversized straps extending from his back, he might appear odd to most, but she viewed him as merely her beautiful, special son, and that was all that mattered. The people would grow to love him, imperfections and all, she had no doubt.

As she sat in the tall grass, Cridon raced past her feet and somersaulted. His straps vaulted him into the air and then cushioned his landing. He was already better at controlling them than Rasi had ever been.

Immersed in watching Cridon, she didn't hear Rasi approach from behind. He put his hand on her shoulder and she leaned her cheek against it. She lifted her gaze to him. "Good morning, Rasi."

He plopped down beside her. *Good morning.* He put his arm around her shoulders, and together they watched Cridon play.

When his boy saw him sitting with Alina, Cridon stopped and ran to them. Rasi opened his arms and Cridon tackled him to the ground. Rasi tickled him, and he giggled and begged him to stop. His straps gently removed Rasi's hand and he went back to fighting imaginary ochrids.

He had turned seven years old that day without a care in the world.

It was the year of Rasi 0001.

THE END

ABOUT THE AUTHOR

Douglas R. Brown is a fantasy and horror writer living in Pataskala, Ohio. He began writing as a cathartic way of dealing with the day-to-day stresses of life as a firefighter/paramedic in Columbus, Ohio. Now he focuses his writing on fantasy and horror, where he can draw from his lifelong love of the genres. He has been married since 1996 and has a son. He has had four books published to date, including his werewolf tale with a twist, *Tamed*, and his fantasy series, *The Light of Epertase* trilogy. Though the publishing company ultimately closed its doors, Douglas has given his work a new home under his own imprint, Epertase Publishing. Visit Douglas at www.epertasepublishing.com or email him your thoughts at epertase@gmail.com.

ALSO FROM EPERTASE

LEGENDS REBORN
THE LIGHT OF EPERTASE, BOOK 1

THE RISE OF CRIDON
THE LIGHT OF EPERTASE, BOOK 3

TAMED

DEATH OF THE GRINDERFISH